Praise for *USA TODAY* bestselling author Jennifer Snow's Wild River series

"Prepare to have your heartstrings tugged! Pure Christmas delight."
—*New York Times* bestselling author Lori Wilde on *An Alaskan Christmas*

"Heartwarming, romantic, and utterly enjoyable."
—*New York Times* bestselling author Melissa Foster on *An Alaskan Christmas*

"Set in the wilds of Alaska, the beauty of winter and the cold shine through."
—*Fresh Fiction* on *An Alaskan Christmas*

"Jennifer Snow's Alaska setting and search-and-rescue element are interesting twists, and the romance is smart and sexy... An exciting contemporary series debut with a wildly unique Alaskan setting."
—*Kirkus Reviews*

"*Alaska Reunion* has a little bit of everything—drama, humor, friendship, and love. It's a well-written story that will draw readers in."
—*Harlequin Junkie*

"This first title in the Wild River series is passionate, sensual, and very sexy. The freezing, winter-cold portrayal of the Alaskan ski slopes is not the only thing sending chills through one's body."
—*New York Journal of Books*

Also by Jennifer Snow

Wild Coast

Sweet Home Alaska

Wild Coast Novellas

Love on the Coast

Wild River

Alaska Dreams
Alaska Reunion
Stars Over Alaska
A Sweet Alaskan Fall
Under an Alaskan Sky
An Alaskan Christmas

Wild River Novellas

An Alaskan Christmas Homecoming
Wild Alaskan Hearts
A Wild River Match
A Wild River Retreat
An Alaskan Wedding

Look for Jennifer Snow's next novel,
Second Chance Alaska,
available soon from HQN.

For additional books by Jennifer Snow,
visit her website, www.jennifersnowauthor.com.

JENNIFER SNOW

Alaska for Christmas

HQN

ISBN-13: 978-1-335-44863-7

Alaska for Christmas
Copyright © 2022 by Jennifer Snow

Love in the Forecast
Copyright © 2022 by Jennifer Snow

Recycling programs
for this product may
not exist in your area.

For questions and comments about the quality of this book, please contact us at CustomerService@Harlequin.com.

HQN
22 Adelaide St. West, 41st Floor
Toronto, Ontario M5H 4E3, Canada
www.Harlequin.com

Printed in Lithuania

MIX
Paper from
responsible sources
FSC® C021394

CONTENTS

To all the bonus moms and dads, adoptive and foster parents, and all the positive role models— you are love and the world is a better place with you in it.

Alaska for Christmas

CHAPTER ONE

GOOSE BUMPS COVERED her skin as the opening beats of "I'll Be Home for Christmas" started to play, the song's lyrics holding a special meaning for her.

Home. This was home.

But standing in the elegantly decorated ballroom of the Sealena Hotel in her small hometown, celebrating the mythical Sea Serpent Queen's 120th birthday that holiday season, Isla Wakefield still had to remind herself that she belonged among that evening's lavishly dressed attendees.

It was the Saturday before Thanksgiving, and the hotel, owned by her family, was decorated for the holidays. They'd opted for a winter wonderland theme—fitting as it matched the weather in Port Serenity, Alaska, snow and ice covering the small coastal town. Sparkling white icicle lights hung from the ceiling, while warm tea lights flickered on the tables' crisp white linen. Large silver-and-white inflatable bulbs bordered the room, mirroring the stacks of mesh faux snowballs that served as centerpieces. Familiar faces were dressed in formal gowns and suits, mingling and laughing, enjoying the festive vibe.

Of course, the focal point of the room was a large ice statue of Sealena. This version of Port Serenity's mythical creature was wearing a Santa hat in honor of the season, looking not at all fazed to be sharing her spotlight with another mythical being. Santa may steal the show this time of year, but Sealena, reported to protect the boats at sea, had turned the sleepy, small town into a tourist destination years before and was regularly honored by locals and tourists alike.

Isla toyed with the crescent-moon pendant hanging around her neck, and when a tray of champagne with frozen cranberries passed, she reached for one. The alcohol should help take the edge off. She took a sip and immediately recognized the expensive Prosecco—her father's favorite. She saw him across the ballroom now, talking to the town's mayor. Dressed in a suit she knew was tailor-made, his hands gestured animatedly as he talked, the mayor seemingly engrossed in whatever story her father was telling. She'd bet it was about golfing. Her parents wintered in Florida and had recently taken up the hobby, only home this year to celebrate the season and the historic Sealena event.

Despite the theme and cause for celebration, the occasion was really about celebrating community. Honoring the men and women who ran local businesses all year round, as well as the local coast guard, who worked hard to keep their waters safe. And this year there was a notable sincerity about it. Dex, her brother, and Skylar Beaumont recently bridging their families, finally ending a feud that had spanned four generations, gave the atmosphere a lively, friendly vibe.

Isla shook her head. A Beaumont and a Wakefield together.

After years of hearing about how their great-great-grandfathers' friendship had ended when the Beaumont put the Wakefield in prison for smuggling contraband into Alaska, she never thought she'd see the day.

Or be okay with it.

But her brother seemed so happy, and Skylar's presence in his life made Isla feel better about traveling the world the way she wanted to, fighting against her overprotective instincts. Since the spring, she'd been to Australia, California and South Africa. She was home for the holidays, enough time to figure out what her next adventure would be.

As long as she could avoid the discussion about her future that she knew her dad would try to initiate when he got the chance. From across the room, he waved for her to join him and the group he was chatting with, people she recognized from his law firm. He was a semiretired defense attorney but still kept a finger on the pulse of the business in Port Serenity, taking on a case or two every year—usually high-profile ones that earned him praise and recognition. He was the best at what he did, helping a lot of innocent people avoid jail time or unfair sentencing, and it was no secret he wished she'd follow in his footsteps.

She pretended not to see the gesture. She needed more time before *that* conversation, and besides, she was there to enjoy herself. As much as she could, anyway. These formal events had always been part of her life, but she'd never quite felt comfortable attending them. She preferred hiking boots and jeans to evening gowns and heels any day.

"Hey, sis!" Dex said, coming up next to her, Skylar on his arm.

"Hi," she said accepting a hug while eyeing Skylar's dress. The tight designer floor-length black gown wasn't Isla's taste, but it suited the coast guard captain perfectly, complementing her flawless figure. Isla knew Skylar was also secretly appraising *her* choice of a Christmas red mini.

"You look beautiful," Isla told her sincerely.

"You too," Skylar said, and her shoulders relaxed a little.

Obviously, they were sticking to the unvoiced pact to leave the past in the past and move on after years of not getting along. Which was good because the huge rock on Skylar's left ring finger was a reminder they'd be family soon.

Family. Was *she* really family?

Instinctively, Isla's hand returned to the pendant around her neck, and she took a quick gulp of champagne before nodding toward the ring. "Congratulations again, you two." She'd been portaledge camping on the side of a mountain in California when her brother had called with the good news. Good thing she'd been harnessed in. Despite knowing the two high-school sweethearts had reunited and were living together, the union hadn't felt fully solidified to her. She'd been nervous that Skylar might have a change of heart about settling down in their hometown.

"Thank you," Skylar said, clinging tighter to Dex. Her brother kissed his fiancée's forehead with tender affection that had Isla looking away quickly. Her brother was definitely the romantic in the family. He'd pined over Skylar for years when his secret ex-girlfriend had left Port Serenity to attend the coast guard academy.

Isla had adopted more of a love 'em and leave 'em approach to relationships.

"New tattoo?" Dex said, glancing at her arm, where the ink was still fresh.

The words *You're fine, keep going* were imprinted in black ink along her inner forearm. It was one of her personal mantras when challenges seemed out of reach. Lately, she'd been tattooing such messages on her body as reminders. Something about the words seeping into her skin made them harder to ignore.

She nodded. "Got it in South Africa the day before flying home." Other people collected trinkets as souvenirs from the places they visited; Isla preferred to commemorate her experiences with tattoos. She knew her brother wasn't a huge fan of the ink, but he nodded supportively.

She and Dex were as different as siblings could be. While she liked body modifications and changing up her style and hair color regularly, Dex liked the same predictable look. He'd had the same haircut since he was six years old. But despite their differences, they were close and could always depend on one another.

Except when it came to a place to stay while she was home.

She faked an annoyed look as she said, "I still can't believe you gave my bedroom to a canine."

Dex had recently partnered with a seizure-alert dog to assist him with his epilepsy, and the beautiful German shepherd, Shaylah, was comfortable in Isla's old bedroom on the family yacht, where Dex and now Skylar lived.

Dex laughed, his blue eyes holding a spark of teasing. "She keeps it cleaner than you did."

Isla swiped at him playfully. Her messy ways weren't a secret. While Dex was organized and structured, she was more chaos and pandemonium. Growing up, she'd negotiated giving him half her allowance every week to clean her room while she was out exploring the outback. He liked the extra cash to take Skylar on dates, and she wasn't forced to stay inside on a beautiful Saturday. Seemed like a fair trade to her.

The festive music came to an abrupt halt, and the microphone on stage emitted a deafening squeal. Isla winced as she turned to see Aaron Segura take the stage.

"Hello, everyone," he said after tapping the mic. "I hope you're all having a great evening. I thought since we're all here together tonight, it might be a good time for a quick winter-safety reminder."

A rumble echoed through the crowd, and Isla sighed.

What a buzzkill.

There was no one on earth more annoying than Aaron Segura. His last name, meaning *safe*, was fitting: he lived up to that reputation without question. He was the self-designated safety officer in Port Serenity, had been since they were teenagers, making it his mission to inform and educate the locals and tourists on backwoods safety any chance he got.

Too bad he was so boring, because he was actually really hot.

Dressed in his chief petty officer uniform, his short, light brown hair gelled to the side and just the right amount of stubble along his jawline, he easily caught the attention of any woman in the room. Oddly enough, he didn't date much. Probably scared women off with a safe-sex lecture before they'd even had dessert.

"As you all know, this time of year, the search and rescue calls nearly triple with accidents in the backwoods, on the ice, the trails..." Aaron continued. "The coast guard station receives even more. And despite our best efforts, for every three people rescued successfully, one person suffers a tragedy."

The mood instantly dulled.

"Ensuring proper safety measures while engaging in these *fun*—" he said the word as though it were a foreign object on his tongue "—activities can reduce the number of calls we receive and help ensure assistance is available for the most hazardous situations. Lives depend on it. The lives of your family and friends depend on it."

Holy shit, Aaron, read the room!

Wide-eyed, Isla nudged Dex and jutted her head toward

the stage. "Do something before he starts spouting statistics," she hissed.

"He's not wrong," Skylar muttered, coming to her crew member's defense, but even she looked like she understood Aaron's timing was off.

As discreetly as possible, Dex waved a hand, catching Aaron's attention on stage, and sent simultaneous thumbs-up and wrap-it-up signals.

Luckily, Aaron caught the hint. He cleared his throat awkwardly. "Right, so anyway, make sure you're prepared for the elements with warm, highly visible clothing, and carry flares whenever possible. Know the weather conditions before setting out and be aware of changing situations. The backwoods are a much different place at night." He looked like he wanted to say more but decided to conclude his message. "All to say, have a happy—and, more importantly, *safe*—holiday season," he said to a round of applause that felt more like relief that he was exiting the stage than appreciation. Music resumed and the guests tried to recapture the festive, upbeat vibe that had been dampened.

Across the room, Isla watched Aaron run a hand through his hair, his chest heaving in a sigh of relief. Huh. He'd been nervous up there. For a guy who lowered himself out of helicopters to rescue people on the open water in death-defying acts of bravery, his apparent fear of public speaking was a surprise.

She'd file that tidbit away to use against him when they were next engaged in a verbal sparring match.

She didn't have to wait long as he joined the group a moment later, right in the middle of her telling Dex and Skylar about her winter plans while she was home. "The ice climbing expedition at the Hidden Glacier waterfalls is a must-do."

"I think I like my waterfalls flowing," Skylar said, shooting a seductive sideways glance at Dex.

"Should we tell her what we do at waterfalls?" Dex said, wrapping an arm around Skylar's waist. Skylar's blush was as vibrant as Isla's dress.

Isla faked a gag as Aaron stopped next to her. "Gross."

She didn't like to think about her brother and Skylar's sex life. But what wasn't entirely off-putting was the mild, manly aftershave scent coming from Aaron. The mix of pine and mint reached her nose, and she secretly savored it. The guy may be irritating, but he always smelled so good. Strong and fresh, like the Alaskan wilderness...

But then he had to speak.

"You know, ice trekking is just as amazing and a lot—"

"Safer?" Isla finished, turning to him with an unimpressed smirk.

Damn, that sexy chin dimple was seriously wasted on this guy.

"Yes," he said, unfazed by her obvious disdain for his opinion on the subject.

"I think I'll stick to my original plan," she said.

"Do you know how many people are injured every year while ice climbing? The weather is unpredictable, and the direct sunlight Hidden Glacier receives midday is dangerous."

From the corner of her eye, Isla saw Dex and Skylar slowly moving away. They were used to this familiar scene and were clearly leaving them to their bickering.

"That's why the expedition is scheduled for early morning."

"That poses its own set of challenges," Aaron said with a nod, armed with more information. "Freezing temps, especially in the hollows between the mountain faces, could dip a lot lower than expected."

She folded her arms across her chest. "That's why you prepare for anything."

"Prepared or not, shit still happens," he said, his jaw tight.

"Look, I've been training for six months, rock climbing all over the world. I'm in the best shape of my life." She flexed an impressive bicep. It was true. She was athletically built and had always been fit, but this past year she'd taken her training to a whole new level. Climbing the challenging rock faces and peaks required dedication and commitment to the strength training and conditioning that was integral to a safe and successful climb. At five foot nothing, she often had to work harder than the taller, beefier climbers, but she relished the challenge.

Aaron's gaze drifted over her, and she caught what she might mistake for attraction, if she didn't know better, before he looked away. "You're not going to change my opinion on this."

Or on her. They'd known one another since kindergarten, where they'd been unlucky enough to be in the same class right up until high school. Almost as though the teachers had been putting them together on purpose to see if they would ever get along. Or more likely for the entertainment of watching them battle it out over absolutely everything.

She knew he thought she was wild, reckless, loud and opinionated. She knew *he knew* she thought he was boring, predictable, annoying and irritating.

Neither one hid how they felt about the other. It was actually refreshing to know exactly where they stood. There was no false praise or interest when she spoke to Aaron, unlike the guys who pretended she was fascinating just to get in her pants.

"Well, I'm flattered that you worry about me," she said with a grin.

He opened his mouth to refute the claim but then said, "I worry about everyone in Port Serenity."

That was true. As annoying as he was, Aaron had good reason to worry about the dangers of extreme sports after losing his sister in a snowmobiling accident during Christmas break when they were teens. Isla didn't know the details, but she remembered him not being in school for a month after her death. As the anniversary was approaching, she suspected this time of year might be more difficult for him.

So Isla cut him a little slack. Just a little.

"I'll tell you what. If the weather conditions aren't great that day or I'm not feeling in top shape, I'll go ice trekking instead."

"No, you won't," he said, sounding half-defeated, but there was also a hint of respect in his tone, drowned out by the opening beats of a Justin Bieber holiday classic.

She laughed as she started shimmying her way toward the dance floor. "You know me too well," she called behind her.

She cast a quick glance over her shoulder to see if maybe he'd follow.

Predictably, he didn't.

THE ICE NEEDED to be four inches thick for ice fishing.

What part of that was so difficult for tourists to understand? Just because this was Alaska didn't mean the weather conditions were always favorable for the popular winter activity. And yet, every holiday season there was at least one emergency call related to a person falling through.

And almost every time, it could have been prevented by checking in with the station regarding the ice thickness.

And to take a snowmobile out there?

This particular call irritated him. A family on vacation from Seattle had driven their snowmobile out onto the ice and set up camp about two hundred feet from the shore. The ice hadn't been able to support the weight, and the vehicle had fallen through, cracking in all directions, preventing the father and his two children from being able to get safely back to land.

One false step and it could be hazardous.

In his gear, Aaron was poised and ready at the open door to drop in once the MH-65 helicopter was over the location. As they approached, he could see the snowmobile disappearing through the increasing gap of the ice pans. A small pop-up tent and several folding chairs were set up, along with fishing gear and a barrel fire that had been snuffed out.

The father and his children stood huddled together in the center of an ice pan that looked unsteady and unpredictable. They had minutes at most before the ice could break away again. Hypothermia would set in within three minutes if they fell into the water, and his job would be that much more difficult. He'd prefer to avoid a freezing plunge if he could.

Seconds later, Aaron lowered himself as his crewmate and helicopter pilot, Dwayne, held the Airbus Dauphin steady overhead. The winter chill was worse out on the ocean, and he struggled with a steady, even descent as wind hit him. The sway made it challenging, but he landed carefully on the ice, braced himself on the uncertain terrain and reached overhead for the basket as it was lowered. A subconscious head count confirmed the man, his two kids, who looked to be around eight and fourteen, and their large husky, who appeared from its hiding place inside the tent.

No one had mentioned the canine.

Too much weight for one trip. They all looked terrified and eager to get off the dangerous ice, but they wouldn't be going together.

"Everyone okay? No injuries?" Aaron asked quickly over the noise of the chopper. If anyone was hurt, he'd have to reassess his plan. A vertical ascent might not be possible.

Luckily, the father shook his head. "We're okay. Just cold and freaked out."

Well, at least they understood the severity of their predicament. Might make them think twice next time. "Okay, let's get the smaller child in the basket with the dog," he yelled.

The little girl looked nervous as she shook her head, blond pigtails beneath her winter hat swishing back and forth. Her cheeks were streaked with tears that were crystalizing on her face in the frigid air. She clung to her father's side, eyeing the long, intimidating ride up to the helicopter. The rotating blades were enough to frighten anyone.

Her older brother put a comforting arm around his little sister, and Aaron's chest tightened. Protective, the way an older brother should be.

He cleared his throat and his tone was calm as he carefully approached and extended a hand. "Come on, it's okay. It's actually kinda fun." His reassuring smile nearly froze on his face as the cold wind continued to blow.

Cracking sounds of the ice around them reminded them of the urgency, and he gestured the little girl forward.

"Maybe I should go first," the father said. "Show her it's not that scary."

Aaron held a hand to him. "Youngest child and dog," he said firmly. The little girl might need more coaxing, but the dog stood at Aaron's feet, ready to go. He reached to assist the animal into the basket, noticing the dog tag on the collar read *Smoky*. The thing weighed a million pounds as he heaved him in. Then he reached for the little girl again. "It's okay. Smoky's in the basket. You won't be alone."

She glanced up at her father, who nodded, and she reluctantly approached. Aaron helped her into the basket and radioed above. "First in position. Ready to be lifted."

The basket started to move upward, and the child's eyes widened with fear.

"It's okay. Hug your dog. Don't look down."

The little girl did as he instructed, and he watched as she was safely lifted up and into the helicopter, where his crewmate, Miller, secured them inside the chopper.

More cracking sounded as a piece of the ice pan separated and drifted away. He scanned the ice and his heart raced. He could see the water below. Nature, especially the frozen ocean, was unpredictable. They had very little time.

The basket returned, and he gestured for the older child. "You're next."

The teen boy didn't hesitate. He climbed in, and Aaron sent the basket up.

"Okay. We will wait," he radioed the chopper.

"Wait?" The father looked panicked as he moved closer, his expression darkening. "What do you mean *wait*?"

"Helicopter is full." Aaron kept his voice calm despite the severity of the situation. The ice pan was now only three feet wide and four feet long. Fishing gear and the tent started to fall into the ocean. His jaw clenched involuntarily.

On top of the human casualties and injuries, there was a great environmental impact associated with rescues like this one. All this pollution entering the ocean could have been avoided.

The man looked ready to argue, but it was futile as the chopper flew off toward the station. He watched it leave, worry etched on his face.

As annoyed as he was by the man's bad judgment call, Aaron sympathized. He had to be feeling guilty about putting his kids' lives at risk.

"Don't worry. Your kids will be okay, and the helicopter should be back in less than ten minutes." He surveyed the ice. Large cracks continued to form in all directions around them. A lot could happen to the ice pan in ten minutes, but he didn't voice his concern.

The structure crackled beneath his boots, and the ice between them separated. He quickly pulled the man's jacket, pulling him to safety, before he was adrift. Aaron's heart raced as the even smaller platform bobbed on the surface of the water.

That was close. Too close.

He was a rescue swimmer, but he preferred to stay dry at this time of year, when the water was so cold.

"Shit," the man muttered, running a hand over his thick beard, which was gathering icicles. "Thanks."

They waited the ten long minutes, not speaking, surveying the ice, mentally preparing to act quickly if necessary. Seeing the chopper reappear in the distance, relief flowed through Aaron as it hovered above a moment later. The basket was once again lowered, and the man hopped in quickly with zero coaxing. Aaron attached himself to the cables and radioed up. "We're ready."

Once inside the safety of the chopper, he sat next to the

father, wrapped a thermal blanket around his shoulders and took a deep breath, his safety speech and reprimand on the tip of his tongue.

Allergic to fun and watching other people have it.

Isla's common taunt chose that moment to echo in his mind, and he clamped his lips shut. Damn, Isla drove him completely nuts. Especially the way she popped into his head, unexpected and uninvited, far too frequently. That smart tongue and sharp mind were always up to the challenge of an argument. She was relentless when she thought she was right, and her inability to listen to the voice of reason—*him*—irritated the heck out of him.

And why he let her opinion of him affect him, he had no idea.

"From now on, just be sure to check with the local station before heading out onto the ice, okay?" he said simply, suspecting a lecture would be lost on the guy anyway.

The man shivered under the thermal blanket, his lips trembling as he said, "Who can I talk to about getting my snowmobile out of the ocean?"

Because it wasn't enough that the coast guard had saved him and his family.

Tourists.

"Yeah, man. It's gone."

CHAPTER TWO

WOULD THIS TIME of year ever get easier?

The sights and sounds of the holidays always caused Aaron's chest to ache. Why didn't he live in a town that kept the decor to a respectable minimum? This time of year, Port Serenity turned into the setting of a Hallmark Christmas movie, and his grinchy heart could barely handle it. The storefronts competed for best festive display, and the town blew their electricity budget on the overhead streetlamps, their poles wrapped in white lights. The large Santa and eight reindeer that hung across the street near the mayor's office were life-size and, in his opinion, blocked sufficient visibility of the only traffic light in town. But his petition to retire the old ornament had been denied at last year's council meeting, so he knew it was pointless to bring it up again.

He hadn't always disliked the season... Things had been different when his younger sister was alive. Amy had loved the holidays. She'd start decorating the minute Halloween was over. Their house had been the most festive on the block with multicolored lights, large inflatables and a family of snowmen on the lawn. She'd always insisted they put up their Christmas tree the day after Thanksgiving, and she helped with all the shopping and wrapping, not caring that she knew all the presents, including her own. She was a true holiday fanatic, which made it hard for Aaron to breathe, seeing all the lights and decorations, hearing the Christmas music she loved and knowing she was no longer around to enjoy it.

That winter break ten years ago seemed like yesterday. The snowmobiling accident that had ended her life along with that of Aaron's best friend, Blake, was something Aaron could never forget. Wouldn't let himself forget. She'd wanted to ride with his friend. She'd had such a crush on Blake. Aaron should have insisted she ride with him. He should have protected her.

He couldn't go back and change the decision he'd made that day, one that had ultimately ended in him losing both his friend and his sister when the snowmobile hit a tree. But he could try to prevent other families from suffering a similar tragedy.

The accident had been the driving force behind his decision to join the coast guard after graduation. He'd volunteered with local search and rescue throughout high school and had taken every safety-training and first-aid course he could. Then after high school, he'd attended the coast guard's Aviation Survival Technician/Helicopter Rescue Swimmer program in North Carolina. The twenty-four-week program had an 80 percent washout rate as candidates simply couldn't keep up with the focus on physical fitness, long hours of pool training, extreme water confidence drills and classroom instruction. Aaron had powered through, fueled by the pain and regret of the past whenever things got tough, remembering Amy whenever he was tempted to quit. There were other positions he could have applied and trained for, but he wanted to do the job not everyone else could do. He wanted the tough, unpredictable, nearly impossible missions that would require him to be at his best. And he now belonged to an elite group of highly specialized coast guard officers. And he was constantly striving to learn more and develop further skills, having recently completing a seven-week vertical-rescue course in California where he'd trained in cave rescues and cliffside assistance.

He wanted to be trained for anything and everything.

Semper Paratus. Always Ready.

He walked along Main Street, his head tucked low inside his thermal winter coat, the snow crunching beneath his boots, and a few minutes later he opened the door to Port Serenity Secondary. His chest tightened even more, entering the school where he and Amy had attended. She'd loved school. Especially during the holidays. She was assistant head of the winter formal committee and would decorate her locker with garlands and lights. She organized a toy drive every year and volunteered at the local food bank after school. Her charitable spirit had been unmatched.

He took a deep breath as he approached the open gymnasium door. His annual talk with the students about winter-break safety was scheduled to start in five minutes and he could see the students already gathered inside, sitting on the floor, while the principal addressed the crowd, settling them down in preparation for the presentation.

He may not be the most exciting speaker, but it was important to educate the kids, as parents weren't always aware of what they were up to in the backwoods. Winter and spring breaks were the search and rescue's busiest times of year. If Aaron's talk could prevent just one student from taking an unnecessary risk, it was worth it.

"Don't worry, they don't bite," a woman's voice said from behind him.

He turned to see Trina Clarkson, an eighth-grade teacher, coming down the hall. He forced a smile at his own former classmate. Trina was pretty with dark curly hair and bright green eyes. She was friendly and patient but had an energetic personality that made her a perfect teacher for hormonal, unruly teenagers.

"Hey, Trina," he said.

"Nice to see you. I haven't seen you at bowling league in a while."

He lowered his head sheepishly. "I was kicked off the team."

She laughed. "What? Why? You were their best player."

"Apparently that's why. The league voted that I take a season off. Let another team have a chance with the trophy." He had eight of them. Joining the team as a teenager as a favor to his dad when they'd needed a fourth player, he'd gotten really good and had come to enjoy the low-key sport. It was a huge contrast to the extreme stress he put his body under in his career. His dad had quit playing when his parents had moved to Florida. They'd been done with the harsh winter weather and unforgiving wilderness—and the countless reminders of Amy and what their family had once looked like.

Aaron couldn't fault them the decision, but he had decided to stay in Port Serenity, a fierce loyalty to his hometown making leaving not even an option. He kept in touch with his parents as much as the time difference allowed, but his crewmates had become his family the last three years.

Trina shook her head. "Well, I for one miss seeing those strikes," she said flirtingly.

Miss staring at your ass was definitely implied.

He cleared his throat but was unsure what to say. Flirting wasn't really his strong suit, and while he liked Trina, he wasn't interested in leading her on. He'd seen the way she looked at him at bowling and whenever they ran into one another around town, and he didn't want to encourage anything he couldn't reciprocate. Unfortunately, there really wasn't anyone in Port Serenity he felt attracted to…

An image of Isla in that smoking-hot red dress at the Sealena party flashed in his mind, and he forced it away. Isla was a solid candidate for *look but don't touch*. He knew better than to allow himself to get burned.

"I think it's really great that you keep doing this," Trina said, changing the subject, seeming to sense his discomfort.

After Amy died, he'd taken all the backwoods-safety courses he could enroll in and had created his own informal presentation covering the essentials. He nodded. "Yearly reminders can save lives," he said, hoping the sentiment didn't sound as lame as Isla often made him feel it was.

Why on earth did he care? And why was Isla popping into his head so often lately, anyway?

She'd been away for six months, and she hadn't crossed his mind once in that time. Okay, maybe a few times, but not as often as she had since the Sealena celebration the week before. That red dress was to blame. And she hadn't been kidding when she said she was in amazing shape…

"Aaron?" Trina waved a hand in front of his face.

"Sorry, what?"

"I asked whether you were free on December 9."

"For another presentation?"

She looked a little nervous as she said, "No, it's a Saturday… It's the night of the staff Christmas party. I was wondering if you'd like to go with me."

"Oh, I'm not really into holiday parties." Only part of the reason he was refusing, but it was true. He'd only attended the Sealena event because coast guard members were expected to be there. But he usually skipped the other holiday-themed events in town.

"Believe me, it's not even really a party. It's sixteen of

us sitting in the teachers' lounge, eating fried finger food, drinking cheap wine and complaining about the lack of resources…" She paused and laughed. "Definitely not helping to sell it, huh?"

Actually it sounded better than a big elaborate party, but still…

"Look, it doesn't have to be a date or anything," she said quickly. "I just hate going alone. Greg tends to hit on the single ladies when he's had too much sugar."

Aaron didn't know Greg very well, but he could understand Trina's desire for a buffer. "So I'd basically be a bodyguard?"

She cocked her head to the side and grinned. "Keeping people safe is your thing, right?"

She was playing that card, and unfortunately, it worked. He sighed. "Okay, I'll go with you."

"I mean only if there's no one special you're seeing…" she said as though fishing for his single status.

Nope. No one special. There had never really been anyone special. He'd dated a bit in the past—mostly tourists on vacation—but he'd never gotten serious about anyone. It was tough to find a connection in a small town. No one really set his heart racing or challenged him or stirred any sexual attraction…

A certain Christmas red minidress didn't count.

"Aaron?"

He blinked. "Yeah?"

"I asked if you were planning to go in?" she repeated with a gentle smile.

"Oh, yes. I was. I am." He had to quit letting Isla Wakefield take up headspace and mess with his dedication to keeping the residents of Port Serenity safe. He hoped she never had a reason to appreciate his diligence.

He followed Trina into the gymnasium as Principal Parks, a short round balding man who'd been the principal since Aaron attended the school, announced him.

"Today, we are lucky to have Petty Chief Officer Aaron Segura back once again to talk about winter safety," he said.

A collective groan rumbled over the group of teens, and Aaron grinned. No one wanted to listen to this, but that would never stop him from doing it. It was too important.

Besides, he wasn't a complete dud. He reached inside his bag and retrieved two hundred candy canes. He handed the bag to the kid in the first row. "Pass these along for me," he said.

The sugar high would at least keep them awake.

THIS TIME OF YEAR would always be significant for Isla.

And not just for the obvious reason of it being the holidays. Main Street in Port Serenity was a winter wonderland this time of year, and whenever she walked the familiar streets, enveloped by the sights and sounds of the season, she remembered the first time she'd experienced it all.

She'd gotten the best Christmas gift ever that year when she'd turned four and the Wakefields had adopted her and brought her home to Port Serenity. Until that point, moving between shelters and foster homes, she hadn't ever celebrated the Christmas season. Being so young, she hadn't even realized it was a special time of year, but that year had been magical. She'd gotten a family with an amazing older brother, and that had been more than enough.

A trip to meet Santa Claus, learning to ice-skate on the outdoor rink, decorating her first Christmas tree, baking holiday cookies and waking up on Christmas morning to all the presents under the tree, Isla had thought her little heart would explode with happiness.

And two seconds later, the fear of losing it all had set in.

This time of year only reinforced how lucky she was. And she wanted to give back any way she could. In her own way. She hummed to herself as she walked along the street in the center of the town, bundled in her warm winter coat, scarf, hat and mittens. She strolled slowly, scanning the storefront displays in all the Wakefield-owned businesses. Her adopted ancestors hadn't just reinvented the town with the erection of Sealena, they'd created employment for so many locals. The appeal of Sealena drew visitors from all over the world, and the Sea Serpent Queen helped fuel the economy.

None of her family members actually ran the businesses, instead providing work opportunities for other families in town. The Walters had always run the Sealena-themed bookstore and museum, which she stopped in front of now and smiled at Carly, who was hanging colorful lights in the window. The pharmacy and convenience store was run by the Grielys, and the spirits and wine store had been operated by the Cranstons for as long as Isla could remember.

There was definitely a sense of pride in being a Wakefield, and the opportunities it had provided her were something she never took for granted.

Unfortunately, she knew her gratitude wasn't entirely enough for her dad.

Everyone said they were a lot alike: stubborn, strongwilled, argumentative and passionate. Key ingredients for a fantastic lawyer, her dad said. But she wasn't sure fighting for justice was what she wanted to do with her life.

She'd been in the system. She'd been a victim of injustice, and besides, she wasn't sure she wanted to live a life spent constantly arguing. Bickering with Aaron Segura was one thing. Fighting in court when there were people's lives at stake was quite another.

She had to do something soon, though, something more permanent. Her parents were supportive of her traveling and discovering herself, but she knew they were starting to worry that she'd simply waft through life. That they'd made things too easy on her and now she didn't know the value of hard work.

It was impossible to explain to other people that it was hard for her to make decisions about her future when there were still so many unanswered questions about her past.

Entering the community youth recreation center a block away, she shivered as a blast of heat hit her. She stomped the snow from her boots on the mat and glanced around. Groups of kids played basketball, indoor tennis and floor hockey in the gymnasiums. The art rooms were full of younger kids making Christmas crafts, and in the drama room a group of young thespians rehearsed for the holiday play that would be featured at the theater hall closer to Christmas.

Mariah Carey's classic Christmas music played throughout the center, and Isla hummed along as she removed her winter outerwear and headed to the indoor rock-climbing room. It was the latest addition to the center. Some anonymous donor had paid for its installation the year before.

"Hey, Isla!" the center's program coordinator said, popping his head around the door frame.

"Hi, Phillip," she said with a smile. The man was dressed in an ugly Christmas sweater, and a snowflake earring dangled from his pierced ear. The kids at the center adored him, and he always made this time of year extra fun and special for kids who might not be getting much holiday spirit at home.

"I have been obsessed with your Instagram all year."

She knew. He'd commented on every photo and video she'd posted of her travels and adventures. "I've appreciated all the comments."

He blushed slightly. "Sorry, I was living vicariously." He rolled his wheelchair into the room and scanned the rock wall. "I reached the top last week," he said proudly.

"That's incredible. Good for you, Phillip. You'll be out on the mountain before you know it, and I'll be commenting on *your* Instagram."

He gave a determined nod. "You better believe it."

"Seems like a lot of kids are enrolled in the class," she said, glancing at the sign-up sheet on the wall.

"The rock wall's been a hit. Wish I knew who to thank for it," he said, eyeing her suspiciously.

She shrugged as the phone rang in his office down the hall.

"Saved by the bell," he said.

"I have no idea what you're talking about," she called after him as he left her to it.

Her own phone chimed with a new text. Opening it, she saw a message from Dwayne.

Great seeing you the other night. That dress—fire!

Isla sighed. She'd suspected her ex would reach out after seeing her at the Sealena event. Though he'd tried to play it cool, keeping his distance, she'd felt his gaze on her more than once throughout the evening. She'd waved once from across the room, but they hadn't spoken. She wouldn't be able to avoid him around town this season. Not with all the holiday events and the fact that they shared the same group of friends. And it wasn't as though she wanted to avoid him. They'd ended things on good-enough terms. They'd dated for three months earlier that year, but she'd called it off when she went traveling again. She'd blamed not being good at the whole long-distance thing, and it was partially true, but it was also an excuse. She liked Dwayne—he was funny and interesting and, as a helicopter pilot for the coast guard, he definitely checked all the right boxes for sexy, successful and daring, things she always looked for in a man. But there had been something missing.

Most likely her fault. Not his. She just hadn't been able to open up and connect with him...or any man, really. Would she ever? Or were casual relationships all she was capable of?

Thanks! Great seeing you too, she texted back. Simple. Platonic.

Dots that he was texting, then:

A group of us are going heli-skiing next week—you in?

Damn, he knew how to tempt her.

Heli-skiing was one of her favorite winter sports. Dwayne's family owned a helicopter tour company in Port Serenity. It was where Dwayne had learned to fly, as a tour guide for his family business, before applying with the coast guard.

His family rivaled hers as the richest in town, with the helicopter business being in their family for generations.

It was something the two of them had in common and one of the reasons Dwayne believed they were so good together. He claimed he had trouble dating as he wasn't sure if women were into him or just after his money. With Isla, he knew he had nothing to worry about. He said they were equally matched. A power couple...

Maybe. Lots of family stuff going on, but I'll let you know, she texted back, then tucked the phone away.

She didn't want to give him false hope of getting back together, but the skiing trip would be fun. As long as he understood they were just friends.

Going into the supply room, she gathered the climbing supplies for the group scheduled to arrive for a lesson. Growing up in Alaska meant incredible access to the most amazing outdoor adventures, but she wanted these kids to learn the proper way to climb before they ventured out onto the mountains. Acquiring the necessary climbing skills in a controlled environment was integral to their safety out in the unpredictable wilderness.

As she checked the harnesses, her cell phone chimed with an email, and her heart raced upon seeing it was from Hunter Investigations in Anchorage. Hands shaking slightly, she opened the email and read the message.

Sorry, Isla. It was a dead-end lead.

Mitchell Hunter was a man of few words. He kept things brief and to the point. She appreciated it most of the time, but sometimes she wished the private investigator could soften the blows a little. She'd hired him two years ago, and he'd yet to discover anything that could help her unravel the truth about her past.

Her hand went to her neck, seeking familiar comfort in the crescent-moon pendant, a gift from her birth mother. The only thing she had connecting her to her early years.

A group of kids noisily shuffled in, dressed in winter gear and carrying heavy backpacks, and Isla quickly tucked the phone away. She forced a bright smile, shaking off the disappointing news as she greeted them.

"Hey, friends! How was school?"

"Boring," eleventh grader Adam Griely said, tossing

his *Walking Dead* backpack against the wall. "We had our annual winter-break safety chat." An eye roll was implied by his tone.

Several of the other kids groaned as well as they filtered in.

"Hey, at least Petty Officer Segura gave us candy," Ariana, a tenth grader, said sucking on a candy cane.

"He needed to provide the sugar rush to keep us awake," another boy, River, said.

Isla hid a grin. So Aaron was still doing his school sessions. As much as she liked to tease him, she thought what he was doing for the school was a good idea. "It's important information," she told the kids.

She was doing a similar thing. Albeit, in a more fun and engaging way…

"I get that we need to be aware of the dangers and know the risks, but all this dude said was, 'Don't do this' and 'Don't do that,'" Adam said, removing his jacket to reveal a shirt that said *Santa Slays All Day.*

So maybe Aaron's way wasn't the best approach with teenagers. In her experience, they often did the exact opposite of what they were told. She'd done her fair share of rebelling at their age. Isla liked to offer guidance without coming across as lecturing.

"Yeah, at least you're teaching us to be safe instead of telling us just don't do it," Ainsley said, reaching for a harness.

She smiled and tousled the kid's long, unruly bed head. "Well, not everyone is as cool as I am. Now, put those candy canes down, and let's get to work."

CHAPTER THREE

DRESSED IN HER winter climbing gear, Isla did squats in her hotel room at the Sealena Hotel. Then she dropped to the floor for a series of push-ups. She'd read on a popular climbing blog that training in full gear helped prepare the body for the excursion, and she was dedicated to being as prepared as possible.

She might give Aaron a hard time about it, but she put safety first too.

When her mindfulness app chimed on her cell phone, she sighed. She didn't have time for her daily meditation that morning, but picking it up, she followed the recommended breathing exercises, repeating the mantra mentally.

Don't allow past experiences to dictate today's reactions. Live in the moment, evaluate circumstances and don't be swept away by emotional assumptions.

The app was a new thing she was trying. Something a fellow adventurer had recommended the year before, when Isla had suffered an embarrassing anxiety attack during a trust exercise with the excursion group. Opening up to people wasn't something she was comfortable with, and the situation had made her feel exposed and vulnerable. She preferred keeping the friendships she'd made along her travels light, casual… Allowing people to get close was reserved for very few…and in those cases, she went overboard with her overprotective nature. As illustrated by her relationship with Dex.

So she had some things to work on. Who didn't? And while she admitted that the daily exercises were helping her to overcome a few personal...*hang-ups*, what really helped was being out in nature.

She packed her gear, carefully selecting only the necessary items. Overpacking could be just as detrimental as not having everything she needed. A mistake a lot of amateurs made. She placed her crampons into her backpack along with her ice axes, a belay device and rope, then zipped it.

She was all set.

Outside the window, darkness still blanketed the coastline, but the day called for perfect weather of just below zero. An overcast sky would ensure they wouldn't have to worry about the direct sunlight Aaron had cautioned against.

She grabbed her cell phone just as it chimed. Seeing a WhatsApp message to the climbing group, she smiled as she opened it. Then her smile faded.

"Canceled?" Apparently, the excursion guide had come down with a bad cold and regrettably had to cancel that day's outing on the glacier.

Disappointment filled her chest as she typed back a *Get well soon* message and then slumped into the chair near the door.

She'd been looking forward to this for months. It was one of the reasons she'd come home for the holidays.

She should never have gone with a different company this year, but she'd wanted to give the new start-up some support. Next time, she'd stick to the company she trusted. SnowTrek Tours out of Wild River was always the perfect choice. With a full staff of qualified guides, the owner,

Cassie Reynolds, never canceled an excursion unless it was absolutely necessary for safety reasons.

Unfortunately, a quick scan of the company's website revealed what she'd expected: all the company's tours were completely booked until mid-January.

She sighed as she opened a Google Map on her phone and checked the route from Port Serenity to the Hidden Glacier. It was a direct-enough drive. She could rent a car and go alone. She'd climbed by herself many times, and she was probably more experienced than the guide anyway... If she got there and felt uneasy about it, she wouldn't do it. The sight of the frozen waterfalls at the glacier would be worth the trip alone. There was no sense sitting around in her hotel room all day.

Having talked herself into it, Isla grabbed her things and headed out.

And an hour later, as she hiked from the parking lot to the base of the glacier's waterfall, she was glad she'd decided to go. Glistening snow and ice-covered mountains were truly breathtaking as the sun started to crest over their peaks. Shimmering, clear, freestanding ice formations from the waterfalls in the distance had her heart racing with anticipation.

This was winter in Alaska at its finest. How could anyone not crave these unique experiences? Isla lived for the moment and lived every moment. So much so that she'd had that mantra tattooed on her rib cage the summer before.

She grabbed her backpack from the car and started the two-mile hike over uneven glacial moraine to the best climbing terrain. There weren't any other groups there yet, but she wanted to make sure she was situated in the best climbing place in case it did get busy with tour groups. She was careful as she made her way over loose, slippery rock, sections of icy mud and steep slopes as she approached the base of the waterfalls.

An hour later, she stopped and stared out at the expansive, intimidatingly beautiful structure that she planned to conquer that day. The unexpected sun was midway high in the sky, illuminating the ice, and she hesitated for just a brief moment before deciding it was still okay to climb. She put on her climbing boots and crampons, checked her gear, then evaluated the ice formation in front of her. The first ten feet of the climb was thin, about shoulder width, so she'd have to climb delicately, but farther up, the conditions were healthier: the ice looked thicker.

She put on her snow glasses and peered up, further preplanning the climb, deciding where she'd place her ice screws along the way. Of course, once she started the ascent, she'd modify her plan as needed.

This was what Aaron didn't understand. She didn't go into things blindly or half-assed. The key to success and safety was to plan. He was right about that. Though, she'd never admit that to him, of course.

If he could see how careful and calculating she was, maybe he wouldn't have so much disdain for her adrenaline junkie-ness, as he put it.

But why she was spending so much headspace thinking about Aaron Segura while standing in front of the most exhilarating challenge of her climbing career, she'd never know.

Pushing all other distracting thoughts aside, ice axes in hand, she took a deep breath and began to climb. Digging her axes in one at a time, she lifted her body onto the frozen waterfall face and then dug her feet into the side. She climbed higher, carefully, until she reached a sturdier, safer height.

The view, even from just those twenty feet up, was breathtaking, and she took a moment to enjoy it. Forecasted clouds hadn't appeared, so the sun lit up the snow-covered valleys and mountain peaks all around her. Tall, ice-tipped evergreens were the only color against the crisp white. The cold air was fresh, and Isla took in a big breath.

Below her in the distance, she saw a group approach on the trail, and she smiled and offered a quick wave when they saw her.

Good thing she'd arrived when she did to secure this primo climbing spot.

She continued her trek upward, her muscles working and feeling the intensity grow stronger, the climb more challenging the higher she went. She stopped to retrieve an ice screw and her crank. With a relaxed position and keeping her weight-bearing arm straight, she fastened the screw at hip level to the side of the mountain and attached her ropes before moving on.

She glanced below to see the group still standing on the trail, discussing and preplanning, getting instruction from the guide, and she was instantly grateful that her tour group had been canceled. This wouldn't be the same with a bunch of people. There was an intimacy with the mountain when it was just her and the rock—or ice, in this case.

"Hey, look out!" the guide called up to her, his voice reverberating off the cliffs.

She turned back in time to hear the ice crack to her right and then see the avalanche of boulder-size ice pans and snow cascading down the side. She moved quickly to the left, just narrowly escaping a large ice boulder barreling toward her.

"Shit, that was close." Her heart echoed in her chest as the avalanche continued down the side, and she hesitated as she glanced upward.

Was her ascent still safe?

A climb down would definitely be too risky, the ice below her already weakening in the sun and heat. The only way off this waterfall was to complete the ascent and hike down the back side as planned.

Below her, the group watched on, appearing to have abandoned their own ice climb for the day, which was probably the right call.

Isla took a deep breath, remembered her training and continued upward. Staying calm and clearheaded was the first step. Precise, confident, safe and calculated movements were the next step... Then it was just one step higher and higher until she reached the top.

Sun glistened off the waterfalls, and she could hear more cracking in the distance. She took a swing with her axe but couldn't break through. She swung three or four times, fearful that too much could cause the whole shelf she was perched against to break free.

The fifth swing connected, and she immediately swung the other side, moving higher.

The group below watched on, and she was further fueled by having an audience.

Half an hour later, sweat pooled under her layered clothing as she swung the axe a final time and propelled her body up onto the top of the glacier.

She'd made it.

Relief, pride and a new wave of adrenaline coursed through her as she positioned herself farther back from the edge and raised her arms in victory.

The group below cheered.

She smiled as she took in the spectacular view and glanced down at the height that she'd accomplished, despite the uncooperative conditions.

Not bad. Not bad at all.

She removed her helmet and jacket, tucking both inside her backpack as the sun and exertion heated her. She opened her thermos and took several big gulps of water before securing the lid and putting it back inside her pack. Grabbing her cell phone, she took several selfies and posted them to her Instagram account with the hashtags *#iceclimb*, *#epic* and *#badass*. Then, removing the crampons and changing back into her hiking winter boots, she surveyed the beautiful Alaskan wilderness a final time before starting her hike back down the snowy side of the cliff.

Adrenaline still pumped through her veins as she walked over the uneven terrain. This was exactly the high she craved, the reason she did these challenges.

Right now, she felt completely invincible.

She took another step, and the ground gave way beneath her on the unmarked path. In an instant, she was plummeting. Free-falling between walls of snow and ice for what felt like forever before she hit ground. Her body crashed onto a shelf of ice, and pain radiated through her from head to toe. Isla blinked, struggling with consciousness, surveying the hazy blue snow and ice walls of the crevasse all around her.

Where the hell am I?

Her final thought chilled her to the core before her eyes closed and darkness took over.

THE *THANK YOU* fruit-and-chocolate basket from Trina that waited in his locker at the station had Aaron blushing as he changed out of his jeans and sweater into his uniform. His presentation may not have impressed the students, but he'd definitely caught the teacher's eye. He was already regretting accepting her invite to the staff holiday party.

It wasn't the first time a visit to a school or youth program had yielded a follow-up request of a different type, and he wasn't oblivious to the fact that he was eye candy in the small town. He worked hard to keep his body in great shape, and the effort had been noticed by more than just Trina over the years.

Unfortunately, the chemistry was never there. The only person who'd ever succeeded in getting his heart racing and blood boiling was Isla. For completely different reasons. He wasn't attracted to her. She just got under his skin. Aggravated him. Occupied his thoughts far more than was necessary.

He refused to think about her any more. She was home for the holidays, but then, she'd surely be off on another adventure, and he could once again put her out of mind. There'd be one less local to worry about. For the next few weeks, they could coexist in the same town: he'd just avoid her as much as possible.

As he left the locker room, a call for assistance coming into the station had him moving fast.

"What's going on?" he asked Dwayne as he joined the helicopter pilot, putting on his gear.

"Incident on Hidden Glacier," Dwayne said, reaching for his jacket.

"A group?" Aaron asked as he donned his own gear in record time.

"Only one woman. Unidentified so far. Another group on site witnessed her fall through a crack in the terrain," he said, hurrying alongside his colleague toward the helicopter pad.

Unidentified woman. Damn. Isla.

She'd said she was heading there that week.

"Were the others climbing?" Aaron asked.

"No. They said the ice was too unpredictable. An avalanche occurred," Dwayne said, filling him in.

His pulse raced. "Was she injured in the avalanche?" Tons of falling ice and snow could be deadly.

"No. Apparently, she made it safely to the top. It was on the trek back down that they saw her fall into a crevasse."

Of course she'd made it to the top. And naturally, that had given her a rush of adrenaline and lowered her perception of continuous risk. Aaron saw it all the time. Waning risk assessment due to the high of completing a challenge. False ground was common this time of year, but if Isla had survived a more treacherous part of her journey that day, she may have downplayed the risk.

"I think it might be Isla," he said. "She was planning a climb while she was home."

Dwayne's terrified expression matched his own as they picked up their pace.

Moments later, they were inside the helicopter and lifting off the pad. As the MH-65 headed toward the glacier about thirty miles away, Aaron's palms were sweating, and his mouth was dry.

Why the hell had she been up there alone? She'd said she was going with a group. With an experienced guide. If the group had canceled due to weather or climbing circumstances and she'd gone anyway… He shook his head as he felt the same irritation rising in his core. The woman was infuriating.

He could see Hidden Glacier in the distance, and attaching his harness, he readied himself as they approached. The large snow- and ice-covered cliffs were jagged and intimidating. Blinding sun glistened on them, making visibility tough. The midday high temperature had small snowdrifts happening already.

"This is going to have to be fast," Dwayne said over the radio.

The helicopter's rotation from above could easily cause the entire mountain of snow to give way. It could be catastrophic to anyone on the trails below, and it could fill in the crevasse where Isla had fallen.

"Copy," Aaron said, readying the basket.

"Location spotted," Dwayne said, moving the chopper directly overhead.

Aaron glanced down toward the deep opening in the snow and ice. It was a long way down, and a quick assessment confirmed the opening was too narrow for the basket. He'd have to bring her up attached to him.

"In position," Dwayne said.

Aaron's heart raced as he immediately began his descent without hesitation. Slowly, carefully, he lowered himself toward the glacier as quickly as was safe. He reached the opening and continued lower, dipping down into the blue, hazy glow of the crevasse. The deep, narrow space was unpredictable as the sun beamed against the crystals. Tall, menacing walls of thick snow and ice bordered all around him. It would be a pretty spectacular sight if he weren't terrified.

This drop could have killed her. Serious injuries were definitely to be expected, and his heart thundered in his chest as he continued lower, scanning all around.

He saw her lying on a shelf a few feet away and radioed the chopper to move farther left. Reaching the shelf, he assessed its depth before stepping onto it.

Isla lay on her back, her left leg slightly bent beneath her. Most likely broken.

But it was the large gash on her head that worried him most. He could see the red in her blond hair, but it was impossible to determine the severity. She'd been lying there for at least thirty minutes. She was no doubt going into shock from the cold and trauma. She wasn't wearing her helmet or her jacket. Just layers of thermal clothing that wouldn't be sufficient for too long without movement in this weather.

"Injured located. Can confirm it's Isla Wakefield."

"Copy," Dwayne said, and he heard the concern in the other man's voice.

The crew would be concerned about any injured person, especially one of their own, but Dwayne had a soft spot for Isla, the two having dated earlier that year. She'd crushed his crewmate when she'd ended things to travel the world. Aaron had served as wingman and designated driver for about two weeks while Dwayne bounced back from the heartache.

He bent next to her. "Isla? Wake up. Can you hear me?"

Nothing.

She didn't stir or open her eyes.

He quickly checked that she was breathing, searching for a pulse. "She's breathing but unresponsive."

"Copy. We need to move fast. Unpredictable cascading snow is heading lower down the mountain."

Shit. He had to get them out of there before snow covered the opening and they were trapped, putting the helicopter at risk as well.

He lifted her carefully, keeping her spine and neck in line as best as possible. He righted the injured leg and attached a clip to the climbing harness still around her.

Her eyes flitted open and she looked dazed, confused. She stared at him as though she didn't comprehend what was happening.

"You're okay. You're going to be okay."

He never said those words unless he knew they were true, and in this case, there was nothing he wouldn't do to keep the promise. Which gave him a whole new sense of terror.

Isla's eyes closed again, and her head slumped toward his chest as he radioed the chopper. "In position. Ready to be lifted."

His pulse pounded in his veins as they were slowly lifted out of the crevasse and up toward the helicopter. He fought to control the sway as he held Isla tight, doing his best to prevent any further injuries, desperate to have her on board the helicopter and off to safety.

She was lucky to be alive. He stared at the drop as they reached the chopper. That fall could have been so much worse. She was breathing, slipping in and out of consciousness. She wasn't out of the woods yet, but at least he had her in his arms, bringing her closer to safety.

An unexpected sense of protection overwhelmed him, and he swallowed the thick fear rising in his throat.

Keep a clear head, and remember the training.

He lifted her into the chopper and placed her on the litter. Dwayne glanced back at them, concern etched into his features.

"Go," Aaron said.

The helicopter took off back toward the Port Serenity Air Station, and Aaron wrapped heated blankets around Isla's body, trying to bring her core temperature back slowly. He surveyed the gash on her forehead. A deep purpling had started around the injury already, and her lips were slightly blue.

Come on, Isla. You're a tough badass. Wake up.

She moaned as she tried to rotate her body, and he gently

held her firm. He had no way to confidently assess her injuries. "Don't move. It's okay. You're safe."

Her eyes opened, and she still looked confused but slightly more conscious, and a small sense of relief ran through him. The temptation to deliver a stern lecture was overwhelming, but it could wait until she was better.

"Where…?" Her voice was hoarse, weak, so unlike her.

"You're in the coast guard rescue helicopter. You fell through the snow and ice into a crevasse." He wasn't sure how much she remembered, but he gave her the facts. "You hit your head and injured your leg. We're bringing you back to the station. Emergency services will take you to the Port Serenity Hospital." The ambulance was already waiting.

"Port Serenity?"

"Yes. Shhh… Just relax."

She nodded, fear in her expression. Something he'd never seen before. It terrified him.

She looked confused as her eyes flitted, struggling for consciousness. She blinked, and her hand searched her neck for something, before dropping back to her side. "Thank you for rescuing me."

Of all the things he'd expected her to say, it certainly wasn't that. He'd almost expected her to demand he bring her back to the trail so she could complete the hike on her own. This woman with her vulnerable, somewhat pleading, desperate expression was not the Isla he'd ever encountered before.

The protectiveness he felt toward her grew stronger, and he moved closer, sensing she needed the reassuring comfort. Isla Wakefield might not be so invincible after all. The feeling made his gut twist, and he realized he didn't like being proven right.

She stared up at him, leaning her body into his. She

***

trembled slightly, and he could see tears welling in her eyes. He touched her freezing-cold cheek gently. "It's going to be okay. I've got you," he said, surprising himself with the deep emotion in his voice.

She nodded, still staring into his eyes. "Who are you?"

He frowned. "What?"

"What's your name?" she whispered, struggling to remain conscious once more.

His heart raced. She didn't recognize him? "It's me. Aaron. Segura."

There was zero recognition in her face as her eyes drifted closed again. "Aaron Segura. Your name means *safe*." Her voice fluttered as she once again gave in to unconsciousness. "I feel safe now."

She might, but *he* suddenly felt ill. Isla didn't know who he was. Amnesia from the head injury?

Shit. What else didn't she remember?

CHAPTER FOUR

THERE WAS SOMETHING unexpectedly freeing about not remembering who she was.

Most people would probably be terrified by that, and she was as she scanned the bruises visible on her exposed arms beneath the hospital gown and felt the bandage around her forehead. But there was also an odd excitement and she knew she'd sound crazy if she voiced her feelings to the three people staring at her who claimed to be her parents and her brother. It felt as if she were journeying into the unknown. Discovering herself, with the potential to become something different perhaps. She couldn't quite explain it, but she felt like maybe this feeling of not knowing who she was wasn't new.

Isla Wakefield, her medical band said.

In front of her were Dex, Brian and Grace. Nice, friendly, concerned-looking people who were obviously rich if their appearance was to be trusted. Her father was in a pair of impeccably pressed dress pants and a button-down under a cardigan sweater, a cashmere coat draped over his arm and expensive leather shoes completing the look. Her mother was in designer jeans and a cashmere sweater, the jewelry she wore looking like it could be the down payment on a house. Her brother was less flashy in jeans and a hoodie. He looked like he'd be a sweet and funny guy. She wasn't sure how she knew that, she just had a vibe.

It was obviously winter as she saw snow falling outside her private hospital-room window, where night had settled, and she'd guess it was Christmas based on the lights shining from a tree visible in the hallway.

Okay, so not great timing for a life-altering injury like amnesia, but she suspected this would have a bigger impact on the family standing in front of her than on herself.

"So…what happened to me?" she asked carefully. All she knew so far was that she couldn't remember anything about who she was.

"You fell into a crevasse while attempting to climb a glacier." It was Dex who answered.

Her eyes widened. Of all the things she'd expected the guy to say, that had to be the last thing. A car accident, a fall from a ladder hanging holiday lights, hitting her head on an open cupboard door, sure, but… "A glacier? I was climbing a glacier?"

Dex nodded and smiled gently. "Sounds nuts to me too, but you do this shit all the time."

Grace shot him a look for the language, and he shrugged. "What? She does."

The woman approached and gently touched her shoulder. "You were lucky. Besides the head injury, you only suffered a sprain in your left leg. The X-ray revealed it's minor and should heal within a few weeks."

Isla nodded. "That's good, I guess. And the memory loss? How long did the doctor say it would last?"

"Could be a few hours," her father said. "Or…longer," he added simply.

In other words, her memory might never return.

She waited for the panic that she assumed would be natural at this kind of news, but only a mild fear gripped her. Mostly for their sake. She had the gift of being bliss-fully oblivious.

"Sorry for the timing... It's Christmas, right?" She nod-ded toward the tree in the hallway when their expressions looked hopeful that she might've remembered something.

Her mother nodded. "Yes, it's Christmas. Well, Thanks-giving today, actually. We are most thankful that you're okay."

A doctor entered and offered a warm smile. "Hey, Isla. I'm Dr. Sheffield. How are you feeling?"

"Okay, given the circumstances," she said.

"Well, your test results showed slight swelling on the temporal lobe and a small lesion near the hippocampus, which we believe is the cause of the memory loss."

"So what does that mean?"

"We're hoping that once the swelling reduces and the brain has time to heal, the memory should return," Dr. Shef-field said.

Should. Not definite.

"Is there anything we can do to help?" her father asked.

Obviously the fixer in the family. He gave the vibe that he'd like to somehow have this situation remedied as soon as possible. That if he could simply pay to have this prob-lem solved, no price would be too high. But he had an air of reserved caring about it that made her believe it came from a sincere place.

"Introduce her to all the familiar things," the doctor said. "Slowly. But try not to tell her too much about who she is, what she likes, what she dislikes. It just clouds who she believes herself to be." He turned to Isla. "Take it one day at a time, and just ease into it. Anything could trigger your memory at any time—a place, a song, a scent. Just remain open and relax."

Remain open and relax. She nodded. "When can I leave?"

He checked her file. "I'd like to keep you for the night, and if your vitals stay stable and you feel okay, you can go home tomorrow," he said.

Home. She wasn't exactly sure where or what that was, but she couldn't stay in the hospital bed. "Thank you," she said.

Her father walked out into the hall with the doctor, and she saw him shake the other man's hand. Obviously, she'd had great care.

An image of the helicopter ride flashed in her mind. Being lifted into it…then arriving at the rescue station where the ambulance waited with flashing lights.

She remembered that part.

"Um…hey, there was a man—a member of the coast guard search and rescue—he rescued me from the crevasse."

"You remember Aaron?" Grace said, looking surprised but hopeful.

"Not really. Just that he saved my life. I remember being lifted into a helicopter…" And a warm, safe sense wrapping around her as she'd looked up at the guy. She'd keep that part to herself. "Is he here?"

Dex shook his head. "He came to the hospital with you in the ambulance but had to get back to the coast guard station to debrief."

She nodded. "I want to thank him."

Dex looked slightly uneasy, but only briefly before the look was replaced by a reassuring smile. "I'm sure you'll get a chance to do that. Just rest for now, okay? Do you need anything? Food? Water?"

What did she like to eat? Or drink? It seemed odd and

embarrassing that she didn't know, so she shook her head. "No, I'm okay. Thank you."

He turned to their mother. "I can pick her up tomorrow when she's released."

Grace hesitated, but nodded. "Yes, good idea. Take her to the yacht."

The yacht?

Yep, these people were rich.

Too bad money couldn't buy her memory back.

HE WAS BACK in the crevasse. His body dangling down the eerily beautiful, dangerous ice cave. He was scanning... searching for something. Someone...

Isla.

He couldn't see her.

He called out, but his voice only echoed on the glistening walls, bouncing back at him.

Where was she? She'd been lying on the crystal slab of ice. He rotated his body as he went lower, searching in the blinding light of the sun reflecting off the surfaces. His own distorted image stared back at him from various angular faces. The look of fear in his expression was foreign.

But he was afraid. More afraid than he'd ever been on a rescue. The normal adrenaline had turned into a chilling, almost crippling, sensation.

This time it was Isla.

He saw her, and as he had in real life, he lifted her to the safety of the helicopter.

The same look of gratitude reflected in those mesmerizing eyes...then her expression changed to one of attraction and instead of thanking him, she reached for his face...

Frozen hands around his cheeks, she brought his head toward hers and kissed him.

His arms instinctively went around her waist, and he drew her in closer. His mouth crushed hers with the intensity of years of bickering, simmering foreplay and the extreme rescue. She was infuriating, and he just wanted to kiss some sense into her. She could have died.

He could have lost her...

Aaron's heart was pounding and the bedsheets beneath him were soaked in sweat when his eyes flew open.

A dream. A very real dream if his body's reaction had anything to say about it.

He threw his arm over his eyes and groaned at the vision of Isla's beautiful face an inch away from his, kissing him, teasing in her expression...

He'd dreamed about rescues before, but this one had felt too real. Even though it was the most far-fetched thing that could ever happen. Isla might have been grateful for his actions the day before, but that was because she'd lost her memory. And gratitude was the extent of it.

Would she even feel that once her memory returned, or would this be yet another source of tension and awkwardness between them? One thing was for sure: he'd never ever mention their moment on the helicopter ride. Even if he knew it would be impossible to forget.

Showered, dressed and at the station less than an hour later, Aaron opened his locker and retrieved his gear. Work would help him shake it off. A few more rescues would put things back into perspective. He'd simply been doing his job the day before.

A knock sounded on the door, and Skylar popped her head around, a hand covering one eye. "Everyone decent in here?"

Aaron laughed. "Depends on your definition of *decent*, but there's no naked people, if that's what you mean."

The coast guard captain entered, dressed in full uniform. "Just wanted to give you an update on Isla."

He nodded, the mention of the woman he'd been kissing in his dream an hour ago making heat rise up the back of his neck. "How is she?" Skylar had already texted him to confirm that Isla had amnesia from the head injury, but he hoped it was a temporary thing. The faster she could remember everything, the faster things could go back to normal.

"Still can't remember much," Skylar said. "She has a sprained leg, but the doctor says her incredible fitness level prevented any serious injuries. The blow to the head is the most concerning."

"Do they know how long the memory loss might last?"

"A day or…forever." Skylar sighed. "Unfortunately, they can't predict how fast she might recover or if she ever will."

"Well, let's hope it's the former."

"Dex is picking her up at the hospital later today, and we're going to take her to the yacht. The doctor said familiar places and faces might help."

Aaron nodded. "Well, tell her I hope she feels like her old self soon."

Skylar hesitated by the door. "She asked about you."

His gut twisted. "Oh?"

"She wanted to know who her hero was," Skylar said with a small grin.

Aaron laughed at the irony. "Did you tell her it was her archenemy?"

"Dr. Sheffield said we shouldn't tell her too much about herself. Let her discover things on her own. Adding our perspective could cloud her judgment and slow her memory regain."

That seemed dangerous in his opinion, but he nodded.

"Okay. Well, I'm sure we'll be back at one another's throats before long. I'll enjoy the reprieve."

Unfortunately, the reprieve from having to see her was short-lived.

When Aaron reentered the station later that day after his shift patrolling the waterways on the cruiser boat, Isla and Dex were in Skylar's office.

What the hell? Dex was supposed to take her to the yacht.

Aaron quickly switched course, away from the direction of the office. He could get his things from his locker later…after she was gone.

"Hey!" Too late. Her voice made him repress a sigh, and he stopped and turned to face her.

"You're out of the hospital," he said, stating the obvious. And other than the crutch she was leaning on and a small bandage on her forehead, there was no sign that only a day ago, she'd almost died at the base of a crevasse. He was happy she hadn't been even more hurt, but he knew that, unfortunately, this small sprain and forgetfulness wouldn't be enough to stop her from taking more risks in the future.

"They let me out for good behavior," she said, almost nervously.

The sound of Isla's voice anything but confident, direct and full of spirited spite caught him off guard. She even looked…softer somehow. As though the chip on her shoulder had broken off in her fall. Her face seemed more delicate, and those lips…

She laughed awkwardly, and he realized he hadn't said anything. He'd just been standing there, staring at her like a moron. He cleared his throat. "Well, take care." He turned and started walking away, but she followed.

"Wait, I wanted to thank you," she said, hopping on her good foot toward him.

"Sure. No problem. Just doing my job. I would have done it for anyone." He was babbling. He slammed his lips shut.

"So I'm not special. Got it," she said with a teasing glint in her eye.

Damn, if only that were the truth. But he knew he'd reacted to this rescue differently than he had to others. Even his damn dreams were confirming how this one had been more intense. The stakes had felt higher...because she was someone he knew. Someone important to the community... important to him?

Jesus. He was in trouble. He ran a hand through his hair. "I just meant—"

"I know. I was kidding." She paused and looked nervous as she continued. "I was hoping I could take you to dinner...to thank you."

His mouth went dry. "You just thanked me."

"Right. But I wanted to really thank you...with food." Her cheeks were flushed with a mild embarrassment. He didn't like putting her through this awkwardness, but there was no way he could have dinner with her. The idea was ridiculous.

"That's not necessary. Really," he said gently.

She looked disappointed, and it was the oddest situation. He felt as though he'd stepped into the middle of a *Twilight Zone* episode. Isla Wakefield wanted to have dinner with him. He could see it now: a nice, quiet meal, and then she'd regain her memory halfway through the main course and stab him with a steak knife.

"You sure? Coffee, at least?"

"We have coffee here...in the break room. I'm set, but thank you," he said awkwardly. This was tough. Prefall Isla would never be suggesting they hang out together. Hell, if she hadn't lost her memory, she definitely wouldn't be there, thanking him for saving her. Her pride wouldn't have let her.

And he would have preferred it that way. Seeing her—rejecting her—was doing things to his emotions that he didn't like.

"Okay... Well, thanks again," she said.

"You bet." He turned and headed out of the station before things could get even crazier. Like maybe he'd actually reconsider and take her up on the unexplainably tempting offer.

CHAPTER FIVE

GOING TO FAMILIAR places might help trigger her memory, the doctor had said.

But staring up at the magnificent yacht, *The Mariana*, later that day, Isla's eyes bulged as though seeing it for the first time. "How rich are we?" she muttered.

Assisting her up the wooden plank toward the boat, Dex laughed. "We're not. Our ancestors were."

Isla nodded. "So all the businesses in town with the Wakefield name on the awning..." She'd counted at least seven along Main Street as they'd driven from the coast guard station.

"Those are the family businesses, but they are mostly run by other local families now."

"Wow," she said, following Dex onto the boat deck. She scanned the marina and the pier, and a warmness enveloped her, but unfortunately no recognition followed. Obviously, this was a place that meant a lot to her, and Port Serenity definitely felt like home. She didn't feel like a stranger or a tourist, despite not fully recognizing her surroundings, as though part of her memory remembered this was where she was from, where she belonged. That was comforting, at least.

Dex unlocked the door and helped her inside. A beautiful German shepherd wearing a therapy vest immediately approached and sniffed her leg. Odd that she could remember the breed of dog but not this specific dog. Animals must fall into the general knowledge and facts category, not impacted like her own personal memories. In the hospital, she'd experimented a bit: she knew the alphabet, how to count, tie her shoelaces… Her muscle memories were all still intact. It was just the details surrounding her own existence that eluded her.

"Aren't you beautiful?" she said, bending as well as she could with her casted leg to cuddle the dog. "What's her name?"

"That's Shaylah, but you may not want to do that," Dex said hanging his keys on a rack near the door.

"Why not?"

"You're allergic to dogs."

"Seriously?" She pet the dog a final time and stood. She looked around the lavishly but comfortably decorated yacht. It was impressive, even bigger on the inside than it looked from the outside. A large, open-concept living room and kitchen made up the main living space, and a spiraling wooden staircase led to a second floor. To her right, she could see a hallway leading to the ship's navigation quarters and a bathroom. A beautiful fireplace and bar were unexpected additions that really made the place feel like a home.

She could see why Dex would choose to live there.

"Well? Anything?" he asked.

She focused really hard, but no memory surfaced. She shook her head. "Nope."

"Well, feel free to wander around. See if something sparks a memory," he said. "I'll make us something to eat."

"Okay. Thanks."

He went into the kitchen, and Isla took the opportunity to tour the yacht. Upstairs, she found three bedrooms. One had been turned into an office, and upon entering, she noted all the books on ship navigation, search and rescue manuals, and novels on the mahogany bookshelf. An old-fashioned typewriter was the focal point on a magnificent, old desk, and pictures of sailors covered the walls. She scanned them, recognizing the family resemblance to Dex and Brian, but nothing sparked any real memory.

She left the office and wandered down the hall to the bedrooms. Dex's was his private space, so she didn't go in. Instead, she went into the room that he'd said used to be hers, which now belonged to the dog. Unfortunately, it was free of any real personal items, and the scent of the canine was starting to make her eyes water. She sneezed several times and quickly left the room.

Downstairs, Dex waited for her with an antihistamine and a glass of water.

"Thanks," she said, gratefully accepting it. She popped it into her mouth, took a gulp of the water and swallowed. "Am I allergic to anything else besides dogs?" she asked him.

"Mushrooms," Dex said as she followed him toward the kitchen.

"Okay…" What else was super important to know? Blood type? They obviously had that on record at the hospital. Her menstrual cycle? Probably not info her brother could provide. "Friends?" she asked. No one had come to the hospital, but that was doctor's orders not to overwhelm her with too much at once. But surely she had people in town who'd heard about her accident by now.

"Other than all our old school friends who still live here in town, your best friend, Jillian, lives in Denver, working as a ski instructor, and I think most of your friends are people you met through your travels… You've hardly been here since graduation." He paused. "Except for last year, when you moved back to help me out after Grandpa died."

She frowned. "Why? What's wrong with you?" she asked, glancing at Shaylah. So, she was some kind of therapy dog.

Dex laughed at her lack of tact. "That sounds like the sister I know. I have epilepsy."

"Oh. Sorry," she said. She'd come back from traveling to help him? That was good to hear. Evidently, she was a caring, compassionate sister. That made her feel better.

He waved a hand as he stirred chicken and vegetables in a pan on the stove. "Anyway, I can reach out to Jillian and anyone else you'd like to update about this…"

She shook her head. "Maybe we should just wait a few days to see if my memory returns." She essentially didn't know these friends, so why reach out just now? If anyone called or texted, she'd deal with it on a case-by-case basis. Maybe she should change her voicemail message to something like *Isla isn't here right now. Please leave a message, and she'll get back to you when she remembers who the hell you are.*

"Okay. Anything else?" Dex asked, dishing up a plate of food.

"Do I work?" Was there an employer expecting her at an office somewhere? Could she lose her job because of this?

Dex shook his head. "Not really. You volunteer with different programs, and you've had a few temporary positions over the years, but nothing permanent."

"So I'm a trust-fund brat?" How did she feel about that? Not entirely good…but she did volunteer. That was something.

"Essentially, but don't stress about it."

"Okay."

"Anything else?"

She hesitated, but it was probably important to know. "Am I dating anyone, or in a relationship?" There hadn't been a significant other present at the hospital. A memory of her rescuer, Aaron Segura, flashed in her mind, and she hoped her brother's answer was no.

He grinned as he set the plate of food in front of her. "You aren't exactly the relationship type. Casual dating is more your thing."

She wasn't sure how she felt about that knowledge. "Because I travel so much?" That would make sense. If she weren't willing to settle in one place for long, relationships would be challenging. Maybe she wasn't ready for serious commitments at this stage in her life.

No job. No boyfriend. Huh. She wasn't quite sure how she felt about these revelations. Obviously, her lifestyle suited her, and she had no choice but to trust that, right?

But Dex looked uneasy as he nodded. "That's a huge part of it."

A huge part but not all. She narrowed her eyes at him. "What are you not telling me?"

He shook his head. "Nothing. Eat before the food gets cold," he said, nodding toward the plate.

It smelled delicious, but she also caught a whiff of non-disclosure. "Come on, Dex. You can't hint at something, then not explain."

He sighed. "You definitely didn't lose your personality in the accident. Still pushy as ever."

"Different part of the brain," she said with a grin, picking up her fork. "Now, out with it."

He folded his arms across his chest and leaned against the kitchen counter. "It's just that...you have issues with trust and letting people get close."

She let that sink in. "Any idea why?"

"Oh, I have plenty of theories," he said jokingly, trying to lighten the mood. "But that's all you're getting from me right now." He handed her his laptop with her open social-media page on the screen. "Start here with your research. See if something looks or feels familiar," he said. "I have to take Shaylah out for her run anyway."

"Thanks," she said, gratefully. She could already tell she was close to this guy. He was being so great with her, and his revelation that she'd come back from traveling to help him the year before made her feel better. She may have trust issues and hesitancies about romantic relationships, but she was clearly tight with her family.

That made her feel better.

Dex grabbed Shaylah's training leash, and the two headed out.

Alone, Isla ate the delicious food as she turned her attention to the social-media platform. There were so many posts—mostly photos captured on adventures with inspirational captions added to them. Some were solo selfies. Others featured groups, probably on excursions or tours, she guessed, as the people in the photos were constantly changing. She appeared to be someone who made friends—or at least acquaintances—easily enough. She scrolled through them, going back several years, seeing her time on a cruise ship, maybe one of the fleeting jobs Dex had mentioned. Family vacations. Lots of outdoor-enthusiast stuff. She seemed to be highly adventurous and up for anything. She seemed happy, always smiling in the photos.

Unfortunately, nothing really triggered any memories of the actual events.

But as she looked at them closer, she did notice something. In every photo she was wearing the same necklace: a beautiful gold crescent-moon pendant on a thin gold chain. It was beautiful and seemed to suit her: simple, elegant, meaningful.

Her hand flew to her neck now, but it wasn't there. The hospital had given her back all of her personal items that day as she'd left. It hadn't been among them.

Damn. She must have lost it.

Oddly enough, it felt like the only thing that might have provided any clarity.

DWAYNE STOOD ABOVE the barbell in the station's gym as Aaron effortlessly cranked out his set of fifty reps of chest presses. It was his second workout of the day, and yet, he still felt an anxious energy that he couldn't quite figure out or get rid of. He'd hoped the physical exertion might help the restlessness he was feeling, but so far it hadn't.

All day, he couldn't erase Isla's look of disappointment when he had turned down her dinner offer. He'd been unnerved to see her so...not fragile exactly, but looking less... intimidating and, dare he say it, approachable and friendly.

The main thing was that she was safe and being cared for by her family. She'd be okay. She did not need him.

He struggled under the weight of the bar as he cranked out five more reps. Hopefully, if he exhausted his body, he'd exhaust his mind enough to stop thinking about her. So far, it wasn't working.

Dwayne let out a low whistle as Aaron finally set the bar back on the rack and sat up to reach for his towel. "Impressive. Soon, you'll be as strong as I am," he said, motioning for Aaron to get up so he could take his turn at the bar.

Aaron stood and started to take several weight plates off the end, but Dwayne stopped him. "Leave them. I got it."

"It's twenty pounds heavier than your set three days ago."

"If you can do it, I can do it," Dwayne said, lying on his back under the bar.

The slight note of challenge in Dwayne's tone wasn't anything new. They'd always had a healthy, friendly level of competition. They pushed one another. But the slight chip on his shoulder today was different. Dwayne was normally carefree and easy-going, but something was up with his buddy, workout partner and co–crew member. Aaron suspected it had to do with the rescue, but he also knew Dwayne wasn't likely gonna talk about it.

Sweating it out in a little weight-lifting catharsis was about as good as it was going to get. Eventually, they'd get over it and move on.

"Okay," Aaron said, poised to spot, ready to catch the bar when it tried to crush his friend. Dwayne was strong, but he trained primarily in cardio. He needed to be flexible, fast and strong enough to keep a helicopter straight in inclement weather. Aaron's body needed to be capable of the impossible—swimming against strong currents and supporting the weight of people in need.

Three reps in, his buddy was struggling.

He reached for the bar, but Dwayne shot him a look that said *Stand down.*

"Man, you're going to pull something and then not be able to work out for a week."

"I got this. Just shut up and stand there," Dwayne grunted. His chest heaved, his back arched in bad form, and his face turned red as he was holding his breath. But to his credit, he finished a set of ten and replaced the bar himself with shaky arms.

"Great job," Aaron said, adding another set of plates for his next round.

Dwayne eyed him over his water bottle as he gulped the liquid. "What are you trying to prove, man?"

"Not trying to prove anything. I'm working out."

"We already know you're the big shot," Dwayne mumbled.

Aaron folded his arms across his chest and took a deep breath. Guess they *were* going to talk about it. "Is this about the rescue?"

"No. It's about Isla and that moment you two had in the back of my helicopter," Dwayne said, standing and reaching for his discarded T-shirt draped across the treadmill.

Ah, so Dwayne had caught that.

Aaron shrugged as he looked away. "That was nothing. It was a stressful moment. She was injured and didn't remember she was supposed to punch me in the face for saving her, that's all."

Dwayne yanked the shirt down over his body. "Her memory was gone, but yours wasn't."

His jaw twitched. He was already battling his irrational reaction to Isla that day, he didn't need his buddy questioning him about it. "What's that supposed to mean?"

"I saw the way you were panicked when you found out it was her. And I saw the way you took risks you normally wouldn't. And I saw the look on your—"

Aaron held up a hand. "Okay, I get it." He took a deep breath. "It was different because it was someone we know, that's all." That had to be all it was.

"We rescue locals all the time. This was different because it was Isla."

"Isla drives me crazy. You know that. With her risk-taking and lack of regard for safety, she put not only herself but also us in danger that day..." Aaron ran a hand through his sweaty hair and sighed. There was no way he would admit to Dwayne that it went any deeper than that. He refused to acknowledge it himself. "Look, let's just drop it, okay? We both did our jobs. She's safe. That's all that matters."

"Only difference is, she didn't invite *me* to dinner to thank me," Dwayne said, tossing his towel into the laundry basket and shoving the swinging door closed.

CHAPTER SIX

PLEASE LET ME remember something.

Opening her eyes, Isla held her breath as she scanned the hotel room. It looked the same as it had the day before, but no other memories surfaced. She knew the hotel had been in her family for generations, an old, run-down place that her great-grandfather had renovated with the Sealena theme, but she didn't have memories of running through the hotel hallways as a child or enjoying Sunday brunch in the dining room the way Dex had recounted the evening before. The clothes spilling out of her suitcase on the floor were nice and to her taste but didn't instill any reminders of shopping trips with girlfriends or amazing online finds. The scents of her perfume and body wash lingering on the bedsheets and pillow didn't trigger anything either.

So far, nothing was different from the day before.

Was she an early-morning person, or did she hug the pillow, hitting snooze a dozen times? Did her usual habits even apply anymore?

She sighed as she tossed the bedsheets back and got up. She set the coffee maker, then hesitated, seeing the empty chamomile tea packet in the garbage can. Was she a coffee drinker or a tea drinker? She craved caffeine, that was for certain.

Taste-test time.

She made both and then took a sip of each.

Preinjury Isla maybe preferred the tea, but Isla 2.0 was going with the coffee.

Her cell phone chimed, and picking it up, she saw a mindfulness app alert, telling her it was *meditation time*. She frowned. She didn't strike herself as someone who meditated. Sitting still for a long time, contemplative, didn't really seem to be her M.O.

The phone rang in her hand, and she jumped at the tinkling holiday tune playing on repeat. Maybe meditation was a good idea. She was definitely wound tight.

Get a grip. It's just a ringing phone.

But what if it were a friend who hadn't heard about her accident? The discussion would be weird and tense… Maybe she should post a disclaimer message on her social-media pages… Would that be in character? To make light of her situation online? Would people expect that of her or think she'd lost her mind as well as her memory?

But seeing *Mom* appear on the call display, she sighed in relief. Grace. "Hello," she said politely.

"Sweetheart, how are you?"

Her mother sounded so hopeful, she hated to disappoint her. "I'm feeling pretty good." She paused. "No memory yet."

"That's okay. The doctor said it could take some time." A silence followed as though that was the main reason she'd been calling and now she had no idea what else to talk about. Was the relationship with her mom strained or awkward? Or was it just the oddness of the situation? "Did you sleep okay?" Grace asked finally.

"Yes, thank you. The hotel bed is amazing." Again with the formal politeness, but she too didn't quite know what to say. Did she and her mother have a lot in common? Did they enjoy the same TV shows? The same music? What would

they normally talk about? Or was it the kind of mother–
daughter relationship that wasn't that close?

"You know you're welcome to stay here. Your old room
is available if you want it."

Isla hesitated. There must have been a reason she hadn't
chosen to stay at her family home that holiday season, opt-
ing for the hotel… She didn't know what it was, but until
she did, it was probably best to stay put. "I'm comfortable
here, but I'll definitely come by. Maybe something from
my old room will trigger a memory."

"Oh… Actually, darlin', probably not. The room is still
there, but we've had it turned into a guest room. Your personal items are in storage."

"Oh." That was to be expected, she guessed. According
to Dex, she hadn't lived there since high-school graduation. Always staying on the yacht or at the hotel when she
was in town.

"We had to, after you moved out," Grace said. "Those
purple and orange walls you'd painted may have been your
way of expressing yourself, and we supported that, but
those colors were a nightmare," she said with a laugh.

Isla had painted her bedroom purple and orange? Her
parents had allowed that? She'd never have pegged them
as parents who'd be that cool and open-minded. She may
have misjudged them based on appearances.

"Well, that's fine. I totally understand."

"But definitely still stop by…anytime. And of course,
you're planning to attend your father's law-firm party at
the house, right? Plus, we will all be together on the yacht
for Christmas. Dex and Skylar are insisting on hosting
Christmas dinner this year."

She couldn't quite tell how her mother felt about
that. Dex had explained briefly about some Wakefield–

Beaumont family feud, but she couldn't dwell on that now. Her head ached slightly. So many family events with strangers were making her feel uneasy.

But they weren't strangers, they were family. *Her* family. "Yes...yeah...of course I'll be there."

"Well, call us if you need anything or if you start to remember," her mother said.

"You'll be the first to know."

"Bye, sweetheart."

Disconnecting the call, Isla sat in the chair near the window and peered out over the beautiful scenery. The marina with its decorated boats, the mountains in the distance covered in fresh snow...

The idea of staying in the hotel room all day didn't appeal to her. What could she do?

Deciding fresh air and exercise might make her feel better, she headed out twenty minutes later to explore the town. She shivered in the cold December chill as she hobbled along the streets on her crutch. She again noted how vibrant the community was, but the day before she hadn't noticed just how much Sealena was part of the aesthetic. The Sea Serpent Queen was everywhere. From the big statue in the town square to the graphics on all the street signs and etched into the sidewalk, wherever it was visible under the crunchy snow and ice.

This was her heritage.

She really should learn about it just in case her memory didn't return. Seeing the Sealena Museum and Bookstore across the street, she made her way toward it. The decorated window featured books and Sealena statues among the Christmas garlands and lights. A large, handcrafted pirate ship was the focal point, also adorned with strings of holiday lights. Inside, a woman who looked several years older than Isla worked behind the counter. She glanced up, smiled when she saw her and waved Isla inside.

Someone who knew her. Her palms sweated a little at what was sure to be an awkward meeting. Though, everyone in town probably knew her. The population was only seven thousand people, and she was a Wakefield... Damn, how many people had she passed on her walk into town who had thought she was being rude when she hadn't acknowledged them? Did everyone know about her accident?

This woman definitely did.

As soon as Isla entered, she hurried toward her and wrapped her in a big hug. "I'm so happy you're okay," she said, squeezing her tight before releasing her.

"Um...thank you," Isla said as she scanned the interior of the store. Sealena-themed items were everywhere: statues, books, T-shirts, hats...a tourist trap for sure. But then she noticed what looked like a small school area in the back with old-looking resource books about the ocean and early captains, the words *Sealena School* written on the whiteboard. An education center. Perfect! That's what she'd been looking for. A crash course on her family's history with the Sea Serpent Queen.

The woman's gaze was sympathetic as she stepped back and eyed the gash still visible on Isla's forehead. She'd removed the bandage because she'd felt silly walking around with it.

"I'm Carly," the woman said. "Guess I shouldn't assume I'm the only person in town you'd recognize."

Isla gave a wry laugh. "Don't take it personally. My own reflection is a stranger these days," she said.

"Well, you are still as beautiful as ever. So happy you're home for the holidays. I'm sure your family is thrilled."

"I think I may be just causing them more stress," she

said, surprising herself a little with her open honesty with someone she currently didn't know. But there was something warm and trusting about the woman with the long, dark hair and caring brown eyes.

"No way," she said. "They love you, and I'm sure they just want you to get well soon. How are you feeling? I heard it was quite the fall at the glacier."

She nodded. "From what I can remember, yeah, but I'm good. Could have been a lot worse." The day before, after studying her social-media page, she'd googled Hidden Glacier and read the coast guard report of the rescue. Seemed like quite an adventure. It was hard to believe she put herself in these risky situations all the time. She hadn't quite reconciled how she felt about that yet. She obviously enjoyed these extreme-sport activities, and she was good at them. After all, she'd made it to the top of the glacier. False ground was unpredictable and not something she could have prevented.

Yep, there was definitely a bit of daredevil still within her if she was already justifying her actions to herself. It was a relief to know her personality might not be completely affected by the damage to her brain.

"All I can say is, I'm so happy that my cousin—and your future sister-in-law—Skylar sent Aaron on all that extra training. If he hadn't been able to do the vertical rescue, they would have needed assistance from the local search and rescue crew. They are amazing, but getting to you by snowmobile or on foot would definitely have taken longer than with the coast guard chopper."

Isla had realized that the fast actions of Aaron and the rest of the crew that day had resulted in her injuries being less severe. In her unconscious state, had hypothermia set in, it could have been a lot worse. But she hadn't realized that her rescuer was a specially trained member of the coast guard.

That made him even more appealing.

"I guess I was lucky."

"Port Serenity is lucky. Aaron is, like, only one of forty-six elite rescue swimmers in the United States," Carly said, then she blushed slightly. "You'd think I had a crush on him with the way I'm gushing. I don't."

Isla did.

But maybe she wouldn't go so far as to confide that in this virtual stranger just yet.

Still, she was curious, so she decided to go for it. "His girlfriend must feel safe having him around." Maybe if he was unavailable it would help lessen the blow to her ego that he'd refused coffee with her.

"No girlfriend. He barely dates. Not that there isn't a string of women interested. Again, not me," Carly said quickly with a laugh.

"I can understand the appeal," she said.

Carly's expression changed slightly behind her teal-rimmed glasses, a fleeting look of disbelief appearing in her eyes before it disappeared just as quickly. "What brings you in?" she asked.

"Well, I don't know how long this memory loss will last, and I'm starting to feel a little weird about not remembering anything about this community and the whole Sealena thing."

Carly smiled, linking her arm through Isla's. "Well, if Sealena knowledge is what you seek, you've come to the right place."

Isla had come for knowledge about the Sea Serpent Queen, but she'd gained far more interesting knowledge about Aaron Segura. Single. Huh. Then, maybe she just needed to try harder to catch his attention.

JUST A FEW more hours, then he was off for a few days, though he'd be on emergency call.

When was the last time he'd looked forward to a break? The last week had taken a toll, and he couldn't quite pinpoint why. There had been a few local rescues, but nothing out of the ordinary and no fatalities or near misses. Certainly not anything he hadn't been able to handle or that'd stayed with him once debriefing was over.

Emotionally, the Isla rescue was still affecting him, and he didn't want to think too long about why.

Aaron poured hot, fresh coffee into his mug and added a packet of sweetener. Normally, he drank it straight, but that morning, he needed the dose of sugar along with the caffeine. He hadn't been sleeping well. There hadn't been any more vivid dreams that he could remember, but he was waking in the middle of the night with a mild sense of foreboding and anxiety. He suspected it was because Isla was still not completely out of the woods, therefore his mission didn't feel over, not fully, and there was nothing he could do about it.

"You ready? Everyone's in the meeting room," Skylar said, stopping in the lunchroom doorway.

"I'll be right there," he said, stirring the coffee and taking a sip.

That day he was training the crew on frostbite. It was a new thing that Skylar had implemented earlier that year. She saw him as a real asset on the team and thought they should all learn some of the specialized skills he had.

At first, he wasn't sure how the crew would respond to him training them, especially the older guard, but so far, the sessions had gone well. And Skylar was right that it did make him feel better knowing that his crewmates had the knowledge to assist in more difficult rescue scenarios.

Frostbite was something that was common in Alaska, not just with tourists or locals enjoying leisure activities but also people who worked outside in the harsh winter environment. It was important to learn how to treat it in those crucial first moments.

He left the lunchroom and entered the meeting, where seven of his crewmates sat waiting for him. Dwayne was in the front row, arms folded, avoiding his gaze.

Okay, so his friend was still pissed.

Going to the whiteboard, he wrote *Frostbite Prevention & Treatment*.

"Oh, come on. Seriously?" Dwayne mumbled.

Aaron's jaw clenched, but he chose to ignore the comment as he turned around. "I know it seems like a basic subject to cover, but this time of year, it's one of the more probable injuries that we're faced with."

"This was taught in Winter Backwoods Safety 101," Dwayne said.

Skylar's gaze met his, and she shot him a questioning look that said *What's his problem?*

Aaron gave a quick headshake and refused to let his friend throw him off course. "Okay, well think of today as a refresher."

Dwayne sank lower in his seat as Aaron started his presentation. "Our bodies are designed to protect vital organs and deep tissues to keep us alive in unfavorable weather conditions. Therefore, protecting extremities from the extreme cold is hard. Once bodies start to cool, they react by shutting down blood flow to extremities it doesn't consider essential for survival—"

"Such as fingers and toes, which are farthest from the body's warm core. Yes, we know," Dwayne interjected.

Okay, this was bullshit.

Aaron turned to him. "What's the freezing temperature of human tissue?"

"It's -0.53 degrees Celsius."

"What causes human cells to expand and burst?"

"When ice crystals form inside the cells."

Okay... "What is autoamputation?"

Dawyne leaned forward. "When destroyed tissues wither and drop off. Any other questions? Sir?"

A low rumble echoed across the room as their coworkers observed the tense exchange. This was unprofessional and petty. But Dwayne had started it.

Aaron's hands clenched at his sides, but Skylar interjected before he could answer.

"Hey, let's take five. Everyone go grab a coffee," she said.

No one moved.

"Go," she said, nudging the coworkers out of the room.

Dwayne stood, but she pointed a finger at him. "Not you."

Dwayne sat back down, and Aaron leaned against the desk as Skylar approached and the room cleared out. "What's going on?" She turned to Aaron first.

"I'm just trying to teach a class."

"This class is a waste of time," Dwayne said.

"Well, what would you rather learn about?" he said, fighting to keep his cool. Everyone always thought the basics were boring, but saving someone's fingers was just as important as saving their life. And while they might not be the most newsworthy or heroic missions, in this Alaskan climate these were the calls they answered most frequently. The crew needed to stay sharp on these skills.

"Vertical rescue?"

Aaron scoffed. Of course. "That's a little hard for most—"

Dwayne shook his head. "Right. I forgot. There's only one superhero per team."

"Look, man, if you want vertical training, go to a vertical training course," Aaron said with a shrug.

Skylar nodded, seeing her opportunity to interject. "Absolutely. I can certainly recommend you for that. I didn't realize it was something you were interested in completing."

It wasn't. Aaron knew that. Dwayne was all talk. He loved flying the chopper—and staying inside it.

Dwayne shrugged. "Maybe I will." He stood. "Hey, listen, since I obviously know my stuff, can I go?"

Skylar hesitated, but sensing it might be best for the rest of the crew not to have a sulking student in the front row challenging Aaron, she nodded. "Sure. Staff meeting at noon," she said.

"Great," Dwayne muttered as he left the training room.

Skylar took a deep breath and looked at Aaron. "What the hell is wrong with him?"

Aaron hesitated. "He's upset about the rescue."

Skylar frowned. "Which one?"

"Isla."

His captain still looked confused. "That was textbook. You both did everything exactly right."

Except that he'd been in the back of the chopper offering support when Dwayne was the one who wanted to be doing it. "He's not quite over Isla yet, and I was the one who was offering the support when she needed it."

"Oh…" Skylar looked like she'd just stepped into a

junior-high love triangle and wasn't sure how to handle this particular workplace dilemma.

He waved a hand. "He'll be fine. We'll be fine," he said infusing as much confidence as possible into his tone.

"Okay. I'm trusting you two to figure this out," Skylar said.

"Yes, ma'am."

CHAPTER SEVEN

ISLA SQUARED HER shoulders as she headed toward the Santa Village with the *almost* one-page résumé she'd put together at the hotel business center. Hopefully they wouldn't notice she'd used a fourteen-point font.

Her mother had mentioned Christmas events, and she'd looked around the hotel room but didn't find any Christmas gifts. She needed to buy some. She couldn't show up to her family's Christmas festivities empty-handed.

Her sequined Gucci wallet held three credit cards that were surely connected to the trust fund Dex had mentioned. But she didn't feel right using them. Especially not to buy gifts for her family.

Merry Christmas! This is what your family fortune bought you from me for the holidays.

No way. She had no choice but to rely on those cards for her hotel stay and necessities right now, but she wanted to give gifts that she'd bought with money she earned.

Therefore, getting a seasonal job was her only option.

Amid the beautiful winter wonderland, the Santa's North Pole Workshop pop-up in the center of Main Street Square was a hot spot for sure. Kids and their parents, bundled up against the cold, all stood in line waiting to see Santa. Photographers and assistants dressed as elves handed out candy canes and helped parents pick out the packages they wanted to purchase.

She could do that. It might actually be fun, and it would be a great way to remeet everyone in the community and really embrace the holiday season. She approached an elf and smiled.

"Hi, I'm looking for the manager."

The elf looked to be about eighteen, and there was no sign of recognition on her expression as she pointed to a small structure named the Elf Hut. "She's in there."

"Thank you," Isla said, taking in the short green velvet costume with candy-cane-striped leggings, pointy shoes with bells, and floppy green elf hat. She'd look cute in that—minus the small issue of her cast...

She bit her lip as she watched the elves move around quickly. They were on their feet all the time... Could she do that?

Nope, she wasn't going to talk herself out of this.

Approaching the Elf Hut, she knocked on the open door that read: *Top Elf: Cherry Madru.*

An older woman with white hair poking out of an elf hat and round wire-rimmed costume glasses glanced up. "Can I help you?"

Propping her crutch against a candy-cane pole, she entered and sat across from the woman. She smiled and tried to pretend she recognized her. She didn't want her memory issue to be the reason she couldn't get the job. "Hi, Mrs. Madru. I was hoping to apply for a job."

Unfortunately, Cherry eyed her slightly disbelievingly. "*You* want to work *here* this season?"

Isla nodded. She would rather a retail position at one of the shops along Main Street or at the local mall, but she had no idea how to fold clothes, use a cash register or sell stuff, and at this time of year, managers were looking for skilled employees, not brand-new hires in need of training. Isla couldn't believe her own dismal résumé.

Rock climbing, traveling... She'd worked on a cruise ship, which was at least something, but she'd been employed as an excursion guide. Basically, she'd gotten paid to do the activities she loved.

But she'd use her people skills as her main selling point.

"I do," she said, sliding her résumé toward Cherry.

The woman replaced the fake glasses with real ones as she scanned it. "There's not a whole lot of experience on here."

"I know, but I'm energetic and great with people." She assumed. "And I pick up new skills really fast." She'd been basically learning everything all over again the last few days, and she was doing well. "I'm adaptable and flexible." So far, she'd been rolling with the memory loss without a meltdown—that was something.

Cherry nodded. "I'm sure you are. But you had a very serious accident..." She nodded to the crutch leaning against the pole. "This job is demanding, fast-paced and requires you to be on your feet for long hours. I'm not sure this is going to work for you."

Isla wouldn't be deterred. "What about a Santa role?" That would allow her to sit all day.

Cherry laughed. And laughed.

Isla forced a laugh too, though she had no idea what the punch line was.

Cherry wiped an eye as an actual tear formed there. "Oh dear...no. Santa is a huge role. The biggest. It takes years to get to that level. We have elves here that have worked with us for six or seven seasons who still aren't ready for that."

"Ah." She could understand that. She glanced toward the Santa seated within the display now. He looked like the real deal and was using sign language to communicate with the child on his lap. There was obviously a lot more to the job than sitting there while kids whispered their Christmas wishes.

"I'm sorry, Isla," Cherry said, sliding the résumé back. "I just don't think—"

The sight of a costume hanging on the wardrobe rack behind Cherry caught Isla's eye. "Hey, what about that one?" she interrupted.

Cherry turned and looked surprised. "No one ever wants to be the Nutcracker," she said with a sigh, as though she'd spent a lot of hours trying to recruit one.

Isla clung to the brief sliver of hope. "Well, you're in luck, because I do."

Cherry frowned. "You do?"

Isla eyed the tan-and-red unflattering costume with the big gold buttons down the front. It wasn't the cute elf costume, but she could add a belt or something. She'd make it work. "Of course!" she said with exaggerated enthusiasm. "I'm perfect for it. I'll even dress up my crutch to match."

Cherry thought about it for a long moment, but then a smile formed on her cherry-red lips. "Okay. Why not? We'll give it a try."

Isla beamed. "Thank you. You'll see, I'll be the best darn Nutcracker you've ever had."

"You'll be the first, so the bar is quite low," Cherry said, but she stood and reached for the costume. She extended it to Isla. "See you tomorrow morning at eight for the staff meeting."

Isla nodded as she stood and took the costume. "See you tomorrow at seven fifty-five."

This might only be her first real job, but she would be the best darn employee Santa's Village had ever seen.

AARON BLINKED SEVERAL TIMES, but there was nothing wrong with his eyesight.

Isla Wakefield was actually dressed as a Nutcracker soldier from the famed holiday fairy tale—one leg and all—leaning on a decorated crutch, made to look like a pole, greeting parents and children at the entrance to Santa's Village.

What the hell had that accident done to the woman?

The oversize uniform was cinched at the waist with a thick belt, and her blond hair peeked out from beneath the tall hat. She made the unflattering costume look good. Better than good.

He took his cell phone out of his pocket and tried to discreetly take a photo because he wasn't sure anyone would believe him without actual proof. He wasn't sure *he* actually believed it even with proof. Unfortunately, he forgot to turn off the flash.

Busted: she looked up and caught him in the act.

Her look of surprise turned into a warm smile, and his gut twisted. She waved, nearly toppling forward as she lost her balance. "Hey! Aaron!" she called when he averted his gaze quickly and hoped she would think he hadn't seen her. Maybe she'd think he'd been taking a photo of the pop-up Santa Village.

He started to walk past, looking everywhere but in that direction, but she called out louder this time. "Hey, Aaron! Over here!"

Oh God.

He stopped and turned back. Hands in his coat pockets, he slowly walked toward her. "Hey, Isla. How you feeling?"

"Festive," she said with a laugh, and her painted cheeks genuinely lit up.

"I can see that." He still couldn't actually *believe* it.

"What are you… I mean, why…?" He gestured to her costume. Up close, it looked even better. He knew Cherry had never had any luck getting anyone to play this role before, but in a weird way, it suited Isla. And unfortunately, the costume had never looked better.

"Turns out other than working as a guide on a cruise ship, I've never actually had a job," she said, lowering her voice.

"No shit," he said in mock disbelief. He knew that. Everyone knew that. Besides her. He felt a tug of guilt at the slight sarcasm in his tone. Bantering and bickering with preinjured Isla was one thing, but she was suffering from a brain injury, so he should maybe cut her some slack. This couldn't be easy on her. Not knowing who she was…or anyone around her. "I mean, good for you."

She nodded. "I wasn't exactly qualified for much, but I'm good with people."

He scoffed and tried to hide it behind a cough.

Unfortunately, she caught it and frowned. "You disagree?"

"No," he said honestly. She was good with people. Just never with him. "Just, uh…" What should he say? That prior to her accident, the two of them would rather jump in a boxing ring than stand around, entertaining idle chitchat? That a week ago, if she'd noticed him on the street outside of Santa's Village, she'd have hidden out of sight? Not called out to him? Twice? "We've just never really…" He stopped. "Never mind. You are absolutely wonderful with people. It's true." He sidestepped a family approaching and watched as she greeted them and handed them the photo packages and candy canes.

"Enjoy seeing Santa!" she said. When she turned back to him, the awkwardness of the moment before seemed to have evaporated. "So are you here with any kids?" She looked around as though expecting a small child to appear out of nowhere.

He shook his head. "No. Just doing some shopping."

"Christmas shopping?"

His chest tightened at the thought. This year would be no different than any other year since they'd lost Amy. Christmas, for his family, would go unnoticed. Just another day. He'd work at the station on Christmas Eve and Christmas Day to allow those with family to have the time off. And his parents would do whatever they did in Florida to try to forget what day of the year it was. He'd get a *Happy New Year* text in January, which was essentially significant of *We survived another season.* But he wasn't about to explain all of that to Isla.

"Nope," he said simply. "Just buying new snowshoes, actually." His old ones had crapped out on him during his last trek through the trails the week before, and it was one of the only low-impact exercises he truly enjoyed. Also, there were zero reminders of Christmas in the middle of the Alaskan outback.

Isla's eyes lit up. "Snowshoeing sounds fun."

He shook his head. Preinjured Isla thought snowshoeing was one of the most boring winter activities. If there wasn't a death-defying element to it, it didn't warrant her time.

How much had her family told her about herself? He knew from Skylar that they'd all been told to let her discover who she was slowly and in her own way, but shouldn't she have some knowledge of her own interests?

Or maybe this was an opportunity for her to develop new ones. Things she had written off, dismissed, never considered. He could see that as a good thing.

"It is fun. You should try it," he said.

"Okay! When?" she asked.

His mouth gaped, and he stammered. She thought he was inviting her to go with him? "Oh…um…I just meant you should try it sometime. On your own. Not with me."

Her expression changed, and she nodded quickly, looking embarrassed to have assumed. "Oh, right. Yeah. That's totally what I meant too. I was just asking what time of day is best to go… You know, weather conditions and all…"

Nice save. There was definitely some of the Isla he knew still in there.

He hesitated, watching her try to hide her disappointment. He must be out of his mind to even be considering this, but… "Hey, why don't you come with me? When your leg is healed enough, of course." By then, her memory would probably be back and she'd pretend she'd never had this conversation, anyway. That thought was unexpectedly disappointing.

What was wrong with him? He didn't actually want to hang out with Isla. Did he?

She sighed. "That could be a few weeks. I'm scheduled to have the cast taken off just before Christmas if I'm lucky."

"Well, the snow tends to stick around here, so I'm sure you'll get the opportunity," he said with a wink, which he immediately regretted as it made the comment seem slightly flirty. Flirting with Isla was not his intention. Was it?

Damn, this entire exchange was weird.

She nodded. "Okay…"

He checked his watch for effect. He had to leave. Put some distance between them to clear the fog that seemed to have wrapped around his common sense. "Well, I should get going. Have fun."

"Yeah…" She gave a little wave, and he started to walk away. "Hey, Aaron."

Damn. So close.

"Yeah?" he asked, turning back to face her.

"I'd like to see you again before I get my cast off—if you know of any other winter activities I should try. I mean, if you're up for it."

He swallowed hard. This was definitely unexpected. Did he want to spend time with Isla? He had never really entertained the idea before. He was physically attracted to her. He wouldn't deny that. Who wouldn't be? She was beautiful and magnetic. But they were so different, and they argued all the time...

Maybe they could get to know one another while she didn't remember they were enemies, but then what? What happened once her memory returned?

Unfortunately, the temptation to show her that he wasn't the boring, safe guy she thought he was overwhelmed common sense. "Sure. There's a lot happening in town this month." He paused. "How do you feel about dogsled rides?"

Her eyes lit up. "I think that sounds wonderful. As long as I don't have to cuddle the dogs, I should be okay." She shrugged and laughed. "Not that I wouldn't want to, but apparently I'm allergic."

He nodded. "Okay, well, let me know when you're available..."

"I have the day off on Tuesday."

Wow, she really was eager to spend time with him. Mixed emotions competed within him, but he'd made the offer. He couldn't take it back now. "Okay. Tuesday it is. I'll pick you up at the hotel around nine?"

She nodded excitedly. "Great! I'll bring my antihistamines."

"Great," he said. Funny how the thought of impenetrable Isla having a weakness at all made her dangerously endearing. "See you," he said, walking away toward the sporting-goods store.

He cast a glance over his shoulder and found her still watching him. Now her turn to be busted, she waved and quickly averted her attention to a group approaching Santa's Village.

Isla Wakefield with a job… He chuckled on his way into the store.

As he perused the shelves in the winter sporting-gear section, Aaron wasn't quite seeing the options on the shelf, still slightly dazed from the encounter. He'd invited her to go dogsledding with him.

What the hell had he been thinking?

"Hey, can I help you find something?" a sales rep, whose name tag read *Parker*, asked as he approached.

"Sure. I'm looking for new snowshoes."

The guy scanned him. "Six foot two, about two hundred and fifteen pounds?"

"You're good," he said. Only off by four pounds.

"It's my job," the guy said. "The biggest factor in choosing a size is weight. The heavier the person, the bigger the shoe. And a lot of folks forget to take into account the weight of the gear."

"Yes. Thanks, I would have," Aaron said.

"My suggestion is the composite frames. They are better for the packed-down and icy conditions we get here in the Alaskan backwoods," he said, reaching for a set.

Aaron studied them. "Bindings?"

"Over here," the guy said, leading the way to the accessories.

Ten minutes later, Aaron was loaded up with heel lifts, wires, snow gaiters and a ton of other things he'd never used before, including a nice, convenient travel bag to carry it all in.

"I think you're all set. Do you need any winter clothing? Thermal gloves? Frostbite's no joke," the guy said.

Aaron almost laughed. Didn't he know it! "You know what? I think I'm good." He hesitated as Parker led the way to the cash register. He'd invited Isla to go when she healed. She definitely wouldn't own all of this already.

"Um, actually, can I get a second set of everything but for a woman who's five foot nothing and a hundred and twenty pounds?" If Isla got her memory back or he came to his senses before then, he could always return the gear.

But he already hoped he wouldn't have to.

CHAPTER EIGHT

ISLA SAT ON the hotel-room bed that evening, staring at an Instagram message from *One Lucky Daredevil*.

How was the climb? Dying to see the photos!

Obviously, a fellow adventurer. She scrolled through their history and discovered it was a fifty-year-old guy named Rick she'd met in Australia. He'd emailed three or four times in the last few months to no response from her. In fact, there were dozens of unanswered messages in the folder, and she couldn't help but wonder why. Did she not like to keep in touch with the people she met? They all seemed nice enough...

Should she post the photos from that day on her account? Her followers might like to see them. They might find it weird that she hadn't been posting lately. But how could she respond to any comments or questions when she didn't remember that day on the ice climb?

Should she at least respond to Rick and let him know what had happened? She suspected most thrill-seeking, adrenaline junkies didn't love hearing about accidents—it would just remind them of their own mortality...

She tossed the phone back and forth between her hands, contemplating.

A soft knock on the door prevented her from having to

make the decision, and she was pleased to see her mother standing on the other side. Grace was warm and caring, and if she was weirded out that her daughter didn't recognize her, she hid it well. She had a calming presence. Dex had told her that it was his mother who'd been a huge source of support for him when he'd been diagnosed with epilepsy at seventeen. His father had had a tougher time with it and wasn't exactly the coddling type. She hadn't heard from Brian since that day at the hospital, but she suspected he dealt with things in his own way.

"Hi, can I come in?" she asked.

Isla stepped back. "Of course. Nice to see you." She meant it. She was glad Grace was there. She wanted to tell her about the new job. Though she was a little nervous: Would her mom be proud or disappointed by the low-level position? She had to start somewhere, right?

Grace entered and scanned the room. "I was surprised when the front desk gave me this room number. I thought you'd be staying in one of the suites."

Isla shrugged. "Maybe they were sold out?" She personally thought the accommodations were wonderful. A king-size bed, a full soaker tub and a small deck to enjoy the view of the marina. She couldn't imagine another room being any nicer, but suites definitely sounded fancy.

Grace shook her head. "There's always a few reserved for the family."

Her eyes widened. "Wait. Do you...I mean, we... Um, do the Wakefields own the hotel?"

Grace smiled warmly as she said, "We sold last year to a hotel chain, actually. One that focuses on unique accommodations. Better marketing tied to the chain, while maintaining the design of the hotel. But they still keep rooms available for us. Would you like me to try to move you to one of them?"

"No...that's not necessary. I'm good, really."

"Okay, darlin'." She removed her overcoat, revealing black, slim-leg dress pants, an emerald-green sweater and a large sequined necklace. The woman was stunning with her dark hair and brown eyes. She was at least five foot seven and had a thin bone structure that made her look so much younger than her late fifties.

Isla tried to see a resemblance between them, but with her five-foot nothingness, blond hair and green eyes, she couldn't. She couldn't claim to look like Brian either, while Dex was the younger version of the man.

Maybe she looked more like a grandparent or an aunt?

"How are you feeling?" Grace asked, sitting in a chair next to the deck doors.

"Better. Lots of sleep the last few days. Still no idea who I am," she said. It had been admittedly fun relearning about Sealena and the town's history with the mythological creature, though. And her old self might never have applied for a seasonal job, which she felt really proud of, so the memory loss wasn't all bad. But she suspected that would be challenging to explain to Grace. No doubt, everyone wanted her to get her memory back as quickly as possible. And she did too—at least, a part of her did. Another part thought getting this opportunity to reinvent herself without biases or prejudgments of who she was before was somewhat enlightening.

Grace nodded. "Well, I went through the boxes in storage and brought you a few things in case any of this might help." She opened her oversize purse and took out several items, placing them on the table between them.

Isla sat across from her and reached for a shaggy, well-loved teddy bear with the stuffing missing from one ear. She laughed. "This guy is ugly." He looked like he could just as easily induce nightmares as offer comfort.

Grace laughed. "We couldn't convince you of that." She looked pensively at the toy. "You used to suck on his ear when you were nervous or afraid. That's why there's no stuffing."

Isla grimaced. "Gross."

"Again, you did not agree when we voiced our opinion on that," Grace said with the gentle laugh of a mother with fond memories.

Isla tucked the teddy bear onto her lap and reached for a lovely handcrafted antique jewelry box. "This is pretty," she said, running her finger over the etched rose carved into the top. Opening the lid, she watched as a ballerina spun in a circle to a song from *Swan Lake*. Beautiful, but unfortunately she didn't recognize it as anything special to her.

"You kept all your trinkets in there," Grace said. "Jewelry, letters, hair accessories…"

Isla frowned. "Speaking of…do you know if there was a necklace among my things at the hospital? I saw photos online of me wearing it."

Grace paled slightly but shook her head. "Sorry, there wasn't." She paused. "Shame if you lost it. You wore it all the time."

"Do you know where—"

Grace cut off the question, her gaze shifting past Isla, noticing the Nutcracker costume hanging on the bathroom door. "What's that?"

Isla recognized the abrupt switch of subject, but she was eager to tell her mom the news, so she smiled and proudly said, "I got a job."

Her mother looked surprised. "In a play?"

A natural assumption. "No. At Santa's Village in town. They had enough elves, so I offered to be the Nutcracker."

"Oh, Isla. You never cease to surprise me," her mother said, her tone holding such endearment as she reached across the table and touched her hand that Isla felt it resonate in her core. Somewhere deep down, some part of her remembered Grace.

She sat back in her chair and curled her good leg under her. "What do you mean?"

"You've always had such an amazing spirit and energy around you. Always up for any challenge, any adventure…" Her mother looked pensive as she recalled a story. "We once had a neighbor who was very old. She lived alone, having lost her husband a few years before. Her kids had all moved away. You saw how lonely she was, so you organized a weekly book club for her with some of the older ladies in town. However, it turned out that her vision wasn't so great, so you recorded your own audiobook for her for each of the books the club decided to read."

"I did that?" It warmed her to know that she had a charitable spirit at least.

"You did. And another summer, your Girl Scout group had to cancel its annual camping trip because of bear sightings at the campsite, so you turned our backyard into a camp, complete with archery training and an obstacle course—even a scavenger hunt." Her mother laughed. "Of course, it was the same night that your father invited two high-profile clients for dinner…"

Isla covered her mouth. "That must have gone over well."

"Your father took them out to dinner instead. Then he came back and taught all of you how to use a compass."

Isla hesitated. "So…Brian…Dad, he's okay? I haven't heard from him."

Grace nodded. "He's worried about you, and this is what he does when there's something he can't fix. He feels helpless, so he distances himself. Don't worry, he'll be fine. We all will, and we will be even better once you get your memory back."

Isla nodded. "Sorry the items didn't trigger anything."

Grace shook her head. "It was worth a try. Anyway, I should go," she said as she stood. "I'm meeting your father now for dinner." She paused, putting on her coat. "You're welcome to join us."

"Thank you, but I have an early-morning staff meeting before my shift starts, so I'll be calling it an early night."

Grace chuckled, giving her a quick hug. "I still can't believe you got a job. Just be careful. Don't overdo it. We'll see you at our place for your father's annual law-firm party?"

"Okay. Yeah. Of course. Dress code?"

Her mother winked as she opened the hotel door and stepped out into the hallway. "Anything but the Nutcracker costume."

JUST BEFORE FIVE O'CLOCK, Aaron poured a cup of coffee and carried it to the table where his computer was set up. He yawned as he rotated his shoulders and then did several jumping jacks to try to wake up. Game face on for the conversation with his parents.

Did everyone need to hype themselves up this way to speak to their parents?

This scheduled early-morning call only happened once a month or so, but he never really looked forward to it the way he suspected most people looked forward to talking to their parents. The conversation always felt strained, as though they struggled to find things to talk about. Neutral things, at least.

As the time on his computer monitor hit 5:00 exactly, he sat and hit the call button. Less than a full ring later, his mother and father appeared on screen.

They were the least retired retirees Aaron had ever seen.

It was nine o'clock for them in Florida, and his father was already dressed in a suit, and his mother was perfectly put-together. Obviously, they had plans for the day.

"Hey, Mom and Dad," he said. "How's the weather in Florida?" Start basic. Safe. Boring casual conversation and run out the clock to dodge any topics he wanted to avoid. Always the game plan.

"Seventy and humid. Can't you tell by my hair?" his mother said, running a hand over perfectly natural gray-streaked strands that he knew women were paying a fortune at hair salons to achieve.

He grinned. Always fishing for a compliment. And he was happy to oblige. "It looks perfect, as usual. Dad, you getting any golfing in?" he asked, then winced inwardly.

Shit, that was danger territory.

"As a matter of fact, we're gearing up for the charity event in the new year. Could use a few extra players on the team. Dates are January 15 to 18."

Not exactly a direct invitation to play, but that's what he was hinting at. Aaron shook his head. "Sorry, Dad, work is busy this time of year. All hands on deck."

"Because of the winter dangers," his mother said tightly.

That didn't take long. So much for staying neutral and running out the clock.

"We read about the rescue in the crevasse," his father said, leaning closer. His dark eyebrows met in the middle as he frowned.

"That one was actually smooth—in and out. No issues." Other than Isla's injuries, that rescue was a success, and other than the stress involved because it was Isla, it hadn't been all that challenging.

"When is the station going to train a few other crew members for that type of rescue?" his father asked. "You can't be the only one they rely on for these dangerous missions."

Same conversation as always.

He appreciated his parents' concern, but they had to start respecting what he did. What would he give for them to just be proud of what he was able to do, the things he'd accomplished? They hadn't encouraged or supported his career decision, but he would have expected that, by now, they'd have at least accepted it.

"I'm actually doing some training with them…" Not anything extensive enough to be relieved of having to take on the more challenging calls, but he liked being that person on the team who could pull off the harder rescues. It gave him a sense of pride and purpose.

"Well, that Isla Wakefield is a ticking time bomb," his mother said. "Wasn't a surprise to read that she was the one needing help." She shook her head disappointedly. "Always a troublemaker, that one."

Aaron's chest tightened, and so did his grip on the coffee cup. "She was trained in ice climbing. The fall could have happened to anyone. It was false ground that caused the incident." Defending Isla was new, but his mother's dismissal and tone rubbed him the wrong way. Isla was a skilled climber, and yes, she'd always been a daredevil, but that didn't equate to causing trouble. In all the years he'd known her, this was the first time she'd ever needed help, and as he'd said, it hadn't really been her fault.

His mother's eyes revealed the surprise. "Since when do you agree with Isla's stunts?"

He fought for patience. "Isla's...stunts...are her business."

"Not when she puts our son's life at risk," his father chimed in.

Aaron repressed a sigh. He couldn't exactly argue with that when in the past it had been his argument as well. "I'm sure she'll be taking it easy while she's home for the holidays." And going dogsledding with him, apparently. He still couldn't quite wrap his mind around that, but he kept that tidbit to himself, not wanting to open a whole other can of worms.

His mother's face twisted slightly at the mention of the time of year, and again he knew he'd messed up. Christmas was another topic to avoid if he wanted to get through this call unscathed.

He didn't even need to ask if they were celebrating. There would be no decorations up at his parents' beachfront property. No gifts, no acknowledgment of the season at all. They wouldn't spout a *Bah, humbug!* to anyone who wished them well, but he knew they were counting the days until the season was over. Focusing on the January charity golf tournament helped keep them busy until the last strand of tinsel disappeared.

He also didn't need to ask whether they'd consider coming home to Alaska for a few days...

But his mother surprised him. "Hey, we were actually thinking about the holidays, and there's a lovely four-day cruise sailing out of Fort Lauderdale that we thought we might take. We'd love for you to join us."

They would? A Christmas vacation? As a family? Too stunned to answer, he sat there, mouth agape.

"It's also a conference for Parents Who Lost Children," his father clarified, obviously sensing Aaron's confusion.

Right. That made more sense. Not a vacation. A support group. He'd love to see his family and spend the holidays with them, but not that way.

It broke his heart that his parents were still struggling so much with his sister's death. He couldn't imagine how hard losing a child must be. Losing a sister was so incredibly difficult. But he thought his parents weren't healing or trying to move forward. They insisted on constantly living in the pain with all the charities and support groups. Reminders of the hurt and suffering and tragic time. Aaron wasn't sure it was completely healthy, but they needed to do things their way.

"What do you think?" his mother asked, hopefully. They really wanted him to get involved in their organizations and support groups. To them, he'd moved on, which translated in their minds to *had forgotten*... That wasn't the case at all, but he knew he was a disappointment to them with his refusal to participate in the organizations they were involved in.

He cleared his throat. "I'd like to," he lied, "but I'm working those days. Letting the guys with family have the time off."

He wasn't sure they'd even noticed the implication he didn't feel he had a family anymore. Hadn't in a long time. To them, the family had dissolved the day Amy died. They'd all felt the loss so hard that their family unity had evaporated, and for years, they'd been three people living in the same house, lost in grief, trying to survive the tragedy in their own separate ways. His parents had found their organizations, and he'd devoted his life to preventing other people from suffering the tragic loss he had.

He recognized his parents' way of healing, he just

wished they could recognize his, even if they never fully accepted it.

"Okay...well, if you change your mind, we will be booking the trip next week," his mother said.

"I'll let you know if anything changes," he said.

His father checked his watch. "We should get going. We're giving a seminar at the church in an hour."

He didn't need to ask what it was about. They gave talks on God's purpose even in moments of heartache and tragedy. Aaron nodded. "Yeah...you go. We'll talk again soon."

"Bye, son," his father said, and the Zoom connection ended.

Aaron sat back in the chair and stared at the screen saver—a photo of him and his sister from when they were little. Regret wrapped around him as it always did when he saw a photo of Amy. Time did nothing to dull the intensity of the loss.

Maybe he should be more active and involved in the charities that his parents supported, but he couldn't imagine it would help ease his own heartache to be surrounded by stories of death.

Still, he logged onto the charity website and found the link for the golf tournament. Hitting the donate button, he left an anonymous contribution, then shut his laptop.

He needed to regroup, clear his head...forget about the ghosts of holidays past that seemed determined to destroy him.

And somehow survive an outing with Isla Wakefield.

CHAPTER NINE

ISLA STILL DIDN'T have her father pegged down just yet, but she was fairly certain the look on his face as he approached the Santa's Village display was one of...disapproval? Or maybe it was disappointment.

She was going with *disapproval* mixed with just the tiniest hint of respect in his expression as well, as though seeing her actually working was a step in the right direction.

He looked as put-together as he had that day in the hospital. A dark charcoal suit, dark green dress shirt and matching tie were visible under an expensive wool peacoat. Despite the thin layer of snow and ice on the road, he wore gray leather dress shoes.

"Hi...Dad," she said when he stopped in front of her. "What brings you here?"

"Your mother told me you were doing this, but I had to see it to believe it." His gaze swept over her in the Nutcracker costume, and she could swear she saw a tug at the corner of his mouth, but no actual smile appeared.

"It's a paying gig, and with a lack of a decent résumé, this is as good as it got," she said, but she smiled. "It's actually fun."

"Fun," he repeated, as though he'd expected that part.

She hadn't learned a lot about herself just yet, but she knew fun was definitely something she lived for. Well, what could she say? The job *was* fun, and who said work had to be terrible? There was no law that said people had to hate their careers in order to be successful. She suspected he enjoyed what he did.

"Can we talk for a few minutes?" he asked.

She nodded. "I have a break in twelve minutes," she said.

"I'm sure Cherry will let you go—"

"I have a break in twelve minutes." One thing she had figured out about Brian Wakefield was that he was used to getting his way. As the latest generation to ostensibly own the town, she suspected no one ever disagreed with him. Well, she wasn't planning on using her last name to get special privileges at her place of employment.

His jaw clenched slightly, but he nodded respectfully. "I'll be at the café. Your usual?"

Though she had no idea what that was, she nodded.

Thirteen minutes later, she entered the café on Main Street near the pop-up and scanned the crowd. The place was decorated for the holidays in a theme of Santas from around the world. Jamaican Santas on the beach, North Pole Santas in sleighs, *Jultomten* from Sweden: it was actually pretty cool. Holiday music played, and the smell of peppermint and gingerbread treats made her stomach growl. Thank God she was only allergic to dogs and mushrooms. If she'd been allergic to sugar or gluten, she might have been tempted to take her chances.

Her father nodded at her from the corner booth near the back, and she made her way to him. On the table in front of him was a straight black coffee and at her place was a chocolate mocha muffin and a peppermint latte.

At least her tastes hadn't changed.

"Thank you," she said as she leaned her crutch against the wall and sat. It felt a little odd sitting across from him, allowing him to buy her break snack, but he was her dad, even if she couldn't really remember the relationship.

"You're welcome," he said. He took a sip of his coffee and studied her over the rim. "How are you feeling?"

"As good as can be expected. No memory yet, but I've been looking at photos and stuff, and it seems like I have a fantastic life."

He nodded. "You do. We're all very fortunate. That's what I wanted to talk to you about."

She peeled the cling film from the muffin and took a bite, waiting for him to continue. The taste of chocolate, coffee and mint tantalized her tastebuds, and it was a struggle to focus on what he said next.

"I'd like to revisit the idea of law school."

"Law school?" She'd been interested in law school? "Have I attended law school in the past?" She couldn't remember any mention of that. Nothing on her social media or calendar that hinted at a class schedule. She took a big bite of the muffin and chewed.

"No. You haven't. But we have talked about that being a possible career."

"Follow in your footsteps?"

"It wouldn't have to be criminal law. It could be in any division of practice you were interested in," he said.

She chewed slowly and swallowed. "Maybe we should wait to have this conversation." The timing felt slightly suspicious to her. As though he were trying to capitalize on an opportunity. She couldn't remember her favorite baked goods, let alone any future plans she'd had of becoming a lawyer. Something that big and important couldn't be decided in her current state.

"Absolutely," he said, sitting back in the booth. "I'm obviously not expecting you to make any decisions until your memory comes back…"

If it came back. She heard that note of uncertainty in his voice and wondered if maybe a small part of her father was hoping it wouldn't. Give him an opportunity to mold her future a different way. He'd call it guidance, of course…

Wow, her memory might be broken, but her gut instincts seemed to still be on point.

She had *issues with trust*, Dex had said. Might have a possible contributor as to why sitting across from her. She wanted to like Brian, trust his motives as pure and believe there was only good in his intentions, but her spidey sense told her to question further.

"What are you expecting right now?"

"Just opening the dialogue. Since you're suddenly keen on working, I just thought maybe you were ready to suspend traveling for a while. You could intern at my firm here in Port Serenity while you take online classes instead of… this." He gestured at her costume.

"I appreciate the offer and your support. I just think, right now, I need something a little less stressful." Dr. Sheffield had said to take it easy. Day by day. Registering for law classes and working with her father seemed a little too much too soon.

"I think it could help give you focus," he countered.

She repressed a sigh. She suspected this pressure was something she'd faced with her father before. A strong sense of determination not to be persuaded resonated from somewhere within her. If preaccident Isla had put off law school, there might be a good reason for it. Therefore, postaccident Isla had no plans to jump on this either. Not without more information and thought.

"I'm sorry. The answer's *no*," she said firmly. "For now."

She wasn't closing the door on the idea, she just needed some time.

Now his expression was definitely disappointed as he stood. "Okay. I understand. I was just hoping we'd be able to revisit this while we were both home for the holidays."

And her accident had obviously derailed his plans.

"Hopefully, we still can," she said. "It's just that I gave my commitment to Cherry, and it wouldn't be fair to leave her without a Nutcracker," she added, to soften her refusal a little.

He touched her shoulder lightly. "I can respect that. I have to get back to the office, but enjoy your day at work."

Isla watched him leave the café. He raised the collar of his coat as a light snow had started to fall.

She sighed. She hated to upset a man who obviously cared about her and had provided a fantastic life, and who still continued to support her and her passion for travel.

But how could she possibly make a huge life-changing decision when her life seemed to have hit pause?

CHAPTER TEN

DRESSED IN HIS winter gear, Aaron sweated as he paced the lobby of the Sealena Hotel Tuesday at 8:50 a.m. Maybe by now Isla would have her memory back and would totally bail on this. The whole idea was ridiculous. He and Isla had never purposely hung out together in all the years they'd known each other. He'd totally been expecting Skylar to text him and let him know that Isla had come to her senses. He'd waited for it...hoped for it. Sort of, at least. Unfortunately, part of him had been hoping for the opposite. For a chance to spend the day with her, which was crazy and even more reason to hope that she bailed.

But nope.

Three minutes before nine, she met him in the lobby, taking the stairs instead of the elevator and getting by amazingly on the crutch. Shouldn't surprise him that she could make hobbling along on a sprained leg look graceful and effortless.

And she looked fantastic in a form-fitting ski suit and a candy-cane scarf with matching mittens and hat. Which were new, judging by the tag still hanging from the end of the scarf.

Her short blond hair poked out the bottom of the hat, and her makeup-free face was radiant with excitement.

To see him. To spend the day with him.

Isla Wakefield had looked at him in many different ways

over the years, but never with the look of sincere pleasure that shone from her now. It was like a gut punch, and he refused to think about just how amazing it felt to be on the receiving end of her smile this morning.

Or how bad it would feel when she got her memory back and he suddenly wasn't.

"Hope you weren't waiting long," she said, stopping in front of him.

"Nope. Just got here a few minutes ago," he said. From the corner of his eye, he saw the hotel check-in staff eyeing them with varying looks of disbelief and suspicion. They had to be wondering what the hell was going on, and he didn't need that discussion ruining the day. "Ready to go?" he asked her quickly.

She nodded eagerly. "I couldn't sleep last night," she said as he led the way to the revolving door.

Neither could he, but for different reasons he'd suspect. Every year, he looked forward to going dogsledding, but having her tag along had him nervous and awkward. What the hell would they even talk about in the truck on the way there? What if she got her memory back during the day and things went sideways? How did he spend the day with a woman to whom he'd always thought his body's reaction was annoyance and dislike but was actually attraction and an undeniable chemistry?

Luckily, if she was struggling with any of these hesitations, she didn't show it as she chatted nonstop on the way out of the hotel toward his truck. "I did some research last night and read that sleds can reach up to twenty miles an hour."

He nodded. They wouldn't be going that fast. He enjoyed the ride at a more leisurely pace, one at which he could take in the scenery and experience a milder thrill. Breakneck speeds could be reserved for elite races like the Iditarod, in his opinion.

Though, maybe she'd find that boring? The old Isla certainly would… Maybe he'd ask the guide to go a little faster that day. He wanted her to enjoy the experience. Enjoy being with him.

He shook his head at the completely crazy thought.

At the truck, she frowned slightly as he opened the passenger-side door. "Um…this might be a little difficult," she said, eyeing the height. At five foot nothing, the hike up into the jacked-up vehicle would be a challenge even if her leg weren't injured.

How had he not thought about this?

Maybe he could use it as an excuse to call it off? *If you can't get into the truck, you can't come.* The comment would definitely escape him if things were normal between them, but he couldn't quite bring himself to say it today.

Unfortunately, it meant he'd need to help her up into the truck.

"Want some help?" he asked awkwardly, sounding as though a frog were lodged in his throat.

"Not sure how I'm getting in, otherwise," she said with a laugh and no sign of having an ounce of anxiety over the fact he was going to have to touch her.

He was the only one freaking out about that. Remembering the way his body reacted to holding her in his arms as he lifted her to safety the week before had his palms sweating and mouth slightly dry. "How do you want to do this?"

She tossed her crutch inside and gripped the frame of the truck. "Just lift me in," she said.

Aaron moved closer and eyed her tiny waist and hips. Damn, she was sexy. He reached out slowly but hesitated before putting his hands on her waist.

Just think of it as though it's a rescue. Nothing sexual. Nothing physical. Just another day at the office.

She glanced over her shoulder at him. "Don't worry. I'm, like, a hundred and twenty pounds. You can do it," she teased, and a hint of the old Isla with her playfully provoking expression made him feel slightly better. He had to stop being so freaked out around her. It was Isla. A slightly different version maybe—and one that had his body reacting in odd and unusual ways—but still Isla. He couldn't break her or hurt her. She was just as strong as ever.

He quickly gripped her waist and lifted her inside the vehicle, establishing that her injured leg was well inside before closing the door.

There. That was easy. Except that his hands felt like they were desperate to get a feel of that waist again. Traitors.

"So did you find snowshoes the other day?" she asked once he was seated.

"Yeah, I did." He wouldn't mention that he'd bought a pair for her too. Memory loss or not, maybe after spending the day together, she wouldn't want to repeat the experience, anyway. To her, this was a first…date? To him, he knew they weren't destined to get along. Not long-term, anyway.

She peered out the window as they drove along Main Street. "I still can't believe my family owns all of these businesses," she said.

He nodded. How much did she know about her family heritage? Had they filled her in on that much, at least? "The Wakefields are credited for saving the community in the late 1800s when the fishing industry didn't provide enough work and income for the families that immigrated to Port Serenity."

She nodded. "Yeah, Carly at the museum and bookstore

was explaining the whole thing, and I've been reading Rachel Hempshaw's blog about the history here. It's fascinating." She laughed. "I guess it sounds weird hearing me talk about it as though I'd never heard any of it before."

"This whole thing is a little weird," he said honestly, shifting in his seat as he changed lanes to take the exit for the highway.

She turned in the seat to face him. "Am I really that different?" She looked like she was struggling with how to act. As though she had no idea what the right thing to say or do was. As though she could possibly make a mistake at being who she was.

And he wasn't helping with the way he was acting. "No. You're not," he said. "You're exactly the same..." Same spirit, same heart, same determination—things he'd tried to find fault with before, but now were just more reasons to be attracted to her. "Some decisions you're making are... surprising."

"Like spending time with you?"

He nodded, but he didn't want to have that conversation. "Among others. Like getting the job at Santa's Village." That was still throwing him for a loop.

She sighed. "Yeah, my parents were shocked by that one too. But I don't know... I mean, I woke up in the hospital with no recollection of who I am and this amazing group of wealthy people telling me that basically I'm a princess with a fairy-tale life and unlimited credit cards at my disposal, and well, it just felt...privileged and wrong to be out spending money that I didn't earn."

"It's a trust fund. The money comes from many previous generations, but your family works really hard. No one can take that away from them."

"I know. But I wanted to buy Christmas gifts with my own money."

That was admirable. He knew she'd worked on a cruise ship before, but other than that, Isla had never held any real employment. No part-time or after-school jobs during high school. She'd interned at her father's law firm for her senior year co-op placement, so she hadn't even had to go out and secure an opportunity like the rest of the class had. Sure, her father's assistant had gone through the motions of an interview with her as per the school's requirement, but there hadn't been any doubt that she'd get the internship. At the time, it had driven Aaron nuts to know that the position would be easy for her and that she would still get the class credit without being expected to do all the menial tasks no one else wanted to do, the way the rest of them would.

"I get that," he said. And worse, he respected her for it. Whatever opportunities she'd been handed in the past, she now seemed intent on earning.

She smiled as though having his support meant something to her, and it was all he could do to keep his focus on the icy highway roads leading to the ranch. They drove along in silence, but it wasn't the awkward, tense silence he'd expected. They seemed to be enjoying the quiet together.

He used to think Isla didn't have it in her to just be still and silent. Every time he'd ever been around her, she'd been practically vibrating with energy, always talking a million miles an hour. It almost seemed as though she were constantly moving, always on to the next thing so that she wouldn't have to take time to stop, feel...appreciate. As though her fear of missing out on the next adventure had her always moving at full speed. This pensive, at-peace version was different. Had she always had this side? Had he just never seen it?

He was grateful to be seeing it now. He snuck a glance toward her at the same instant she turned to look at him, and the two shared a smile that had his palms sweating against the wheel.

A few minutes later, she leaned closer to peer out the windshield as he parked in the lot of Champion Racers. "Wow, this place is beautiful," she said.

The ranch-style facility was amazing. Owned by Dru Dean, a champion and famous musher who'd run the Iditarod eight years in a row, coming in the top three each year of the thousand-mile race across Alaskan wilderness, it was one of the most popular dogsled experiences in Alaska.

"The view from here is fantastic," Isla said, admiring the breathtaking landscape of Denali in the distance and the miles of snow-covered mountain terrain all around them.

Aaron was thrilled that she was already excited and felt an unexpected surge of pride in having suggested something he knew she was going to love. Something that fell somewhere between her adrenaline-junkie comfort zone and his slower, yet still exhilarating, pace.

A common ground, maybe? Finally a means to meet halfway?

He climbed out of the truck, and she opened the passenger door as he met her to help her down. "I got it," she said, expertly jumping down on one foot and then reaching back for her crutch.

Damn, he'd kinda been looking forward to lifting her again.

They walked across the snowy parking lot and entered the visitor center where a welcome blast of heat from the roaring fireplace greeted them. Huge windows and open-beam wood ceilings made the place feel cozy yet majestic. Memorabilia such as older sleds and trophies were displayed throughout the center, along with photos of previous generations of racers. The sign on the check-in desk announced that staff would be back in five minutes.

Above the desk, a monitor displayed a video featuring Dru and his championship sled team. He explained the year-long lifestyle of a dog musher. Isla stood back to watch as the video showed footage of the previous years' Iditarod, the harsh weather conditions making the already-difficult race that much more challenging. "They are truly incredible," she said, admiring the gorgeous team of powerful, fast huskies leading the sled down the various trails.

"This is the trail they take," he said, motioning to the ten-foot map on the wall. Trails leading through Denali and all the way to the Bering Sea.

Isla scanned it and shook her head. "I'm sure I should know all of this, but it's actually spectacular discovering it for what feels like the first time."

Only Isla could put such a positive spin on memory loss. His admiration for her was growing, and if he weren't careful...

"Aaron! Nice to see you again," Dru's wife, Maria, said warmly, coming inside through the yard door.

Isla glanced at him. "You've done this before?"

"This guy comes out at least a few times a year. Someday, we will get him training for the race," Maria said, offering a hug to them both.

He grinned. "And someday, I'll take you up on that challenge. Maria, this is my...friend." The word stuck in his throat, and Maria read it wrong. She thought he'd struggled to not say *girlfriend* while in fact he'd struggled to withhold *pain in the ass nemesis* and sent him a knowing grin.

"This is Isla Wakefield," he said.

Maria's eyes widened. "The *legendary* Isla Wakefield?"

Uh-oh. He may have communicated his irritation regarding Isla to Maria and Dru on several occasions...

Isla laughed nervously. "You told them about me?" she asked him, looking intrigued and amused.

"Oh, we've heard..." Maria started.

But Aaron quickly jumped in for damage control. "Maria is just referring to your many adventures," he said quickly, before turning back toward the facility owner. "Isla actually just had an accident. She's suffering from memory loss, so details about her *legendary* status might be blurry."

Isla shot him a look that said *What are you not telling me?* Which he conveniently ignored, knowing the conversation would probably pop up again.

Maria nodded and offered a sympathetic look. "Oh my God, I'm so sorry. I hadn't heard."

Isla shook her head. "Thank you. It could have been a lot worse if this guy hadn't been there."

"You rescued her?" Maria was looking back and forth between them with the dreamiest expression as though she thought this turn of events had *romance movie* written all over it.

Aaron cleared his throat and looked at his watch. "I think we should get started."

"Yes, we should get you two moving. Let's tour the kennels so you can meet the dogs," Maria said, leading the way out of the visitor center and across the field to the dog-boarding facility. A large, fenced-in field was set up with forty individual dog kennels, small red houselike structures with each of the dog's names on them. Paths between the kennels allowed them to walk around.

Immediately, the dogs appeared in the doorways and outside, barking and demanding attention. Isla moved a little closer to Aaron, and he smiled down at her. "Don't worry. This is their way of showing their excitement," he said.

Maria waved a hand to silence them all. "They love to run and show off for new guests," she said. "They want you to choose them for the run today."

Isla admired the beautiful huskies. "How on earth do you choose?"

"Each dog has their own skills and personality. We train all of them together, but it quickly becomes apparent which dogs work best together as a team. Some are fast, some are strong, and their skills work to complement one another."

She stopped at several kennels. "This is Lightning and Bolt," she said, gesturing to two huskies, sitting obediently on the ground but looking eager to get hooked to a sled. "Brothers. They work really well together because they are both so competitive. They push one another to be the best."

Isla turned to look at Aaron, and he nodded. "I've seen them in action. Definitely something to observe."

Smaller, weaker-sounding barks coming from the other side caught their attention, and Maria smiled as she led the way toward a house with three husky pups playing outside together. "These pups are our latest trainees," she said.

They were so adorable as they fell over one another, playing and fighting for attention.

"I'm taking one of those home," Isla said, gushing over the pups.

Maria picked up the tiniest one and extended him to Isla. "Want to hold?"

"Uh, Isla's allergic..." Aaron said.

But she shook her head, accepting the puppy and immediately snuggling into it as though she'd never give it back. "I came prepared. Double dose of antihistamines. There was no way I was going to resist puppy cuddles." She buried her head into the dog's fur, and Aaron felt an irrational sense of jealousy of the dog.

Maria handed him another one, and they spent far too much time getting attached before she said, "There's Dru now. He'll be setting up the sled. Time to go back," she told the pups.

Aaron reluctantly put his back, and Isla made a motion of pretending to tuck hers into her jacket, before a sneezing fit hit and she gave in. "Okay, small doses only." She gently placed the puppy on the snowy ground and whispered, "I'll come back and visit."

As they followed Maria toward the prep area, he saw Dru preparing a bigger sled than he'd reserved. "Oh, hey, Maria, we just reserved the two-seater..."

Maria looked slightly confused. "Ashley on the desk said the reservation was changed last night."

He turned to Isla with a suspicious look. "What did you do?"

"After checking the website, I may have called and changed the reservation to include the Christmas-tree-cutting option," she said excitedly, looking pleased with herself that she'd pulled off the surprise.

"Christmas tree?" he said, feeling his heart thunder in his chest. He hadn't even known the company offered that option. Made sense since they also owned acres of tree farmland on the adjacent property. He swallowed hard. Was it too late to change it back? Could he without hurting Isla's feelings? She thought she was doing a nice thing for him. He didn't want to make her feel bad, but the idea of cutting down a Christmas tree made him break out in hives. He hadn't had a tree...since the year Amy died.

"Oh no! Are you an artificial-tree guy? Because if so,

I'm not sure we can be friends," Isla said teasingly, reading his reaction completely incorrectly.

He shook his head and took a deep breath, drowning in the irony of her words. There were so many reasons they'd never been friends. This was only a tree. He could survive cutting down an evergreen if it would make her happy.

"Definitely not an artificial-tree guy," he said, offering what he hoped was a sincere-looking smile, despite the feeling of uneasiness in the pit of his stomach.

AARON'S REACTION TO her change of plans wasn't exactly what she'd been expecting. When she'd taken a look at the company's website the day before in anticipation of the outing, she'd been excited about upgrading the trip. But, maybe he wasn't the kind of guy who liked his plans changed without notice. He didn't strike her as the macho type whose ego would take a blow from something like this...

But there had definitely been a moment when he'd paled and looked slightly freaked out.

Oh no. Maybe he didn't celebrate Christmas. Shit, had she offended him somehow?

She pulled him aside as Dru selected the excited huskies for that day's excursion.

"Hey, if you want to skip the tree thing, it's totally fine."

"No, I don't want to skip it. I think it will be fun," he said, and to his credit, he sounded believable. "I was just worried it might be too early...but it's a fresh tree so it should last..."

"You two ready for an unforgettable experience?" Dru asked as he hooked the dogs to the packed and ready sled.

Isla glanced at Aaron, and he smiled at her, deep dimples appearing in his flushed cheeks. "Absolutely."

Her heart raced, and she wasn't even on the ride yet. It

had already been an unforgettable day for her. She liked being with Aaron. It felt natural, comfortable…easy. She didn't feel nervous around him the way she did with her family. With him, she didn't worry about saying the wrong thing or doing something out of character.

While everyone else seemed to be looking at her cautiously, waiting for her to regain her memory at any moment, Aaron seemed to be completely accepting of this new situation. Unfazed by it. Which made her feel better.

And the sight of him in the hotel that morning had only solidified her attraction to him. Dressed in black ski pants and a red ski jacket with the coast guard logo on it, he'd looked amazing, and the slight air of authority from the jacket patch revealed she was definitely a sucker for a guy in uniform, the subtle reminder that he was an elite rescue swimmer dialing his already-scorching hotness up a few more degrees.

"Okay, climb in," Dru said, and Aaron helped her onto the sled, securing her crutch in the front with the other supplies.

He joined her on the seat and draped a thick blanket over their laps as Dru took his post behind the sled.

"Will the sled really go twenty miles an hour?" she whispered to Aaron. Now that she was seated there, she was a little nervous. Adrenaline coursed through her, and her stomach was queasy, like that feeling when waiting for a roller-coaster to start. This fear of the unknown, of relinquishing control.

"Only ten to twelve today," he said.

"Only?" she said with a nervous laugh.

"Trust me, you like speed," he said, staring into her eyes.

Her tongue felt thick in her mouth as she stared back into the most incredible blue eyes. She liked speed. That might be true, but she wasn't sure how she felt about how fast her feelings were developing for her rescuer.

She didn't have long to contemplate it as Dru gave the signal and the dogs started to run.

Within minutes, wind whipped against her cheeks, and she was smiling so hard her face hurt. Holding onto the sled as it sped over the trails, the sun casting a glow against the crisp white snow, it was so much better than she had even anticipated.

Next to her, tucked up in the blanket, Aaron smiled. "Fun?"

She nodded. "Best thing I've ever done." She paused. "Definitely the best new memory."

She reached across and touched his hand, and his gaze flew to hers with a mild look of panic. Oops. Had she read things wrong? She thought things had been going well. She felt a connection to him. Maybe he really wasn't into her. Maybe she'd forced him into this outing with her persistence.

She quickly went to pull back, but he gripped her hand, squeezing it tightly in his. Her shoulders relaxed. They were on the same page. She hadn't imagined the attraction in his gaze.

"To the right!" Dru called out.

They turned their attention toward an opening in the tree line and saw a family of red foxes traveling along the trail near a cascading frozen river. It was an image straight out of a children's book. The largest fox turned to watch them as they approached, with a confident stance and unrelenting presence. The sledders were the visitors here. This was the foxes' home. "Wow, they are beautiful," Isla said, as the sight whizzed past far too quickly.

Aaron leaned closer and whispered, "So are you."

Her heart swelled, and she moved closer, allowing her body to snuggle into his. He wrapped an arm around her shoulder and drew her in tight. And there was nowhere else in the world she wanted to be, nor anyone else she wanted to be with.

A few minutes later, Dru reduced their speed and brought the sled to a stop. Isla looked around. They hadn't reached the evergreen lot yet.

"Anyone want to take over driving?" he asked, climbing off the sled and checking the dogs. Their furry friends looked annoyed to have stopped and were eager to get going again.

"I do!" she said quickly, then pouted. "Can I? With my leg?"

Dru hesitated, but nodded. "I can't see why not. As long as we don't go too fast and Aaron holds on to you."

Her cheeks flushed, and she was almost afraid to look at him for his reaction to that.

"Absolutely. No problem," he said, getting out of the sled and extending a hand to her.

She carefully climbed on the back and rested her foot against the wood. She grabbed the reins from Dru, and after a few instructions, the musher moved to the seat and relaxed as she and Aaron took the helm.

When his arms wrapped around her waist, Isla felt heat coursing through her entire body. The smell of his cologne filled her senses, and his warm breath on the back of her neck had shivers dancing down her spine. She wasn't sure the last time she'd been this intimately close with a man, but her body's reaction suggested it was far too long.

Or was it just this man in particular?

"Ready when you are," Dru said.

"Ready?" Aaron asked her.

"Ready," she said. For this and for a whole lot more.

He gave the signal and held her tight as they set off on the thrill of a lifetime.

"NIGHTFALL'S COMING," DRU TEASED as Isla took her time perusing the trees on the acres of tree farm. They were all so beautiful and majestic-looking. Large evergreens, covered in snow. Walking through the rows of them, the smell of sap and pine evoked memories within Aaron. But it wasn't the painful longing for holiday traditions past he'd been expecting. It was almost comforting in an unexpected way.

He knew it had everything to do with Isla being there. Cuddling her in the sled and holding her tight as they'd run the dogs, emotions he'd never experienced before had nearly knocked him on his ass. There was no denying his attraction to her, but there was also no denying there were real feelings involved, a deep caring he hadn't expected or felt for anyone in a long time. He'd wanted to keep holding her for as long as possible, and that was definitely new to him.

"How does anyone decide?" she asked, looking seriously conflicted.

"Define the perfect tree," he said. If they had parameters, that would help narrow it down, at least.

She bit her lip as she thought about it, then said, "Full, but not too full. Tall, but obviously I need to be able to reach the top..."

"A three-foot tree it is," he said, unable to resist teasing her about her five-foot-nothing height. It was actually one of the things that he'd always marveled at—how much scrappiness was contained in such a small woman.

Isla's personality had always been anything but small. Fiery, passionate, argumentative, determined...

He wondered how much of her independent, wild spirit

was because of her upbringing—before and after being adopted? It was something he'd always wondered about her, but they'd never been close enough to talk about. He knew her earlier years hadn't been easy—in and out of foster homes before being adopted—and he knew that had to have shaped her personality, even at such a young age that she probably didn't remember much of it.

She playfully slapped his arm, then gasped. "That one," she said, pointing to a five-and-a-half-foot Douglas fir.

"Great choice," Dru said, admiring the one she'd chosen.

"That one it is," Aaron said, accepting the axe from Dru and getting to work. Before long, he was sweating. Removing his coat and rolling the sleeves of his red sweater, he noticed Isla's appreciative gaze when she looked at him. He couldn't claim to have seen that look directed his way before.

And he liked it a lot more than was wise.

Unfortunately, he doubted she'd still look at him that way once her memory returned, and she might even be more annoyed than usual that he hadn't bothered to tell her that the two of them didn't like one another. He hated that common sense had chosen that moment to appear, dampening his joy in the moment.

He hit the trunk hard a final time. "Timber!" he called as the tree toppled over.

Isla clapped and smiled at him as he and Dru secured it to the back of the sled.

"She's going to look great in your apartment," she said as they climbed back onto the seat, and his heart nearly stopped.

"Wait. My apartment?" He hadn't agreed to a Christmas tree. His palms dampened even more than they had a few minutes before. He'd cut it down for her.

She frowned as she nodded. "I'm living in a hotel this holiday season. Where did you think it was going to go?" she asked.

Aaron hadn't exactly thought it through.

"I guess my apartment it is," he said, climbing back onto the sled beside her.

She pulled the blanket up around them and rested her head against him. "Don't worry. I'll help you decorate it."

Now he was really sweating.

CHAPTER ELEVEN

ISLA KNOCKED ON the door of the Top Elf hut at the end of her shift the next day. Cherry sat behind a desk, with her elf hat askew and looking frazzled with her cell phone to her ear. "No, you can't watch that… Because your brother will have nightmares… No, you can't lock him in the pantry until the movie's over." She glanced up and saw Isla standing in the doorway. "Mike, I have to go. Do not watch that movie until I get home." She disconnected the call and sighed.

"Everything okay?" Isla asked, entering the office. Cherry looked stressed, and she hoped the woman hadn't called her in to let her go. She thought she'd been doing a good job, but maybe the customer suggestion box on her desk held some critical reviews of Isla's portrayal of the Nutcracker?

"My great nephews are visiting for the holidays. Well, the whole family is, but the boys got out of school early, so they arrived last night. I forgot how much work teenagers are." She yawned and rubbed her eyes. "They were up all night, and they've called me fourteen times this morning already. Apparently, there's some *Santa Slay* movie— a Christmas horror flick—that one wants to watch but the other isn't allowed…"

Isla nodded her sympathy, her eyes still on the stack of customer comments on the desk. She didn't see any with *Nutcracker* written on them. "You wanted to see me?"

"Oh, yes," Cherry said, reaching behind her to retrieve an envelope from the employee files. "It's payday," she said, handing it to Isla.

Payday. Phew!

She accepted the envelope and a sense of pride wrapped around her as she took out the check. Her first paycheck doing a job that couldn't possibly be considered playtime. She'd stood at the entrance of Santa's Village for hours, constantly smiling and greeting guests with a warm welcome. She'd been cheerful and fun with the kids while they waited. She'd sweated in the costume and stood on one leg… She deserved this…

A hundred and eighty-six dollars?

How could that be right? She'd worked four shifts…eight hours each at ten dollars an hour.

"Um… Cherry? Is this amount right?"

Cherry glanced at it and nodded. "We deduct the cost of the costume from the first check," she said, pointing to the deduction on the statement attached.

The cost of the costume? She'd assumed it was a rental. "I get to keep this?" She glanced down at the ugly costume.

Cherry shook her head. "No that's the rental fee as we have to have it dry-cleaned after use…" Her cell phone rang and she groaned, looking at it. "The boys again. I swear to the baby Jesus… I gotta take it. Sorry, Isla. Have a good day," she said, dismissing her as she answered the call.

Isla stared at the meager amount on the check as she left the hut.

Okay, so it wasn't what she'd been expecting, but it was hers. All hers. She'd earned it. Maybe she should not cash it and frame it instead, she mused.

She changed out of her uniform, then after a quick stop at the local bank, where thankfully the teller behind the counter recognized her and agreed to cash the check, she made her way to the yacht and knocked on the door. She had a key, but it didn't feel right to just barge in on Dex and Skylar.

Skylar's expression was one of disbelief when Isla revealed the reason for her visit as though she had suggested they take the Polar Bear Plunge in the Arctic. "What? It's just shopping," she said in Skylar's silence.

She'd invited her future sister-in-law to spend the evening Christmas shopping for two reasons: first, she wanted to get to know her better, and second, she had no idea what to buy her family as gifts for Christmas. What did everyone want? What might they need? Probably not much. More than anything, she needed help figuring out how to buy for four people with a hundred and eighty dollars.

"I know…" Skylar said. "It's just…" She sent a look to Dex, who shrugged, looking similarly surprised but happy. Skylar turned back to her. "It's just we…you and I don't usually…I mean, we don't hang out much. Together. Alone. Without the rest of the family around."

Isla frowned. "Why not?" Seemed odd that they wouldn't be friends. They were only a few years apart, and if Skylar was going to be part of the family, she would hope they'd be like sisters.

Skylar looked at Dex, urging him to answer. Dex shook his head and pretended to resume watching the football game on television.

Isla sighed in exasperation. "Come on, you two! I know I'm supposed to figure things out on my own, but I need some help."

Her brother stood and approached. "You and Sky have just never really been friendly…"

"We're just different," Skylar added quickly.

"So?"

Her brother's fiancée didn't seem to have an answer. At least not a good-enough one to get out of Christmas shopping. "I'll get dressed," she said.

As Skylar disappeared up the winding staircase to the bedrooms, Dex chuckled.

"What's so funny?" Isla asked.

He shrugged, his hands deep in his jeans pockets. "Just never thought I'd see the day, that's all."

But he certainly looked happy about it, and that gave her a good feeling about the decision. "Well, maybe this injury has its benefits. I'm making new friends."

Dex eyed her. "Like Aaron?"

She felt her cheeks flush at the mention of him. They'd had an amazing time the day before, but there had been just a slight awkwardness when he'd dropped her off at the hotel. After cuddling in the sled and holding hands, having his arms around her and him telling her she was beautiful, she'd been hoping for a kiss when he helped her out of the truck. But instead he'd offered a one-armed hug and had quickly gotten back in the vehicle. She hadn't heard from him since and hadn't reached out either, unsure of proper after-date etiquette and not wanting to come across as too eager. She'd basically forced him into spending time with her already; the next move was on him. "Maybe," she said casually, because it was true. She did like Aaron but had no idea what exactly was going on between them.

Dex looked slightly concerned as he touched her shoulder. "I'm happy you two are spending time together. He's a good guy. Just be careful, okay?"

"Is this a big-brother speech warning me about boys?" she asked with a grin.

"Something like that," Dex said as Skylar reappeared,

dressed in black leggings, a red thermal jacket and hiking boots. He approached her and gave her a kiss.

Isla averted her eyes to give the two privacy, but when the kiss went on and on, she cleared her throat. "Stores will be closing soon," she said.

Dex laughed and finally released his fiancée. "Have fun," he said, still sounding amused by the whole thing.

"So where are we headed?" Skylar asked as they made their way down the pier.

"Wherever I can buy Christmas gifts with a spending cap of forty-six dollars a gift," she said.

Skylar looked confused as she turned to look at her.

"I got my paycheck from Santa's Village."

Skylar laughed. "Working for a living isn't what it's cracked up to be. Don't worry. We're hosting Christmas this year, so you can be in charge of filling stockings."

Isla smiled in relief. Filling stockings was the perfect idea. "Thanks, Skylar."

"You're welcome," she said.

With Skylar's help, she'd checked off everyone on her list in an hour, finding fun and zany items and candies and chocolates at the local shops to fill the family's stockings with. Skylar made her look away while she bought the items for Isla's.

Sitting across from one another at the Serpent Queen Pub, the bar attached to the Sealena Hotel, shopping bags filling the booth next to them, it was just after eight when the two clinked martini glasses.

"To a successful evening of shopping," Isla said before taking a sip. "Mmmm, this is delicious." The Grinch-themed martini was the perfect blend of mint and lime. Refreshing and sweet with the tang of the alcohol to balance the flavors.

Skylar sent her a soft smile from across the booth.

"I drink these all the time, don't I?" Isla said, feeling slightly embarrassed. She had to look like a complete moron to everyone else. Acting as though everything she saw was new, everything she tasted was foreign. Entering the bar, she must have looked like a tourist, scanning all the Sealena memorabilia and the history of the community portrayed in photos on the pub's walls. The old-school charm of the place made it feel cozy and warm: she could see why it was the locals' favorite watering hole.

"You came up with the festive-drink menu," Skylar said softly.

Isla sighed. "This is getting frustrating. At first, it was kinda fun rediscovering things."

"Only you would be brave enough to look at it that way."

Skylar's compliment made her feel a little better, but it just further emphasized that she had no idea how preaccident Isla would be dealing with this. "The thrill is wearing off. I feel like a fool or, at the very least, a tourist in my own life."

"Don't feel that way. This isn't your fault, and believe me, there are some things I'd love to experience for the first time again. Port Serenity is a truly magical place, and sometimes it's easy to take it for granted."

She sent Skylar a grateful look. Her brother's fiancée was amazing. Why hadn't they gotten along much before? She couldn't find fault with her. Kind, caring, successful, a badass coast guard captain...

"Can I ask you something and you'll tell me the truth?"

Skylar shifted uncomfortably in her seat.

"Please, Skylar. It's important."

Skylar nodded but sucked her lips back as though debating with herself.

"Am I an asshole?"

Skylar laughed out loud, then sobered when she saw that Isla was serious. "Oh…um…" She seemed at a loss for the right words.

"I think that answers my question," Isla said with a sigh.

"No! Really, you're not," Skylar said quickly. "Not at all. You're determined and strong-minded, and you like to do things your way. You're fiercely protective. You don't take any bullshit from anyone. You're just a little…guarded."

"Guarded?" Weird, because right now, at a time when she was probably the most vulnerable she'd ever been in her life, she didn't feel the need to be guarded. Why had she before? Had she been hurt?

"You're careful with who you let get close, that's all."

She nodded. Dex had said the same, and Aaron had too in a different way. She twirled the liquid around in the glass, letting the information settle in.

"But I'm grateful for this opportunity to get to know you. I wish it hadn't taken a head injury," Skylar said gently. "And I hope you won't regret this when you regain your memory."

"I won't." She knew she wouldn't. Maybe letting her guard down was something her former self wasn't so great at, but as long as she had no reason to be closed off, she wouldn't be.

A COFFEE MUG clutched in his hands, Aaron stared at the five-plus-foot Douglas fir that barely fit in his apartment, the urge to take it down and toss it outside overwhelming. It was just a stupid tree; it shouldn't hold this much power over him, and yet his chest had felt tight since he'd unloaded it from his truck and lugged it up the three flights of stairs by himself. Without a proper tree stand, it was propped against the wall in an old fishing bucket he'd found in the basement of the building.

What the hell was he going to do with it?

Decorating the tree had been Amy's favorite part of the holidays. She'd always insisted that the family do it together on December 1, and each year, they bought a new ornament with their names and the date on it. They took turns selecting the design, but he always gave his turn to Amy as she always seemed to find one she just had to have, and as a teenage boy, it had really made no difference to him. He had no idea where those family heirloom ornaments were now...

How had he let Isla talk him into this?

It hadn't taken much, actually. All she'd had to do was ask. The day of the sled ride had been the best day he'd had in forever, and in the moment he hadn't minded chopping down the tree. She'd made the event fun, and he'd been able to treat it almost like a new tradition, not haunted by the memory of the last time he'd had a Christmas tree. It was as though being with her had shielded him from the usual pain and hurt he associated with the holidays. He wasn't sure what the hell had happened but his feelings for her had completely changed...or maybe he was finally recognizing them for what they were.

But could he really start falling for her, developing feelings? What happened when she got her memory back? As soon as she realized that she didn't like him, this thing between them would end...and he wasn't sure he'd recover from that.

He hadn't heard from her, and he hadn't reached out either, unsure what to say.

Thanks for a great day.
Thanks for the tree.

Thank you for causing my emotions to spiral in an uncontrollable, terrifying way.

His cell rang and he sighed, reaching into his jeans pocket. Retrieving it, he frowned, seeing a FaceTime call from his parents. They hadn't scheduled a call, and it was rare that they'd call out of the blue.

His heart raced as he tapped to connect. "Mom, what's wrong?" he asked as her face appeared on the screen. She looked healthy. Not panicked...

"Wrong? Nothing, dear. Just wanted to check in," she said.

Right. His heart rate settled, but the uneasiness in the pit of his stomach lingered. Something was up. "Everything good in Florida?" he asked, carrying the phone and his coffee to the table and sitting.

"Yes, the weather's been perfect. No more humidity," she said, tossing her hair as if to prove it.

"Looks perfect," he said. "I'm just getting ready for work..." It was a white lie, as he had three hours before his shift started, but he needed her to get to the purpose of her call fast. The longer they engaged in idle chitchat, the more anxious he'd get. She obviously had an agenda.

"Well, the reason I'm calling is that the head of the parents' support group here in Florida is launching a new organization... It's for siblings of lost ones."

He thought he might actually be sick. He swallowed the bile rising in the back of his throat and fought to keep the phone steady as his hand trembled. Identifying as a sibling of a lost one was hard enough without an organization putting a label on it. He was distrustful of these organizations that always seemed to be raising money through their support groups; meanwhile, he'd never witnessed how the money benefitted real families in real ways.

No amount of money could bring Amy back.

"Alan, the organizer, loves the work your father and I have been doing, so he wanted us to invite you to—"

"No." He couldn't even let her finish the sentence.

"But, it's just a—"

"Mom, no," he said firmly. How many times did they have to go over this? He wasn't interested in being a spokesperson for these organizations. He'd attended a support group for a year in Port Serenity after Amy died—mostly at the insistence of his parents—but he'd been a minor and hadn't had a say. That group had only made him feel worse, having to keep telling the story of the day that forever haunted him. Having to rehash the decision he wished he could remake…

"Darling, look, we just think it will help you heal if you give back—"

"If I give back?" he asked, anger bubbling up within. "You mean like being an active member of the coast guard? Rescuing people from danger? Saving families from similar tragedies?"

His mother looked pained. "That's all wonderful. But we do a lot of good too. The money from the golf tournament in January is going to cover medical bills for a local family who recently lost their daughter after a long cancer battle. And last year's funds covered the costs of funeral arrangements for a family who couldn't afford it."

Okay, so maybe the charities did some good, but Aaron wasn't able to be a part of it. He just wasn't strong enough. "Mom, the answer's *no*."

She nodded, looking annoyed to have been shut down. "Okay. If that's how you feel."

"It is," he said as his father's face appeared on the screen behind his mother. He'd obviously been listening as he added his own look of disappointment to the guilt trip. Aaron sighed. "I'm sorry." He was and he meant it. "I just can't."

His father squinted as he peered through the screen. "Is that a Christmas tree?"

Shit.

"It is, yes," he said, fighting to keep his voice even. He hadn't thought it was possible for this call to get even worse.

His father nodded slowly. "Okay, well, I guess there's not much else to talk about. Bye, son," he said, and the Face-Time call disconnected abruptly.

As if the Douglas fir leaning against the wall in his apartment was the ultimate act of betrayal.

CHAPTER TWELVE

HER CELL PHONE chiming on the bedside table woke Isla.
She groaned as she rolled over and picked it up. After too
many Grinch martinis with Skylar the night before, she'd
been looking forward to sleeping in a little. She squinted
at the phone through tired eyes, a light hangover headache
making her temple throb.

It was a calendar reminder making all the noise.

Community Center 9:00 a.m.

What was at the community center? A quick glance at
the time revealed whatever it was started in an hour.

She sat up and started to text Dex to ask him if he knew
what that was about, but then decided against it. She needed
to figure this stuff out herself. If it was on her calendar, then
it was obviously a commitment she'd made. She climbed
out of bed, showered and got dressed.

Then, googling the directions to the community center
and seeing it was only a ten-minute walk, she headed out.
The air was cool, but not too cold, as she walked along
the marina. Big ocean waves crashed against the rough,
rocky shore in the distance. Skylar was right: Port Serenity truly was a magical place. Nestled between the most
incredible mountain ranges, vast wilderness all around and
the view of the sea—she understood why it was so popular with tourists.

The coast guard station in the distance caught her eye,

and she slowed her pace a little. Maybe she could stop by to say hi to Skylar...then she remembered the other woman wasn't working that day. She stared at the building as she drew closer. Was Aaron at work? She didn't see his truck in the parking lot.

Not that she could actually stop by to see him if it was. He was at work, and she refused to become a stalker. She sighed as she continued on. Not hearing from him was disheartening. She thought they'd had a great day together, but the radio silence since was making her think it had been one-sided. But he was probably just busy. Work had to be crazy this time of year.

Besides, she had things to do too.

She pushed through the doors of the community center two minutes before nine. The sights and sounds of Christmas were everywhere. A large artificial Christmas tree stood in the corner, a group of kids nearby stringing popcorn to hang on it. Holiday music played as kids and teens participated in festive activities. Apparently, it was the place to be on a weekend in Port Serenity, and her mood instantly lifted.

She scanned the center, unsure of where she was supposed to be. Was she meeting someone there? Was she volunteering?

"If you're looking for Phillip, he's in the rock-climbing room!" a kid playing basketball called out, noticing her standing there.

Phillip. The center organizer maybe? Sounded like the best place to start. "Thanks!" she said, heading in the direction he was pointing.

Inside, there was a ten-foot rock wall and all the necessary climbing gear. Safety-instruction posters hung on the wall, and climbing-themed T-shirts and sweatshirts for sale hung on a rack.

A man in a wheelchair turned and greeted her as she entered. "Hey, stranger! How are you?"

"Feeling good. Phillip?" she asked.

"Still don't remember this handsome face, huh?"

Isla laughed, feeling instantly at ease with the man. He was obviously a friend. "Unfortunately not." She placed her crutch against the wall and removed her mittens and hat. "My calendar said I had something going on here at nine."

He nodded. "You teach a beginner climbing group for teens."

That might be difficult. She eyed the wall that wasn't entirely menacing, and she knew by her social-media photos that this wall wouldn't normally pose any challenges. But how was she supposed to teach kids when she couldn't remember the terminology or technique?

Phillip sensed her dilemma as he said, "Maybe start by attempting the wall."

She hesitated. "I'm not sure I can do it with the cast."

"I climb it every day. You'll be fine," he said.

She hid her surprise as she nodded and removed her jacket. He handed her a harness and instinctively she knew how to attach and secure it. Huh. That muscle memory must be strong.

She approached the wall and a feeling of excitement bubbled up within. Mentally, she saw the climbing path unfold like a live map. She reached for the first two handholds, lifting her feet off of the ground. The weight of her body settled on her arms and she immediately felt energized, strong. Having her muscles engaged in physical activity felt great.

"Keep your Ls," Phillip said.

Keep your Ls.

She knew what that meant! It was the first real familiar thing, something direct from her memory that she'd experienced. She instinctively bent her arms at the elbows, feeling the tension shift to her biceps, which now helped to control her entire body. She reached for the next two and climbed higher, using only her upper body to complete the climb.

She had to be careful. If she fell, even with the harness, she could seriously reinjure the leg that was otherwise healing nicely.

"You've got this," Phillip said as he watched from below.

And he was right. She did.

She reached the top, hit the victory buzzer and carefully used the harness to lower herself back to the floor.

"That was fun," she said. One perk of this amnesia was that it was as though she were encountering so much for the first time. Her body might remember the thrill and ensure she could still do things she was good at, but her mind seemed to be treating it as a novel experience.

Phillip laughed. "Well, you're the best at it, and your group of miniworshippers will be here around nine thirty."

"Miniworshippers?"

"You're something of a local superstar for these teens."

"No pressure." She hoped they all knew to lower their expectations given the circumstances. Hopefully someone had filled them in about her injury and limitations.

"I'll tell them to go easy on you," he said as he left the room.

"Appreciate it," she called after him with a laugh.

Twenty-two minutes later, four kids entered the room, chatting and laughing and making some joke about a substitute teacher. Isla forced a deep breath as she smiled. They were just teenagers. Harmless.

They stopped talking when they saw her and looked at her as though she'd grown an extra head.

So this was awkward for everyone.

"Hi," she said with a quick wave. "You all know who I am, but I'm going to need a refresher," she said, hoping to break the mood with a joke.

Having four teens rush toward her and hug her was the last thing she'd been expecting, and they nearly knocked her off balance.

"We were so scared when we heard the news," one girl said.

"Are you okay?" a boy asked.

An unexpected lump formed in the back of her throat, and her laugh sounded strangled as she detached herself from the kids and nodded reassuringly. "I'm fine. Thank you all for being concerned, but the good news is muscle memory is a real thing, and I can still climb this wall."

Relieved expressions responded to her.

"But it doesn't solve the problem of your names so..." She reached into the supply kit and retrieved name tags and markers, handing them out. "Please, just for now, until I remember again."

An hour flew by, and she was exhausted and her ribs hurt from laughing as she wrapped up the lesson. She could definitely understand why she'd volunteered with these teens. They were smart, funny and up for the challenging climbs. She high-fived each of them on their way out and felt a genuine sense of pride.

She might have only recently gotten a real job, but she felt like she certainly made a difference here. With these kids. That was something.

"Looks like it went well," Phillip said, appearing in the doorway.

"Yes. I think so," she said. "Great group of kids."

Phillip chuckled. "You know, none of them wrote their actual names on those name tags."

Isla's mouth gaped. Those little monsters. She should have known. She'd thought *Fabio, Enrique, Esmeralda* and *Bono* seemed a little far-fetched. She shook her head and laughed. "Guess they got me."

Her phone rang, and she frowned seeing Hunter Investigations on the call display.

Who was that?

"I'll let you get that. Great job today. Good to have you back," Phillip said, leaving her alone to answer.

But she hesitated. Maybe she should let the call go to voice mail and return it once she figured it out. She bit her lip as the phone continued to ring, but something in her gut told her not to ignore it.

"Hello?"

"Hey, it's Hunter," a man's deep voice said.

"Hi…"

"I think I may have found her."

Isla frowned. "Found who?"

"Your birth mom," he said.

Her what?

"This is Isla, right?" the man asked, sounding concerned that he may just have breached client confidentiality by not confirming her identity first.

She was almost too shocked to say anything, but she finally found her voice. Sort of. "Yes, it's Isla. I'm sorry…I recently suffered an accident so I'm not exactly myself these days." She didn't want to admit that she had absolutely no idea what he was talking about. She suspected this was information she really should know. Her *birth mother.* The words felt foreign. Wasn't Grace her mother?

"Right, okay. Well," Hunter said, "no guarantees, as always. But after the last dead-end lead, I wanted to update you that I've found another possibility. I need to do a bit more investigating first..."

Last dead-end? She'd been working with this man for a while? To find her birth mother... It still wasn't making sense. She'd think he had the wrong number if he hadn't confirmed it was her he was speaking to.

"Oh, okay. Of course. That's great," she said, her hand trembling. Was it? She had no idea...

"I'll keep you posted."

"Yes, please do," she said.

Because her family certainly wasn't.

ISLA BARELY FELT the cold breeze as she made her way across town moments later, toward her family home. Walking almost on autopilot, her feet moved in the direction suggested by her phone's GPS, but it felt like more muscle memory propelling her. She barely saw her surroundings as she walked, the nice houses lining both sides of the street a blur as she passed. A few people waved in greeting, but she hardly noticed them.

Her birth mother. Which meant she must have been adopted. It was both difficult to wrap her mind around and yet it wasn't the deep shock she'd have expected. Obviously somewhere in her mind, this knowledge existed. But all she was experiencing was confusion and curiosity.

How was she going to broach the subject with her parents? No one had told her this detail of her life. Why? Was it something they didn't talk about? Was it something they never really acknowledged?

She was adopted.

The thought spun in her mind, and her emotions seemed

reluctant to settle on just how she felt about it. Right now, she had no idea who she was, her past was a mystery... Had that always been the case?

"Your destination is on the right," the female voice of the navigation system said, and she stopped.

She wasn't surprised to see the biggest home in Port Serenity. The white three-story house had to be at least five thousand square feet with a three-car garage and large plot of land. She could see a pool in the back that was covered for the season, but a hot tub bubbled on the expansive deck. White Christmas lights framing the exterior and a wreath on the door were the only holiday decorations.

Tasteful, classy...like them.

Isla hopped up the front steps and raised a hand to knock. Then, deciding that would be an awkward way to start what was sure to be an awkward visit, she opened the door and entered the magnificent foyer. A winding staircase and elegant chandelier greeted her in the slightly cool interior. Big, impressive-looking pieces of modern art hung on the wall, and a large vase holding fresh flowers stood on an entrance table. To her right, she could see the sitting room with a large, rock-face fireplace and elegant furniture. And to her left, a large den with floor-to-ceiling bookshelves. Each room had a slight museum vibe, as though it were staged and no one actually lived there. It was beautiful but lacked the warmth she felt on the yacht with its old furnishings and family photos.

No surprise that she'd enjoyed living on the boat with Dex or opted to stay at the Sealena Hotel while home for the holidays. This place didn't feel cozy or inviting. She knew her family was nice and friendly and caring, but a certain level of warmth was missing from the house.

Was that why she was searching for her birth parents?

Did she feel something missing in her life? Or was it just curiosity? Would her parents have those answers? Or would the question just hurt them?

She hesitated. She had no idea what the situation was. Maybe she should wait to bring it up... She'd headed there from the community center in a haze, thinking it was the logical thing to do, but the last thing she wanted was to hurt anyone.

"Hello?" her mother's voice called from somewhere in the house.

Too late. She was there, and she couldn't wait for these answers. She'd never be able to act normal around them with such thoughts constantly plaguing her. Better to face the issue head-on.

"Hey...Mom? Dad?" Those titles had felt odd to call supposed strangers before; now they were unsettling. She was adopted. No one had thought to tell her that detail. Sure, the doctor had said it was best to let her discover things on her own, but this was huge, especially considering she'd apparently been trying to track down her birth mother.

She'd been caught too off guard by the call from the investigator to question the man further, but someone needed to fill her in. This was one detail of her life she couldn't be left in the dark about any longer.

"In the kitchen," her father called out.

If only she remembered where that was. She headed in the direction of his voice, and after just one wrong turn into the formal dining room, she found the kitchen, a beautiful, commercial one that looked like it could cater large parties and events. Like her father's annual law-office party that was coming up soon.

"Hi, darlin'. How are you?" her mother asked, pouring a cup of coffee.

"I'm adopted?" The question just seemed to pop out.

The coffeepot slipped from her mother's hand, crashing to the tiled floor at her feet. She jumped back, but not before the dark liquid covered the base of her tan dress pants.

"Shit, sorry," Isla mumbled. This was a bad idea. Or at least she could have approached the topic a little more gently.

Brian jumped up from the table to go to Grace's aid, scanning her for signs of injury. "You okay? Did you burn yourself?"

"I'm fine," she said, but her voice sounded strained.

"Stay still. Watch the glass. I'll grab the mop," Brian said, and it didn't escape Isla's notice that he avoided looking at her as he opened the utility closet in the hallway and retrieved the mop.

"I'm sorry," she repeated. "I didn't mean to just blurt that out."

Grace sent her a strained smile. "It's okay. Let's just get this cleaned up, and we can talk."

Isla nodded, and several minutes later, the three of them were seated at the large kitchen table, fresh coffee sitting untouched in front of them. No one seemed to want to speak first, and the tension was making her palms sweat.

Her father finally cleared his throat. "You're starting to remember things?"

Isla shook her head. "No. I got a call from a private investigator in Anchorage."

Now it was their turn to look caught off guard. "You're trying to find your birth parents?" her father asked.

Shit. Obviously, they hadn't known. A lot of revelations were happening today.

"I guess so," she said with a shrug.

"Why?" her mother asked softly.

How would she know? She'd literally just discovered this fact an hour ago. She took a deep breath. "I don't know. But I can only assume it's important for me to know who I am." Funny how she'd been searching for her identity, her past, when it had been taken from her once again.

Her father stared into his coffee. "You're Isla Wakefield. Our daughter," he said, and the rare show of emotion in the man's voice was almost enough for her to simply accept that. Obviously, this was hard on them, and she hated that she'd brought up a painful topic, but what was she supposed to do?

Her mother touched Brian's hand gently, before turning to look at her. "Darling, we had no idea you were interested in knowing. Forgive us. This is just a bit of a shock."

For her too.

"I'm sorry. I'd like to pretend that I didn't get that call today. Upsetting you both is the last thing I want to do, but I think you're going to have to bring me up to speed again," she said, slumping into her chair to listen to a story that she suspected hadn't been all that easy to hear the first time they'd told her.

Brian shook his head quickly, as though he couldn't be the one to tell it, but stayed seated at the table as Grace took the lead.

"We adopted you from a center in Anchorage when you were four years old. You had been in the foster-care system for about a year and a half before that." She paused and hesitated before continuing. "Your mother was in jail at the time, and, well…no one knew who your father was. He wasn't listed on your birth certificate."

In jail? Her mom was a criminal? And her father had been MIA since birth? Isla clenched her hands together on her lap as she listened to the unsettling news.

"Your father was actually the lawyer on her case," her mother said. "Defending her," she added quickly.

That was a relief, at least.

"What did she do?"

"Petty theft, mostly. She was just trying to survive. Before she went to jail, the two of you had been moving around a lot." She paused. "She wasn't a bad person." She touched Isla's hand. "And she loved you."

"How do you know?"

"Because she did what was best for you by allowing us to adopt you instead of keeping you in the foster-care system indefinitely." Her mother glanced at Brian, who was still staring into his cup. His shoulders had sagged, and it was the first time the man looked his age. Wrinkles had appeared around his eyes and forehead, and it broke Isla's heart that this was causing him so much pain.

"She also wrote you a letter," Grace said. "I think it might be best for you to read that instead of hearing this from us."

A letter from her birth mother.

It all seemed surreal, yet part of her felt like she'd always known something was missing, that she was searching for a part of herself, even before her memory loss. It was almost a relief to know she could trust her gut instincts, even if she couldn't rely on her memory.

She nodded then hesitated before asking, "Do you know where she is? Did we keep in touch?" Had her mother cared enough to keep in contact with the Wakefields all these years? Maybe hiring the investigator hadn't been necessary, if she'd only come to her parents sooner. Though, now she realized why she hadn't.

Her mother shook her head. "We really don't know. She served a four-year sentence, but then we lost track of her whereabouts. The terms of the adoption were that there wouldn't be any contact, so she's never reached out. The agency suggested the terms, and we all thought they were for the best."

Isla nodded silently. She had no idea whether that were true. She couldn't imagine how her parents had made these decisions. How her birth mother had made the decision to give her up. But based on the life she knew she had, she could only believe that all the tough decisions they'd made had given her an amazing, stable and secure life. One she may not have had otherwise.

The three of them sat there for a long moment, lost in their thoughts. Then Grace stood. "I'll get you the letter and some of your things. You used to write in journals... Maybe those might help. Take your time to process, and if you want to talk again, I'm here. We're here," she said, leaving the kitchen.

Tense, thick air seemed to linger around them as she sat with her father. She wanted to say something—anything— but she didn't know how to make things better. She had no idea what he was thinking. Whether he was angry or just hurt.

Finally, her father looked up at her and offered a supportive nod. "This isn't easy for me. Just know, whatever you learn, whatever you find, you're my daughter. Always."

Isla swallowed the lump in her throat as she simply nodded, not trusting her own voice to speak. Moments later, Grace returned, and Isla accepted the old, worn journals from her with appreciation. Then her mother handed her an envelope. "All the details of the adoption, including the letter," she said.

"Thank you," Isla said.

Her mother hugged her tight and kissed her forehead. "We love you."

There was no doubt in Isla's mind that was true.

Back in her hotel room half an hour later, she sat on the bed and stared at the journals. Floral notebooks, hardcover diaries with tiny locks… A few hours ago she'd wanted answers, but now, faced with a stack of information, she wasn't sure she was ready for them. Where did she even start?

She picked up the adoption file and slowly opened it. Inside were the legal documents that outlined the process and stipulations. She scanned them and was relieved to see that her name hadn't changed. It had always been Isla. She wasn't sure why that was so important, but it was. She then saw her birth mother's name: Ariel Hopkins. Father: Unknown.

She flipped through the pages outlining the terms of the adoption.

No contact. Closed file. A large amount of money was deposited into an account for Ariel for after her release.

A photo of her as a child made Isla's throat tighten. Her little smiling face was grinning at the camera, and her little arms were wrapped tightly around a woman's neck. Her mother. She was thin and pretty with light blond hair and the same green eyes. She looked scared…sad.

Isla swallowed another lump in her throat as she noticed the crescent-moon pendant hanging around the woman's neck. The same one she noticed herself always wearing in the photos of her online.

A gift from her birth mother.

And she'd lost it. The only thing she had. Something that had obviously meant a lot to her if she wore it every day. So, this search for her birth mother hadn't been a new thing. She'd always been wondering...

She saw the letter in the back of the file, and with a shaky hand, she reached for it. She knew this was going to destroy her, but she had to start somewhere. Her mother's own words might be the most important thing she was missing, searching for...

Taking a deep breath, she read.

Dear Baby Girl,
There is so much I want to tell you, and I have only a solitary page to do it in. This will be the only letter from me that you'll receive, so the pressure to wrap all the emotions I'm feeling into it is overwhelming, but I'll try.

I'm not able to be a mom, but that doesn't stop the intense protective instinct within me, demanding to do what's right for you, precious girl. And I know the right thing is to give you the chance to have the best life. A life you deserve. With a family that can give you everything I can't.

I'm not ready to raise a child, but that doesn't stop the images of all the things that I'll miss out on from tearing a hole in my heart. But those images also give me peace, knowing you'll have the security of loving arms to help you back up when you fall. You'll shine like a star in everything you do, and you'll feel all the support and encouragement and love from everyone around you.

I'm not ready to kiss your beautiful little cheek a final time, but I will, because you, my baby girl, are the most important thing in my world. Know you'll always be on my mind and in my heart.

Your first Momma

Tears ran down her cheeks, and Isla let them fall as she clutched the letter to her chest and leaned back against the pillows on the bed.

She had no idea who she was, and now she felt even more lost. If she hadn't been sure who she was before her injury, could she ever discover it now?

CHAPTER THIRTEEN

THE LOOK OF disappointment and hurt on his parents' faces continued to play in his mind as Aaron finished his shift at the station. He'd gone over the conversation with his mother a dozen times, but he couldn't agree to what they were asking. For years, he'd longed for a way to reconnect with them, try to rebuild their relationship, become a family again in some way, but he was starting to lose hope of it ever happening.

Not unless he gave in and held on to the past the way they were.

Heading into the staff room, he poured the cold contents of his travel mug into the sink and rinsed it before securing the lid. Next to the sink, he noticed a stack of Christmas Train Ride tickets. The local annual event started that evening and ran until Christmas Eve, and they always donated tickets to the station for the crew's family and friends to participate free of charge.

He'd never actually gone. This year probably wouldn't be the year either.

How could he possibly participate in holiday events when he was already feeling so guilty about having an undecorated tree in his apartment?

Didn't matter, anyway. The event was for families—people with children. Or, at the very least, someone special to share the season with.

That wasn't him, and after his call with his parents, he'd realized that as much as he liked Isla, felt a connection to her, he couldn't keep seeing her.

Cooling things down was better for her sake.

He entered the locker room and removed his jacket, hanging it inside.

A knock sounded on the open door before Skylar entered. "Hey, do you have a sec?"

"Something wrong?" He could hear it in her voice.

"Isla had a rough day," Skylar said.

Aaron sighed, wishing that didn't have as much of an impact on him as it did. But he couldn't deny that since their dogsledding date, he was all kinds of messed up. He'd known there was sexual chemistry simmering beneath the surface of their resentment all these years, and he was definitely attracted to Isla physically, but that day had revealed another level. They'd connected in a different way.

A dangerous way.

He needed to pull back. It wouldn't take much to lose his common sense regarding her—or at least this new version of her that he was getting to know.

"What happened?" he asked.

"She found out that she was adopted," Skylar said with a sigh. "We really should have found a way to tell her, but it had just seemed like such a big thing…"

It was a huge thing, and not something that she should have discovered on her own. His chest tightened at the thought of how hard that must have been on her. "Is she okay?"

"Dex reached out to her, and she said she was 'processing.' I guess Grace gave her some old journals and her adoption file."

"I'm sure she needs time," he said.

"Well, I was hoping maybe you'd reach out to her?" Skylar said. "I know you two have a thing going on…"

He sighed. "It was just one day. We hung out and had a good time, but I don't think it's a good idea."

"I just think she could use support that isn't family right now. She's a little upset with us for keeping this from her," Skylar said, a note of pleading in her tone.

Just like she was going to be upset with *him* for not telling her about *their* history. There were a lot of things that Isla didn't know, and the more she figured out, the more she'd pull away from him.

"She's going to be upset when she gets her memory back and learns that the two of us would rather murder one another than have dinner together," Aaron said.

Skylar entered the room. "That was before. You two have been getting along, connecting…"

"I feel like I'm deceiving her." Even worse, he was lying to himself by thinking things could actually work between them.

"You're not," Skylar said quickly. "She's the one who has been initiating this time with you. She's getting to know you, and so far, she likes what she's learning. Things she never allowed herself to discover when the two of you were too pigheaded to acknowledge the intense attraction between you."

He sighed. "I don't know, Skylar. Things have already gotten complicated." The Christmas tree in his apartment was evidence of that. It wasn't just the tree: Isla had opened up past wounds within him as he'd struggled with wanting to celebrate the holidays this year, to finally enjoy the season again. With her. But he couldn't rely on this temporary connection for healing. If he did, he'd be doomed when it ended.

"I understand. I do," Skylar said. "I just think that you two could really be good for one another. I know this time of year is hard on you too. You could be there for one another, that's all."

Unfortunately, that wasn't all. Not even close.

But the idea of Isla hurting and conflicted and not feeling like she had anyone she could confide in or talk to made his protective instincts kick in. They had connected, and he'd be an asshole to keep avoiding her now when she could use a friend. "Okay. I'll reach out to her. Any ideas for making her feel better?"

Skylar smiled as she handed him a set of the Christmas Train Ride tickets. "She mentioned wanting to do this while she was home."

He glanced down at the tickets and sighed. More holiday-themed activities. Wonderful.

SHE'D OFFICIALLY RUN out of tissues. A big pile of used ones littered the hotel bed next to the old journals as poring over her entries from ages ten through eighteen had Isla's emotions spiraling. One minute she was laughing at her young antics, and the next she was sobbing, as teenage turmoil spilled onto tear-stained pages.

Her parents may not have known the struggles she'd been facing back then, but in those tough adolescent years, she'd really fought with her sense of identity, not knowing where she'd come from. She'd wondered what her birth parents were like, where they were, if they'd ever thought of her or regretted giving her up.

The entries were always full of conflict as her younger

self felt a sense of betrayal of her family for even having these thoughts. These secret hopes and desires and fantasies of someday meeting her birth parents. Guilt over feeling there was something missing when she had everything.

Some entries were full of angst as she planned out what she'd say if that day ever came and she was face-to-face with them. Would she be angry and reject them in turn? Tell them she didn't need them, that she was fine without them? Or would she be happy and accept them back into her life, relieved to have the mysteries solved?

The entries all seemed to have one major thing in common, one written between the lines: a struggle with not feeling good enough. Despite getting good grades, having nice friends, working hard and achieving success in all her extracurricular activities, she battled a lack of self-worth. If her real parents hadn't wanted her, why would anyone else? Why would anyone else accept and love her for who she was?

As a teenager, it had evidently been a huge issue for her to come to terms with.

At least Isla had solved one mystery: the lack of trust she had in others had developed in her time in the foster-care system. Her earlier diary entries had mentioned those years from age two to four. Memories, surely clouded by time and being so young, but ones that were so deep-rooted they'd had an impact on her. Recollecting how she'd carried her few belongings in a black garbage bag from one home to the other, or having her doll stolen by another child. Lack of attention, being left all alone in a bedroom for hours… Just reading about it had made Isla's chest ache for the lost little girl she used to be.

The biggest takeaway from reading her journals was

understanding why she'd felt such a great source of freedom after losing her memory. Why there had been a sense
of relief that overpowered any fear or frustration she'd felt
that day in the hospital. For the first time in her life, she
hadn't known that she was supposed to be closed off and
guarded, she hadn't had all of these painful reasons not to
trust, no constant sense of searching…

She sighed, putting a journal aside as she noticed the sun
dipping lower in the sky outside her window.

Her parents had texted once to ask if she was okay, and
she'd responded that she was. Dex had reached out as well
to say he was there if she needed to talk or just wanted to
hang out.

She worried about the impact this had on all of them.
They hadn't known she was searching for her birth parents,
which meant she'd been keeping it from them for a reason.

That reason had been evident on her father's face. She
hoped he could understand why this search might be important to her. Though, could anyone really understand it?

Her phone chimed with a new message now, and she
was surprised to see it was from Aaron.

Heard you wanted to check this out. Still interested?

Attached was a picture of tickets for a Christmas Train
Ride.

He hadn't texted since the sled ride, and she'd thought
maybe he wasn't interested in seeing her anymore. But the
timing of his message couldn't have been better. She was
eager to see him and spend time with him again, and after
the emotionally taxing day, the train ride looked like a fun
way to let it all go for a while.

She checked the details on the tickets. They were for that evening's ride at seven o'clock. It was already after five. She wouldn't have to wait long to see him.

Meet you outside the hotel at six thirty?

His reply was immediate: I'll be there.

Odd how those three little words seemed to hold so much more meaning, just when she needed them most.

CHAPTER FOURTEEN

"I FEEL LIKE we should have a kid," Aaron said as they arrived at the train station just outside of town that evening.

Isla grinned at him. "This is only our second date, but I'm game if you are."

"I mean to board this train," he said as he took in the Alaska Railway's Holiday Train. Every inch of the train's magnificent glass enclosure was decorated with garlands, lights and snowflakes. The staff were dressed as elves as they took tickets and welcomed excited families onboard.

Isla pointed to a family with six kids, all wearing Christmas onesies under thick winter gear. "We could ask to borrow one of theirs if it makes you feel better."

He laughed as he gently shoved her. "You really don't feel awkward going on this as a twenty-three-year-old adult?"

"Nope," she said.

He was relieved to see she was okay, despite the news he knew she'd discovered that day. He'd actually been surprised when he'd picked her up and she'd greeted him with a smile and only slightly puffy eyes that hinted she'd been crying. It broke his heart to think of her so upset. She was Isla Freaking Wakefield: he'd never seen her cry in all the time that he'd known her, so the knowledge that something earlier that day had caused tears made his own chest ache.

They approached the train and handed their tickets to the

attendant, who was dressed like an elf. "Welcome aboard!" the cheery man said, moving back to allow them entry.

Using her crutch, Isla carefully climbed the stairs. "Where do you want to sit?" she asked, scanning the rows of seats.

"Wherever you like," he said and followed her to the last seat in the back of the train car.

She propped her crutch against the wall as she sat near the window and removed her hat and gloves. "This is really nice," she said, taking in the decor.

The train had certainly been transformed into what looked like the Polar Express on its way to the North Pole. Christmas lights were strung around the windows, and holiday classics played over the speakers. There was a level of excitement in the air as the magic of the season surrounded them.

Aaron hadn't allowed himself to enjoy the season in so long the feelings of warmth and happiness felt slightly overwhelming. Ignoring the festivities, claiming it was just another day and working at the station to distract himself had helped to dull the pain, but it had never fully gone away.

This year with Isla was magical in ways he hadn't even considered the holidays could be. He glanced at her as she peered out the window. She looked breathtakingly beautiful with her short blond hair in loose waves and a hint of makeup on her face. Her bright green eyes sparkled in the glow of the holiday lights, and her happiness was contagious.

After the day he knew she'd had, he was glad he'd invited her out.

Damn, he should have reached out days ago.

"Hey, sorry I was MIA the last few days," he said.

"Were you? Hadn't noticed," she said, but he heard the

note of teasing and mild annoyance at what could have been considered ghosting on his part.

"Work was busy…" *Nope. Try again.* "Truth is, I got a little freaked out."

She nodded. "Well, I'm glad you got over it."

He wasn't sure about that. In fact, he was fairly certain that he would only get more and more freaked out the more time they spent together and the more his feelings grew. But it was a chance he was willing to take. Earlier that day in the station, his resolve not to see her again had come from fear of getting hurt…but now he was going all in.

"And your timing was good," she said softly, with a deep sigh. "I got some news today."

Admit that he knew, or let her tell him?

She continued before he could decide. "I'm sure you know I'm adopted."

He nodded.

"And apparently I've been looking for my birth mom."

That he hadn't known.

"Anyway, I don't really want to talk about it. I'm still processing…but I just wanted you to know that being here with you is making me feel better than I have all day, so thank you."

"You're welcome," he said, as the train whistle blew, indicating the last chance to board. He wrapped an arm around her as they sat back and watched the festive scenery pass outside the window when the train started to move.

The helper elves walked down the aisle, handing out Christmas carol books, and one pushed a serving tray of hot chocolate heaped with marshmallows and big chocolate chip cookies.

Aaron took two cups of hot chocolate and handed one to Isla. "Cookie?"

"I think the hot chocolate is plenty," she said, taking a sip, her lip covered in marshmallow.

The temptation to lean forward and lick it off her lip vanished only when she beat him to it.

He sipped his own and watched as the family of eight devoured their cookies in record time, chocolate all over their tiny faces. "Those kids are going to be up all night," he said.

Isla laughed as she glanced toward the family. "Do you want kids?"

The question caught him off guard, but he thought about it. "I can't say I've really given it much thought. My career has been my main focus for a long time. The training is demanding and, well, the job's dangerous." He wasn't entirely sure having a family would be fair to them when he was constantly putting his own safety on the line.

He didn't add that the idea of family was hard to envision when he hadn't had one in so long. That he'd basically accepted that he'd probably be alone forever, never really considering a life with someone else.

"You?" he asked.

"I'm not sure either," she said. "I mean, who knows what my former self wanted, but I guess I don't feel any real maternal instinct or pull toward having kids. Not yet, anyway. Maybe that will change."

He liked that they were on the same page on this. No real definitive answer either way. No pressure or need to hurry into that stage of life. Odd. He'd never thought that he'd be on the same page with Isla Wakefield about anything.

"Have you given any more thought to law school?" he asked. She'd mentioned it in passing on the way back from the dogsled adventure a few days before. He hadn't known she was entertaining following in her father's footsteps. But then he'd never been in her inner circle.

"I have, but I'm still not sure. Dad's really hoping I will, but I don't think I'll be able to truly decide until things are back to normal. If they ever are." She shrugged. "I just know I'm disappointing him by not agreeing to it right away."

"Brian can be fairly demanding and opinionated. I'm sure he just wants what's best for you."

"He seems to leave Dex alone," she said.

"Dex set boundaries years ago when he moved out of the house and onto your grandfather's yacht. But I know Brian had envisioned a football career for Dex." It had been harder on Brian than it had been on Dex when Dex had been diagnosed with epilepsy, ending any hope of professional football.

"So Dex is the brawn and I'm the brains?" she asked.

"You are anything you want to be." He paused. "For the record, I think you'd make a fantastic lawyer."

She turned in the seat to face him. "I get the impression I'm slightly argumentative?"

Slightly was an understatement.

Now was the perfect opportunity to gently suggest there had been tension between them. Broach the subject slowly, and reveal everything over time. He wasn't about to tell her about the *Anyone but Isla* club he'd started in third grade just yet, but he said, "You and I may have had some heated debates on certain subjects."

She looked intrigued as she urged him to continue. "Subjects such as?"

"Your daredevil nature and my aversion to unnecessary risk-taking may have come up a time or two."

She seemed to think about it for a moment. "You probably weren't always wrong. I mean, look what happened to me," she said, pointing to her head, where the bruising had turned a pale purple and yellow hue.

What had happened to her was that she'd suddenly become an open and vulnerable version of a woman he'd always found fascinating and intimidating.

"I wasn't always right," he said. He could acknowledge that now. Truth was he was so afraid that she'd get hurt because he'd always liked and cared about her more than he'd admitted. Even to himself.

He gently touched the bruise on her forehead, wishing he could erase any hurt she ever felt with his touch. Their eyes met and held for a long moment, heat vibrating between their stare, and anticipation flowing through him. He leaned forward and she moved closer, titling her head upward slightly, inviting the kiss.

His hand slid down her cheek and brushed her blond hair back from her face as he lowered his head toward hers. The full pale pink lips so deliciously tempting and the smell of chocolate still on her breath.

Damn, he wanted to kiss her so bad… Could he? Could they cross that line?

If they did, there would be no turning back. At least not for him. He was already developing feelings for her, and his attraction was undeniable.

Her gaze shifted slightly to the right, and she pulled back with a flushed look. "Um…I think we have an audience," she whispered.

He turned to look where she pointed. Leaning over the back of the seat in front of them, three little children were staring at them. Engaged and fascinated.

Aaron cleared his throat and laughed. "Okay, show's over," he told them.

They giggled as they turned around in their seats, their parents shooting him an apologetic look.

So close… He'd been seconds—and inches—away from kissing her. He knew he wanted to, and he knew she wanted to. Now, it was only a matter of time…

For now, he pulled her in tight to lean against him and whispered, "I'm leaning toward no on that whole kids thing."

She giggled as she snuggled closer, and Aaron held her in his arms as he sat back to enjoy the seasonal atmosphere enveloping him, filling him with happiness instead of a sense of dread, allowing himself something he hadn't in a long time.

Something that was long overdue. Something he was desperate to hold on to.

THE NIGHT HAD been magical. The Christmas-themed train ride through the beautiful Alaskan mountain range, singing Christmas carols and drinking hot chocolate, feeling Aaron's arm around her, had been the perfect way to end a stressful day.

And it would have been that much better if she'd gotten that kiss.

She liked kids, but damn, they had the worst timing. In fairness, they had been on a family-friendly train ride. A full-on make-out session wouldn't have been appropriate. Not that that would have stopped her. He was so incredibly handsome, and his easy-going nature fiercely contradicted the butterflies she got when she was around him. He made her feel comfortable, yet nervous—and she suspected his kiss would have made her feel all kinds of ways.

The train hadn't been the right place or time for a first kiss, but now they were in the privacy of his truck as they headed back to the hotel. Would he attempt it again? Soft holiday music played in the vehicle while snow fell outside. There was a romantic mood that had lingered all evening.

It definitely felt like a date. Did he consider it a date? Like the dogsled ride, they'd cuddled, held hands, had an almost-kiss...

She glanced his way as he drove. She somehow suspected he'd reached out that night because he'd known she'd needed a friend. Tipped off by Skylar, maybe? Was spending time with her really what he wanted to do, or had he felt guilted into another date with her? Only a kiss would confirm that he was seeing her because it was what he truly wanted...

Unfortunately, she couldn't just grab him and kiss him while he was driving along the highway, even if it was tempting.

He glanced her way and caught her stare. "You okay?" he asked.

"Yeah...better than okay. Tonight was exactly what I needed." Seeing all the families together had reminded her that having people who loved and cared about her was most important. It didn't matter if they were blood-related or not. And the Wakefields were her family.

"If you want to talk about what happened today, I'm here. No pressure," he said, sounding sincere.

She realized she did want to talk to him about it. At least some of it, so she took a deep breath and said, "My mom gave me some of my old journals."

"Are they helping?" Aaron asked.

"They've been enlightening. Turns out I've always been quite the badass," she said.

Aaron laughed. "I'd agree with that."

"The thing that struck me most is just how unafraid I was. Of anything," she said.

He glanced her way. "Isn't that a good thing? Not allowing fear to hold you back?" he asked, flicking on the windshield wipers as the snowfall picked up a bit.

"I guess. But I also think it depends on why. Some of the entries I read seemed to highlight a lack of fear of consequences, which is a little scary." She could appreciate her fearless, daredevil, risk-taking ways, but part of her had wondered if they stemmed from a dangerous place. She'd had a rough start in life, and those defense mechanisms she'd built in those early years were still at play—or at least, they had been. Did it go further than that?

"These entries were from when you were a teen?" he asked.

"Yeah…"

"Then, I wouldn't worry," he said reaching across and taking her hand in his. "We all struggled with identity and finding our way during those adolescent years."

She held his hand tight, finding comfort in both the gesture and his words. "You're right." She wondered about him and his troublesome teen years. It struck her that in her current state she knew very little about him. He was a rescue swimmer for the coast guard, he enjoyed Alaskan winter activities, he was incredible sexy…but what else? Did he have family in town?

"I'm almost afraid to ask, but anything in those journals about me?" He checked over his shoulder to switch lanes.

She shook her head but then laughed. "There is someone in there that I've affectionately called Colonel Bore who I seemed to bicker with a lot during high school."

Aaron swerved slightly, and she gripped the door handle.

"Sorry, black ice on the road," he explained.

"I don't know who this person is, but they really seemed to get under my skin. They're in every second journal entry… Honestly, it sounds like I had a crush on this person," she said, sounding slightly amused. "I mean, we often tease the ones we like, right?"

"Only if you're a narcissist," Aaron muttered.

"What?"

"Nothing," he said, pulling into the lot of the hotel. "I was just kidding."

Isla eyed him as he put the truck in Park in a stall close to the entrance. He hadn't pulled up in the drop-off zone, so that was a good sign. She was reluctant to see the night end… Would he come inside if she invited him? Was she ready for that?

Not that anything had to happen, but it might give the wrong impression if she invited him to her hotel room. It hadn't failed her notice that he hadn't invited her back to *his* place that evening.

Speaking of… "Hey, have you decorated the tree yet?"

He shifted in his seat as he turned to face her. "No. Not yet."

"I did promise to help," she said. Okay, so maybe she sounded slightly desperate to see him again, but she was afraid that the minute she climbed out of his truck, he'd go MIA on her again for days. She liked spending time with him, and she wanted to spend *more* time with him. Locking down a future time and date seemed like the safest bet.

"That you did," he said. He ran a hand through his hair, a look of mild frustration appearing on his face. "Look, Isla…"

Fuck it, she was going for it. Before he could talk his

way out of seeing her again. Before he denied the attraction between them or how great it felt being together.

She leaned across the seat and, gripping his face between her hands, she pressed her mouth to his. A small gasp of surprise escaped him before his arms encircled her waist and he pulled her in close. His mouth melded with hers, and she moaned softly as they both gave in to the kiss.

Her arms went around his neck, and her hands slid up the back of his head, her fingers tangling in his dark hair as she pressed her upper body closer. His tongue separated her lips and explored the interior of her mouth.

Frantic, urgent kisses followed, bodies pressed together, inhibited by their bulky winter clothing. Lips, mouths and tongues danced together in a perfect rhythm as though they'd been kissing one another for years.

He held her body close as he deepened the kiss, and relief ran through her. She hadn't imagined their connection. He wanted this just as badly as she did.

She pulled back slightly, her eyes opening and meeting his stunned, intoxicating gaze… "Maybe don't go MIA on me again?" she murmured against his lips.

"I don't think I could even if I wanted to," he said, kissing her again. Long, hard and full of passion.

She'd never felt so elated in her entire life. The rollercoaster of emotions she'd experienced that day made it impossible to believe that it had only been twenty-four hours.

A long, breathless moment later, Aaron reluctantly pulled away, and his gaze burned into hers. "I think we should call it a night," he said.

"Because you're tired?" she asked.

"Because I'm not at all tired, and if I had my way, I'd sit here kissing you all night."

She shrugged, wrapping her arms around his neck once more. "I have nowhere else to be," she said as seductively as possible.

Aaron pulled her closer again and kissed her as though the night were young and they had hours of moonlight to kill.

CHAPTER FIFTEEN

NEVER IN HIS wildest dreams could he have imagined making out with Isla Wakefield. If someone had told him three months ago that he'd not only be dating her and enjoying it but he'd spend two hours in his truck, parked in a hotel lot, kissing her and holding her and touching her, never getting quite enough of her, he'd never have believed it. But waking up that morning with the taste of her peppermint lip gloss still on his lips proved it hadn't been a dream.

The passion between them had been ignited; it was a flame he knew he should put out immediately, before he got burned, yet he was willing to take his chances. He'd never been with anyone who had such an effect on him, and it wasn't just physical. He liked being around her, as crazy as it sounded. She was funny and smart and seductive and sexy. He was discovering so many new qualities about her, ones he was sure had always been there but he'd never allowed himself to notice.

She'd needed a friend the night before, someone to help her cope with the stress of the day, but he hadn't expected how much *he'd* needed the time with *her*. He'd been keeping her at bay, not reaching out because he thought that was the right thing to do, what was best for her, but he knew it was his own fears holding him back. Isla was therapeutic and helping him through the holiday season in ways he'd never thought possible.

He'd actually sung Christmas carols.

And today he was going to decorate a Christmas tree.

He rolled to his side and reached for his phone to text her, then saw she'd already beaten him to it. The message had arrived two minutes ago. Must have been what woke him. It was good to know she was thinking about him this morning too.

Meet you on Main Street in an hour?

He smiled at the profile picture he'd attached to her number: a selfie shot of the two of them on the train ride, goofy expressions on their faces, marshmallow topping covering their upper lips. She was amazing, and even on her worst days she could find happiness in the moment. She was a breath of fresh air and the hopefulness he'd been craving for such a long time. Never ever expecting to find it in someone who was his complete opposite.

See you then, he texted back as he tossed the sheets back and climbed out of bed.

After a quick shower, he looked at the tree in his living room, still leaning against the wall, pine needles collecting on the floor beneath it, and shook his head. Not only had the thing not been tossed to the curb, but in a few hours, it would be illuminating the small space with a warm festive glow.

Who would have thought?

This holiday season he could be setting himself up for a fall, but there was nothing he could do about it. He'd never actually won an argument with Isla, and he suspected there'd be no winning now either. Especially with his heart on the line. And for once, it was a battle he was happy to avoid...or at least put off for as long as possible.

But an hour later, Aaron was more than a little out of his comfort zone. Standing in the middle of Sealena Trinkets and Gifts, in front of a large display of Christmas decorations, the competing artificial scents of pine, cinnamon and gingerbread burning his nostrils, and the blare of dogs barking out Christmas music making his brain hurt, he didn't trust his legs not to bolt any minute. It was all just a little much.

He took a deep breath. He needed to loosen up and get into the spirit.

It was just a tree. It was just decorations.

And the important thing was that he was spending the day with Isla, who looked sexy as hell in a form-fitting thermal jacket and faux-leather leggings, a pair of knee-high black suede boots completing the look. His gaze swept over her, taking in the sexy curves, and the tightness in his chest eased.

Damn, she looked good in red. Where was that red mini she'd worn to the Sealena event? He hoped that dress made another appearance in his life sometime soon.

That's it. Just keep focusing on that body.

"Okay, let's talk color scheme," she said, turning toward him. Unlike him, she was buzzing with excitement about that day's activity. She really loved the holidays, and it reminded him of how fanatic his sister used to be about it. For a brief moment, he chose to let the feelings of nostalgia wash over him instead of pushing them down and trying to fight them. Amy would love that he was doing this. That made him feel better.

"Color scheme?" he asked.

Isla stopped and picked up two sets of round plastic balls. A silver and blue set in one hand and a red and gold set in the other. "Which one do you prefer?"

He eyed both. "Red and gold?"

She laughed. "There's no wrong answer. This isn't a test. I could have pegged you for a traditionalist." She grabbed several boxes of the ornaments and placed them in the basket he carried. He followed as she moved farther down the aisle. "Next decision: garlands or tinsel?"

"Both?" he said because he couldn't remember the difference.

She nodded. "A little busy, but okay." She picked up a pack of shiny silver strands and several lengths of sparkling red and gold garland and added them to the basket. She thought for a moment, then snapped her fingers. "The most important part—lights!" She led the way to another aisle where dozens of options overwhelmed him. White lights, colored lights, warm hues, bright LEDs, flashing, twinkling—how did one choose? He scanned the boxes of lights and felt dizzy.

The barking dogs' rendition of "Jingle Bells" over the store speakers grew louder, and the overpowering scents mingling were making him ill.

"You know, I think I'll leave the decoration decisions up to you. I'm really out of my element here," he said, wiping sweaty palms on the legs on his pants. He tugged at the neck of his sweater. It was really hot inside the store.

Isla frowned as she studied him. "Are you okay? You look a little flushed."

"Yeah, fine." He cleared his throat. This must seem weird to her, but he couldn't really explain it right now. "Hey, why don't you get the lights and any ornaments you like, and I'll go get us some hot chocolate?" He needed to get out of that store before he embarrassed himself with an anxiety attack.

Isla looked confused and more than a little worried about

him. "You know, if you really don't want to decorate the tree, we don't have to. I feel like I've pressured you into this."

She had, but that wasn't a bad thing. "No, it's okay. Really, buy any decorations you want, and I'll meet you outside." Truth was, he wanted to spend time with her. And shockingly, he wanted to have a Christmas that year. He needed to be able to celebrate the holidays again, and this was a good first step. But it was just a little too much, too soon.

"Okay…" she said, and he hated that he'd deflated her enthusiasm.

He set the basket down and reached for her, wrapping his arms around her waist and pulling her close. "Look, it's just the competing smells in here are making me nauseous," he said, and she looked a little relieved.

"So no scented candles. Got it," she said, pressing her body closer and placing a soft kiss to his lips. Soft, but affectionate. A taste of something he was once again craving.

"Besides, the faster we get the shopping over with, the faster we can go back to my place," he murmured against her lips, squeezing her tight before slowly releasing her to finish the shopping.

He fully intended on surviving this tree-decorating by stealing her breath through passionate kisses whenever he needed to stave off an anxiety attack.

DEFINITELY A BACHELOR PAD.

Isla scanned Aaron's apartment as they entered with the decorations an hour later. The one-bedroom, eight-hundred-square-foot space was more like a man cave. Sparsely furnished with just a small love seat in the living room and a tall bar-style kitchen table that was set up more like a desk with his laptop and several rescue manuals on it. She suspected he ate at the slim kitchen island, where a well-used lone stool sat.

A large map of Alaska was the focal point on the walls, other than a flat-screen TV that had to be at least eighty inches.

Priorities, she mused.

The apartment smelled like Aaron—fresh, manly, with a hint of pine from the…

Christmas tree?

Isla's mouth gaped as her gaze landed on it. Propped up against the living room wall, the thing looked a little worse for wear. Pine needles covered the floor beneath it, and the tips of the branches were turning brown.

"Oh my God, have you even watered it?" she asked, dropping her bag and heading toward it. They'd cut it down four days ago.

"I was going to," Aaron muttered.

She fingered the branch and frowned. "For someone so concerned with safety, this thing could be a serious fire hazard. Good thing I bought LED lights or it might go up in flames the moment we light it," she chastised gently, but it was true. She was relieved she hadn't gone with the old-school bulbs she'd been eyeing.

"There was water in the bucket," he said.

She glanced in. If there had been, it had long been sucked up by this poor dehydrated tree. "Okay, well, let's try to save this thing before all that's left are bare branches." She removed her jacket and tossed it over the back of the sofa, then rolled up the sleeves of her V-neck shirt.

Time to get to work. She was hoping once the thing was decorated and lit, Aaron might start to ease up a little. He'd certainly been on edge at the shop, and she was desperate to figure out why. He seemed to be struggling with the whole Christmas thing, and yet, he'd invited her to go on the Christmas Train Ride and had appeared to be enjoying himself.

This hot-and-cold relationship he had with the season was certainly confusing.

Aaron approached with the bags and retrieved the tree stand. "I guess we should start with this?" he asked.

She nodded. "Yep, if you can lift the tree, I can secure it at the base."

"No problem." He grabbed the tree trunk and lifted it with ease as Isla lay on the floor and wiggled her body underneath, securing the base of the tree into the stand. Dry needles rained down around her, confirming that maybe the tree had been a little neglected.

"There," she said, shimmying back out. "Now water."

"Right. I'm on it," he said, filling up the water base and placing it under the tree.

"Hopefully we weren't too late," she said with a grin.

Aaron looked sheepish as he stared at it. "Sorry I didn't take better care of it."

Isla walked toward him and wrapped her arms around his waist. "The tree will be fine." She paused, staring up at him. "But will you?"

"What do you mean?" he asked.

"I mean, Christmas seems to have you conflicted," she said, holding him tight, hoping he could feel the safe space she'd created for him to tell her what was going on. He hadn't mentioned any holiday plans—or any family, for that matter. She'd been so preoccupied with her own issues that she hadn't really asked how he usually enjoyed the season or if he even did at all. But she hoped he could see that he could open up to her, tell her anything.

He took a deep breath, staring into her eyes, a look of pain reflecting in his as he said, "This time of year is a little hard on me, that's all."

Okay, they were getting somewhere…

"Do you have family that you spend it with?" Maybe he was usually alone. That would definitely be cause not to celebrate. But this year, he didn't have to be alone. She'd be there if he let her.

He cleared his throat. "My parents are in Florida. They moved there about six years ago. They don't come home, and they don't celebrate." He cleared his throat, and she sensed there was more, so she remained silent. "My sister, Amy, died this time of year," he said, a deep note of sadness in his voice. "A snowmobiling accident while we were on winter break."

Her gut twisted and instant regret ran through her. He'd lost his sister during the holidays. No wonder the sights and sounds in the store earlier had made him go pale. "I'm so sorry," she said, holding him tighter. "And I'm sorry you're having to tell me this. I assume I already knew that?" Remorse nearly suffocated her. No doubt she had known all of this already. Making him rehash it was horrible. And making him do Christmas was even worse. Her gaze slid to the tree, and her shoulders sagged.

No wonder he'd left the thing for dead.

"I'm so sorry, Aaron. I shouldn't have shoved all this holiday spirit down your throat."

He slid a finger under her chin and titled her face upward. He shook his head as he gazed affectionately into her eyes. "No. Don't apologize. I haven't had any of this in so long, and yeah, this time of year is hard, and it always will be, but you're actually making it a little easier."

She wanted to believe that, but she feared she'd caused

him pain. The last few days she'd inadvertently caused a lot of people she cared about pain. She was suddenly seeing the severity of her injury and memory loss—the impact it was having on those around her.

"Hey," he said gently. "Don't beat yourself up over this. You didn't know, and I'm glad you didn't know. I've been having a really great time with you, Isla." He gripped her face between his hands and lowered his lips to hers.

Tension seeped from her body as she sunk into him, wrapping her arms around his neck and deepening the kiss that was erasing all her guilt and remorse. He smelled so good and tasted incredible and being in his arms was the only place she wanted to be.

He pulled back reluctantly, and she pouted. "I wasn't done kissing you yet," she said playfully.

He grinned. "Tree-decorating first, then kissing. Otherwise the tree will stand there naked and wilting all season."

"I'm fine with that," she said, suddenly caring a lot less if the baubles and garland ever came out of the shopping bags.

He laughed, releasing her gently. "Get to work. I'll follow your lead."

She sighed but then retrieved the bags of decorations as Aaron flicked through the television stations for an old black-and-white Christmas movie. *"It's a Wonderful Life,"* she said, marveling again at her ability to remember certain things.

"It used to be one of my favorites," Aaron said. "Even though I cried like a baby every time."

"Your secret's safe with me," she said as she opened the bags and took out the decorations. The two of them got to work, each keeping an eye on the sentimental holiday classic.

Once the tree was decorated, they stood back to admire their work. "Looks good," she said with a smile.

"Let's light her up and see what happens," he said, plugging in the lights.

The tree illuminated with a bright, warm glow, the ornaments and tinsel sparkling.

"What do you think?" she asked him.

He stood behind her and wrapped his arms around her waist, drawing her into his body as he stared at the tree. "I think my sister would love it and she'd be happy that I'm finally embracing the spirit of the season again," he said, kissing the top of her head.

One of the bells jingled on the tree, and both he and Isla turned to look at it.

"Every time a bell rings…"

CHAPTER SIXTEEN

THE CALL COMING in to the station as Aaron arrived for his shift the next day was an unusual one. A private plane flying over Denali had gotten into trouble when its navigation system failed and was requesting assistance. The pilot had circled the area too long before running out of fuel and had had to crash-land in the backwoods, five miles from Port Serenity. Local search and rescue were asking them to air respond.

"Single passenger onboard, the pilot. He's reporting moderate injuries and requesting immediate extraction. He's stuck in the plane and there's leaking fuel."

The briefing was quick, and the crew launched into action within minutes.

Dwayne, Aaron and Miller were suited up and the helicopter was headed toward the crash site in record time. It was the first rescue responded to since Aaron and Dwayne's bickering session in the training room the week before. They hadn't spoken outside of work either. Aaron just hoped they could at least put aside their issues at work.

Of course, he wouldn't be mentioning the time he'd been spending with Isla, and he struggled with his lingering feelings of guilt.

From his position in the helicopter doorway, Aaron spotted the wreckage in a clearing west of the Denali Glacier. The small, private plane was in pieces, metal and fiberglass littering the forest and black smoke spiraling up from the wreckage. It was a miracle the pilot was still alive.

"Crash site spotted," he said over his headset to Dwayne. "I've got eyes."

Dwayne's response irritated him. At the station, at the gym, at the pub, his buddy could keep the attitude, but on a rescue, he'd expect his crewmate to act professionally and keep the personal shit out of the chopper.

Miller shot Aaron a questioning look that said *What's his problem?*, but Aaron shook his head. The drama bullshit could wait.

"Ready and in position," he said as Dwayne hovered the helicopter over the crash site. *High* above the site. "Can you get any lower?"

"Not without risking hitting the tree. Afraid of the drop?"

Damn, they needed to hash this Isla thing out and fast. These rescues were dangerous enough without him having to put his life in the hands of someone who might be hesitant to save his ass if needed. He knew if it came down to it, he could trust Dwayne, but he'd like to feel a little sounder in that belief.

"Lowering now," he said through gritted teeth, determined not to let Dwayne's unprofessionalism distract him from the task.

As he lowered from the chopper, he scanned the area. The windshield of the tiny private plane was shattered, and the wings had broken off. The tail end was smashed, and the door was hanging off its hinges.

The pilot was trapped under metal from the front of the plane and waved both arms as Aaron lowered. He took in the wreckage and spotted the fuel leak, gas and other fluids seeping over the snow.

One wrong move and the plane could go up in flames.

Aaron reached the ground and approached the pilot. The man looked relieved to see him but was clearly in pain. A deep gash on his forehead was worrisome. "Local coast guard," Aaron said, identifying himself. "Where are you pinned?"

"My leg. It's crushed under the front control panel."

Aaron nodded and approached the heavy piece of metal keeping the man pinned. He accessed the area and then lifted, struggling under the weight. "Quick, slide out," he called to the man. He wasn't sure how long he could actually hold the thing up.

The man pulled his body out of the plane and moved as far away as possible as Aaron carefully set the slab of the plane back onto the ground. He approached and, keeping an eye on the plane, assessed the man's leg. The damage was extensive, the leg crushed from thigh to ankle. He was bleeding, and on the ground it was impossible to determine the extent of the injury. The man started to tremble as shock and cold set in. He had to move fast, but a vertical ascent with the man harnessed to him wasn't the best option. "Can I get a litter?" he radioed up to Miller. He'd have to do the horizontal lift.

"Copy," Miller said, and a moment later, Aaron saw the litter being lowered toward them.

He turned to the injured man, who was barely remaining conscious. "Hey, stay with me a little longer, okay?" he said as he reached for the litter and placed it on the snow. "I'm going to lift your upper body first, then your lower half. I'll try to make this as smooth as possible, but it's going to hurt."

The man nodded, his eyes drifting closed.

Shit. So much for getting this guy to help with the transfer.

Aaron stood behind him and, lifting under his arms, he carefully transferred him to the stretcher. Then he lifted the lower body, wincing as the mangled leg bent in unnatural ways. The man was lucky to be alive, but Aaron had his doubts that the leg would survive.

The sound of a branch snapping to his right caught his attention, and he turned to look between the thick trees behind him just as Dwayne's voice sounded over his radio. "Looks like you got company."

A brown bear approached the wreckage on all fours. He sniffed and pawed at the metal on the ground, searching for food among the mess, his massive paws flinging pieces of the plane aside.

"Holy shit," the pilot said, suddenly awake again as he saw the bear.

"Stay still," Aaron instructed him quietly. The bear had yet to notice them, but it wouldn't be long. Brown bears weren't uncommon in these backwoods, and he'd seen many while on hikes and camping. Usually, he enjoyed sightings of the majestic, strong creatures, with their big paws and thick fur, but this visit was something Aaron could have done without.

He reached into his gear pack and took out a flare. With so much leaking fuel, this could be a big mistake, but there was no way to get the man hoisted up into the chopper without risking the bear making an attack, and that could cause the chopper to waver.

"Going to try to scare off our friend here," he said calmly over the radio.

"That flare could cause the entire wreckage to blow," Dwayne said, concern in his voice.

"The litter and I are detached. Get ready to move off if you need to," he said as he lit the flare.

"Not leaving without you, even though you're an asshole," Dwayne said, a hint of the friend he knew returning to the other man's tone.

The bear turned in his direction, and Aaron moved quickly toward it, waving the flare in front of the animal, yelling at it and not retreating as the animal stood on its hind legs, roared and looked ready to attack.

"Back! Go!" he shouted with authority, keeping the flare high as he directed it at the magnificent creature.

The bear growled, baring its huge teeth.

Shit. Sometimes this worked. Sometimes it didn't.

Aaron continued to wave the flare, aware of the leaking fluid covering the ground near his boots.

The bear lowered himself back down on all fours and began moving away.

Aaron released a breath of relief and lowered the flare.

Unfortunately, the bear kicked at the wreckage as it passed, as though saying *Fuck this shit*, and the plane ignited. Flames instantly engulfed the front of the plane and the liquid all around them.

His heart racing, Aaron turned to the pilot. "Okay, we gotta go. Now." He secured the man in the litter and signaled for Dwayne. "In position."

"About time," his buddy mumbled in response.

Moments later, after a dicey ascent watching the forest below them go up in flames, he and the litter were brought on board the helicopter with Miller's assistance.

Dwayne glanced over his shoulder at him with a slightly annoyed look as he navigated the chopper away from danger and back toward the station. "Enough excitement for you?"

Aaron grinned. "Just the way I like it." His friend may still be mad at him, but it was good to know that in a crisis, they still had one another's back.

"THE SPRAIN HEALED quite nicely," Dr. Sheffield said, looking at the X-ray during Isla's follow-up appointment at the hospital later that day. "A credit to your level of physical fitness. I'm not sure I've ever seen anyone heal so fast."

"So, I don't need the boot cast anymore?" Isla asked, stretching her leg on the examination table. Her leg did feel better, and it would be great not to have to wear the annoying thing anymore.

"Nope," he said. "Just take it easy, okay? No major climbing for another few weeks, but some walking and hiking would do you good."

"I can live with those conditions," she said.

"How are you feeling, otherwise?" the doctor asked, using a light to look into her eyes.

"Okay. I mean, I still can't remember anything. I've been going to familiar places and reading old journals..." She shrugged. At first it hadn't really bothered her. She'd assumed the memories would come back. But the last few days it had become painfully evident how not remembering her past could impact both her and those around her.

"It could take time. The MRI shows less swelling on the temporal lobe, but there's still some, and the lesion is still healing, but that too will take time."

As before, it sounded like all she could do was wait. She bit her lip as she nodded. "What if my memories don't come back?" That was a possibility, and with each passing day, she had to at least entertain the thought.

"Then, you make new ones," he said gently.

Make new ones.

The doctor didn't know just how impactful those words were. Sometimes, the past really didn't matter. What mattered was the here and now. It wasn't as though she could go back and change anything…and her future had always been hers to discover. Her path was always hers to carve.

She smiled as she climbed down from the table. "Thanks, Doc."

"Take it easy, okay?" he said as she left the office.

Outside the hospital, she breathed in the cool, fresh air, enjoying the freedom from the cast.

Her phone chimed, and she smiled, reading the text from Skylar.

Girls' night at the yacht. You in?

She hesitated briefly. She'd been looking forward to seeing Aaron again. The day before had been a little rough in the beginning, but he'd opened up to her, and they'd really connected. They seemed to grow closer the more they were together, and she liked where things were headed.

Another text from Skylar arrived, and she laughed as she read it.

Aaron's working a double shift if that helps in your decision-making. ;)

I'll be there, she texted back.

And a few hours later, she was really glad she'd accepted the invite—and that she was the first one to arrive. It gave her a few minutes alone with Skylar.

"Wine?" Skylar asked as Isla removed her coat and hung it on a hook near the door.

"Need something to wash the antihistamines down," she said with a laugh. Dex and Shaylah had gone winter camping, but the scent of the dog lingering in the room already had her eyes watering.

Skylar handed her a glass of white wine, and she took the meds.

"No cast?"

"Got it off today," she said. "Feels good to not have to wear it."

"That was fast," Skylar said.

"I'm a fast healer," she said. "Well, my bones are, at least. Wish my broken brain would hurry the hell up."

"No luck with the journals?" she asked gently.

"They've been interesting…but I feel like I'm reading about a stranger." She hesitated before confiding, "I don't feel like the person in the journals. That's weird, right?"

Skylar shook her head. "I don't think so. I mean, you have been different lately."

Isla nodded. "It's just hard to make decisions not knowing what my preinjury self would have wanted or chosen to do. I feel like I'm betraying Old Isla or something. Like I can't make a decision in case my memory comes back and I regret the choice I've made." She must sound completely crazy, but it truly felt like there were two versions of her. Who was she really? What did she want?

Skylar offered a sympathetic smile. "I think whatever decisions you make now will be the right ones. You're more open to things, and that can't be a bad thing, right?"

"I guess so." She paused again. "I know Dad wants me to go into law, and I don't want to disappoint him, but I'm not sure it's what I want." She'd been thinking about it the last few days, and the idea hadn't excited her. She'd even looked into the online classes he'd mentioned earlier that day while she'd waited for her appointment at the hospital, but it had been more out of a sense of guilt over the whole birth-mother bomb she'd dropped on her family and not any real interest in pursuing the career.

Skylar nodded. "I get it. I mean, I always knew I wanted to be a captain in the coast guard. That was never in question, but there was a lot of pressure to follow in my grandad's and father's footsteps, coming back here to Port Serenity. I know all about family pressure and wanting to find your own path."

The fact that Skylar got it made Isla feel a little better. "But ultimately, you decided this is what you wanted?"

"Dex had a lot to do with that," Skylar said, sipping her wine.

Isla bit her lip, hesitating. She felt like she could confide in Skylar. That the other woman was someone she could trust. So she said, "In my journals, I talk about being interested in social work."

Skylar's eyes widened. "Really? Wow."

"Yeah, and now that I know more about my birth mom and how I was in the system, I think I want to look into that career a little more," she said.

"Then, that's what you should do," Skylar said.

"You think so?"

"Absolutely. I think you'd be fantastic. You're great with kids, especially teens, and if it's something you're passionate about, you can't fail."

The words of encouragement meant a lot and actually helped to better support the possibilities that had been percolating in her mind.

But still, she wasn't sure. "Brian is pretty adamant about the law-school thing…"

"Brian is a tough one," Skylar said, "but only because he loves you. He'll accept and support whatever you decide."

Isla hoped Skylar was right, because the more she thought about it, the more the idea appealed to her. If she could help others who were in the same situation her mother had been in, then maybe she'd find a sense of purpose and feel closer to the mother she'd never known.

"Thanks, Skylar." She raised her glass to the other woman.

"Anytime," Skylar said as the doorbell rang, announcing their friends had arrived.

Isla sipped her wine, feeling more at peace and content than she had in days. The doctor was right: she'd focus on making new memories, new decisions, new life paths, and if her memory came back, then her past self would just have to deal with who she'd become in the meantime.

CHAPTER SEVENTEEN

"I'M NOT SURE I like you having such a dangerous job," Isla said Friday evening as Aaron recounted the rescue involving a brown bear. The entire thing sounded wild and incredibly risky. A plane about to explode was more than enough.

They were cooking pasta together in his kitchen, the glow of the Christmas tree lights illuminating the apartment with a warm, festive glow, and it was a struggle to hide how happy she was to be there with him, doing this simple, everyday thing. It felt even more intimate than their previous dates as they moved around one another in his tiny kitchen. Her reaching over his head for spices in the cupboard, him reaching around her for a knife from the drawer, their bodies always so close, but never quite touching...

Heat coursed through her that had nothing to do with the steam coming off the boiling water on the stove.

"Now you know how I feel about your daredevil ways," he said, wrapping his arms around her waist as she added the noodles to the boiling water.

She laughed as she fell back against him, loving the sensation of his body around hers. "Well, I promised the doctor I'd continue to take it easy for another few weeks."

He kissed the side of her neck quickly, causing a tingling sensation to vibrate throughout her body. Goose bumps surfaced on her skin despite his warm breath. But far too soon, he was moving away.

Damn, he was always doing that. Teasing her with these fleeting kisses, these brief embraces. She was desperately craving more. A lot more. The night before, all she'd thought about was the next time she'd get to be with him. Now that they were alone again in his apartment, she was desperate for him to make a move—or she'd have to. The sexual tension building between them was going to cause her to implode. "Hey, you can't just do that, then run away," she said, reaching out to pull him back in.

"I have a surprise for you. Wait here," he said.

She sighed as he left the kitchen. "I'd prefer more kisses," she mumbled.

"You'll get those too," he said, reentering almost immediately with a shopping bag behind his back.

Now she was intrigued. "What do you have there?" She leaned to one side to try to read the logo on the bag. Some sort of sporting-goods store.

He handed it to her, and she opened it. "Snowshoes?" she asked, looking up in surprise. Inside the bag were all the accessories for a day out on the snowy trails.

He shrugged. "That day at Santa's Village, you said you'd like to go with me. I was already headed to the store so…"

Her eyes widened. "You bought these that day?" At the time, he hadn't seemed exactly thrilled at the thought of having her tag along. That had changed in the time since, but she was shocked he'd bought these back before they'd gotten close.

He shrugged in an attempt to look nonchalant. "I figured I could return them if you changed your mind."

Isla set the bag aside and stepped into his arms. Hers encircled his neck, and she stood on tiptoes to kiss him softly.

"Why on earth would I change my mind about spending time with you?" she whispered against his lips.

"I thought maybe you'd be sick of me by now," he said teasingly, but she heard the small hint of sincerity. As though he actually thought that was a possibility. She didn't think she could ever be sick of him.

"Is that why you keep teasing me with these brief kisses?" she asked. "To keep me keen?"

He held her tight against him. "Is it working?"

"Yes."

She saw him swallow hard as he stared into her eyes. "Believe me, I've only been torturing myself."

"Well, stop," she said, pressing her body closer. What on earth did she have to do to get him to grab her and kiss her senseless?

He hesitated only a fraction of a second before bending slightly and lifting her off her feet. He set her onto the counter and wedged himself between her legs before crushing her mouth with his.

Thank God…

Since that night in his truck, they hadn't had a full-on make-out session, and this was long overdue. She could appreciate him taking things slow, given the circumstances of her injury and the inner turmoil they'd both recently been challenged with, yada, yada, yada, but she wanted him to know that she wasn't going to break, and that moving a little faster, acting on this attraction between them, was completely okay.

Better than okay.

Her hands tangled in his hair as she held his head close and deepened the kiss. His hands wrapped around her thighs, and his fingers squeezed, digging into her flesh beneath her jeans. There was no trace of the restraint he'd

demonstrated before. Now his kiss was eager and demanding, challenging her to respond. As though he expected
her to retreat.

Not a chance.

His tongue teased her bottom lip, and a moan escaped
her. Damn, he was hot when he let go and took what he
wanted.

He could have it. He could have her.

He pulled her even closer until every part of their bodies
touched and she pressed herself to him. Her hands fisted his
T-shirt at his chest, and she wrapped her legs around him,
preventing any attempt at escape. His tongue circled hers
as his hands moved upward on her thighs, inching higher
and higher, causing her entire body to spring to life. She
couldn't get enough of him. She never wanted this kiss to
end—this moment to end.

The shrill sound of the smoke detector made them both
jump, and she hit her head on the cupboard door. "Ow!"

"Oh my God, you okay?" Aaron asked, bending at the
knees to look at her as she rubbed the aching spot on her
head.

She nodded then stilled.

His eyes widened with a look of panic. "What? What's
wrong?"

"Nope. Still no memory," she said teasingly.

He shook his head, shooting her a look. "Not funny."

"It was kinda funny," she said jumping down from the
counter and turning off the once-boiling pot that was now
charred pasta noodles stuck to the bottom.

Aaron grabbed a dish towel and waved it below the
smoke detector until the wailing stopped. "See?" he said.
"This is what happens when you try to seduce me."

She grinned as she took his arms and wrapped them

around her, placing his hands on her ass. "Maybe if you didn't make me work so hard, I wouldn't have to nearly set your apartment on fire."

He laughed, drawing her hips into his body. "Fair enough," he said. "But just for the record, I tried to take things slow."

"Just for the record, I didn't ask you to," she said as she stood on her tiptoes and kissed him again.

He groaned as he returned the kiss then, pulling back, he rested his head against hers. "You are killing me, Isla Wakefield."

"You say that like it's a bad thing," she said with a teasing wink as she eased out of his arms. "Now, what are we going to do about dinner?"

Because now that she'd caught him, it was his turn for the chase.

THE NEXT MORNING, Aaron knocked on Isla's hotel-room door just before eight o'clock. Dressed in his ski suit, hat and gloves, he was sweating after the hike up the stairs, not willing to wait for the elevator. They were getting a head start on the snow trails before a forecasted ice storm hit later that afternoon, and he was excited to get the day rolling. Right now there wasn't a cloud in the sunny, crisp morning sky, but that could change in a heartbeat. Snowshoeing was his favorite winter activity, and he couldn't wait to share the experience with Isla. He had the perfect trails in mind, ones which would provide enough of a challenge and thrill but wouldn't be too hard on her still-recovering leg.

He was on call with the station in case of emergency, but he really hoped people stayed safe so he'd have no reason to end their time on the trails before the weather forced them back inside.

He heard her footsteps approaching the door, and the same anticipation flowed through him as it always did at the thought of seeing her. He'd only dropped her off here ten hours ago, after take-out Chinese food and an attempt to focus on a *Die Hard* movie marathon, but it felt like forever since he'd seen her.

Isla Wakefield had him losing sleep—and for different reasons these days.

When she opened the door, his mouth went dry. She stood in a towel, her hair still wet and hanging around her shoulders.

"You're early. Come on in," she said.

He tried to look anywhere but at the sexy cleavage escaping the top of her towel or her incredible set of muscular legs as he entered the room. He was a few minutes early, but not that early. He suspected this was all part of her plan to torture him into making more moves.

But if she kept this up, he wasn't sure how long he could maintain the good-guy act. He was only human, and she was irresistibly sexy.

"I'll just be a few minutes," she said. "Make yourself comfortable."

"No rush."

He scanned the hotel room. The bed was made, and all of her clothes—including the red dress of fantasies—were hung in the closet. Her shoes and boots were lined up under the window and her makeup and accessories were neatly arranged on the vanity.

Huh, not the incredibly messy Isla that Dex had always complained about.

It was baffling how so many of her character traits had been altered by the head injury, yet she was still the same

Isla deep down. Her personality might be less edgy and prickly, but she was still a sharp-witted smart-ass.

Just a neater version, apparently.

He saw an old teddy bear that looked like it had seen better days lying on the pillow, and he laughed as he picked it up. "This thing would give me nightmares."

"Apparently, I refused to sleep without it," she called from the bathroom, where the door was still open a crack and he could see her slide into a pair of dark blue leggings.

He'd like to be the thing she refused to sleep without.

He averted his gaze as he saw her reach for a lacy bra draped over the towel rack.

She was definitely doing this on purpose. Teasing him, tempting him—and it was definitely working. But what was she expecting? Him to barge in there, rip her clothes off and make love to her? Spend the day kissing every inch of her body? They'd only been seeing one another a few weeks, and she still didn't know that, before that, she didn't even like him. What would she do if he did act on the impulse to change the day's plans?

Damn, it was hot with all this gear on.

He placed the bear back on the pillow, desperate to turn his thoughts to something a little less boner-inducing as his ski pants felt restrictive in the crotch.

He noticed her open laptop on the desk. Social work online-course listings filled the screen. Social work? Wow. "Are you thinking about taking these?" he asked, turning toward her as she exited the bathroom.

She nodded slowly, running a brush through her hair. "Yeah. A few start in January, and I think I'll apply. My high-school grades were high enough, and they take mature students based on life experience and an admission letter."

"That's amazing. That's not an easy career." Especially

compared to her Nutcracker job. But she was definitely smart enough and hardworking enough to achieve any career she wanted. That was part of what had made it so frustrating that she'd seemed content traveling the world with no career path or plans. Though, if that had made her happy, who was he to judge? "What happened to law school?"

"Law school would be great too, and I really did give it some thought, but I want to do something where I'm making a difference to help people going through the social system." She paused. "I know Brian—*Dad* would like me to follow in his footsteps, but I feel like I'm being called toward this. I can't explain it."

It made sense that Isla would be drawn to this type of career. Having been involved in the system herself, he understood where her motivation was coming from. Understood it and respected the hell out of her for it. He walked toward her and cupped her face with his hands. "That is a great idea."

She looked relieved to hear him say it. "Thank you." She pressed her body into his and placed a soft, teasing kiss to his lips. She tasted like peppermint lip gloss, and he wanted to lick her like a candy cane.

"What's *not* a great idea is answering hotel-room doors in only a towel," he said, the heat returning.

She grinned. "Caught that, did you?"

"I'm only going to resist temptation for so long," he said.

She removed his hands from her face as she sashayed back into the bathroom. "Promises, promises," she called over her shoulder.

CHAPTER EIGHTEEN

As Hidden Valley Trail came into view, Isla could barely contain her excitement. Sure, she'd been teasing Aaron in the hotel room with the towel and giving him just a glimpse of her getting dressed in the bathroom, but she was really looking forward to the day out on the snowy trail. The weather was crisp, and a cold wind rustled through the trees in the distance, but the early-morning sun was bright. She peered through the window as he parked his truck in the ice- and snow-covered parking lot, reading the sign at the beginning of the trail.

The five-mile hike was a moderate difficulty level and was expected to take about two and a half hours. According to the map displayed, the trail took them near the river's edge and along the base of the mountain range, boasting several points of interest and viewing places along the way.

"Sure you're feeling up to this?" Aaron asked, turning in his seat to face her.

"Yes. My leg feels great, and the exercise will be good," she said.

"Okay, let's get the gear." He climbed out of the truck and opened a rear door, retrieving everything before leading the way to the back of the truck. He dropped the tailgate and lifted her up onto it.

She laughed at the unexpected gesture, loving how he could just pick her up so effortlessly, like he had the night before in his kitchen: it was sexy as hell. She stared at him as he helped strap her boots into the new snowshoes he'd bought for her. He attached the climbing rails and adjusted the height on her poles.

"All set," he said, helping her down.

He put on his own gear, and they set out. She was grateful for all the warm clothing she'd worn as they started along the trail that was still shaded by tall trees. The sun wasn't yet high enough in the sky to break through, and the snow beneath their snowshoes felt crunchy. It wasn't long before she'd gotten the hang of it, and her body heated after the first few inclines along the trail.

"Hadn't expected such a workout," she said, slightly out of breath five minutes in.

Aaron laughed as he moved effortlessly alongside her. "I've been telling you for years this isn't as easy as it looks."

She frowned. She still didn't quite understand why the two of them had never been friends before. He was kind, funny, smart, sexy and he made her feel comfortable. His support in the hotel room regarding her plan to pursue social work as a career had meant a lot. She knew her family—particularly her father—might not be completely thrilled about it, at least not at first, so it felt great to have Aaron's encouragement.

The two of them seemed to get along great, and the chemistry between them was undeniable, so why had it taken so long—not to mention a head injury—to get to this place?

She was about to bring up the subject again when the first point of interest marker appeared on the trail. As they moved through the trees into an open clearing, Isla's eyes widened.

The view of the mountains and the river with waterfalls trickling into it was absolutely breathtaking. Glistening sun reflecting off the water and the ice all around were worth the hike.

"Beautiful, right?" Aaron asked, taking it in.

"You've been here before?" she asked.

"This is one of my favorite trails," he said, smiling at her. "But this has to be my favorite time being here, seeing this."

She warmed to her core at the words. "Thank you for inviting me to come along."

He moved closer and slid his snowshoes outside hers to wrap his arms around her waist and draw her close. He kissed her forehead, her nose, her cheeks, his breath warming her skin before his lips finally landed on hers.

Isla wrapped her arms around his neck and pressed her body closer. This moment felt incredible. Being there with him, the only two on the trail. It felt like they were the only two people in all of Alaska, as the quiet stillness of nature was all around them, the only sounds the running river and the rustle of a breeze through the trees. Peaceful, serene and full of beauty.

He deepened the kiss, his tongue slipping between her lips to explore her mouth. Her hands crept upward to cup the back of his head as her tongue danced with his. He tasted so good, a hint of coffee on his breath, and smelled incredible, his soft aftershave mingling with the fresh air on his skin. He hadn't shaved that day, and the stubble along his jawline was rough and tickled her flesh, but she loved the feel of it.

His hands gripped her rib cage, squeezing gently as the kiss grew more passionate. A sense of urgency that continued to grow until they were both struggling for breath. She didn't care about breathing, she just wanted to stay there in this perfect moment, kissing for as long as she could.

Panting slightly, he pulled away reluctantly, and desire burned in his eyes when they met hers. "You are the most incredible woman I've ever known," he said.

"Then, why did it take this long for you to realize it?" she asked with a note of teasing, but also a level of real curiosity.

"Maybe because I never thought I'd get this chance to be with you. Never dreamed that you could ever want a guy like me."

"A guy like you? You mean, courageous, brave, sexy and caring?" she asked, kissing him gently again.

"You think I'm sexy?" he asked with a grin as he reluctantly released her and they headed back onto the trail.

"I would have thought that was obvious," she said with a laugh. "And I'm most likely not the only one in town to think so," she said, shooting him a sideways glance. How was it that he was still single? He had to be one of the most eligible bachelors in Port Serenity. Odd that no one had caught his eye…

He shrugged. "I get some attention, but I'm pretty sure it's just the uniform," he said with a wink.

Isla was fairly certain the uniform played a part in it, but it was the man inside it that made her knees weak and her heart race. And as much as she was enjoying this time with him out on the trail, she was looking forward to being alone with him where she could continue showing him just how sexy she thought he was.

THE DAY HAD been perfect and even the weather had held out for the five-mile hike through the trails. Locals and tourists had avoided getting into any trouble requiring his assistance, and his on-call shift was officially over.

He was free to spend the evening with Isla uninterrupted.

The Christmas tree was the only light illuminating the space, and warmth from the electric fireplace on the wall provided a cozy, romantic vibe. He barely used it, but he was happy to have it that evening as he tried to set a mood.

Isla thought he was sexy, and she sure as hell had been trying to seduce him that day. Maybe he'd try a little seducing of his own that evening.

Aaron propped several pillows behind his back as he relaxed on the sofa, stretching out his stiff legs in front of him. The exercise and cold air had felt great, but it was nice to be inside where he planned to cuddle Isla all evening. The passionate kiss they'd shared on the trail had left him craving more all day, and he hoped she wasn't intent on watching any of the holiday movies he'd invited her over for.

His cell phone chimed, and the temptation to ignore it was strong. The only person he wanted to talk to right now or give any attention to was already there in his apartment, in the kitchen, making them hot chocolate.

But what if it was important?

He reluctantly reached for the phone and read the text.

Are you on your way?

Aaron frowned at the text message from Trina. On his way? On his way where?

His eyes widened. *Shit. What was the date?*

He checked his calendar and saw it was December 9, the night of the teachers' staff Christmas party.

Damn, he'd totally forgotten he'd agreed to go with her. Panic seized his chest. That was before he and Isla had started dating, but it was already after six o'clock. How could he bail on Trina at the last minute? That would be a douchebag move...

But how did he tell Isla he had a date this evening? He wanted to be with *her*, desperately so. The day had been wonderful, and the mood in his apartment was just right, and he'd finally talked himself into making more moves... But he knew he had to fulfill his promise to Trina to be her buffer with gym teacher Greg.

He glanced up as Isla entered the room with their hot chocolate, topped with large dollops of whipped cream and chocolate sprinkles. "I may have overdone it on the sprinkles," she said with a laugh, handing him a mug.

He forced a laugh. "Never too many sprinkles." He took a sip, the hot liquid beneath the cream burning his top lip.

"Careful, it's...hot," Isla said too late.

He set the cup on the table and cleared his throat. "So I, um...forgot about a commitment I made for tonight."

"Oh...okay," she said, and he knew she was trying not to seem disappointed as she settled in next to him on the sofa.

"I have to head out in about five minutes." He'd have to forgo a shower, quickly change into something appropriate and then drive like a maniac across town. With the bad weather, he'd be lucky to make it a half hour late.

"Okay," she repeated, jumping up. "I can get going, but I'm taking this with me." She hugged the mug to her chest.

He stood and touched her shoulders. "I really don't want to go, but I have to," he said, wanting her to know that. He'd been looking forward to cuddling on the sofa with her, more passionate kisses... Now he had to abandon that for an evening with another woman.

"It's totally fine. You have a life and your own plans." She stood and collected her jacket.

He sighed as he hesitated. He had to tell her what those

plans were. But how? He didn't want her to think that he was into Trina or that it was a date. Especially after she'd alluded to the fact there might be other women in town who might find him attractive. He was a hundred percent single and available and not interested in anyone but her, but how could he make her believe that with what he was about to say? He cleared his throat. "It's just a staff holiday party."

"At the station?" she asked as she wrapped her scarf around her neck.

"No, at the elementary school. I kinda told Trina Clarkson, a teacher there, that I'd accompany her—not as a date or anything, just to prevent Greg, the gym teacher, from hitting on her. And it was before you and I—" What? How did he describe what they were doing? They hadn't really put a label on it. What did he want it to be? What did *she* want it to be?

This timing couldn't be worse.

Isla looked slightly amused by his anxiety. "It's fine." She paused. "And it would still be fine if it *were* a date."

It would? Why? He'd hoped she wouldn't want him dating other people. Was she planning on dating other people? He hadn't really thought about it. "You'd be okay with that?"

She shrugged. "Well, I don't love the idea…"

That was a relief.

"But, I mean, we're not exclusive or anything. You're free to date anyone you want."

Which meant she too was free to date anyone she wanted. That thought didn't sit well with him at all.

Damn, he had to go and go now, but he really didn't want to leave with this matter unsettled. It seemed as though it were something he needed clarity on.

She headed toward the door, and he reached for the end

of her scarf, drawing her back toward him. "It isn't a date," he said. "I don't want it to be a date."

"I'm sure Trina might see it differently," Isla said with a quick kiss on his cheek and a wink as she took her scarf from him and headed toward the door. "Have fun," she said as the door closed behind her, leaving him standing there, knowing he'd think of nothing else all evening except making sure he got clarity on their relationship. ASAP.

Twenty minutes later, he was apologizing to a freezing-looking Trina as she waited for him on her front step.

"Sorry I'm late!" he said, meeting her at her door and helping her descend the slick steps in her high heels. She'd definitely gone to some trouble that evening—her hair and makeup were perfect, and a short black dress was visible under a red cashmere coat. Aaron instantly felt guilty. Even more so. He'd given Isla the wrong impression by going through with this event, and he was terrified he was also giving Trina the wrong impression.

There really didn't seem to be any winning this evening.

"It's okay," she said with a smile. "I'm glad you were still able to make it."

"Of course. Bodyguard at your service," he said teasingly, but with the intention of reminding her of their arrangement.

At the truck, he opened the passenger-side door for her and was relieved when she had no trouble hoisting herself up inside. Somehow lifting another woman up into his truck would feel like a betrayal to Isla.

Man, this whole thing was really making him uncomfortable. He was technically single, but this still felt wrong. He'd never dated more than one woman at a time. For good reason. Things got complicated, and feelings got hurt. Fast.

He'd seen it with some of the other guys at the station, and it just wasn't for him.

As he climbed into the driver's seat, Trina used the mirror to apply a layer of red lipstick to her lips. He couldn't help but compare it to Isla's pale pink gloss that tasted like peppermint.

Lip gloss he'd been hoping to overdose on that evening…

"This weather is crazy, huh?" he said in an effort to focus on Trina and not be distracted by thoughts of the woman he'd wanted to spend the evening with.

Trina nodded, peering out the windshield as the wipers tried to keep up with the blowing snow. "I swear we get this crappy weather for our staff party every year. Last year, the storm got so bad that we were all trapped at the school for the night."

His mouth went a little dry. That couldn't happen this year. There'd be no explaining that to Isla.

Luckily, the school wasn't far from her home, and four minutes later they pulled into the nearly empty lot. Only seven other cars were parked there—all staff, there for the party. He helped Trina down from the truck, and they carefully made their way toward the door. "Why do they hold the parties at the school?" he asked. A local pub or even the bowling alley or pool hall would be more fun.

"Lack of funds," she said. "This plus a ten-dollar limit on a Secret Santa exchange is as good as it gets," she said, removing her coat once they were inside.

The black dress was sleeveless with a plunging neckline, and once again, guilt washed over him. Trina was a beautiful woman, and she'd obviously dressed to impress this evening. She deserved a real date with a guy who was genuinely into her and whose thoughts weren't constantly returning to someone else and somewhere else he'd rather be.

Unfortunately, they were nowhere, and she was stuck with him. He'd help her enjoy the evening, keep Greg at bay and, next year, hope Santa brought her better options for a date.

He extended an arm to her as they approached the staff room, where voices drifted from inside. She tossed her hair over her shoulder and cuddled in closer as they entered the room.

Oh no. She was getting a little too close for comfort.

He scanned the room and saw the familiar faces of the school staff mingling and drinking what he suspected was spiked red punch. Everyone looked their way and greeted them, and he noticed Greg eyeing Trina with definite interest. The former football player was a giant, with huge bodybuilder muscles. He'd always seemed shy and soft-spoken to Aaron. It was surprising that he could blur the lines at work. He wouldn't have pegged him as that kind of guy.

But Trina hadn't been wrong. The gym teacher really did look taken by her. But then he averted his gaze quickly, and she turned her attention to Aaron.

He didn't say anything, but suddenly she was laughing loudly and hitting his chest playfully. He frowned in confusion until he saw her gaze shift toward Greg who was watching them again with a look of annoyance on his face.

Holy shit.

"Wait a second... Are you trying to make Greg jealous?" he asked quietly. It certainly appeared that way. "Is that why you invited me?"

Trina gave him a sheepish look, pulling him to the side. "Okay, yes," she whispered. "I'm sorry. I like you, Aaron, but I'm using you."

And he'd thought she was into him and would be disappointed when he had to resist any flirtation that evening. A sense of relief ran through him with only the slightest hint of annoyance that he was being used.

"But I thought you said Greg got handsy and you needed someone to protect you," he said.

"I may have exaggerated the truth a little," she said. "We started seeing one another when the school year started. Casually. Off the record for a few weeks. But then he ghosted me just before Halloween."

Aaron repressed a grin at the irony of that. "Did you ask him what happened?"

"I just assumed he wasn't interested," she said, looking exasperated as she snuck another glance at the man, refilling his glass.

Aaron shot a glance toward the gym teacher too. Dude was definitely interested. He could pretend not to watch them, but he wasn't fooling Aaron. He felt daggers coming from the other man. "Believe me, he's interested," he said.

"How do you know?"

"Because he can't keep his eyes off you." The same way Aaron couldn't keep his off Isla, even back when he used to claim she irritated the hell out of him. There really was a fine line between love and hate.

"So what do I do?" Trina asked.

Aaron had officially switched positions from bodyguard to wingman. He wrapped an arm around her shoulder as he ushered her farther into the room. "Let's make him jealous, and I'll bet he'll be texting you first thing tomorrow morning."

Trina sent him a grateful smile, and Aaron repressed a sigh as he accepted his new mission for the evening.

At least he wouldn't have to let Trina down gently.

STANDING AT THE bathroom sink, wearing the soft terrycloth robe and slippers with the Sealena Hotel logo on them, Isla applied a seaweed face mask. It wasn't the evening she'd originally planned, but a night of self-care was the next best thing.

It'd be lying to say it didn't bother her a little that Aaron was at a staff holiday party with Trina. A quick social media search had revealed the teacher was young and pretty, but he'd made the commitment before they'd started to get to know one another intimately. Plus, he had seemed disappointed to have to rush out on her...

Still, she was going to make him sweat a little. The *Thinking of you* text he'd sent an hour ago remained unanswered. It was killing her not to respond, and she would... soon. Truth was she missed him too. A lot more than she'd expected to.

A knock sounded on the door, and she quickly dried her hands in a towel.

Her ice cream sundae!

After the hot chocolate that evening, she'd been craving the creamy whipped dessert, and the room-service menu had caused her to cave.

Ice cream was a requirement for self-care.

She grabbed several bills from the table and headed toward the door as another knock sounded. Opening it, her eyes widened. "Aaron?"

It had only been two hours since she'd left his house. She'd expected him to still be at the staff party. With Trina. Not standing outside her hotel room with what looked like an icicle pressed to his left cheek. "What are you doing here? And what happened to you?" she asked, seeing a deep bruise forming beneath the ice.

"I wanted to talk to you," he said, looking a little nervous. "And I was slugged by a gym teacher."

Both statements made her heart pound. Had something happened with Trina? He'd said it wasn't a date, but…had he gotten into a fight with the other man over Trina?

"What's going on?" she asked as she stepped back to let him enter. She caught her reflection in the vanity mirror and gasped. Oh God! She still had the seaweed mask on her face. "Before you start, let me go wash this off."

He reached for her, stopping her from escaping into the bathroom. "Leave it. It's cute," he said with a crooked grin before wincing in pain. "Smiling hurts."

"Let me see," she said, leading the way to the bed, where she coaxed the melting icicle down from his cheek. It didn't look too bad yet, but it would be nasty in the morning. "Why did this guy hit you?"

"Turns out Trina invited me to make the guy jealous. And he was," Aaron said.

Isla couldn't help the laugh of relief that escaped her.

"I found the whole thing less amusing," Aaron said, sounding more on edge and a little grumpy. She'd never seen this side of him before; something was definitely bothering him, and she didn't think it was entirely the punch to the face.

"I'm sorry. You're right, it's not funny," she said, sucking in her bottom lip. It wasn't funny that he'd gotten hurt, but she was secretly thrilled that Trina wasn't competition.

"But it turns out that the punch from Greg wasn't the worse part of the evening," he said.

"It wasn't?"

"No. I was at the party, but all I could think about was how I wouldn't be okay with you going out with someone else, and I'm not sure how I feel about you being okay with it."

She hid a grin. "So what you're saying is you wanted me to act like a jealous, controlling girlfriend?"

"Yes! I mean, no." He shook his head quickly and turned toward her, taking her hands in his as he released a deep breath. "Not controlling or jealous but maybe someone who'd like to be…"

"Like to be what?" Her heart pounded so loudly she thought for sure he could hear it. What exactly was he saying?

"I don't know…exclusive?" he said, looking nervous and hopeful when his gaze met hers. "I mean, if it's too soon—"

"No!" she said quickly. It wasn't exactly the label she'd been wanting, but it was a step closer. It had only been a few weeks, but technically, they'd known one another their entire lives. There was no one she'd remet recently that made her feel as happy and calm as he did.

He climbed off the bed and knelt in front of her. "So what do you say, Isla Wakefield? Are you cool with dating only me?"

"Do you have any other previous commitments you need to get out of the way first?" she teased.

"No," he said as he kissed her hand.

"Then, yes," she said. She stood and gently pulled him to his feet, then shoved him gently toward the door. "But now you have to go."

He turned back in surprise. "You're kicking me out?"

"You were the one with other plans tonight, and now I have a rom-com marathon to binge and an ice cream sundae on its way." As much as she'd love to let him stay and spend the evening wrapped in his arms, she'd made alternate plans for the evening.

He laughed. "Guess I can't compete with that." He stopped by the door. "Can I see you tomorrow?"

Her heart swelled as she nodded. "I'm off work at five."

"I'm off at three, so I'll pick you up?"

"Already looking forward to it," she said as she opened the door in time to see the room-service attendant arrive with the mouthwatering three-scoop sundae.

Letting Aaron leave was just the tiniest bit easier.

CHAPTER NINETEEN

APPARENTLY, SHE'D BOOKED some sort of winter-camping expedition while she was home for the holidays. The text message reminder from Bird's Eye View Glamping about her upcoming weekend confirmed she'd booked two nights in a yurt in the middle of the forest. In winter.

She knew she was adventurous, and she suspected this was one of the least insane things she typically participated in, but maybe she should cancel. The dogsled ride and snow-shoeing were one thing, but a quick Google search of the company revealed a long, treacherous hike into the camp-grounds and yurts that were positioned far enough away from one another that they were fairly isolated.

Did she want to be all alone in the woods?

She glanced at Aaron as he drove along Main Street after picking her up from her shift at Santa's Village. Could she really invite him on an overnight? The night before they'd become exclusive, but what exactly did that mean? They weren't seeing anyone else, but what did it imply for their situation? How fast would the relationship move now?

"Yes to whatever you're about to ask," he said, not even turning to look at her.

Her cheeks flushed slightly. "Who says I was going to ask anything?"

He turned her way with a grin. "Because you always

run your index finger along your bottom lip when you're contemplating something."

She did?

She was doing it right now. How had he noticed?

"What is it?" he asked as he turned into the parking lot of the Serpent Queen Pub where they were having dinner.

"Some winter-camping trip I booked. Bird's Eye View. In Willow." She had no idea where Willow was. It could be an hour away or eight hours away.

But Aaron nodded as he cut the truck's engine. "I've heard of it. A few of the guys at the station go during the summer mostly. Great fishing out there."

"But going in winter might be a bit much, don't you think?" The yurts looked cozy, but it would have to be freezing in the middle of the night once temperatures dropped below zero, and she hadn't noticed mention of a bathroom in the accommodations.

He reached for her and pulled her closer. Her heart raced as he stared into her eyes. "I'll go with you if you want to go."

She didn't necessarily want to do this winter-camping thing, but two nights in a yurt with Aaron was definitely appealing. She'd been wanting to move their relationship to a new level, and two days and nights alone together in the woods would be a great way to see if the relationship was moving in the right direction. "I think it might be a fun experience."

"Me too," he said, moving closer.

"And you're sure you're ready to...you know?" Her cheeks flushed. How did he feel about the overnights?

"I'm sure we could ask for separate beds," he said with a grin.

She flushed and nodded her head quickly. "Oh yeah, I

wasn't talking about that. I just meant are we ready to go away together? That's two full days—" and nights "—together…"

"I think I can handle that." He touched her cheek and then slid a finger under her chin to lift her face up toward his. Her pulse raced as his gaze flitted from her eyes to her lips. The smell of his cologne encircled her head, and heat radiated from him as she moved closer and wrapped her arms around his neck.

His lips approached hers, and she met him halfway, her eyes closing as their mouths met. His arms went around her waist, and picking her up, he placed her on his lap to straddle him as he deepened the kiss. Soft, teasing, barely-there caresses, then urgent, desperate, searching kisses.

She knew she must have kissed many men in her lifetime, but these kisses with Aaron felt like the first ones. Was it just because she couldn't remember any others? Or was it because when she was kissing him, it felt like no other kiss could ever take her breath away like his did?

His hands slid higher to grip her rib cage, his fingers digging into her skin. She pressed her body closer, grinding her hips onto his lap, feeling the effect she was having on him under her leg.

Her tongue danced with his as her hands tangled in the back of his hair. Heat coursed through her, and she knew she'd never wanted anyone as badly as she wanted Aaron in that moment.

He pulled back reluctantly, slightly out of breath, still holding her tight.

"Still think camping is a good idea?" she whispered against his mouth.

"I'm sure the beds can be pushed together," he said, before kissing her again.

That weekend couldn't come fast enough.

AARON KNOCKED ON Skylar's open office door the next morning. Christmas music played from her computer as she reviewed a new training manual on her desk. She was dressed in her uniform, but he could see she'd kicked off her boots under the desk.

"Come in," she said glancing up. "Oh my God, what happened to your face?"

He waved a hand. "A misunderstanding, that's all." Flirting with Trina had definitely worked to get Greg to act on his attraction to her, but it turned out spiked punch and jealousy were a bad mix. Greg had texted him to apologize already, and they were all good.

"Heard about that bear on the rescue last week. Well done," she said with a look of sincere praise. "I'm not sure I'd have been so quick thinking with the flare."

"Aw, bears are just the sharks of the forest," he said.

"Yeah, I don't intend on meeting too many sharks either," she said with a shudder as he entered the office. "And thanks again for taking Isla out the other night." She lowered her voice. "I know she was feeling a little confused about the whole adoption thing."

Isla was handling it like a pro. That knowledge being dropped on anyone else might not have been received so well. Plus, it had spurred her interest in going into social work. Had she shared that information with anyone other than him yet? Told her family her plans?

"Yeah, it was no problem." He placed the time-off request he was carrying on her desk. "I know it's fairly short notice, but I was hoping to have the weekend off."

Skylar eyed him as she picked up the form, where he'd filled in the reason for request as *None of your business ;)*. He knew she'd take it as a joke but hoped she wouldn't ask for further info. He knew she wanted him to be there for Isla, but an overnight camping trip might be a bit much...

Or maybe she already knew Isla's weekend plans. Had the two women talked about him and everything that was going on?

"Are you able to be on call?" Skylar asked. "That way, I can still pay you."

It was a nice offer, but there was no way he was working that weekend unless there was an emergency in Port Serenity with all hands on deck. And he really hoped there wouldn't be. Since Isla had asked him to go—or rather, he'd invited himself along—he couldn't think about anything else. He'd never thought he'd ever be looking forward to two uninterrupted days alone with Isla Wakefield, but here he was.

"No, I don't think so, but thank you."

"You going out of town?" she asked.

"A few hours away," he said, rocking back and forth on his heels. Willow was about two and a half hours south of Port Serenity. Close enough to make it back if absolutely necessary, but far enough away to truly feel like a getaway.

"You know, Isla mentioned something about going away this weekend too," Skylar said, a knowing look on her face.

He sighed. No sense lying about it. "She had booked the winter-camping trip, but she was nervous about going alone..."

Skylar nodded, a look of worry etching across her features. "Look, I'm thrilled that the two of you have been hitting it off...and I know I was the one encouraging it, but just be careful, okay?"

"You know I'd never let anything hurt Isla. Including myself," he said. He'd do anything to protect her. Bears, wolves and coyotes didn't stand a chance. And the way he was feeling about her, he knew there was no chance of him breaking her heart either. The other night he'd wanted to ask her to be his girlfriend, but he'd chickened out and gone with the lame *exclusive* idea. If it were up to him, he'd jump in headfirst. But taking it slow was the right thing to do given the circumstances.

"I know," Skylar said sincerely and hesitated before continuing. "*Isla* just has a way of hurting Isla, and I'm worried that *you* could get hurt in the crossfire."

Right. Isla was bulletproof, whereas he was the one who could shatter if things went sideways. He gave a weak smile as he shrugged. "A chance I'm willing to take, I guess."

Skylar nodded as she signed the time-off sheet. "Okay. Well, have fun. Not too much!" she called after him as he left the office.

The level of fun would be decided by Isla. Aaron was just happy to take all the time with her that he could get.

MUSIC CRANKED IN the vehicle, shoes off and her feet propped up on the dash, Isla sang off-key as Aaron drove along the highway that Friday evening. The weather and road conditions were perfect for the trip. He grinned as he glanced her way then opened his mouth. She reached across and popped a piece of chocolate chip cookie into it. The gesture felt so comfortable. As though they'd been together for years instead of just a few weeks.

He reached for her hand and placed it on the gearshift under his, and a warmness flowed through her. All week she'd been excited about their time away. She'd expected to feel nervous or anxious about it, but those feelings didn't come.

She was only happy and comfortable being with Aaron. There was no doubt that the two of them had a connection. One they both felt...one they both wanted to explore further.

Whatever their history was, it no longer mattered. To either of them.

She was grateful for the opportunity to get to know him in ways that she might not have ever entertained before.

Her gaze drifted out the window as they drove along the highway. Snow-covered evergreens and icy mountain-tops all around them, the scenery was breathtaking in the valley. A river ran parallel to the highway, and there was a sense of peace as she watched the water flow over the rocks. It was no wonder that no matter how much she traveled, she always came home to Alaska. She couldn't imagine a more magical place, especially in the frost-covered shimmer of winter.

Aaron took an exit and switched gears, moving her hand under his.

It was sexy the way he led her hand through the gear changes. An unexpected masculine thing that had her more than a little turned on.

"Skylar was okay with the time off?" she asked.

He nodded. "She's onto us, though."

"Well, I'm not exactly trying to hide it." Unlike her brother and Skylar who had hid their relationship from everyone based on a decades-old family feud, Isla had no reason to hide her feelings for Aaron from anyone. She didn't care if everyone in Alaska knew she was dating the sexy rescue swimmer.

He pulled the car into the parking lot of Bird's Eye View campground ten minutes later, and Isla eyed the large lodge that looked cozy and inviting. Decorated with multicolored holiday lights, the evergreens on the lawn lit up as darkness started to settle over the forest. It was only five o'clock, but night fell fast this time of year with only seven hours of daily sunlight in this part of Alaska. The frame of the lodge featured white icicle lights and oversize holiday wreaths on the exterior. Smoke billowed from a chimney, and the smell of wood burning was definitely a familiar scent.

There was no doubt about it, camping was something she loved to do if the warm familiarity wrapping around her was any indication. It made her even more excited. Maybe this trip would help trigger some memories.

Either way, she'd be making new ones.

"This place looks great," Aaron said as he shut off the truck and looked through the windshield to take in the campgrounds. There were yurts and small cabins spaced out along the property and a firepit next to what she was relieved to see were shower facilities. The place was even better than the website had described. Much more modern. And while rustic in appearance, it was obviously a high-end establishment with all the comforts of home.

A hot tub was next to the lodge, and they could see several couples sitting in it, the steam rising in the cold air as they drank champagne out of flutes.

It might be nice to have that to themselves at some point...

"I'm sure we can sneak out once everyone else is asleep," Aaron said.

She slapped at him playfully. "Stop reading my mind."

He grabbed her hand and kissed it. "It was just wishful thinking on my part."

Oh God, this weekend was already going by too fast. She wanted time to slow down so she could enjoy every minute of being here with him.

They climbed out, and he retrieved their bags from the back of the truck. She reached for hers, but he shook his head. "I got it." He slung both bags over his shoulder and reached for her hand as they headed toward the door marked *Reception*.

Inside the lodge, they were greeted with the heat from the large stone-crafted fireplace, and Isla shivered inside the warmth. The open-beam A-frame was decorated for the holidays with fresh garlands of holly and bows draped around all the dark wooden structures. The mantel featured a Nativity set and a North Pole village. Hand-knitted white stockings hung by the fire, and two large Nutcrackers stood guard at the base of the spiral wooden staircase that led to the rooms on the upper two floors of the lodge.

Maybe she should have booked one of those.

Old Isla might have been excited about the yurt, but this version of herself would have preferred something a little more romantic and cozy—at least now that it had turned into a couple's getaway.

A group of friends sat around the fireplace, enjoying hot chocolate and laughing, and a man played classical music on a grand piano in the lounge. The mood throughout was festive and warm.

"Hi, can I help you?" a woman at the front desk asked with a warm smile as they approached. Her name tag read *Marsha*, and underneath were the different languages she spoke: English, French, Spanish and German. It was no surprise that they had visitors from all over the world. This place wasn't your typical campground, and for a second, she worried about the cost. Her second paycheck from Santa's Village had been just over three hundred dollars. She'd be breaking into the trust fund for this one. But she wouldn't worry about that now. She'd find a way to pay it back. "Reservation for Isla Wakefield," she said, taking out her credit card.

The woman entered the information into the computer's registration system and smiled. "Perfect. We have you staying for two nights."

"That's right."

"In the Bird's Eye Nest," the woman continued. "Amazing choice."

Isla frowned. "Oh, no. I had a yurt rented."

"The reservation was changed earlier this week," the woman said. "You were in luck too, as that accommodation had been previously occupied, but the couple had to cancel."

Isla swung around to look at Aaron suspiciously. "You did this?"

"Consider us even," he said, with a smile.

Isla's heart swelled. He'd upgraded the reservation to something a little nicer… That had to mean something.

She slid her credit card across the desk, but the woman shook her head. "The room charges have already been paid."

Isla turned to Aaron again. "You have to at least let me pay. This was my idea."

He shook his head as he accepted a key and a campsite map from the woman behind the desk. "Not a chance."

"The Bird's Eye Nest is through this exit, down the back trail and just a ten-minute hike up the mountain. The snow and ice have been cleared, and at this time of year, the extra holiday lights on the trees illuminate it quite well, so it shouldn't be too tough a climb, but be careful. It's getting dark, and the path could be slick." She pointed to the lodge cafeteria behind them that looked more like an elegant five-star restaurant. "Buffet breakfast is included with your stay and is served from six to ten, then we have an à la carte dinner from six to midnight. The snack bar is always open, and the hot tub is first come, first served, but a lot of guests are happy to share and meet one another. There are snowmobile, skate and cross-country ski rentals at the hut next door. If you need anything, don't hesitate to contact the front desk."

"Thank you," Aaron said, picking up their bags.

"Enjoy your stay," Marsha said.

Isla smiled and nodded as she followed Aaron through the exit that led to their accommodation. The winter-evening chill had her zipping her jacket higher, but anticipation helped to warm her as they located the path to the Bird's Eye Nest. "You really didn't have to upgrade the reservation. I was fine with the yurt," she said as he took her hand and they started along the trail.

"I would be happy in a sleeping bag on the snow, but I figure, it's Christmas and it would be nice to stay somewhere extra nice." He lifted her bare hand to his lips and kissed it.

Despite the chill in the mountain air, Isla was toasty warm inside her coat as they made the hike to the Bird's Eye Nest. And moments later, she stared up at the magnificent treehouse cabin.

This upgrade was amazing. As Aaron helped her carefully climb the slippery wooden steps up to the entrance, Isla took in the view from the elevated height. Views of the Chugach mountain range in the distance, a beautiful frozen lake, a waterfall and snow-capped mountains, and snow-covered evergreens all around, decorated in white lights.

Being the only cabin in that section of the campground provided a secluded intimacy that had her spine tingling in anticipation. He'd done this for her.

On the large wraparound deck was an open-air kitchen and barbecue. A table for two and two wicker chairs were positioned side by side. A small outhouse served as the bathroom, but it contained running water and plumbing. Not exactly roughing it.

But what caught her attention was the two-person hot tub on the deck. Already full and bubbling, steam rising, it looked like heaven. She hadn't even thought to pack a swimsuit. Did that matter?

Her cheeks flushed when Aaron caught her stare and grinned as though reading her mind.

She'd felt their attraction grow over the last few weeks, but it was more than that: she'd opened up to him, and he'd done the same with her. It was crazy to think they'd known one another their entire lives. Lived in the same town, attended the same school, shared a lot of the same friends. They weren't strangers.

"That looks seriously tempting," he said, nodding toward the tub.

"Would be a shame not to use it," she said, happy they were on the same page.

He set their bags down and used the key to unlock the door. He opened it and gestured for her to enter first.

Inside the cabin, their own wood-burning fireplace had already been lit, and the smell was one she knew was a favorite, given the flood of pleasure that flowed through her. The queen-size bed was made of exposed, stained wood and featured a Christmas-patterned quilt along with a soft, furry throw. The rustic, wood vibe was so warm and inviting.

Damn, only two nights?

Behind her, the sound of a hip-hop Christmas song started, and turning, she saw Aaron dancing his way toward her.

She laughed as he took her hand and twirled her around.

"Never pegged you for a Biebs fan," she said. She remembered the song!

Aaron smiled. "I'm not. This is reportedly your favorite Christmas song."

Her chest warmed once again, and she felt such a sense of relief over just one familiar thing. He turned her around and pulled her back into his arms, swaying them both seductively, their bodies pressed together as he sang the lyrics into her ear.

She swallowed hard, and her body tingled with an awakening at the feel of his hands on her hips, moving her body in rhythm with his. Dancing with him felt amazing, natural, as though they'd always moved in perfect harmony together.

She turned her face toward his, and he kissed her gently as the song ended. Then he pulled her closer, and she wrapped her arms around his neck as a softer, romantic song started to play on what was obviously a holiday-themed playlist he'd made for that weekend.

He lowered his mouth to hers, squeezing her tight and lifting her off her feet. He kissed her softly, teasingly...over and over again. She reached up and tangled her fingers into his hair, forcing his head to stay close, needing more of those lips. Needing more of him.

His hands under her ass squeezed tighter as she separated his mouth with her tongue and deepened the kiss. He was so hot. This treehouse was magical. The fireplace, the glow of the holiday lights and the music had really set the mood.

There would never be a more perfect moment.

She reached down to lift his sweater and T-shirt over his head in one motion and tossed them to the floor at their feet. He didn't seem surprised by her actions, as though having come to the same conclusion himself. This moment was the perfect time to take things to the next level.

"Arms up," he said.

She did as he directed, and he lifted her sweater off. He smoothed the staticky, flyaway strands of blond hair, and then holding her face between his hands, he kissed her again, backing them toward the bed. "You sure you don't want to enjoy the room first?" he murmured against her mouth.

"I am enjoying the room." She couldn't think of a better use of the romantic space, and right now, she was craving only him. They could savor the view and the hot tub later.

They fell onto the bed and continued removing articles of clothing, kissing in between. His body was even more amazing than she could have imagined. Chiseled shoulders and arms, solid, muscular chest, abs for days. He had to be physically fit for his job, but damn, this was perfection.

Isla's body was alive, and her heart pounded in her chest as she eyed the man in front of her, his own look of appreciation reflecting in his eyes as he took in her petite but muscular body.

She would remember how to do this, right? She didn't know how long it had been since she'd been with a man...

"Muscle memory," Aaron murmured against her lips, once again reading her mind.

She laughed. "You're in my head again," she said as he stared into her eyes.

"I want to be in much more than that." He touched her chest over her heart for clarification that he didn't just mean her body.

He was already there. She knew she was falling in love with him. It might have only been a few weeks of dating, but technically, Aaron had been in her life forever. A part of her felt that long-lasting connection. He didn't feel like a stranger. Not when they touched, not when he looked at her—as though some part of her remembered him the same way the smell of the wood burning had been a memory. She might not recall every conversation, every detail of their past, but she trusted her gut feeling that he was someone who'd always meant a lot to her.

How had they never realized how perfect they were for one another?

A question that continued to plague her. Maybe the timing had never been right. After all, she did travel a lot...

He gently laid her down against the soft down-filled pillows and continued to kiss her as his hands trailed the length of her body, tickling her as his fingers caressed her chest, her ribs, her stomach.

She shivered, and goose bumps surfaced on her skin. He covered them with the blanket before following the trail of his hand with his mouth, kissing every inch of her.

Every inch. He wasn't missing a spot, moving in the tiniest of increments.

She laughed in pleasure as she ran her hands through his soft, dark hair. "This is going to take all night at this rate," she teased, but she was enjoying every last kiss. The feel of his mouth on her, his breath against her skin was the best feeling she'd ever experienced.

Aaron continued his mission. "I've got nowhere else to be," he said against her flesh, making her entire body tremble.

And he wasn't kidding. He wasn't in a rush. And while she could tell he wanted her as badly as she wanted him, he wasn't quickening the pace to selfishly take the pleasure he craved. This seemed all about her. All about pleasuring her.

But it also seemed as though he were getting just as much out of it, savoring the taste and scent of her skin as he went.

Kisses covered her stomach, her arms, her thighs, all the way to her feet.

"Roll over," he said. "Other side."

She laughed but shook her head, reaching for him. "Keep the back for tomorrow."

"Or later tonight," he said. "You weren't planning on sleeping this weekend, were you?"

Holy hell. "Sleep is definitely not on the agenda," she said.

He fell back onto the bed on top of her, and she opened her legs to allow him to lie between them. He nuzzled her neck and fondled her breasts, and she arched her back to press herself closer. She slipped a hand between their bodies, trailing her fingers over his chest, down his six-pack, then lower, to grip him and stroke. He was so incredibly sexy, and while he was thick and hard, he took his time with a sexy sense of control that was intoxicating. He moaned as her hand wrapped around him, and his gaze was full of desire when he stared down at her.

"I want you, Isla," he said.

"I'm yours," she said, and she knew in that moment that it was true. She was so into him, and every moment they spent together was better than the last. She didn't think she could possibly enjoy being with anyone else as much as she loved being with him.

He brushed the hair away from her face as he kissed her again. His expression was loving and full of desire—a combination that stole her breath away and made her feel confident in this decision to be with him. Fully.

He sat up and slowly climbed off the bed. She watched

as he reached into his discarded jeans pocket for a condom and raised an eyebrow.

"You came prepared?" she said. So, he'd been planning on it happening that weekend. Or hoping, at least. So glad they were on the same page. That he was finally giving in to the temptation.

"Always. Safety first," he said with a grin as he tore it open and slid it on before rejoining her on the bed.

He lay next to her and pulled her on top of him, holding her tight as he kissed her. She could feel his erection between their bodies, and heat coursed through her at the thought of having him inside of her. She deepened the kiss with a passionate sense of urgency, grinding her hips into him, telling him she was ready. Ready and desperate for him.

His eyes opened, and he broke the contact with her mouth. "You sure?" he asked.

"Absolutely," she said.

He sat up slowly and lifted her into a straddled position on his lap and gently lowered her down over him. He groaned in pleasure, and his head fell back. Isla took a deep inhale as she felt him fill her completely. She clutched his shoulders as they started slowly, then picked up the pace as their desperation for release grew. His gaze locked with hers as he kissed her, as though staring deep into her soul. She couldn't tear her own gaze away from the love and affection reflected in his eyes.

She rode him up and down, feeling their bodies moving together in perfect synchronicity. She ground her pelvis as close to him as possible, taking him deep within her body. It felt so incredible. He felt so good. She never wanted the sensations to stop.

Aaron held her ass as they continued to make love, lifting her up and down over his erection, plunging in deeper, with each stroke of her body coming down over him.

He rested his head in the crook of her neck, his fingers digging into her flesh. "Isla... Damn, Isla..."

Her name on his lips was everything as she heard all the emotion in his voice. He wanted her just as badly as she wanted him. He was feeling this connection as much as she was. In that moment, this was all that mattered.

She felt him harden even more as the first waves of her own orgasm toppled over. She clung to him as she moved faster, desperate for release. He held her tight as he submerged himself as deep as possible and stilled, his own orgasm erupting in time with hers.

Outside, the snow fell in big flakes, the fire crackled and roared, and the sound of the holiday music made it the most amazingly romantic moment Isla imagined she'd ever experienced.

She didn't need her memory to know this was the best one yet.

UPGRADING THEIR ACCOMMODATION had been the best decision he'd made in his life. Not that he cared where he spent the weekend with Isla. He wasn't lying when he said he'd be happy on the ground in a sleeping bag made for two, but this was so much better. Romantic, cozy, warm...

Aaron lay on his back on the bed, one arm folded behind his head, the other wrapped around Isla as she cuddled into his side. The Christmas playlist he'd made still came from his cell phone, and it was dark outside the cabin, but the solar-powered white holiday lights had come on, giving a magical glow that illuminated the forest around them. The heat and ambience from the fireplace made it the perfect moment. He didn't regret their actions one little bit. Making love to Isla had surpassed any expectations. Never in his wildest dreams could he have imagined something as incredible. Especially when she'd been just as ready to take that next step with him.

"This place is so beautiful," Isla said with a contented sigh.

She was beautiful. Every inch of her. Inside and out. He could touch her and kiss her for hours and never be satisfied. How had he never known that the feelings he'd had for her were ones of attraction and affection? His irritation with her was just caring. Intense, deep caring. And from knowing she was with the wrong guy whenever that guy wasn't him. He wanted to be the only man she wanted. The only man for her.

And he'd do anything to be that man.

He held her tighter as she traced her fingers over his chest. "Do you have any tattoos?" she asked. "I don't remember seeing any."

"Nope. None."

"Not a fan?"

"Not a fan of needles," he said with a laugh. In fact, he'd gone four times to the local tattoo shop and chickened out each time they started the gun. But he wasn't sure he wanted to reveal how much of a wimp he was.

"You fight bears in hand-to-hand combat, but a tiny needle freaks you out?"

"Yep. It's the noise the machine makes," he said. He held up her arm and examined her tattoo that said *You're fine, keep going.* She had several such phrases tattooed on her skin. He liked them; they each sounded like something that was important to her, things that motivated and inspired her. He thought it was sexy.

"This didn't hurt at all?" he asked.

She laughed. "Not that I can remember."

He shook his head. "Smart-ass."

Isla traced the shape of a scar on his shoulder. "Where did this come from?"

He glanced down at it. The three-inch white mark was something he considered a badge of honor. It represented something to him just as her tattoos did to her. "My first week of rescue-swimmer training," he said. "We had a rappel challenge, and my harness got tangled. I was trapped, suspended in air for over twenty minutes, and the pressure from the weight of my body dangling tore into my skin."

"Ouch."

"Yes, exactly." It had hurt. Like hell. But it had made for an invaluable—if painful—lesson about making sure safety equipment was properly inspected before use.

"You're a real tough guy, huh?" she asked, propping herself up to look at him.

He wouldn't say that. *Tough guy* would imply he was impenetrable, that nothing could break him. He knew that wasn't true. This little five-foot, hundred-pound tornado of a woman could crush him with ease. "I train a lot in order to be prepared for anything, to be able to protect myself and the people I love," he said. From physical danger, at least.

"Nothing can hurt you?" she asked, straddling him and pinning his arms above his head.

Only the breathtakingly beautiful woman staring into his soul right at this moment. Other than that, nothing. And she had the power to completely destroy him.

In one quick move, he'd reversed their position, and now she was at his mercy. Staring up at him with the most intoxicating, breathless look of desire in her mesmerizing green eyes.

"Nothing," he said, desperately hoping that she never decided to test that theory.

CHAPTER TWENTY

HE MIGHT HAVE slept all morning, he was so comfortable and warm wrapped in the thick Christmas quilt, Isla's body draped over him, if his stomach weren't growling so loudly. They'd skipped dinner the night before, and Aaron was starving.

He slowly, quietly and gently slipped out from under her and grinned, taking in the messy blond hair and the slightly gaped mouth, drooling on the pillow he'd just vacated. Wearing his T-shirt, one leg outside the blankets, she was a sight he'd never thought he'd ever have the pleasure of seeing. He'd been with women before, but no one had impacted him like Isla.

Pulling on his discarded jeans and a thick hoodie, he quietly opened the door and slipped outside onto the deck. He opened the icebox and took out the bacon and eggs. The buffet was included in their stay, but he was in no rush to leave the privacy of their cabin, and nothing could beat a breakfast view like the one they had.

Moments later, the smell of food cooking outside on the open fire had his stomach rumbling appreciatively. He breathed in the scent, combined with the fresh outdoors, and took in the surroundings.

He'd never thought he'd be celebrating the season again, but being there in this magical winter wonderland, the sights of the holidays no longer gave him a sense of dread or anxiety. As Christmas approached, he was only looking forward to spending it with Isla. This year was already special because of her.

"Oh my God, that smells amazing," her voice said from behind him.

He turned to see her step out onto the deck in her boots, the thick quilt wrapped around her shoulders. Her hair was still tousled, and he was happy to see that she hadn't immediately dived into the bathroom to freshen up. He wanted her in this adorably messy state for as long as possible.

"I wanted to stay in bed, but I thought my stomach would wake you up," he said, opening his arms to her. She stepped into them, and he hugged her tight to his chest.

"Last night was...fun," she said, glancing up at him. Her expression was one of slight apprehension, as though gauging whether he regretted it. She had nothing to worry about.

And it was so much more than fun. It was earthshattering and meaningful, but he was terrified his feelings might scare her, so he nodded. "It was definitely fun."

The bacon sizzled on the pan, and he reluctantly released her to get their breakfast before he burned the food. Setting up the plates, he dished up the meal and poured their coffee, then sat across from her at the two-seater table where she immediately dug in.

"This is delicious," she said, after swallowing a piece of bacon.

"Food always tastes better outside," he said.

"I have to agree," she said, sipping her coffee. She gazed out over the forest and curled her hands around her mug. "I could stay here all winter."

He could too. But hopefully this weekend with her wasn't a limited-time deal. They weren't on borrowed time. They both lived in Port Serenity, and she had no immediate plans to leave town after the holidays. Plus, she'd talked about taking the online social-work classes in January. Things between them were just getting started: there was nothing to worry about.

So why did he suddenly feel as though at any minute the spell would be broken and the holiday magic bringing their unlikely hearts together would fade once the Christmas lights and garlands all disappeared for another year?

He struggled to push the feelings aside as they set out on their day an hour later. As much as he wanted to stay in the cabin with her all weekend, there was so much to see and enjoy at the campgrounds, and it would be a shame not to experience it fully.

Six hours later, he was exhausted as they hiked back from the main lodge to the cabin. Skating, cross-country skiing and a rousing game of Scrabble with a couple they'd met in the lodge had him yawning. The fresh mountain air was partly to blame along with the lack of sleep the night before.

Still, he hoped another sleepless night awaited them.

Watching Isla's sexy curves in her ski suit as she made her way up the hill toward their cabin had his mouth watering. He couldn't wait to get her inside and peel off that suit and everything beneath it. He was glad she'd turned down the other couple's offer to join them for an evening soak in the lodge hot tub. The unsettled feeling that had enveloped him that morning still lingered, and he wanted her all to himself. He wanted to kiss her and hold her and make love to her again, to reinforce the connection he knew was growing between them, and shake off the anxiousness he'd been battling all day.

He saw her bend to scoop up a handful of snow on the

trail ahead of him, and before he could dodge it, it hit him square in the chest.

He faked a look of shock. "Did you just throw snow at me?"

"Yep. What are you going to do about it?" she teased as she walked backward on the trail.

"Oh, it's on," he said, dipping to collect his own handful of wet, heavy snow. He threw it at her, but she ducked, and it missed by a mile.

"That all you got?" she asked, picking up another huge ball of snow and bouncing from one leg to the other, egging him on, threatening to throw it.

Aaron ran and tackled her to the snowbank before she could pummel him with the ball in her hand. She squealed in surprise as they fell into the snow. He landed on top of her and she struggled for air. "You're crushing me," she said, laughing.

"I'm not falling for that," he said, but he pushed himself up onto his arms, relieving her of his weight. Her face was flushed from the cold and exertion, and her eyes sparkled brighter than the Christmas lights all around them. She was so gorgeous. She'd always been the most beautiful woman he'd ever laid eyes on, but over the last few weeks, her beauty had been amplified by this sense of vulnerability, an openness that she hadn't seemed to have before.

He knew it was because she was no longer inhibited by years of knowledge and reasons to be cautious. He just hoped she could hold on to this feeling when her memory returned. Remember how fantastic it was to not be closed off.

He brushed her hair away from her face and lowered his mouth to hers. She tasted like peppermint and chocolate, and he could savor the taste all night. She reached up and wrapped her arms around his neck, drawing him closer. She moaned softly across his lips as he deepened the kiss, pressing his body to hers. The way she was always turned on and responded to his kisses with her own passion was intoxicating. It helped ease his anxiety...

But then he felt freezing-cold snow on his back beneath the neck of his jacket.

He jumped back up, and she laughed. She'd actually snow-bombed him while he was kissing her?

"Cold...cold..." he said, trying to scoop the snow out of his jacket.

On the ground, she was still laughing.

He stopped and stared at her. "Oh, now you're really going to get it."

She was on her feet in a flash, dashing away from him, struggling to run in the deep snow. For someone who'd sprained a leg just weeks before, she could certainly sprint.

But with his height and long legs, he easily caught up to her and backed her up toward the base of a large evergreen.

"Okay, truce. I'm sorry," she said, holding her hands up in surrender as she realized she had nowhere to run.

Her back hit the large tree trunk behind her, and he pressed his body to hers, slipping his hand down the front of her ski pants and underwear.

"Cold!"

"Now we're even," he said.

Instantly, she seemed to forget all about the cold fingers as he slid them along the opening of her folds. She was so warm and moist, and he felt himself harden in the front of his own ski pants, uncomfortably so, as he gently stroked her. The gesture had been meant to tease her, but he was torturing himself.

She closed her eyes and clung to him as he slipped a finger inside. He ran his tongue along her bottom lip, savoring the delicious taste of her.

Damn, he'd like to be licking her everywhere. He'd bet every inch of her tasted just as sweet. The thought made him nearly burst through the front of his ski pants.

She bit his lower lip, and he groaned. He wanted her so badly. They were still at least ten minutes away from the treehouse cabin. He'd never make it that long. Her hands stroking his back underneath his jacket and the way she spread her legs as wide as her ski pants would allow to give him better access to her body had him craving her right now.

She was the sexiest woman alive.

Her mouth crushed his as she deepened the kiss, her breath escaping in small pants between their lips told him that she was just as eager for him. He pressed his palm against her mound and rubbed his thumb against her clit as he slipped another finger inside her tight body.

He wished he were inside her, feeling her body tighten and clench around his penis instead of his fingers.

With his free hand, he unbuttoned his own ski pants and slid his hand inside. Instant relief flowed through him as he stroked his erect cock, immediately followed by an intense desire for satisfaction.

Isla's eyes opened, and she watched as he lifted his penis out from his underwear and pumped himself up and down as his fingers moved in and out of her body in the same rhythm.

"Are you sure we should be doing this here?" she asked, out of breath, tossing her head back in pleasure.

"Do you think we could stop?"

"No," she said, reaching out to circle the tip of his cock with her thumb. He raised his hand, allowing hers to wrap around his straining, throbbing cock and, placing his hand over hers, he guided her up and down.

She slid her other hand inside her ski pants and guided another one of his fingers inside her body. She inhaled sharply at the additional pressure, then moaned in pleasure, the sound nearly toppling him over the edge.

Guiding one another, they continued to pleasure each other until they were both panting and desperate for release.

He pressed his body closer to hers and buried his head into the crook of her neck, kissing, sucking and biting gently on the soft skin. She smelled so delicious, and when his lips brushed hers again, he devoured her mouth, never wanting to stop.

When he was kissing her, touching her, pleasuring her, he could forget all the insecurity that had come on suddenly that morning. When he was holding her in his arms and stealing her breath with his kisses, he didn't experience the fear of losing her. If only he could hold on to these moments forever. Moments when he knew she was feeling their connection as strongly as he was.

She closed her eyes and picked up her pace on his cock, stroking and massaging under his direction. He was close to the edge, ready to come at any moment.

The creaking of tree branches on the trail nearby had his heart nearly stopping.

Shit. There were people coming.

Isla's eyes opened and widened. He stilled, but she moved his hand, gesturing for him to continue. "Hurry before we get caught," she whispered against his mouth.

Fuck, this was the hottest woman on the planet.

They picked up speed, increasing the tempo of their actions as their urgency grew to the sound of footsteps and voices growing louder as the people approached. Knowing they could be caught at any moment had his heart racing and his body aching with a whole new level of desire.

"Hurry, Aaron, faster," she moaned, pumping her hand up and down over his cock.

Man, he was so close...

She panted and gripped his shoulder, urging him on.

He felt his orgasm mount and topple over at the same time he felt her vaginal muscles contract and clench. Her throbbing matched his as she exhaled as slowly and quietly as possible. A moan escaped him, and she kissed him to muffle the sound.

His body went limp as he came, and he slowly removed his fingers from her body. She quickly adjusted her pants as he tucked himself back inside.

Just in the nick of time.

His pulse still thundering in his veins, he turned to see the other campers on the trail about ten feet away.

Damn, that was close.

"That was exciting," Isla said, grinning at him. She looked so beautifully flushed, a look of satisfaction on her pretty face as she waved at the group approaching. It took all his strength not to go another round, audience or not.

For the first time in his life, he wasn't so opposed to Isla's daredevil ways.

AARON HANDED HER a cup of mulled wine as he sat next to her on the deck outside the cabin much later that evening. The thrill of the day competed with her exhaustion, and she suppressed a yawn. She couldn't believe what they'd done on the trail. Her own impulsivity and inhibitions had surprised her.

"Thank you," she said as he wrapped the quilt around their legs, and she moved closer to him.

She couldn't get close enough. That weekend was going so much better than she could have imagined. She liked being with him. He was fun and sexy and attractive. True, she didn't have a reference point, but she couldn't imagine ever enjoying being with a man as much as she was enjoying this time with Aaron. It wasn't just the physical attraction. She felt a pull to him, a connection that ran much deeper than just superficial lust.

But that would be impossible—to fall so quickly…right? Then again, they'd known one another their entire lives, even though she couldn't remember it.

He wrapped an arm around her shoulders, and she snuggled closer, sipping the hot spiced wine. He felt so great, and being in his arms felt so natural.

"You having a good time?" she asked, glancing up at him. She'd sensed that something might be bothering him earlier as they'd participated in the outdoor activities. He'd seemed happy, but there had been just a hint of something else… Anxiety maybe?

But his gaze was peaceful now as he stared out at the snow-covered forest. "The best time."

"Good," she said. "Me too."

There was so much she was wondering, but she didn't want to ask him what he was thinking. She was desperate to hear that his feelings were growing just as quickly, just as strong as hers were, but she wasn't sure how to coax that information out of him without revealing her own feelings, and she didn't want his confession to be a forced response to hers.

"Hey, you know I'm falling in love with you, right?" he said, once again displaying that uncanny ability of his to read her thoughts.

A smile broke across her face as she turned to face him.

He was looking at her now with a look of affection so strong there was no room for any doubt.

"How do you always do that?"

"Do what?" he asked, brushing her hair back from her face.

"Know what I'm thinking."

He pulled her closer and kissed her forehead gently. "We've known one another a long time. I guess we're in sync."

"In sync. I like that," she said. She leaned up and kissed him. "I like you. A lot. More than *like*, actually."

He stared deep into her eyes and held for a long, soul-gazing moment. He looked as though he weren't sure if he could believe it, could trust it...

"Why do you think it's taken us this long...to get here?" she asked. She'd asked a similar question before, but she couldn't get any really satisfaction or clarity in the answers. It shouldn't matter, but somehow it did.

Aaron hesitated, then cleared his throat. "Maybe it was because we thought we were too different. But I think we had preconceived ideas about one another, and we just didn't look close enough. Didn't see what was really there." He paused, then staring deep into her soul, he said, "But I see it now. See *you* now. All of you."

Her chest swelled with love as she nodded, staring up at the man who was making up for all she'd lost that holiday season.

CHAPTER TWENTY-ONE

As he parked his truck at the marina Monday morning, Aaron was already counting the seconds until he could be with Isla again. The weekend had changed things. For the better.

Before, he'd been nervous about them seeing one another, questioning what it meant and what could happen once she got her memory back. He had been operating under the assumption that she was only with him because she couldn't remember the reasons she shouldn't be.

But this weekend, they'd connected on a deeper level.

They'd admitted their growing feelings. And while he hadn't been a hundred percent transparent with her, he'd told her the truth when she asked why they'd never gotten to this point before. They *had* been blind as to who the other person truly was. He'd never allowed himself the chance to really get to know her, to understand and accept her, and in turn, he'd never had an opportunity to show her that there was so much more to him than what she saw on the surface.

This weekend, that had changed.

His phone chimed with a text, and he grinned as he read the message from Isla.

Miss you already.

Miss you more, he responded.

No more games. No more playing it cool. They were

going all in on the feelings they had for one another, and it felt great.

Grabbing his gear, he hummed a holiday tune as he climbed out of the truck and headed into the coast guard station. A rental car was parked in front of the front door, blocking the lane. He sighed. Tourists. If they were there to get the local weather and ice forecast, they could at least park in the lot like everyone else.

At least they were enquiring about safety info.

He entered the building and headed to the locker room, where he changed into his uniform. Before he knew it, Skylar was on his heels as he headed down to the meeting room.

"So?" she asked.

"So what?"

"How was the weekend?"

Mind-blowing, intoxicating, magical, glorious... "Good."

She let out a sigh of exasperation. "Not going to give me anything, huh?"

"I think you'll have to talk to Isla if you want any...details." He wasn't sure if women talked about things the way dudes did. Not that he'd be telling anyone anything that had happened between him and Isla on the weekend. The only person he'd normally share any personal stuff with was Dwayne, and his buddy was still being a bit of an ass. He certainly wouldn't want to hear about what Aaron and Isla had done together.

"Fine," Skylar said with a shrug. "I guess I'll just have to text her and invite her out tonight."

Damn, that meant he wouldn't get a chance to see her that evening. "Hey, Skylar, wait up—"

But too late, his boss had already changed from curious friend to captain. "See you at the staff meeting," she called over her shoulder.

Aaron yawned as he entered the kitchen. He hadn't gotten much sleep on the weekend—not that he was complaining—but he'd need caffeine to stay awake for the end-of-year meeting when Skylar was going to go over the stats regarding that year's rescues.

Normally, he enjoyed the recap, but he could appreciate that it wasn't all that exciting. Not like, say, finger-banging against a tree with an almost-audience.

Damn, Isla had really put things into perspective for him. He couldn't help the smile forming on his face as he entered the staff room.

"Ah, there's the man you were looking for," Dwayne said to someone Aaron couldn't see.

Aaron turned to see who his coworker was talking to and had to do a double take.

His parents sat at the table. His parents were in Port Serenity.

"Mom? Dad? What are you two doing here?" And at the coast guard station of all places. Since Amy's accident, they'd held little respect for the local search and rescue crews and came nowhere near the stations.

Too many bad memories, his mother claimed.

Dressed in their usual professional attire—his father in a gray suit beneath his long overcoat, and his mother in a black, knee-length dress, leather boots and lavish coat—they always looked like they were on a mission.

His mother stood and gave him a quick hug as his father drained the contents of his mug and remained seated. "Hi, honey. Great to see you," she said, but it lacked the warm affection that he assumed most mothers would have when surprising a son they hadn't seen in person in years.

He was still struggling to actually believe they were there. "Hi…"

"We went by your apartment several times when we got into town yesterday afternoon, but you weren't home," she said.

Dwayne shot him a look before saying, "I'll leave you three to talk. Ben, Jackie, always great to see you." He tapped Aaron on the shoulder as he passed, but it wasn't a friendly tap, it was more of a your-parents-are-here-so-you're-in-shit tap. "Take your time. I'll cover for you at the meeting."

As Dwayne left the room, Aaron turned back to his parents. "I thought you were going on a cruise?" Had they changed their minds? Decided to come home for Christmas? Seemed unlikely, so he didn't allow any hope to seep in that they might have had a change of heart and wanted to spend the holidays with him. His gut told him they had an agenda, so he kept his guard firmly in place.

"We still are," his father said. "But we wanted to talk to you."

They'd flown all that way just days before their own holiday plans to talk? He stood straighter and folded his arms across his chest. "About?"

His mother touched his arm and took a deep breath. Her forehead wrinkled the way it always did when she was stressed.

Here we go.

"We know you said you weren't interested in being part of the new organization, Siblings Left Behind," she started, and Aaron's gut tightened. Just the name of the organization sounded so depressing.

"But we thought maybe if you met Alan, the organizer, and spoke to him about what he's hoping to achieve, you might change your mind," she finished quickly.

They were back to this again? They'd flown all the way

to Alaska to try to strong-arm him into this? Unbelievable. "I already told you both I'm not doing it." He'd been very clear on their last call.

"Just meet him. That's all we ask," his father said as though it were a reasonable request.

Meet him? "He's here?" Had the man really flown all this way with his parents to convince Aaron to...what? Give up his life here in Port Serenity, the career he loved—the woman he was falling in love with—to move to Florida and become some figurehead for pain and suffering? His temple throbbed.

His mother nodded. "It was his idea to come here and meet with you. He's a great man, and he has a wonderful idea about launching a program here in Port Serenity, so you wouldn't have to move to Florida..." She continued on in an excited tone as though this should be an easy *yes* for him. Maybe they weren't asking him to relocate, but what they were asking was still huge.

He held up a hand. There was no way he was meeting with this guy: his parents had wasted a lot of time and money coming there to try to change his mind. "I've already given my answer. I have to start my shift. You two should go." He'd known there was a purpose for their visit, but it still hurt being right.

"Aaron," his mother started, pleading in her tone. She reached toward him, but he pulled back. "Think about all the good you could do. You could honor Amy's memory by telling her story and—"

"Mom, I said no!" he said, his voice rising.

She pulled back in alarm, and regret filled him, but damn, they were pushing too much. He was honoring Amy's memory, and it tore a hole through him to hear that they thought he wasn't.

"Do not speak to your mother in that tone, young man," his father said, finally standing.

Aaron fought to control his patience. He hadn't had a mother in forever. Hadn't had either of them in his life in any real, significant way in years. They hadn't supported him or been there for him as he'd finished high school, then gone into the coast guard. They hadn't been there to help him through his pain and grief, too focused on their own. When Amy died, it was as if they'd lost their only child. They hadn't cared enough to try to keep their family together for his sake. He couldn't imagine how difficult losing a child must have been, but he'd given up hope that they'd realize they'd lost two of their children back then, just in different ways, and that time was running out to reconnect with the one they still had.

He shook his head. "You're both wasting your time," he said, his voice breaking. He cleared his throat before continuing. "You know the way out." He stalked out of the room and away from his parents for what felt like the last time.

ISLA KICKED OFF her winter boots and curled her legs up onto the seat across from Skylar at the Serpent Queen Pub later that evening. Inside the local watering hole, Christmas music blared from the speakers, the holiday lights were set to blink, creating an almost strobe-light effect, and the place was packed with several holiday parties and festive get-togethers. They were lucky to secure a booth as another group vacated it.

Aaron had texted earlier that day to say he was working late at almost the same moment Skylar's text had arrived to ask if she was free to meet that evening for drinks. It was a little suspicious. As though Skylar had pulled rank for a girls' night out.

Her suspicions were confirmed as Skylar leaned forward on the table and said, "Start at the beginning, and don't leave anything out."

She pretended not to know what Skylar was talking about, but her brother's fiancée was obviously eager to hear the juicy details of Isla's weekend with Aaron. "I don't know what you're talking about." She eyed the drink menu, not really reading the choices. She was excited to tell someone about her and Aaron. All she could think about that day was the incredible time they'd had together.

"I approved the time-off request. I know you two went away together this weekend."

Isla laughed as she eyed her pointedly. "Do you gush about you and Dex?"

Skylar raised an eyebrow. "Do you want me to gush about my relationship with your brother?"

"Nope. You're right. That's gross," she said with a laugh. Even though she'd only really gotten reacquainted with Dex over the last few weeks, she suspected Skylar had a point. There were some things she was better off not knowing. "Do you really want to hear about me and one of your crew?"

"As long as it's not one I'm related to, then yeah. Come on. I'm dying to hear how it went. He wouldn't give me anything today at the station."

Isla's ears perked. "What did he say?"

"That it was *good*."

"*Good*. That's it?"

"I knew it! It was spectacular, wasn't it?"

That was one way she'd describe it. "It was…incredible," she said, feeling heat rush to her cheeks. She couldn't deny it had been amazing, and she was actually excited to tell Skylar about it. "He canceled my yurt-rental reservation and booked one of the treehouse cabins." She opened her cell phone and showed Skylar the pictures she'd taken of the cabin and the surroundings.

Skylar scrolled through the pics and stopped at a selfie of Isla and Aaron wrapped up together in bed. She cleared her throat and raised an eyebrow.

"What? I told you it was amazing." Isla sipped her martini, her cheeks flushing with heat as she avoided Skylar's gaze. "All of it."

"Oh my God! You're falling in love with him."

No sense in denying it. She didn't want to. It felt so great. So right. She nodded. "He said he was falling for me too."

Skylar sat back in the booth and shook her head. "I can't believe the two of you are together." She looked slightly worried as she asked, "Have you two talked about your past? You know, that you might not have always been this close?"

Isla took another sip and nodded. "We did, and we came to the conclusion that maybe we were just prejudiced against one another without really knowing each other."

Skylar looked relieved. "I'd agree with that." She smiled. "So, you're going to continue dating?"

"We are." Unless anyone could think of a good reason why they shouldn't, Isla was going all in.

All in in love.

A waiter arrived at the table with a fresh round of shots, and Skylar frowned as she shook her head. "Sorry, we haven't ordered yet."

The server nodded toward the pool tables where two men were playing. "These are on Dwayne."

Skylar's smile looked forced as she raised one of the shot

glasses in the men's direction. Isla grinned. "Should I tell my brother that he has some competition?"

Skylar nearly choked on the liquid. "Hardly," she said. "These are because of you."

"Me?" Isla glanced toward the men, but she didn't really recognize either of them, though one was staring at her with unconcealed interest. It made her slightly uncomfortable. "Am I supposed to know the tall younger good-looking one with the Ryan Gosling grin?" Her memory of hot movie stars had clearly been unaffected in her accident.

"That's Dwayne. He was the helicopter pilot that rescued you from the crevasse."

"Oh…" She should have remembered to thank the others involved in her rescue that day.

"And…you two dated for a few months earlier this year," Skylar said.

She'd dated him? Isla glanced back at the guy quickly, trying to see the attraction. He was good-looking and muscular and had a confident air about him, but there was nothing stirring inside her to indicate that there were any feelings of attraction there. Or had ever been.

She shrugged. "I don't recognize him."

"Aaron didn't mention the rift you've caused between them?" Skylar asked.

Isla's eyes widened. "No! I'm causing trouble between them at work?" That had never been her intention. She hadn't known there was any friction between the two men. How serious had she been with this Dwayne guy? Was there some sort of bro code between crew members? Had that been part of Aaron's hesitancy to date her in the first place?

Skylar waved a hand. "It's nothing. They'll get over it," she said.

Isla could still feel the other man's eyes on her as she

sipped the shot. A dry gin flavor. Gross. She pushed the drink aside, feeling as though drinking it would somehow be betraying Aaron.

"Anyway, Aaron has bigger issues right now besides your past with Dwayne," Skylar said, a worried expression crossing her pretty features.

Isla frowned. "Why? What's going on?"

Skylar sighed. "He didn't tell you?"

"Tell me what?"

"His parents are in town, and from what I overheard in the staff lunch room today, they are trying to get him to head up some sort of grief organization," Skylar said, sympathy for Aaron in her voice. "They've really been pushing him to be more involved in their charities since his sister died."

Isla's heart lurched slightly. He hadn't mentioned anything by text that day… "They came by the station?" They hadn't talked about his family much, but from what Aaron *had* confided, his parents were totally unsupportive of his chosen career. It must have been a shock to see them there.

Skylar nodded. "He seemed pretty messed up after they left. That's why he offered to take the double shift. I think he just needed to stay busy—preoccupied, you know?"

Isla swallowed hard but forced an understanding look as she nodded. "Of course, yeah…" But it was hard to understand why he wouldn't have told her, relied on her… She thought they were close enough that he'd confide in her with something this important.

But he hadn't mentioned anything about her previous relationship with Dwayne or how that was impacting things at work either. They needed to talk. As much as she appreciated him wanting to protect her from things while she struggled with trying to regain her memory, she needed him to know that this relationship was a two-way street. She was there for him too.

It was difficult to think about anything else as she finished her drink with Skylar, and the moment the two women parted ways, Isla headed to Aaron's house. It was just after ten o'clock, and she saw his truck in the driveway and the apartment lights on.

He looked surprised when he opened the door to her a few moments later. Dressed in just a pair of gray pajama pants, his hair messy and his five-o'clock stubble turning into a messy beard at his jawline, she'd never seen him looking anything but confident and in control. This evening he looked like a hot mess.

"Hey, you. I thought you were out with Skylar tonight?" he asked, running a hand through his hair.

She stepped inside and wrapped her arms around him tight. She may not be able to help solve the issues with his family, but she could hold him and be a source of support, the way he'd been to her throughout all of the things she was dealing with.

His arms immediately went around her, and she felt his body sag slightly in relief that she was there. "Skylar mentioned my parents' surprise visit?" he asked, his voice sounding strained with emotion.

Among other things. But right now that was most important. She'd ask him about Dwayne another time.

She pulled back slowly and studied his pained expression. She'd never seen him this way. "You should have told me you needed me. I could have come over," she said.

He pulled her inside, wrapped his arms tight around her, and Isla felt some of the heaviness he was feeling ease a little as he said, "I do need you. Thank you for coming over."

She looked at him, and the hurt in his expression broke

her heart. She touched his face gently and stood on tip-toes to kiss him. Talking could wait. Right now she sensed he could use a different kind of comfort. She pressed her body closer and deepened the kiss, feeling his grip on her waist tighten.

Breaking contact with her mouth, he bent and scooped her into his arms, carrying her into the apartment and toward his bedroom.

Inside his room, he removed her jacket and placed her gently on the bed.

She watched him remove his sweatpants and underwear, immediately turned on by the sight of him naked in front of her. She lifted her arms for him to remove her sweater. He tugged at the waistband of her leggings, seductively rolling them off over her legs.

She lay there in her bra and underwear, anticipation coursing through her as he climbed onto the bed and moved toward her. He gripped her face between his hands and kissed her hard, as though he couldn't control the force of his desire for her—as though the cure for the stress of his day was in her kiss.

She wrapped her arms around his neck as he unhooked her bra and removed it. He massaged her breasts with one hand as he held her body close.

"Damn, Isla, I've never known passion like this. You're everything I want. Everything I crave," he said. "You make everything better."

Her heart pounded. She felt the same way. She wanted every inch of him close to her. All the time. This obsession couldn't be healthy, but it felt as though she were filling an overdue need, something she'd deprived herself of for too long...

He turned their bodies over so that he lay on top of her.

He lowered his mouth to her neck, and she tilted her head back as he kissed his way down, along her collarbone to the swell of her breasts. His hands massaged as his mouth savored. Her body tingled, and the ache between her legs got stronger.

She reached down to remove her underwear, lifting her hips to lower them down her thighs. Aaron removed them the rest of the way and sat up to take her in. Exposed and vulnerable. He ran a hand along her thighs, up over her hip and stomach, all the way to her heart. His hand rested there as his gaze burned into hers. "I need you," he said. "And I don't just mean your body. I mean you. All of you. Your heart, your soul, your every breath, every heartbeat…"

"You have it." Part of her suspected he always had.

He lowered himself between her legs and, taking her hands, he lifted her arms above her head as his mouth found hers. His kiss started slow, teasing, his tongue tracing her lips before slipping between them.

She opened her legs wider, and he rested between as she arched her back to bring their bodies closer. She needed to feel him inside her. She wanted to comfort him, make him feel better any way she could. He reached for a condom and slid it on slowly. Then he entered her ready and eager body.

With her hands pinned above her head, Aaron filled her body with his big, thick cock. She swallowed hard as he plunged deeper and harder.

"Look at me," he said.

She opened her eyes and stared into his as he continued to move in and out of her, quickening the pace and intensity as their desperation grew.

"I love…being with you," she said, chickening out of the full disclosure at the last second.

"I love you," he said, his voice full of emotion.

She smiled, feeling all the warmth and affection enveloping her. "That's what I meant."

"I know," he said as his mouth found hers once more, and they enjoyed the sensations of lust and love that she thought she'd never get enough of. There was still so much they needed to talk about, but in that moment, she could feel him healing through their physical connection, and she was happy that she could be there for him in this way.

For now, that was all that mattered.

CHAPTER TWENTY-TWO

HER CELL PHONE ringing woke her the next morning, and Isla reached for it quickly and climbed out of Aaron's bed where he still slept soundly. She'd stayed the night, and they'd barely slept, holding one another. He didn't talk much about his parents' surprise appearance or the reason for the visit, but she knew he was happy to have her there.

The private investigator's number lit up the call display, and her heart raced as she headed out of the room. Keeping her voice low, she answered the call. "Hello?"

"Hey, Isla?"

"Yeah."

"Did you get the email I sent?" Straight to the point as always.

She sighed. "No. I'm still having some memory issues, and apparently I've never written down any passwords." She'd need to eventually reset everything, but she'd been hoping she'd have regained her memory by now.

"Okay. Well, give me two minutes, and I'll send the photos to your phone by text, as long as you are okay with receiving them that way," Hunter said.

"Photos?"

"Of your birth mother—or at least, the woman I've identified as a possibility."

Her birth mother. He said it so casually, as though it were just another day at the office. For him, she suspected it was. He didn't get attached to his clients or the cases, but her throat felt thick as she answered, "Yes, please send them by text."

"Will do. Talk soon."

The call disconnected, and Isla's hand shook slightly as she waited for the texts to arrive. She paced the hallway. What would she do if he had found her? Would she actually go through with meeting the woman? Right now, she couldn't remember the family who'd raised her. She was already dealing with so much. What could she even say to the woman given the circumstances? It wasn't as though she could recount her childhood or convey any emotional turmoil she'd experienced by being put up for adoption when she had no memory of any of that. Her journal entries were far too raw. She could never share those—and she'd lost the necklace.

Meeting the woman under these circumstances didn't seem like the best idea.

Her phone chimed, and she jumped, as though she'd forgotten she was waiting for something.

"Hey, you okay?" Aaron asked, appearing in the hallway behind her before she could open the messages.

A sense of relief washed over her. She was grateful she was there with him. She'd come there the night before to support him, but it was her who could use the support this morning. "The investigator looking for my birth mother sent photos…"

His arms immediately went around her waist, and he held her tight. "You don't have to do this right now if you're not ready."

Was she ready? Could she ever be ready for something like this?

She took a deep breath and raised the phone between them. "I can't not look."

"Do you want privacy?" he asked.

"No. I want you to stay right here. Keep those arms around me."

"You got it," he said, looking almost as nervous as she felt as she clicked on the first message and looked at the slightly blurry image of a woman going into an apartment building.

She brought the image closer, zooming in on the side profile of the woman's face. Light hair, streaked with gray, high cheekbones on a thin face. Impossible to tell if it was the same woman in the photo in her hotel room.

She clicked on the next one. The woman had turned to face the camera, a mild look of surprise in her expression as though realizing she was being photographed.

Isla's stomach turned. It felt wrong somehow. As though she'd hired someone to stalk this woman. Having some man following and photographing her mother, or maybe even worse—a stranger—made her feel slightly ill.

"This seems wrong," she said to Aaron. "I mean, it's been more than twenty years. If this woman wanted to be found, if she wanted to reconnect with me, she would have by now, right?" It was unfair to pressure someone into meeting her if she didn't want to, if she'd never had the desire to herself, if she'd accepted the decisions from the past and moved on with her life. Maybe she had a new family now. One that didn't know about Isla. She couldn't disrupt this woman's life out of her own selfish desire to know her.

"Maybe she couldn't. You said the terms of the adoption prevented her from contacting you," Aaron said gently.

"That was when I was young. Now I'm an adult, so those terms wouldn't still apply."

"Well, maybe she has searched for you too, but had no luck."

She appreciated his attempt to try to make her feel better, but she knew deep down that wasn't the case. She sighed as she stared at the photo of the woman, looking for any sign of familiarity. Some family resemblance… "I don't know if this is a good idea, and I have no idea why I started this process in the first place. My parents are certainly not on board with it. Dex didn't even know I was doing it, and I feel like it's something I would have at least shared with him. They all seem disappointed that I'm looking for her. As though they somehow all failed to give me everything I needed."

Aaron placed his hands on her shoulders and bent at the knees to look into her eyes. "Hey, this isn't about them. I'm sure they know that. I'm sure they understand."

She wasn't. She hadn't spoken to either of her parents since the day she'd talked to them about it and her mother had given her the journals. Over a week ago.

"Either way, it doesn't matter. *You* deserve to know. To have any questions answered. Know where you came from," Aaron said supportively.

But did it truly matter? She had a wonderful family who'd given her everything she could ever want and more—a full, amazingly privileged life. Why wasn't that enough? What answers were so important that she needed to do this?

"I'm here, whatever you need. Whatever you decide," he said.

Isla sighed as she hugged him tighter, grateful that at least her past didn't have any effect on this connection with Aaron.

HE'D HAVE PREFERRED staying in bed with Isla all day. With the emotional toll the last twenty-four hours had taken on both of them, he was exhausted, and he couldn't imagine how conflicted she must be feeling after the call from the investigator. He may have issues with his parents, but hers seemed more complicated. He had no idea what she would decide to do, but he would be there to support her in any capacity. Her coming to him the night before had been exactly the support he'd needed, even if he hadn't wanted to ask for it.

Telling her he loved her had been easy. He did love her, and hearing that she felt the same way was the only thing propelling him forward today.

"The forecasted snowstorm has been upgraded to a full blizzard warning..." Local news reporter Monica Mallard stated on the television in the locker room as Aaron changed into his uniform for his shift.

Great.

He shut the locker and headed toward the meeting room just as a call came in from local authorities. A fishing boat had capsized ten nautical miles offshore. Three men onboard, now all overboard.

Skylar brought the crew together, and Aaron shook off his exhaustion and all distracting thoughts as they launched their rescue plan. Less than five minutes later, he followed Dwayne and Miller to the waiting chopper.

The weather was frigid with blowing snow and poor visibility. The men shouldn't have been out in the first place.

"This is bullshit," Dwayne mumbled as they climbed in.

First thing the two of them had agreed on in a long time.

Noticing the fuel gauge, he nodded toward the fueling station. "Better fuel up." Something Dwayne should have done after their last rescue. This would waste precious time, but Aaron kept his annoyance in check.

Dwayne shook his head. "No time. They aren't far off the coast. We'll be fine."

An argument was on the tip of his tongue, but Dwayne was the pilot; he had his own job to focus on. He needed to rely on and trust his coworker's judgment call.

Inside the chopper as it lifted off and headed toward the men's last-known location, Aaron braced himself for the freezing plunge he was about to take. Three men in the water meant three times he'd have to jump into the tossing waves to bring them all to safety. His thermal wetsuit would only keep him warm for so long.

"Boat spotted," Miller said over the radio as the tiny fishing vessel came into view.

"I can't get any closer," Dwayne said, struggling to keep the chopper steady in the forty-mile-an-hour winds.

"Dropping in," Aaron said. He jumped from the helicopter and free-fell what seemed like forever. He braced himself as an instant freeze enveloped him as his body hit the water, and he started swimming against the current toward the capsized boat. All three men were holding on and staying afloat as best they could as it was tossed about on the waves. They'd been in the water for almost an hour. Hypothermia and exhaustion would have set in, and they'd be useless in helping with their own rescue. This was all on him.

The pushback from the current made the swim that much more challenging, and Aaron's limbs ached under the strain of his fast pace.

He reached the vessel and grabbed the closest man. He quickly attached the harness and once the man was secured, he motioned for Miller to hoist them. The man was conscious, but his lips were blue, and he was moments from passing out.

The second plunge was even harder, and the third had Aaron's fight-or-flight reactions kicking in, challenging him mentally as well as physically.

He could do this. One more. Push through.

You're fine, keep going.

Isla's forearm tattoo and the words she told herself in challenging times echoed in his mind as he swam harder against the waves toward the last man. He'd let go of the boat and was drifting lower beneath the surface of the water.

Unhooking from the harness attached to the chopper, Aaron took a deep inhale and plunged beneath the icy waves. He scanned and spotted the man trapped beneath the capsized boat. He made his way toward it and wrapped an arm around the unconscious victim, then struggled to bring them both up to the surface—where he saw the helicopter move back toward the shoreline. Back toward the station.

What the hell was Dwayne doing?

"Too low on fuel," Miller's voice came over the radio.

Damn. He'd told Dwayne they should refuel.

Aaron's legs felt like jelly as he treaded water, desperate to keep them both afloat. The man had to weigh over two hundred and fifty pounds, and the additional deadweight made it nearly impossible. His arms ached, and his chest was tight.

Remain calm. Remember your training.

With his gear, he could last in the water maybe twenty minutes, but the other man was in serious danger. Aaron held on to him tight, kicking against the strong current, heading in the direction of the shoreline. He'd never make it the full way, but at least the swimming made his muscles move and helped to elevate his body temperature. Of course, it might also make them harder to locate, having moved from the original rescue point, but staying still would definitely be worse. Blowing snow made it hard to see which direction he was swimming in, but he continued on, hoping he wasn't putting them more at risk.

Moments later, exhaustion and a numbing sensation in his limbs were provoking a sense of panic. He wasn't sure either of them were going to make it. He could hear the chopper in the distance, but it sounded far away.

Too far...

Frigid waves crashed over him, and they dipped below the surface. Aaron struggled to hold on to the unconscious man as he continued to move his limbs through the water, back to the surface.

Then it felt as though a force from beneath him was pushing through the current in front of him, leading the way and reducing the force of impact against him. He squinted through the snow and crashing water.

Sealena?

A sense of calm enveloped him, and he found renewed strength as he continued to swim. Had the Sea Serpent Queen come to his rescue? Or was the cold numbness impacting his imagination? Either way, he no longer felt terrified, the panic eased, and he was able to once again think clearly.

He saw the chopper overhead and stopped swimming as the harness was dropped. He grabbed it and secured them both. His body leaving the water gave him a rush of relief. They were going to be okay.

He scanned the water below as he was lifted, but only the tumultuous waves were in sight. No sign of anyone—or anything—else out there.

Safe inside the chopper, Miller helped secure the patient, wrapping warming blankets around them both.

"Sorry about that, buddy," Dwayne said over the radio, a deep-sounding remorse in his tone.

"No problem, man. Another day at the office," he said, shivering and exhausted as the chopper headed back to the station.

Unfortunately, Skylar wasn't so forgiving three hours later.

"You knowingly went with low fuel," she said, her voice tight as he, Miller and Dwayne sat in her office for the rescue debrief.

"Low fuel meant I could get there faster," Dwayne said. "The men had been in the water for too long. I was following my gut."

"And it was wrong. You put everyone's safety at risk. You put your crewmate's safety at risk," Skylar said.

Aaron didn't disagree, but he also couldn't say that Dwayne's instincts on it had been completely wrong. In hindsight, it was impossible to say what might have happened if different judgment calls had been made, so he didn't remind his coworker that he'd suggested refueling.

"If the idea had been Aaron's, you'd have no problem with it," Dwayne said.

"That's not true," Skylar said, but even Aaron could hear the slight wonder in her tone whether she might be treating the situation differently. She cleared her throat, a note of authority to her voice. "You're suspended for two weeks."

Dwayne looked at her in disbelief. "One of the most hazardous times of year, and you're taking me off duty?"

Skylar nodded, and to her credit, she didn't seem to be wavering, despite what Aaron suspected was one of the hardest decisions she'd had to make so far in her career. The crew were close. They were all friends, and they were like a family. This wasn't just a disciplinary thing: it hurt on a personal level.

"Skylar, I know the decision seemed hasty, but it didn't end badly," Aaron said, coming to his buddy's defense.

"It could have," she said. "My decision sticks."

Dwayne stood abruptly, his chair hitting the wall. "I don't need you fighting my battles," Dwayne said to him, shoulder-nudging Aaron as he stalked out of the office. A moment later, they heard the slam of his locker door down the hall.

Skylar looked distraught as she shook her head. "That sucked."

"Two weeks? I'm not questioning your call, but are you sure it's not too harsh?" Dwayne may have been wrong in his assessment of the situation, but he was right about them needing him this time of year especially.

"You could have died," Skylar said. "And I need him to get his head on straight and not let personal issues cloud his judgment. I'll talk to him privately."

She thought Dwayne's beef with him over Isla had maybe impacted his actions that day. Aaron refused to believe his friend would take things that far, but he nodded. "Understood."

Unfortunately, now his safety was in the hands of a less qualified pilot during one of the most treacherous times of the year.

THE MOST CHALLENGING part of dating a local hero was listening to the rescue story and hearing how he'd had to put his life on the line. But if Isla wanted to be with Aaron, she had to accept his chosen career. After all, he'd been nothing but supportive of her.

And she did have to admit that the idea of him rescuing three people was insanely sexy.

Sitting next to him in the booth at the Serpent Queen Pub that evening, Isla clung to his hand under the table, not wanting to let go as the crew celebrated that day's successful rescue. Unfortunately, Aaron seemed a little stressed.

"You okay?" she whispered.

He nodded and offered a weak smile. "Just still feel shitty about Dwayne."

She'd quickly noticed that the pilot wasn't there that evening, and he'd explained what had happened and Skylar's decision.

"I hate that I've played a part in this," she said.

"It's not your fault. This goes deeper than just you and I dating," Aaron said.

No doubt it had to be difficult for the other alpha males on the crew to accept that Aaron was the best they had with his extra elite training. It couldn't be easy on guys like Dwayne.

"Why didn't you mention I'd dated Dwayne?" she asked, sensing the opportunity.

Aaron shrugged. "It hadn't seemed serious for you, but I guess it was for him."

Her eyes narrowed. "How do you know it wasn't for me?" She knew it mustn't have been. She felt zero attraction to the handsome helicopter pilot, and while he seemed like a nice guy, there wasn't any lingering spark or tension. Had there ever been? Maybe that was the way she'd preferred things before: casual, no strings, no real feelings, no potential to get hurt...

Aaron thought for a moment. "You two just didn't seem passionate about one another."

She nodded slowly. "And what about us?"

"There's definitely passion between us," he murmured, drawing her into him.

It was true. She could feel the heat of their intense attraction to one another every time they were together. When she was with him, she wanted to crawl into his arms and stay where she felt safe and secure—and loved. When she was away from Aaron, he was never far from her thoughts, and she looked forward to the moment she could see him again.

They'd admitted their feelings, and she knew hers were only growing stronger each day, every moment they spent together.

"Well, I'm sorry for driving a wedge between you two," she said sincerely.

"It will work out," he assured her.

She really hoped so, because she hated the thought that Aaron was putting his safety in the hands of a guy holding a grudge.

AT THE COMMUNITY CENTER the next morning, Isla waved to her rock-climbing group as they left. Great group of kids, especially when they weren't trying to prank her with fake names.

The door reopened, and she saw her mother enter with a box of clothing donations. She smiled nervously as Grace approached. She'd been meaning to reach out to her, but she still had no idea what she was going to do about the investigator, and it seemed like a challenging conversation to have.

"Hey, just dropping off some donations," Grace said, giving her a quick hug. "You're still teaching the rock-climbing course?"

Isla nodded. "Yeah. Apparently my muscles remember what to do even if I don't."

"That's great. And you got your cast off," her mother said, pointing to her leg.

"Not too long ago." Damn, she should have at least reached out to let them know that. "I'm feeling much better."

"No memory yet?"

"Not yet," she said.

A silence fell between them, and Isla shifted her weight from one foot to the other.

"Hey, I wanted to—"

"Your father and I—"

They both spoke at the same time and then laughed.

"Go ahead," her mother said.

"I just wanted to say that I'm sorry about the other day. I really didn't mean to upset you."

Her mother shook her head. "No, you have every right to look into your past. Your father and I want you to know we are here to support you in this. You don't have to do it alone."

A warmness enveloped her as she smiled. "Thank you." She hesitated. "Actually, there is something you could maybe help me with." She took out her cell phone. "The investigator sent photos of a woman…" She opened the messages, and Grace glanced over her shoulder at the images.

She enlarged the photo on the screen and nodded slowly. "It's been a long time, but yeah, this could be her."

Unexplainable emotions confused Isla further as she tucked the cell phone away. "Thank you."

"Are you…planning to meet her?" her mother asked.

Was she? She had no idea, but she did know one thing. "I haven't decided, but if I do, will you and Dad come with me?"

Tears shone in the back of her mother's eyes, but she

smiled warmly. "Of course we will." She hugged her quickly. "Whatever you decide, we'll do it as a family."

Isla hadn't realized just how incredible her family truly was, but she knew she'd never do anything to risk what she had.

AARON SET THE WEIGHTS back on the rack and reached for his towel later that day in the station's workout room. It sucked not having a spotter. As much as Dwayne had been a pain in the ass lately, he missed his friend and coworker. The whole thing had gotten out of hand, and Aaron just hoped his buddy could eventually accept him and Isla together.

He hoped more than just Dwayne could. Isla had invited him to attend her father's work party with her that evening, and he'd easily agreed, but the more he thought about it, the more nervous he was. He'd known the Wakefields his entire life, but what would they think about him dating their daughter? Especially given their history?

A knock sounded on the door, and he glanced toward it.

"Your parents are here," Miller said, popping his head in. "Want me to tell them to take a hike?"

Tempting, but Aaron needed to face them and this issue head-on. "I'll be right out," he said. He took several deep breaths and pulled his T-shirt on as he left the gym and met his parents in the front office of the station. "Hey," he said, folding his arms across his chest and preparing for another repeat of the same old argument. Hopefully for the last time. As much as it would hurt, he knew it was time to cut ties with them. He'd never be able to give them what they wanted, and they'd never appreciate his way of dealing with loss. The relationship had become a toxic one.

"We're headed to the airport, but we just wanted to stop in to say goodbye," his father said.

Goodbye.

The word sounded so finite. They'd obviously reached the same conclusion he had.

Aaron nodded. "Have a safe flight home."

His mother looked slightly pained as she glanced at his father and stepped toward him. "We also wanted to say that we're sorry."

His arms fell to his sides. Hadn't been expecting that. He wasn't quite sure what to say, and he still wasn't convinced this wasn't just another ploy, another manipulative attempt, to get him to agree to what they wanted, so he remained silent and waited for her to continue.

"We heard about the rescue yesterday," she said. Tears burned in her eyes as she touched his arm gently, quickly. "You were very brave."

The words hit him straight in the heart, and a lump rose in the back of his throat. For the first time they were acknowledging what he did—the good he did in his own way.

"You saved three people's lives...and you were out in that water for a long time," his father said. A deep look of respect crossed the older man's features, and Aaron was left speechless, so he simply nodded.

"We are proud of you," his mother said.

Aaron thought his knees might actually give out from beneath him. He'd never expected to ever hear those words from his parents. Hadn't realized just how much he needed to hear them. Maybe this didn't need to be the end. Maybe this was a turning point in the relationship. He cleared his throat. "Thank you. That means a lot." Everything, actually.

His mother stepped closer and hugged him, and Aaron squeezed her tight before releasing her. His father extended a hand toward him, and he shook it, feeling a sense of peace that had eluded him for so long.

"Merry Christmas, son," his father said.

"Merry Christmas," he said, his voice thick with emotion as his parents waved goodbye and left the station.

CHAPTER TWENTY-THREE

"So...HOW ARE YOU at boring, obligatory dinner parties?"
Isla asked casually later that evening in Aaron's truck when
he picked her up from the hotel. He seemed happier, lighter
that evening, and she suspected it had everything to do with
the small step toward reconciling with his parents earlier
that day. She was so relieved that his parents were finally
seeing him for the amazing man he was.

"The best," he said just as casually, pulling her toward
him for a kiss.

"Small talk?"

"My specialty," he said, leaving a trail of kisses along
her neck.

Goose bumps surfaced on her skin despite the heat of
the truck, and she moved away slightly. If he kept doing
that, they'd never make it to her parents' house for the party.
"And what about meeting the parents? Does that freak you
out at all?" Might be a little late in asking. He had already
agreed to go, but she wanted to make sure he was really
okay with it.

"I've met your parents at least a dozen times, so no."

She laughed. "This is in a different capacity..." Her parents might know Aaron, but they didn't know the two of
them together. Showing up at her father's holiday do with
Aaron as her date might be a little awkward. But she wanted
him there.

"What capacity, exactly?" he asked, putting the vehicle in Drive.

He wanted her to put a label on them? She'd been hoping he would. "Well, I guess we are seeing one another."

He nodded. "Exclusively."

"Right. And you did confess that you were falling in love with me, so we're more than just dating…"

He grinned as he sent her a quick look. "Isla Wakefield, will you—" he took a deep breath and looked very serious as he finished "—be my girlfriend?"

"Your girlfriend?"

He grinned wickedly. "What did you think I was going to ask?"

She leaned across the seat and kissed him. "Yes, I'll be your girlfriend."

"Great, that's settled then." He sent her a wink and took her hand in his as they drove the rest of the way to the Wakefield family home.

But her anxiety rose moments later as they entered, and she heard the sound of Dwayne's voice coming from the living room.

Dwayne's loud, slightly tipsy-sounding voice.

"I hadn't realized he'd be here," she said quickly to Aaron. It struck her that she had no idea who was on the guest list for that evening. It hadn't really seemed to matter.

"His mother works with your dad. Makes sense," Aaron said, obviously trying to sound like he was unfazed. "Don't worry. It will be fine," he reassured, straightening the red tie, which he'd bought to match her dress, beneath his suit jacket.

Isla held his hand as they entered the main room where all the guests were gathered. About twenty formally dressed men and women mingled and chatted, drinking champagne.

Classical piano Christmas music played, and the event held an air of elegance that she'd come to associate with her family.

A slight feeling of being out of place struck her, and she tugged at the hem of her red minidress. Maybe she should have worn something a little more reserved. She spotted Skylar and Dex across the room and wished she'd opted for a long black formal like Skylar had. She should have talked to the other woman first.

"You look amazing," Aaron whispered next to her, and her anxiety eased just a little. "I've been dreaming of this dress since you wore it to the Sealena anniversary party."

But when Dwayne's gaze fell on them, Aaron only held her hand tighter, and the tension around them instantly thickened. This was the first time the two of them had been in the same room together since Dwayne's suspension.

"Hey, darlin'. Hi, Aaron," her mother greeted them pleasantly. "Drink?"

"Sure," Isla said, glancing at him. He nodded.

Grace reached for the champagne and handed two glasses to them, but Dwayne called out, "Hey, Isla, come do a shot!"

Her eyes widened as she shook her head, laughing awkwardly. Everyone in the room had turned to look at her.

"I'm okay with the champagne, thanks," she said.

Dwayne scoffed. "You've been hanging around with this guy too long." He nodded toward Aaron before downing his own shot with a shrug that said *Suit yourself.* He refilled the shot glass as several guests watched the interaction.

Isla's pulse raced. Things were a little more awkward than she'd expected with Dwayne being there, and she suspected they weren't going to get easier as her father approached.

"Hey, sweetheart. Glad you could make it," Brian said, kissing her cheek. As usual, he was impeccably dressed and oozed a quiet confidence. "Aaron," he said, shaking hands with him, but Isla could hear a note of disapproval in his tone.

Which part did he disapprove of?

"Can I borrow her for just a sec?" he asked.

Aaron reluctantly released her hand. "Of course."

"There are a few partners I want you to meet," Brian said, and Isla's chest tightened. She should have expected this evening would be another attempt at getting her to pursue a law degree. She sighed and sent Aaron an apologetic look as her father took her arm and led her away.

So much for a pleasurable evening, introducing her new boyfriend to her family.

HE REFUSED TO feel intimidated by the room full of rich people.

Most of them he'd known his entire life. Half of them he'd helped in times of danger, or their family members. He had no reason to feel out of place or inferior.

Just because Dwayne's family status matched equally with Isla's didn't make the other man the better match for Isla. She'd invited him there that evening, and he'd have to get used to events like this with her family if he wanted to be with her.

Which he desperately did. Whatever that meant.

He strolled through the house, sipping his champagne. He saw Isla chatting politely with several lawyers from her father's firm. She sent him a desperate look, and he sent back a supportive one. Obviously, she hadn't mentioned her intentions of a social-work career to her family, and Brian was still pushing the law route.

He'd been looking forward to showing up there on her arm, presenting themselves to her family, but now he was looking forward to the night being over. He suspected this was more stressful for her than fun.

Entering the den, he saw Brian pat Dwayne on the back as the two men drank scotch together. "I think you made the right call," the older man said. "Those Beaumonts don't always know what's best."

So the family feud between the Beaumonts and Wakefields might not be as buried as everyone in the community thought.

Noticing him, Brian waved him inside the room. "Come on in. We were just talking about the rescue. Impressive," Isla's father said, pouring another glass and handing it to him.

He wasn't a scotch guy, but he accepted the glass and the toast with his girlfriend's father and his crewmate. They clinked glasses, and he took a swig.

"I think Brian here would love to hear what your intentions are with his daughter," Dwayne said with a smirk, steadying himself against the bar.

Great, his friend was drunk and intent on making a scene.

"Isla and I are seeing one another. Things are going well," he said tightly. He wouldn't allow his friend to make him look like a fool. He wanted to make a good impression on Brian. It was important to him to be accepted by the family.

"Well, we know how long Isla's attention span is, now, don't we?" Dwayne said with a cold-sounding laugh.

Aaron's gut twisted, and his jaw clenched at the insult.

"Enough of that, Dwayne," Brian chastised before Aaron could defend her.

Dwayne held up his hands innocently. "What? I'm just stating a fact. Isla doesn't like commitment."

Aaron turned to see Isla enter the room, a look of confusion on her face as she took in the scene and heard Dwayne's words. Brian gestured her forward. "I think she's matured a lot in recent months. She's actually considering law school."

Isla looked uncomfortable as she stood with her father's arm draped across her shoulders. "Um, actually, Dad, I'm not. I've decided to go into social work," she said confidently. Clearly, it wasn't the way she'd wanted to tell her father.

Aaron was proud of her for telling him. He knew it couldn't have been an easy declaration to make, especially given the circumstances and the event.

Brian frowned. "Since when?"

"See? Classic Isla. I'm sure she'll change her mind," Dwayne said, cutting off Isla's chance to speak.

"Okay, that's enough," Aaron said. He was done with his friend's bullshit.

"Because you say it is?" Dwayne said, advancing toward him.

Aaron set his drink down on the bar and met the man toe-to-toe. Dwayne couldn't continue insulting Isla in her own home. "I think you've had too much to drink, and you owe Isla an apology."

"Going to make me, big man?" Dwayne challenged, snarling at him.

"That's enough, you two," Brian said, extending an arm between them.

There was no way Aaron was going to give Dwayne the satisfaction of losing his cool. Not in front of Isla and her family and her father's colleagues. He wouldn't escalate this in the family home, or elsewhere. His buddy wasn't worth it. He relaxed his shoulders. "No one is making you do anything, but it's probably time to leave."

Dwayne looked ready to argue, but then he shrugged, set his drink down and stalked out of the den. The front door slammed a moment later.

Aaron turned to Brian. "Sorry about that." He touched Isla's shoulder. "You okay?"

She nodded. "Fine," she said, though she sounded unsure as she turned to her father. "I hope you're not disappointed."

Brian shook his head. "No. Just surprised. I had no idea you were interested in that career."

"I am, and it's not a new thing. In my journals, I mentioned my interest several times. I've enrolled for classes starting in January," she said, reaching for Aaron's hand.

Brian nodded slowly, then smiled. "Well, I think it's a great idea."

"You do?"

"Whatever—and whoever—makes you happy is fine with me," her father said, raising his glass once again to Aaron.

Relief ran through him at her father's acceptance. He might not be rich, but he loved this man's daughter as much as he suspected Brian did, and it felt great to have the older man's approval.

To feel like part of a family again.

CHAPTER TWENTY-FOUR

THREE DAYS UNTIL CHRISTMAS, and the kids were in frantic mode getting their last-minute wish lists to the big guy. Isla's face hurt from the plastered-on smile she had four hours into her shift at Santa's Village. She was happy she'd gotten a job that season, but she'd cross off customer-service positions from her list of possible future careers. This was exhausting.

With local schools bringing kids on field trips for the last day of school before Christmas break, it was utter chaos with teachers trying to wrangle sugar-hyped children and keep them occupied while in line. She'd heard every rendition of every Christmas carol ever written in the last four hours.

Another hour and then she was off. This was her final shift for the season. Santa was headed back to the North Pole the following day to get ready for his big night.

A new school group approached, and Isla ushered them inside. "Hey, friends! Is this your first visit to see Santa this year?"

Most kids nodded, but several shook their heads. One little girl broke out of the line and approached. Her peeling name tag on her school uniform said *Tess*. "Hi. You're Isla Wakefield, right?" she whispered.

"Yes, I'm Isla. Do we know each other?"

"Sort of. I'm Tess Klein. My dad is the lighthouse keeper."

"Oh…hi." The lighthouse stood high on the hill overlooking the marina, but she hadn't realized anyone actually still did that job.

"This is my second time to see Santa this year," the little girl said, "but I have a question."

"Okay."

"I know this isn't the real Santa, but he can get wishes to the real one, right?" she asked, her tone urgent.

Isla bent lower and nodded, feeling slightly guilty for deceiving the child, but maybe she could hear what the kid wanted and convey it to her father. If her father was the lighthouse keeper, that should make him easier to find. "I'm pretty certain he can, yes."

"Perfect," the little girl said, looking relieved.

"Is it something I can help with?" she asked, knowing the big guy probably wouldn't remember each of these children's requests. He was a good Santa, but this late in the season, with these large crowds, he must be starting to tire as well.

Tess eyed her in the Nutcracker costume. "I don't think so. You're not even an elf. No offense."

"You never know... Can't hurt, right?"

Tess hesitated. "My dad says your family invented Sealena."

Isla couldn't tell by her tone whether the child's father thought that was a good thing or not. "My family invited Sealena to be a part of our community, yeah." The mythology of the Sea Serpent Queen had existed in Alaska long before the Wakefields.

"If she's so powerful and cares about the community, how come she can't save everyone?" the little girl asked.

Why had she opened this conversation with the child? She had no idea how to explain the Sea Serpent Queen as a myth. "Um…I'm not sure, sweetie. Sometimes she's not there when she's needed?"

"Like with my mom and sister," she said sadly.

Isla's heart clenched. Damn. This child had lost family at sea?

"Anyway, I'm here to ask Santa to find them. He travels all over the world, so if anyone can find them, it's him."

Isla swallowed the lump in her throat as the teacher called out for Tess to rejoin the class back in line. The child was planning on asking Santa to bring her family back. That was heartbreaking, and it killed her to know that Tess was probably not going to get her ultimate wish this holiday season.

Returning to her post, her cell phone vibrated, and she hurried to take it out of her pocket. She glanced around for Cherry as she saw the investigator's number on the call display. Phone calls during her shift weren't allowed, but this might be important and there were no other groups approaching the front of Santa's Village at the moment.

She answered quietly, turning toward the wooden structure. "Hey, Hunter. I'm at work right now—"

"This won't take long," he said, and her heart fell at the discouraging tone in his voice. "There's no easy way to say this, but unfortunately, the woman I found isn't your birth mother."

It was impossible to discern how she felt about it. She'd yet to come to a conclusion about whether she'd have met the woman anyway, or what it was that she ultimately wanted to achieve with this. With reopening her past.

"Okay, well, are you planning to keep looking?" She had no idea what parameters she'd established with this investigation.

"I think the search is over. I'm sorry, Isla, but your birth mother died last year. She was serving time for robbery and died of pneumonia. It was a challenge locating her because she'd moved to Seattle."

Her mother was dead. Now there was no possibility of ever meeting her; having that option whisked away made her stomach turn. She swallowed hard several times, but the lump lodged in the back of her throat refused to go down. Tears burned her eyes, and she cleared her throat. "Okay… Well, thank you."

"Of course. I'll return the funds to you right away."

"Funds?" For his services? Was it one of those situations where she didn't pay unless he found the person? Seemed odd that someone would offer a service like that in this unpredictable industry where success rates were probably low.

"The money you wanted me to give her," he said.

"Wait, so that's why I wanted you to find her?"

"You said you wanted to help her, correct? It was an anonymous donation."

"So I never planned on meeting her?"

"I don't think so," Hunter said gently, a rare hint of sympathy in his voice. "You mostly just seemed concerned with making sure she was okay."

A tear cascaded down her cheek, and she swallowed again. "Okay, well thank you for trying."

"Have a nice holiday."

"You too," Isla said as the call disconnected. She stared at the phone in her trembling hand. Her birth mother had died before she could ensure that she was okay, financially stable… Her chest hurt as she mourned the life of someone she'd never truly known. Now she'd never have that chance.

She took several deep breaths, wiped the tears from her cheeks and turned back to another group of students approaching with their teachers. She forced a smile as she took her place, but on her unsteady legs, she stumbled backward against the wooden structure. Her shoulder knocked into the sideboard, and she quickly stabilized the wreath on the door before it fell.

Above her, the structure shifted, and a shelf containing a row of Nutcrackers in various shapes and sizes slipped off the hardware holding it in place.

"Hey, look out!" a little boy in line yelled, pointing to it.

Too late, Isla looked up, unable to avoid the large, open-mouthed, wooden Nutcracker falling straight toward her.

The next thing she saw was a dozen little faces staring down at her.

She blinked, struggling to focus as bright Christmas lights blinded her. Her head throbbed, and she reached up to touch a spot on the left side of her forehead. A small bump had formed, and it was tender. How long had she been lying there?

"Are you dead?" a little boy asked.

"No, I'm not dead," she said.

"You looked dead," he said.

"Well, I'm not." At least she didn't think so. The after-life wouldn't be so…annoying.

"Move away, kids. Give the lady space," Cherry's voice said as she approached. She stared down at Isla, concerned. "You okay?"

Was she? "Um…I think so." Isla frowned as she sat up and surveyed her surroundings. Nutcracker statues were all around her. She picked up the largest one that had broken after it had hit her head. She must have blacked out for a moment. Something felt odd: a surrealness surrounded her as though nothing was real, as though she were dreaming.

"Take your time getting up," Cherry said.

"I'm okay…" she started, but the sound of "I'll Be Home

for Christmas" playing inside the Santa's Village hut had those same familiar goose bumps surfacing on her skin.

Home.

Her entire life seemed to play in a montage in her mind, causing her surroundings to blur. Her heart raced, and her thoughts spiraled like a whirlwind.

She knew where she was. She knew *who* she was.

Her memory was back. Relief flowed through her, followed immediately by a sense of dread.

Holy jingle bells…

What kind of mess had this impostor made of her life?

AARON READ THE text from Skylar several times, not sure if he was being pranked.

Isla got hit on the head by a Nutcracker, and her memory is back.

There was so much to unpack in the text. His heart was racing, his mouth dry, and his palms were sweating as he texted back.

Is she okay?

That was his primary concern. Another head injury wasn't good.

She's pissed. With everyone.

Aaron's legs felt like rubber as he lowered himself onto the bench in the station locker room.

Shit.

Isla had every reason to be upset with him. He'd allowed

them to get close, to fall in love without being completely honest with her, but she couldn't hold her family accountable for that. They'd been letting them get to know one another—without interferences.

This was his fault.

He changed out of his gear and into his jeans and a sweater. He had to go see her. They needed to clear the air right away. She hadn't reached out to him, and his gut told him that she'd ignore any calls or texts from him. He needed to go to the hotel and have this dreaded conversation face-to-face.

All he could do was hope that she loved him enough to forgive him.

SHE FELT LIKE A FOOL.

The past few weeks had been incredible. But she could fully contest that they'd been the best four weeks of her life now that she had memories to compare them too. She'd fallen hard and fast for Aaron Segura.

And she'd been duped.

Everyone in town must have found it hilarious to watch her chase after Aaron and then fall all over him. Everyone knew their history. Everyone had heard her say repeatedly that he was the last man on earth she could ever be compatible with.

Her stomach hurt, and she couldn't decipher which emotions were bothering her the most—embarrassment, anger, hurt…or the deep longing she felt now that it was all over. Part of her wished she'd never gotten her memory back.

Now she remembered everything and all the reasons she'd kept herself closed off. All the reasons she'd avoided opening up in relationships. Why she'd avoided dating men that she might actually fall for.

She'd never thought Aaron was in that category, but it all made sense now.

Fighting with Aaron, refusing to acknowledge her attraction and allowing herself to believe they were too different to ever get along was a defense mechanism to protect herself against this.

A deep, painful yearning for something that hadn't been real.

She searched through her suitcase for her workout clothes. Her leg felt better, and she needed to go for a run. Clear her head. Burn off the negative energy overpowering her. If she didn't shake this off, she'd probably climb into the hotel bed and not resurface again until sometime in the new year.

So much had happened that day. Finding out her birth mother was gone had been difficult to hear without the context of her memories; then the weight of the disappointment had truly set in as her memories had spiraled back.

She'd been searching for her birth mother to help her. Her main goal in locating the woman was to give her an anonymous donation of money to help her get on her feet. The cash was her own, money she'd made working on the cruise ship, not from her trust fund. It wasn't a lot, but it was something.

And she hadn't involved her family in it because hurting them, upsetting them, hadn't been her intention. She'd never planned on meeting the woman. She had everything she needed with the Wakefields. Sure, as a teenager she'd been curious and confused at times, but that had passed. In adulthood, she realized that the decisions her parents and her birth mother had made were for the best, and while she'd always felt a little like an outsider, that hadn't been the Wakefields' fault.

Then she'd gone and let her guard down with everyone, allowing them all to see she was vulnerable and fragile. Allowing them to think something was missing from her life, something that needed to be fulfilled.

She wanted to scream.

She sighed as she sat on the edge of the bed and laced up her running shoes. And when a knock sounded on the hotel-room door, her gaze shot to the window in search of an escape. She didn't want to talk to anyone right now. Unfortunately, she was too high up and essentially trapped.

"Isla, it's me." Aaron's voice drifting from the other side wasn't a complete surprise. She'd suspected Skylar would have told him. Her embarrassing incident had spread through the small town like wildfire by now.

Well, if he'd heard she had her memory back, then he should also know that she wasn't in the mood to hear anything he had to say.

She remained quiet and still. If he thought she wasn't there, he'd leave.

"I'm not leaving. If you're not in there, I'll wait," he said from the other side of the door. She heard him lean against it and a quick peek through the hole revealed he was sitting on the floor. She could see his legs stretched across the hallway.

Now she was really trapped.

What should she do? She couldn't avoid him forever, even though that's what she'd prefer to do. Hashing this out would be useless. It would get them nowhere...and she was terrified that she'd lost the ability to hide her true emotions. One look at him would make her cave if she wasn't careful, wasn't armed with enough anger.

He'd deceived her. He hadn't been honest with her from the beginning. How could she believe anything now?

She reluctantly unlocked the door and saw him jump to his feet.

Stay strong. Do not let him get to you.

Keeping her expression as neutral as possible, she squared her shoulders and opened the door.

Aaron looked nervous and distraught.

Good, he should be. For weeks, he'd allowed her to believe they had a connection. And maybe she'd seen him in a different light, maybe she'd actually changed her mind and heart about him, but he couldn't possibly have changed his opinion of her, because she hadn't been acting like herself. They hadn't crossed this bridge together, finding a better path on the other side. He'd had full awareness while she'd been wandering through the dark, being misguided by the people she thought were supposed to care about her.

Had they all wanted her to become something different? Something she wasn't?

"Hi… How are you feeling?" he asked.

"Fine. Better than fine, actually. Things are clear again," she said coldly.

Only they weren't clear at all. Seeing him standing there with a deep look of remorse and concern clouded things in her mind and her heart. Where did they stand now? How did they move forward?

"Can I come in?"

"I was just heading out."

"Isla, we need to talk."

"You need to talk. I don't."

"Please, Isla. Will you just hear me out?"

This was harder than she thought it would be.

Shut this down. Shut him down.

Yet, she owed it to him and herself to end this officially.

End it now before things went any further, then not leave an opportunity, an open door...

"I'm not sure I want to hear anything you have to say when you haven't been completely honest with me this whole time." She folded her arms across her chest, needing some sort of shield, a barrier between her conflicted emotions and the words that might cause her to cave, to understand, to forgive...

"I told you we didn't always get along."

Isla scoffed. "Understatement." They'd made a life out of arguing. Every memory she had of the two of them together was a tension-filled, heated one—the ones from the last four weeks tense and hot for other reasons, but she pushed those out of her mind.

Aaron reached for her. "That was before we got to know one another. Truly got to know one another."

She moved out of reach, and he let his arms drop to his sides. "I may have gotten to know you, but you liked a different person. Not me."

He shook his head. "Not true. I've always cared about you and been attracted to you. That's why our relationship was so strained. I had this complex dichotomy inside that I couldn't figure out. Fighting with you was as close as I could get to you. I knew I didn't have a chance with you." He ran a frustrated hand through his hair. "You were always too guarded and anti...*me* for me to get close." He dared a step toward her. "But over the last few weeks, I got that chance."

"You didn't fall for the real me."

"Bullshit. These past few weeks you've been a more sincere version of yourself than you've ever been."

She looked away. "That's not true." At least she couldn't admit to any truth in that. She needed him to believe it was the head injury that had clouded her judgment, made her...different.

"It is. You let your guard down. You let me see another side of you—not a different version. Who you were before the accident was still in there, but you also allowed me to get to know you on a different level."

Oh, they'd gotten to know one another on so many different levels. Deeper, more intimate, passionate levels. Thinking about them now made her stomach turn.

"And *you* pursued *me*. I tried to keep my distance for fear of exactly this..."

So he was making excuses, turning this around? "That was a mistake. I made a mistake," she said, her chest tightening. He was right. She was partially to blame for this too. She had thrown herself at him and forced him into spending time with her. But how could she trust him when he'd allowed her to believe their relationship wasn't what it was? He should have been completely transparent.

"Isla, don't do this. Don't push me away," he said gently yet urgently.

She hesitated, emotions spiraling through her. She wanted to step into his arms and keep moving forward with what they had developed, but common sense demanded she see things for what they were. She and Aaron were too different. She wasn't going to change who she was for him. Soon, she'd piss him off with her adventurous ways just as she always did. She wouldn't be the woman he'd fallen for—one who'd been more fearful and cautious— and then he'd walk away from her. Though...*was* she still the old Isla?

She couldn't process everything that had happened in the last twenty-four hours. She rubbed her forehead as pain radiated in her temples.

"You okay?" he asked, stepping closer, concern in his expression.

"I don't know." This was exactly why she'd always guarded her emotions, refused to let anyone in. Really in. Now her protective shields were gone, and how was she supposed to protect herself from hurt and disappointment? Waves of confusion washed over her as she battled with the knowledge of who she was—or had always been—and the depth she was capable of these past few weeks. Who did she want to be now? Could she somehow be both and not feel this terror bubbling up inside of her? Fear was such a foreign feeling as she'd never allowed it power, but now it was threatening to take hold, shatter her.

"I have to go," she said quickly. She reached behind the door for her jacket and room key, then moved past him into the hall.

"Isla…"

Nope. She couldn't do this anymore. She'd given him enough time, heard too much already. She needed time and space to figure things out without her feelings for him influencing her. She did care about him. She had fallen in love with him this holiday season.

But now she had no idea what to do about it.

"Merry Christmas, Aaron," she said as she headed down the hall, away from him and all the emotions she wasn't sure she'd be able to run far and fast enough away from.

CHAPTER TWENTY-FIVE

HE ALMOST WISHED there would be an emergency call.

Sitting in the station with nothing to occupy his mind and thoughts for two days, all Aaron could think about was Isla. She was upset, and he understood that. He should have tried harder to tell her the truth about them.

Maybe he shouldn't have allowed her to get close to him at all...

No, he couldn't regret that. Spending the last few weeks with her had been everything. He'd fallen in love with her, a fact that hadn't been as clear as it was these last forty-eight hours. If he hadn't, then accepting her dismissal would be easier. Moving on from her rejection wouldn't be this hard. He'd be able to turn off these thoughts of her, remembering every moment, everything she'd said to him. He wouldn't be constantly fighting this urge to be with her, to reach out, to try to get her to give him—them—another chance.

He ran a hand through his hair and sighed. Anxious energy coursed through him that no amount of working out could diminish. He couldn't sit still, he couldn't sleep, couldn't eat.

Isla Wakefield had him all kinds of messed up.

This holiday season had been the best one he'd had in so long. It had been hard for him to open up and accept the season, but he'd felt safe in doing it for Isla. Now, without her, the holiday was even harder to survive.

It was Christmas Eve and he was alone, missing the woman he loved.

He leaned back in his chair in the staff room and stared at the snow falling outside.

What the hell should he do?

She didn't want him. Could he just accept that? Did he have a choice? Isla was the most stubborn and determined woman he'd ever gone up against. Only before, they'd been fighting on opposite sides. He had to believe that this time they both wanted the same thing—to come out of this stronger and hopefully together. They just didn't know how to get there.

Damn, he hoped that was true, because he was changing course. Nothing in his life had ever come easy. He'd worked hard and persevered in every challenge he'd ever faced.

So instead of continuing to wallow in self-pity and regret, he was going to fight for the woman he loved.

He'd given her time and space to think things through, figure things out, but he loved her, and he knew she loved him. She thought he'd fallen in love with her because she'd been different, but that wasn't true. He understood her better all around; now, he just needed to show her.

And there was only one way he could think to do that, but he needed help.

Climbing the stairs to Dwayne's house after his shift, he took a deep breath as he knocked. He hadn't seen or spoken to his buddy since the party at the Wakefields', and he hoped his friend was ready to move past all of this.

He danced from one foot to the other, tucking his neck further inside his jacket as the cold wind blew snowdrifts around him. He rang the doorbell and waited.

Come on, man, open up.

Both Isla and Dwayne had every reason to avoid him.

He'd hurt them both. But he needed a chance to make things better.

Dwayne looked like he'd just woken up when he finally answered the door. "Hey, man. What are you doing here?"

"I came to tell you that I'm sorry about everything," he said. "I didn't realize your feelings for Isla were as strong as they were." Having now lost her himself, Aaron could sympathize with his friend's heartache. "I didn't mean to fall for her, but I did…" He sighed. "I'm a mess without her, man, and I need your help to get her back."

"Dwayne? You coming back to bed or what?" a woman's voice said from inside the house.

"You've got company?" Aaron asked in amusement. Maybe his buddy wasn't still pining for Isla. That would hopefully make things a little easier.

"I'll be right there," he called back. "Melissa, the yoga instructor from the community center," he whispered to Aaron. "She's been keeping me company while I've been grounded," he said with a look that said he still held Aaron partially responsible for that, but Aaron could hear that all was forgiven in the other man's tone.

"That's what I need your help with," he said, feeling relieved. "Time to get you back in the air."

"My suspension is lifted?" Dwayne's eyes and hopes rose.

"Not exactly. I need you to fly one of your family's helicopters."

Dwayne frowned. "Where exactly are we going?"

"Probably better that I don't tell you until we're in the air," Aaron said. "But it's for Isla."

"You're really asking me for help to get your girl back?"

"Yes. Look, man, this conversation is overdue, but I love her, and I hope you and I can be…cool."

There was no hesitation from Dwayne. "Of course we can be cool, and I'm in," he said reaching out a hand to clap Aaron's and draw him in for a hug.

"COME ON, ISLA, OPEN UP!"

Isla cranked the music higher on her headphones, ignoring her brother knocking on the hotel-room door. As far as she was concerned, they could all kiss her jingle bells. It was Christmas Eve and her holidays had gone from magical to complete shit. She wasn't even sure how she was going to spend Christmas Day with her family with so much tension surrounding them. Eventually, she'd have to talk to them, accept what had happened and move on, but not yet. Deep down, she knew they weren't at fault for what happened with Aaron, but she was still pissed and needed a little more time.

"Isla, I'll ask the desk for a key," Dex called out.

"That's an invasion of privacy!" she yelled back.

"Okay, fine. If you won't open the door, I'll just yell through it," he said.

Isla sighed. Great, and have everyone in the hotel know their business and disrupt the guests. She sighed, getting up and opening the door. "What?"

Dex stopped pacing the hall and turned toward her with a look of desperate frustration. "You have to stop ignoring us. We're worried about you."

"I'm fine. Except that I'm surrounded by a bunch of liars," she said, holding her chin high. Aaron might have gotten to her, with his timing so close to when she was feeling raw. But she'd had two full days to start building her shields back up. She'd never let Dex know how torn she was.

"No one lied to you," Dex said gently.

"No one was exactly forthcoming either." Hands on her hips, she fought for patience. How silly must she have looked these past few weeks going around town with Aaron? Everyone must have been snickering and getting a real kick out of it. Had that been Aaron's motivation in the beginning? To trick her for how she'd always treated him—to humiliate her?

She wished she could believe he'd do something like that, but she knew he never would. Which made it harder to keep pushing him away and remain resolved that it was over.

"The doctor said…"

She wagged a finger at her brother. "Do not blame the doctor. He said to let me figure out who I was on my own. He didn't say keep things from me so I looked like a fool."

"Why do you think you look like a fool? Because you fell in love? Sis, it happens to the best of us," he said.

"I fell for Aaron without knowing who he really was."

"That's not true. You know him better now than you ever did. You just didn't have your preconceived notions about him anymore, blocking your ability to see how perfect the two of you are together. None of us wanted to ruin what you two had going."

She'd ruined it. That was all on her. But what even was there to ruin? It wasn't as though the two of them were actually going to stay together. They fought all the time and had different viewpoints on everything—at least, they did back when they'd been so blind about their own prejudices that they didn't allow themselves to truly get to know one another…

Dex's shoulders slumped, and he looked desperate for her to see things a different way. "All I'm saying is that you have been happier the last few weeks than I've ever seen you. You let your guard down and—"

"Exactly!" she said, exasperated. "I let my guard down. And I was duped."

"That's not what happened. Aaron wasn't dating you as a joke. He fell for you too."

"How do you know?"

Dex sighed. "Because he's out on the mountain right now, rappelling down into the crevasse he saved your ass from to try to find your necklace."

Isla's chest felt like it might explode. Dumbfounded, her mouth gaped.

He's doing what?

Dex shot her a look. "Now do you believe this was all some sort of con?"

No, she didn't.

But *now* she was terrified that the man she loved was going to get hurt proving it to her.

ISLA HAD EVERY RIGHT to be angry with him.

Their entire life, the two of them had never seen eye to eye or gotten along. He'd never indicated that the feelings he had for her went deeper than he'd let on. So of course she didn't believe it now.

How could she trust anything he said after he hadn't told her about their tumultuous relationship leading up to her accident?

He couldn't rely on just words. He had to show her. Which was why he was harnessed and ready to drop into the deep crevasse that she'd fallen into weeks ago. Well, not ready, but doing it anyway.

"In position," Dwayne said. "This weather won't give us much time."

"Copy." The weather had quickly taken a turn for the worse, with thick, blowing snow reducing visibility and a wind from the north that was reported to reach a forty-mile-an-hour speed within the next few hours.

This was dangerous, and he'd dragged his friend into it.

It was amazing that they'd even found the crevasse exposed and still accessible. He had the recent temperatures and lack of big snowfalls to thank.

Aaron lowered the rope and dipped down over the edge. The long, ice-crystal formations all around him were like mirrors reflecting his image as Aaron descended farther in the direction of the ledge where he'd found Isla that day.

It was a beautiful sight—the ice in ragged shapes all around him, clear, blue-toned glass that hung, menacing and majestic. Unlike the last time he'd been in there, his heart wasn't pounding, and adrenaline didn't make his pulse race. Isla wasn't in danger today, but still, there was a lot on the line.

If he could find the necklace that meant so much to her, it would not only prove that he cared about her but that he could be okay with the lifestyle she loved. Yes, he'd worry about her when she went out exploring the world, pushing through boundaries, but he wouldn't be so adamant about the dangers anymore. He'd accept her choices, respect them and maybe open himself up to more challenges as well.

Like the one he was currently embarking on that he'd never have done a month ago.

"Wind's picking up," Dwayne said over the headset, and Aaron moved faster, lowering himself farther.

This was a long shot, but she had lost the necklace that day, and it made sense that it could be here. He knew out of everything he could possibly give her this holiday season, this would mean the most, especially now that her birth mother had passed. Aside from the letter, it was the only thing Isla had from the woman, the only thing she ever would have.

He quickly scanned the area, squinting in the glare to try to locate the ledge where she'd been lying the day he'd found her. The structure had changed over the last few weeks, parts of it melting away, some covered by snowdrifts, so it was hard to tell exactly where she'd landed.

He turned to get his bearings, positioning himself as close as possible to the place where he'd been weeks before and continued moving farther down into the crevasse toward a larger ledge protruding from the ice shaft.

He spotted the shimmer and sparkle of the gold crescent-moon pendant and smiled. He lowered himself down onto the ledge, careful it could support his weight as he bent to reach for it. He couldn't believe it was actually there, this very important item that Isla thought was gone forever.

"Item retrieved," he said over the speaker.

"Shit, that was lucky, man."

He was lucky. Lucky to have a buddy crazy enough to help him pull off this stunt. "On my way back up."

Overhead, he heard cracking and the sound of rumbling. The definitive sound of an avalanche.

He glanced above just in time to see the first falling crest of snow cover the crevasse, partially blocking his exit. More cracking and rumbling sounded, deep and menacing.

"Mountain's giving way!" Dwayne said.

Aaron didn't pause to consider his next move. Quickly, he detached the harness, letting the rope free. He couldn't risk the chopper being dragged down by the cascading snow, covering the crevasse. "I'm detached. Go," he said.

"Are you crazy? No. Reattach. I'll pull you up."

"Too late. Just go."

"You'll be trapped in there."

"Then, come back with a shovel," he said in an attempt to lighten the mood, but his palms dampened, and his heart raced as a huge chunk of the crevasse caved in under the weight of the avalanche. There was no more opening at the top. He couldn't see the chopper or the sky overhead. There was no way to get out by climbing up. The terrain was too unstable, and the snow was too thick.

He heard the chopper moving farther away. All he could do was wait and hope that help arrived quickly—before the entire structure caved in around him.

For the first time in his life, Aaron was the one waiting for rescue.

HELICOPTERS AND SNOWMOBILES could cause the avalanche to give way even more, so they were snowshoeing their way up the trail toward the crevasse.

Dwayne's call to the station and the local search and rescue crew had everyone moving quickly. They all understood the urgency in getting Aaron out of the crevasse as fast as possible. The weather conditions had gotten worse. With limited visibility and early darkness fast upon them, they were racing against the clock.

There was no way Isla was sitting in the hotel room or waiting at the station. She'd go crazy feeling helpless, so she was making her way through the blowing snow alongside the others.

Cold wind bit into the exposed flesh on her face, and the resistance made the hike harder. Pushing through the deep snow slowly and carefully, so as to not set off the cascading snowdrifts, they moved as quickly as they safely could.

Her heart pounded in her chest, and her stomach twisted at the thought of Aaron down in the crevasse. Her own fall had been sudden, but Aaron's situation was unpredictable and getting worse the longer it took to reach him. It was freezing and getting dark.

If the crevasse caved in... She swallowed hard.

"Hey, he's going to be okay. We're almost there," Dwayne said next to her.

Obviously the two men had made amends, and that made her feel a bit better, but why the hell had their first bonding exercise been something so dangerous? Going to find her necklace was thoughtful and endearing, but she was going to strangle Aaron when she saw him. "I can't believe you two did this," she said, her words lacking conviction in her anxiety.

"He wanted to do it for you," Dwayne said. "To prove to you that he cares, I guess."

"He could have sent flowers," she muttered.

He shook his head. "We both know you're too stubborn for that. It takes something extreme to get you to take notice."

She was silent as they continued on. Dwayne was right. She was stubborn. Foolishly so. Why the hell had it mattered so much that she'd felt fooled? The love between them had been real. Their connection had been real. Her feelings for him had been real. That should have been enough.

It was enough.

God, please let him be okay.

She needed to tell him that she was sorry for pushing him away and that she loved him.

"Hey, I, uh, wanted to apologize," Dwayne said. "For what I said at the party."

Isla nodded. "Apology accepted. And I'm sorry too." When she'd called things off with him, she hadn't realized the extent of his feelings. "I never meant to hurt you."

He winked at her. "I'm getting over it." He stopped and gestured for everyone else to stop. "This is it. Everyone stay back. False ground could be anywhere," Dwayne said as they reached the marked spot on the mountain.

Shovels out, they started to dig. Slowly, moving in closer as they went.

"Here's the edge," a search and rescue crew member said after a few moments. The group picked up speed as they uncovered enough of the crevasse to see into the hole. Isla peered over the edge, relief flowing through her as she saw Aaron sitting on the ledge where she'd fallen. The sight of the crevasse brought her back to her own accident, falling through and then seeing Aaron as he'd lifted her to safety. She'd never felt so protected in her entire life.

She wanted to feel that again, and with Aaron, she knew she'd always feel that sense of security.

He looked up and saw them, offering a wave as Dwayne harnessed up and got the litter ready. He slowly descended over the edge.

"Be careful," Isla said.

"I've got him," Dwayne said confidently. And ten long, excruciating minutes later, he did, and Isla released a huge sigh of relief. Then prepared to give the man she loved the lecture of his life.

As she approached the litter, he saw Isla fight back tears as she lectured him. "Are you insane? You could have died."

The sight of her had him instantly forgetting about the nerve-racking two hours he'd spent inside the sealed crevasse, hoping the entire thing wouldn't cave in on him. She was flushed and looked so beautifully distraught, it warmed him to the core. He hated that he'd put lives in danger, having to be rescued, but he couldn't regret that it had brought them back together. "You'd have missed me?" he asked.

"Yes, you idiot! Of course I would have missed you," she said, emotions so thick she choked on the words.

A lump formed in his own throat. "Why?"

"Why what?" she asked.

"Why would you have missed me?" he asked.

"You're really going to make me say it, aren't you?" she asked as the first few tears froze on her cold cheeks.

"I really am," he said with that grin.

"Because I love you. So much. Even though you're annoying and—"

He cut off her words with a kiss. Deep, passionate, long.

"I love you too." He opened his hand. "I think this is yours."

"Oh my God. You actually found it?" Fresh tears formed as she took the necklace from him with a shaky hand. "I never thought I'd see this again."

"For a moment, trapped in there, I never thought I'd see you again. Glad we were both wrong," he said gently, caressing her cheek and kissing her again. For two days, he'd been miserable without her, afraid he'd never get the chance to touch her, kiss her, hold her ever again. It made this whole thing worth it. Given the choice, he'd do it all over again.

"Hate to break up this beautiful reunion," Dwayne said with a note of mock annoyance, "but we should get off this mountain and out of the weather before it gets worse."

The sky was already darkening, and the snowstorm was progressing. Another hour and it would be dangerous. Not the best weather for being trapped on a mountainside but perfect for curling up by the fire.

Aaron climbed out of the litter and reached for Isla's hand as they made their way down the side of the mountain.

"When we get back to Port Serenity, do you think maybe you'd spend the rest of the evening with me?" he asked.

"I can't think of any other way I'd want to spend Christmas Eve," Isla said, smiling up at him with only love in her expression. When she wrapped an arm around him and held on tight, Aaron knew this was going to be the best Christmas he'd ever had.

EPILOGUE

THIS HAD TO be the ballsiest thing he'd ever done. Non-careerwise.

Staring at the ice pans bobbing on the surface of the water, Aaron shivered despite still being dressed warmly in his ski suit.

That was about to change.

In just over a minute, when the clock hit 9:00 a.m. on New Year's Day, he'd be plunging almost naked into the freezing water with Isla and about thirty other people on the annual Polar Bear Plunge.

"This is actually really good for you," Isla said, as she removed her own ski suit.

"I'm not so sure about that," he grumbled as he disrobed along with the others. The cold January wind was numbing all his extremities, and he wasn't even in the water yet.

But there was one thing he was sure of, and that was that he wanted to spend his life with the courageous, adventurous, beautiful woman he was taking this plunge for.

"Three, two, one!" the unofficial organizer, a man in his late sixties who'd been participating in this every year for over four decades, yelled as the clock struck nine, and the group went running.

"Ready?" she asked, her excitement contagious as her green eyes sparkled.

Aaron took a deep breath and grabbed Isla's hand in his as they plunged together.

His breath came in short gasps, the cold water instantly paralyzing his extremities.

"Oh my God! So cold!" Isla said, laughing next to him. She danced from one foot to the other in the water and wrapped her arms around her body as she started to head out. "Okay, that's long enough."

"Wait," he said, reaching for her.

She turned back and shot him a quizzical look. "It's f-f-freezing. Come on." Her teeth chattered.

He wanted nothing more than to get out of that water, but… "There's another plunge I need to take first," he said, extending his free hand toward her and opening it.

Isla's eyes widened as she saw the ring on his open palm. Her hand went to her mouth and she looked at him in wide-eyed disbelief, freezing ocean water momentarily forgotten. "Are you serious?"

He nodded. "I love you, Isla. I always have. Over the last month, you've changed my life for the better, and I don't want to live a day without you in it." He paused. "In case the question wasn't implied—marry me?"

She shivered, and her teeth chattered. "Yes! I'll marry you!"

His heart filled with love as he slid the ring on her shaking finger, then drew her into his arms in the icy Pacific Ocean.

"Are you sure you're up for a life of adventures with me?" she asked against his lips, her loving gaze warming him as it burned into his.

"I can't wait," he said, and he meant it.

His entire life, he'd lived cautiously, worried about what could happen if he took a risk and let go. But now he wasn't afraid of the fall, as long as it was with her.

* * * * *

ACKNOWLEDGMENTS

Thank you to all my readers! I couldn't continue on this journey without you! Your emails, reviews, comments and encouragements mean so much. Thank you to my agent, Jill Marsal, for all your support and guidance, and my editor, Dana Grimaldi, for the notes and feedback that make each book stronger. Thank you to the HQN art department and marketing team who continue to bless me with beautiful cover art and cover blurbs. Biggest of thanks to my family, who are my biggest inspiration and source of motivation.

Happy Holidays!
Jen

Love in the
Forecast

CHAPTER ONE

WIND DANCER WAS the most beautiful thing Keith Beaumont had ever seen.

Or at least she would be once he gave her a fresh coat of paint, rebuilt the damaged section of the bow and attached a new rudder and a new mast for the sail.

The cruising sailboat would be the best one on the North Pacific Ocean for the annual coast guard–sponsored Astronavigation Contest. Next weekend, bragging rights over who was the best sailor in Port Serenity, Alaska, would be up for grabs again, and Keith was ready to defend his title, alongside his best friend and cocaptain, meteorologist Bob Bartlett. The other man lived in Siren's Bay and had yet to see *Wind Dancer*. They normally rented a boat to compete, but this year the glory of a win would belong to Keith's new pride and joy.

He might have embellished *Wind Dancer* a little last time he spoke to Bob, so he wanted the sailboat to be in tip-top shape when his friend arrived in five days.

"Can you hand me that plank of wood?" Keith asked his daughter, Skylar, who was his *living, breathing* pride and joy.

She handed the teakwood plank to him and stood admiring the work they'd done so far. She laughed as she wiped her arm across her forehead. "Funny to be working on a larger-scale model this time."

He and his daughter had a long-running tradition of building model boats together. Since she was three years old, Skylar had helped him build a new one each year. They'd bonded over their passion for boating and love of the ocean throughout the years, and it was a joy to be working on a real boat with her.

Owning a cruising sailboat had always been a dream of his, but now that he was officially retired from the Port Serenity Coast Guard, leaving the station in his daughter's capable hands, Keith had finally taken the plunge and bought the secondhand boat from an older gentleman in Anchorage.

He hadn't mentioned his plans to Skylar yet, but he intended to sail from Alaska to Florida on a two-month course he'd plotted. Not exactly a direct route, and he didn't intend on cruising at high speeds. He wanted to experience life on the open water in a way he never had before—being at the mercy of nature, with the control and confidence of over thirty-five years respecting the ocean and her mysteries.

It was a journey he'd talked about with his wife before she'd died seven years ago, and he was certain that she'd still want him to take the trip. The thought of going without her made his chest tighten, but he knew—as always— she'd be with him in spirit.

"Think she'll be ready for the contest?" Skylar asked as he knelt to hammer the plank of wood in place, her diamond engagement ring sparkling in the July midday sun. She'd recently gotten engaged to her secret high-school love, and Keith felt better leaving on his journey knowing she was settled in her career and in love.

"More than ready. She's going to win her first time out, aren't you, darlin'?" he said, standing and gently stroking the port side of the hull.

Skylar shot him a look. *"Darlin'?"*

"She's the second love of my life," he said, readjusting his tool belt around his waist.

"You know...speaking of love—"

Saved by the bell. His daughter's speech about how he should consider dating again was cut short by Keith's ringing cell phone. They'd had the conversation countless times in the year that Skylar had been back in town, and his response was always the same: he wasn't ready. What he'd had with Skylar's mother had been a once-in-a-lifetime love, and he wasn't ready for another relationship. He wasn't sure that was in the cards for him.

"Hold that thought," he said, holding up a finger as he answered the call. "Bob! How's the best cocaptain in Alaska? Hope you've been brushing up on the upcoming weather patterns."

"About that... Sorry, Keith, but I won't be able to participate this year." On the other end of the call, Bob lowered his voice as he continued. "Marsha has her heart set on a trip to visit Alison and the grandkids."

Bob's daughter and grandkids lived in Iceland, and due to health reasons he and his wife hadn't been able to travel in recent years. Now that Marsha was feeling better, she must be eager to see her family. But this contest happened every year. Who knowingly planned a trip for those dates? Visitors from all over Alaska and beyond came to Port Serenity for the event. "Can't you leave a few days later?" Marsha could head out, and Bob could meet her there. The couple took separate vacations all the time, so it wasn't unreasonable to suggest.

"Afraid not. We're using flight points, and there are all these blackout dates and restrictions." Bob sounded less than thrilled about missing the contest too, and Keith suspected it may have been a source of tension and debate in the Bartlett home. But ultimately, Marsha—with the assistance of blackout dates and restrictions—had won out.

Keith sighed. "Okay. Well, yeah, that's fine." What could he say? By now, the tickets to Iceland would already be booked, and his friend had a wonderful marriage. "Happy Wife, Happy Life," right? Keith wouldn't mess with his friend's relationship. He wouldn't be that single friend who constantly needed a wingman.

That's what his daughter didn't understand. Even if Keith was interested in meeting someone, everyone he knew was happily married and watching reruns of *NCIS* on Saturday nights. He couldn't exactly go clubbing with her fiancé, Dex, or hit up the hot spots alone. He wasn't a creeper, and besides, he had no idea where to meet single ladies his age. Online dating or apps weren't his thing.

"Sorry, buddy. Next year," Bob said, sounding truly remorseful.

"Next year," Keith said. "Have a safe trip."

He sighed as he disconnected the call and tucked the cell phone into his jeans pocket.

"What's wrong?" Skylar asked, lifting her blond hair into a ponytail as the hot midday sun beat down on the deck of the boat.

"That was Bob. He's out."

They'd been partners in the contest for years. With his expertise in celestial navigation and Bob's experience as a meteorologist, they made the perfect, unbeatable team. They'd held the first-place trophy for five years running.

"Aw, sorry, Dad," Skylar said sympathetically. If anyone knew how important this yearly event was to Keith, it was Skylar. She understood his desire to prove that the old-school methods of navigation were just as valuable as the new technologies. The contest sparked a renewed interest in astronavigation, and the media attention surrounding the event helped ensure time-tested teachings were still included in sailing courses. "What are you going to do?"

"I don't know." Keith would hate to pull out of the contest this year. Especially when he was eager to test out *Wind Dancer*. He'd been confident the boat would be just the good-luck charm they needed to secure a sixth-year win.

But contest rules were clear: each team required a navigator and a meteorologist. Two sailors from start to finish. Bob was the only qualified person he knew.

Who was he going to partner up with now?

THE SIGHT OF her ex-husband flirting with another woman shouldn't have this effect on her more than eleven months post divorce. But Monica Mallard wasn't sure she could ever really get used to it.

Watching him laugh while charming the pants off the new twenty-five-year-old network intern at the Station Five News office made her stomach flip-flop.

It wasn't that she still had romantic feelings for Brent Clauson—the handsome, charismatic news anchor—or that she didn't agree that ending their relationship was for the best... It was just that when she saw him smile or wink at another woman around the station, it reminded her of how their relationship had started.

Eight years ago, her third week on the job at the local station, she'd fallen hook, line and sinker for Brent. And their whirlwind love affair had taken the whole community by storm. Self-proclaimed Never Settling Down forty-five-year-old Brent had finally found his match.

Or so went the buzz around the small coastal town.

Turned out, Brent was definitely better suited to being

a bachelor. He wasn't a bad husband. Not at all. They'd gotten along fabulously. They never argued and had similar interests and the same taste in food, music and movies, which had made life comfortable and Friday nights debate-free. They loved and respected one another, but Brent just couldn't fully commit to the lifestyle.

In hindsight, it was a good thing that he'd never sold his condo overlooking the marina to move into her larger home near the lake.

Being married hadn't been the problem, it was the label of *husband* that gave him mild anxiety attacks. As though wearing a wedding band changed who he thought he was. Changed the public's perception of him as a carefree, unattainable bachelor that every woman wanted and every man envied. Eventually, they realized that staying married would only hurt them both.

Brent had wanted to continue seeing her, dating her, maintaining a physical relationship after the divorce, but Monica wasn't built that way. It would never make her happy. She'd needed the clean break and the ability to move on…

Unfortunately, that was tougher to achieve when they still worked together.

Sitting across from him now in the Monday-morning meeting, he winked at her, and she smiled back. Luckily, and maybe surprisingly to all their coworkers, they were still great friends. The best of friends. They still confided in one another and asked one another for advice. And they had dinner once a week.

It was nice that they'd both agreed that losing their friendship would be silly, and so far neither of them had acknowledged that things might get weird or complex if one of them were to become involved in a new relationship.

The news director, Calvin Helmes, entered the board-room and took his place at the head of the long table. The station's mascot, an old but beautiful husky named Static, sauntered in behind him and lay at his feet. Static was a famed former racing dog from Calvin's Iditarod days, and she was as much a part of the team as anyone else in the room. The dog had found a second career as Port Serenity's beloved on-camera pet in a short daily segment called *Static's Stunts*, where she and her trainer, Jackie, performed tricks and taught the audience tips on how to train their own dog.

Calvin referred to his notes and addressed the room. "Biggest story this week is obviously the Astronavigation Contest. Monica will be reporting live from the marina for the two days, and Brent will be in studio."

The Astronavigation Contest was one of her favorite stories. Most local-interest pieces went to the other on-staff reporters, but anything to do with the weather was all hers. The forecast for this weekend was perfect: clear skies and warm temperatures, seasonal for summer in Alaska, and Monica was excited to spend time at the marina and, with any luck, out on the water.

Calvin turned to her. "Be sure to get the contestant listings from the organizers at the coast guard station, and see if you can arrange a few earlier interviews, featuring their contest prep, that sort of thing."

"Absolutely," she said, making a note.

Once the meeting wrapped up, she grabbed a fresh espresso from the machine in the hallway, then headed toward her own office. She paused outside her boss's door when she heard the conversation inside.

"It's just time for young blood in the position," Maxwell Taylor, the head of Station Five News, was saying.

Monica frowned and continued to walk slowly. Several coworkers caught her eavesdropping, but she kept her ears peeled to hear the rest of the discussion.

Who were they considering firing?

"She's been here eight years. Viewers love her," Calvin said.

Monica's heart raced. *She'd* been here eight years. And according to the network stats, viewers loved *her*.

They were thinking of replacing her. With young blood. At forty-eight, she was aging out of the career she loved. She had known it would happen sometime, but she hadn't expected it so soon. Fifty was the new forty, and she'd kept herself in great shape over the years. This was ageism.

Her chest tightened, and saliva gathered in her mouth as she turned on her heel and headed toward the washroom. Her skin felt clammy, and she thought she might be sick.

"Hey, Mon!"

Brent's voice behind her made her feel even more nauseous. He was five years older than her, but *his* aging looks were deemed *handsome*. The soft lines around his eyes were *endearing*. His salt-and-pepper hair was *distinguished*. He'd never age out. He'd get to choose his own expiry date.

She folded her arms across her chest as she turned. "What?" A little harsher than she'd intended, and heaven forbid a woman show negative emotions in the workplace.

Brent frowned, immediately concerned. "You okay, sweetheart?"

He still called her that, and it might break her heart the day he ever stopped. She relaxed her shoulders and nodded. "I'm fine." He'd throw a fit if she told him what she'd just overheard. He was supportive of all aspects of her life, but especially her career, and she knew he'd probably threaten to quit if they fired her, but she didn't want him to feel that responsibility toward her. She never had. Their individual careers were their own to manage and navigate. "What's going on?" she asked.

He extended a piece of paper toward her. "The coast guard just sent over the contestant list. Looks like Captain Keith Beaumont announced that his partner dropped out at the last minute, and he's looking for a meteorologist to fill in."

She didn't even hesitate. "I'll do it." If the network was going to fire her anyway, why not abandon her position in front of the camera and participate in the event? They could offer the segment to whoever they were thinking of replacing her with. She ignored the tug in her chest at the thought.

Brent smiled. "Great, because I already told the contest organizers that I knew the perfect replacement."

CHAPTER TWO

NO ONE COULD really replace Bob. His best friend could predict wind changes and weather patterns even before Mother Nature made the call. But the other option was sitting out this year, and Keith didn't want to do that. Especially with his new boat. He wanted to see what she was capable of before he took her out for a long trip on the seas.

He stood on deck, the contest-route map laid out in front of him. They changed the course each year, but it was still a hundred-mile trip in the North Pacific in two days, with checkpoints set up on buoys and marking points along the shore. The team would collect a colored flag from each one.

This route was definitely more challenging than previous years, and without a teammate he trusted, Keith's confidence faded slightly. He checked his watch. Race check-in at the marina office was in an hour, and his mysterious new partner had yet to arrive.

Not off to a great start.

"*Wind Dancer.* What a great name," a woman's voice said from the dock below.

"Afraid I can't take credit…" Keith turned toward the voice, and his mouth dropped. TV meteorologist Monica Mallard was standing there dressed in a pair of white, wide-legged, flowing pants, a navy tank top that clung to her curves and accented her shapely figure, low wedge sandals on her feet and a white-and-blue-striped bandanna covering her wavy red hair. Keith's tongue swelled in his mouth at the sight. He'd always thought the woman was the prettiest on TV, but in real life she was breathtaking.

Carrying an overnight bag, she covered her eyes with her other hand and smiled up at him as he stood there starstruck. "Permission to come aboard?"

"Onboard?" She wanted to come onto his boat? She must be covering the contest for the network, as she did every year. She'd interviewed him and Bob after their win the year before, and Keith hadn't been able to say much, leaving the talking to his friend. "Uh, yeah, sure…" He reached for her hand as she approached on the gangplank and helped her onto the boat. Her skin was silky soft, and her nails were trim and covered in a clear polish. No fuss. He liked that.

She glanced around the boat with a look of appreciation. "Beautiful cruiser," she said.

"Thank you. I just bought her and did some finishing work," he said.

She strolled across the deck admiring the new flooring and mast.

"Are you covering the contest again this year?" He scanned the dock for her camera operator but didn't see anyone approaching.

She turned to him with a slightly confused smile. "No one told you?"

"Told me what?"

"I'm your new partner," she said.

Keith's heart raced as he processed the information. Monica Mallard, the most beautiful woman in Port Serenity, was his partner in the contest. She was going to be on his boat with him for the next two days. He could barely remember his own name in her presence: navigating the vessel would definitely be a challenge.

But what could he do?

The contest was starting in less than two hours. There was no time to request another partner...and besides, it would be terribly rude to have her replaced.

"Just think of me as the weather to your stars," she said with a smile.

A smile that Keith knew would be a major distraction for the next two days. He already knew he could kiss his winning-streak goodbye, and it had nothing to do with his new partner.

And absolutely everything to do with her.

WAS HE HAPPY about the news or not?

Monica waited for Keith to say something, but he continued to stand there with a dumbfounded look on his handsome face. She'd seen him around town over the years and had interviewed him after the race the year before. Or, rather, she'd interviewed his partner while he stood there a little camera shy. She'd thought it was cute how nervous he'd been to be on television. She knew his reputation as one of the best captains of the local coast guard and had heard all the stories about the Beaumont–Wakefield family feud that had lasted generations, but she hadn't quite realized how handsome he was.

He was recently retired and had a daughter in her mid-twenties, so he had to be late fifties at least, but he was still in great shape—broad, thick shoulders and muscular arms visible beneath his light blue polo shirt that matched the color of his eyes. No sign of an expanding middle. His salt-and-pepper hair was thick and trimmed in a stylish cut, and the stubble along his chin gave him a George Clooney vibe.

She'd heard that his wife had died years before, and the sight of his wedding ring still on his finger quite possibly made him the most endearing man in Alaska.

"Don't worry. This isn't my first time sailing," she said quickly. "My family owned a fleet of racing sailboats in Anchorage and taught courses at the marina. I assure you, I'm quite capable." She had years of experience on the water, and she wanted him to know she was serious about the contest.

Maybe she should have dressed a little less yacht-clubish, but in truth, whenever she was a little nervous, she always felt better when she dressed the part. But she hoped he didn't think she was just along for the ride. She was ready to roll up her metaphorical sleeves and get to work.

Keith shook his head and cleared his throat. "Oh, I'm sure you'll make a great partner," he said. "Sorry, I'm just... well...starstruck, I guess."

He looked slightly embarrassed by the admission, and she laughed, relieved that was all his silence was about. "I'm just a news reporter, not a movie star."

"Pretty as a movie star," he said, then blushed again.

Damn, the man just kept getting more and more attractive. He was so different than most of the men she knew. *Confident to the brink of cocky* was the way she'd describe her news-anchor coworkers. She'd been attracted to Brent for his charismatic charm and smooth-talking ways, but she was surprised to find Keith's soft-spoken nature also very appealing.

"Well, thank you, Captain Beaumont," she said.

"Keith. Please call me Keith."

"Okay, Keith. Where do we start?"

He checked his watch. "Check-in is in forty-five minutes at the marina, then the horn will blow, and we'll be on our way."

"On our way where?" she asked, seeing the route map on the table. She moved closer and scanned it. The hundred-mile path would take them along the south coast of Alaska, eastward out to sea, then looping back. She pointed to the checkpoints. "Scheduled stops?"

"Only long enough to capture the flags."

"Right," she said, and he gestured her to follow him inside the cabin.

It was a lot bigger than it looked from the outside. An open-concept kitchen and living area with regular-size appliances and comfy, slightly worn furniture. There was no television, but there was a stereo system.

Keith gestured to the shelves that held trophies from previous wins. Under each was a collection of colored flags with the coast guard logo on them.

"Five years in a row—wow! No pressure," she said with a laugh.

Keith waved a hand. "Oh, I'm not worried about winning…"

She suspected that was a little white lie to make her feel better. Captain Beaumont may be quiet and easy-going, but he was definitely someone with a reputation to uphold, and she'd be damned if she was responsible for breaking his winning streak.

"Well, you better get your game face on, because I compete to win," she said with a smile.

And there was the speechless, dumbfounded look again. How incredibly sexy.

TWO HOURS LATER, after the official contest horn sounded, they were out on open water.

Keith glanced at Monica out of the corner of his eye as he sailed *Wind Dancer* out of the inlet. She hadn't been lying when she claimed to have sailing experience. While he'd set the sails, she'd maneuvered the boat out of the marina like a professional. And in record time. It was early in the contest, but they'd already taken the lead.

Already working well together.

"Light winds from the north that will definitely pick up by evening. Based on the current, keeping with our pace, we should reach the first checkpoint by 18:14," she said.

She really was trying to reassure him that she knew what she was doing, and her competitive spirit made her all the more attractive. She turned and caught him staring, and Keith looked away quickly. "Would you like to take the wheel while I make a few calculations?" He'd better start pulling his weight and doing his own job of navigating.

They were allowed only the map, a sextant, a watch and nature. No GPS or any other navigation equipment. He used the position of the sun and his watch to set their course as Monica watched.

"You learned to do this in the coast guard?" she asked, taking over the wheel.

"Back when I was at the academy, it was a required course. It was my favorite thing to study."

"Do they still teach it?" she asked.

He nodded. "They didn't for a while, back in the late nineties, but a few years later they realized the importance of knowing nontechnological ways of navigation and brought it back. A modified version, at least." The old-school ways were difficult, and it took a real passion for navigating to devote time and effort to learning them.

Monica looked impressed as she scanned his charting calculations. Keeping one hand on the wheel, she leaned over him as he worked, and her closeness was more than a little distracting. The soft scent of her perfume drifted on the salty sea air, and the sun had warmed her exposed flesh, giving her a beautiful glow. He hadn't been alone with an incredibly beautiful woman in such a long time, and there was an intimacy about being out there on the water...alone.

With a dozen other sailboats on their tail, closing the gap fast.

He needed to stay focused.

He moved away slightly, and she cleared her throat. "I'm crowding you. I'll give you space," she said with an apologetic laugh.

Keith didn't really want her to go anywhere. He was enjoying her company. "Would you like to learn how to do it?" he asked. "I mean, it's not your job, but..."

"I'd love to," she said enthusiastically, and he felt his heart skip a beat. This beautiful, interesting woman wanted to learn the complexities of how to navigate using nature's elements and some mathematical equations.

She might just be the most perfect woman in the world.

CHAPTER THREE

BY NIGHTFALL, THEY'D REACHED two of the eight checkpoints, and as they sat on the deck, across the table from one another, they clinked their glasses together to toast a successful first eight hours. They'd be sailing through the night to reach two more checkpoints; therefore, they were celebrating with cranberry juice instead of wine.

"You did really great today," he said, picking up his sandwich and taking a bite. He'd packed the sandwiches and snacks that he and Bob always enjoyed. So he was relieved to see Monica take a big bite of the tuna and Swiss on homemade bread and look like she was genuinely enjoying it.

"It was fun. Especially the crash course in navigation," she said.

It had felt great sharing his knowledge and passion with someone. It had been a long time since he had, and it had helped him relax a little around her. She was easy to be with. As they'd sailed, there had been moments of talking and laughter as he'd told her about his plan to sail the following month, but also moments of comfortable silence as they'd enjoyed being out on the water, the mild breeze blowing and the hot sun beating down. He'd quickly realized that she was a woman who could sit with her own thoughts, and he hadn't needed to keep her entertained. But there had been no doubt that she was having a good time.

"Maybe tomorrow you can teach me how to read the weather patterns," he said.

"Deal," she replied with that beautiful smile of hers that made his palms sweat. He couldn't remember the last time a woman had had this effect on him. He liked her. A lot. And he'd only truly met her eight hours ago.

"You must be so thrilled to have your daughter home, following in your footsteps," she said.

He nodded as he sipped his drink. "I only ever wanted her to follow her own dreams, but it was definitely *my* dream to have her here in Port Serenity." His daughter had left for the academy just weeks after her mother had passed away. Having both of them gone had been terribly lonely. The house had felt different: cold and joyless. It had taken him a long time to figure out how to live without them both. He'd struggled to find new routines, different ways to occupy his free time. So much of his life had revolved around his wife and daughter that he'd been a little lost.

Having Skylar return to Port Serenity the year before had filled a huge, gaping hole in his heart, but he'd never wanted to pressure her into it. "Luckily, I know she isn't here to make poor old Dad feel better but for a certain se-cret high-school sweetheart, slash soon-to-be husband," he said proudly. Skylar and Dex made a wonderful couple, and more importantly, any man that made his daughter happy was the right choice in his book. No matter the last name.

"Ah, the Wakefield–Beaumont feud," she said with a smile.

Generations of Beaumonts had been civil servants in Port Serenity, whereas the Wakefields were rumored to have made their family fortune in questionable ways, in-cluding smuggling contraband into Alaska. The families had divided the town's loyalty for too long.

"There's definitely a lot of history there. My dad always said you could never trust a Wakefield, but I'm happy that Skylar and Dex being together has resulted in a long-overdue truce."

"Skylar's a wonderful captain and a lovely woman. You raised her right," Monica said.

"My wife gets all the credit for that," he said.

Monica offered a sympathetic look. "I'm sorry for your loss. Cancer, right?"

He nodded. "We'd thought she'd beaten it, but it came back. Stronger and faster the second time."

"That must have been hard," she said, and her gaze landed on his wedding band. In the years his wife had been gone, he'd never been able to take it off. He didn't think he ever would.

He fingered it now as he said, "It's a part of me. Just like she is." The deep grief and pain had subsided. His heart had healed, and he'd learned to move on, but she would always be in his daily thoughts, and he'd always love her.

He cleared his throat in the silence, struggling for something to say to turn the conversation toward lighter territory. He didn't know much about Monica except that she'd moved to Port Serenity from Anchorage and had been married to a news anchor at the station. They'd recently divorced, and though it seemed amicable enough, he wondered how it was, still working together, but he chickened out, deciding to stick to a safer subject. "Do you have kids?" he asked. He didn't know of her having any in Port Serenity, but maybe they were in Anchorage.

"No," she said softly with just a hint of remorse as she wiped the corners of her lips with her napkin. "I wanted them at one time in my life, but they just weren't in the cards, I guess. My career was the main focus."

"Not too late," he said.

Monica grinned and shot him a questioning look. "How old do you think I am?"

Uh-oh. That was a dangerous question. A smart man knew never to answer that honestly, but she couldn't be over forty. She was fresh-faced, and her green eyes were bright and vibrant, especially now when they caught the glow of the moonlight. Lost in them, he nearly forgot to answer the question. "Late thirties?"

She laughed. "Try adding ten years."

His jaw dropped. "Impossible."

"Nope, it's true, but thank you. I guess being in television, I'm not really allowed to age so the pressure to stay looking a certain way has helped slow the aging process."

"That must be exhausting, though." He couldn't begin to comprehend the pressure she must be under in a public-facing role.

"You have no idea." She paused, looked conflicted for a brief second, then added, "And I think the network is looking for a replacement."

Keith frowned. "What the hell would they do that for? You're the best meteorologist we've had since Francine Walsh. You almost always predict the right weather, and your humor makes it the best part of the five-o'clock news report."

Her laugh was rich and smooth as it echoed on the silence all around them. "Thank you...but, um, I think they want to find someone a little younger."

He shook his head. "When did the world get so narrow-minded? Older generations used to be respected for our wisdom and experience. Now it's like we turn a certain age, and they think we need to be put out to pasture. I retired young, and I'll admit, I'm not as limber or capable as I used to be, but youth isn't always better than experience," he said. "You are incredible, and they'd be idiots to fire you." He reached across the table and touched her hand.

An instinctive, impulsive move, but when she turned her palm up to intertwine her fingers with his, his heart pounded in his chest. He stared at their hands and swallowed hard, conflicted. He didn't want to pull away. It felt nice. Real nice.

But it had been so long…and he wasn't sure he was ready to move on with a new relationship.

He cleared his throat and gently pulled his hand back. "Maybe you should grab the first shift for some rest."

She nodded. "Good idea."

Was it? He'd prefer to sit out there on deck chatting with her and looking at the stars all night. Not exactly the experience he'd have shared with Bob, but he was quickly warming to his new partner.

Maybe dangerously so.

She stood and headed toward the cabin. "Night, Keith," she said.

"Sleep well," he said as she disappeared inside.

He sighed and sat back, staring up at the night sky. The sound of the lapping waves all around him and the cool, light breeze providing no answers to soothe his conflicted emotions.

CHAPTER FOUR

THEY STOOD ON DECK, after each getting only four hours of sleep the night before—less for Keith as he'd tossed and turned after she'd appeared on deck to relieve him a little after three o'clock. He hadn't been tired and would have preferred continuing at his post, but she'd insisted on taking a turn at the helm.

"So why meteorology?" Keith asked.

He couldn't help but admire her dedication to the partnership. She was a fine woman, and that news anchor she'd been married to must have been a fool to let her go.

Coffee cups cradled in their hands, they headed toward the fourth flag, visible on a buoy in the distance.

Monica smiled. "I've always loved weather. All kinds of weather. Most people have a favorite season, but I have a sincere appreciation for them all. I love the cold and snow in winter, the beautiful frost and the chill that settles over the town. The deep freeze that seems to cause everything to stand still. Then in spring, the milder weather helps everything come to life. The late sunlight and early dusk are magical. Summer here in Alaska is uniquely precious because it's so short. I cherish every hot, sun-kissed day, and fall holds a desperate longing of trying to hold on to the heat, the length of the days…" She laughed as she stopped. "That all must sound so weird."

Keith shook his head. "Not at all." He knew exactly

what she meant. He loved the changing seasons too. Each one seemed to last just long enough, the other arriving in time to remind the residents of Port Serenity that life was ever-changing.

Monica looked to the sky and frowned. "I think we're in for a storm," she said.

Keith eyed the morning sky as the sun crested the horizon in a warm, red glow. The old adage *Red sky in morning, sailors take warning* sounded in his mind, but he wasn't convinced that was always true. He'd sailed some very nice days that had started just like this one. "You sure? Weather forecast didn't predict any this weekend. You didn't predict any," he added with a smile. It was one of the safer weekends of the year to hold the event as history proved rainfall and inclement weather were rare.

Monica nodded slowly. "There was a storm pattern hitting Nunavut that was supposed to bypass the northern coast of Alaska, but those clouds in the distance and the fierceness of the wind make me think we may see a tail end of it at least."

"You're the expert," he said. He'd trust her on this.

"I think we should slow the pace, lower the sail and wait a few hours. We don't want to move toward it," she said.

Keith hesitated. Waiting a few hours could put them severely behind…if she was wrong. If she was right, it could save them a lot of trouble, not being in the thick of it and having to rechart their course to go around it. "Okay," he said.

Monica looked slightly surprised, as though she'd expected an argument. Or at least for him to offer his own opinion. "Okay," she said.

They got to work lowering the sail and positioning themselves away from the clouds rolling in overhead.

Unfortunately, an hour later, she started to doubt her assessment as the darker clouds seemed to change direction. "Huh, maybe I was wrong," she said.

Keith shrugged. "No worries. Let's just raise the sail and keep going." They'd only lost an hour.

But as they readied the sail, a clap of thunder sounded in the distance, where they were headed. Followed by a quickly darkened sky and a big bolt of lightning several miles away.

The storm that had seemed to be blowing over was now fast approaching. A violent wind came out of nowhere, and rain started to fall within minutes.

Securing the sail, they ducked inside the cabin as the torrential downpour started.

"Well, you were right," Keith said, handing her a towel to dry her hair. He peered outside as the waves grew stronger and fiercer, tossing the cruiser around like a toy sailboat.

"Thank you for trusting me," she said softly, drying water droplets from her bare skin.

His gaze met hers, and he swallowed hard. "Of course."

The boat tipped on a wave, sending her stumbling toward him, and he reached out to steady her before she fell. His hands on her shoulders, he held tight as their eyes met and held for a long, tension-filled beat.

"Keith…" she said, her voice low but full of something he hadn't heard in a long time. Desire.

Without thinking, he pulled her toward him. He stared into her eyes as he drew her into his chest, her hands pressed between their bodies as he lowered his head toward hers. He refused to think, moving only on impulse.

She tilted her head up and closed her eyes, and Keith kissed a woman for the first time in seven years.

KEITH WAS RIGHT about one thing. With age definitely came experience.

Monica wrapped her arms around his neck and drew his face closer as she deepened the kiss. One that was so fantastic, it caught her completely off guard.

Not that Keith seemed like a man who didn't know how to leave a woman breathless, but this was more than just a physical connection. Her stomach fluttered, and a warmness was flowing through her. There was a passionate longing, yet sexy reservedness, about the way he held her that made her legs go weak.

And the kiss itself had caught her by surprise. She'd felt Keith's attraction to her, but she hadn't expected him to act on it.

She moved closer to him and savored the taste of his lips, breathed in the manly aftershave and the scent of the outdoors lingering on his skin, enjoyed the feel of big, strong arms holding her tight as the boat continued to sway beneath their feet. She hadn't kissed anyone since her divorce. She hadn't even entertained the idea of a new relationship. It seemed still too fresh, too new... Her feelings about the whole situation were still a little undecipherable.

But kissing Keith brought a new clarity. It erased any doubt about whether she was ready to move on...to give her heart to someone else. She'd missed this physical closeness—this connection—with a man. She knew she didn't want to spend the rest of her life alone.

He broke away, slightly breathless, and she wanted to reach for him and bring his mouth back to hers, but she sensed the kiss had shaken him a little. His expression held a hint of cautious hesitation when his eyes met hers. He cleared his throat as he gently released her and took a step back. "Sorry if that—"

She shook her head quickly. "No. That was…" Wonderful. Spontaneous. She'd hazard to say the best kiss of her life.

He shoved his hands in his pockets and nodded. "Why don't you take the opportunity for some sleep," he said. "It might be another late night, trying to get back on course."

He was trying to distance himself. The kiss had completely freaked him out.

"Okay. Sounds great." She took a deep breath as she headed toward the bedroom, though she knew she probably wouldn't be able to sleep. "Wake me up when you want to switch off," she said.

Inside the bedroom, she lay on the bed and pulled a blanket up over her. The sound of footsteps pacing above her head confirmed it. Keith was panicking.

Should she go back out there and assure him that the kiss was okay? Or was he regretting it? In which case she should probably go out there and tell him that it hadn't meant anything and reassure him that she wasn't reading anything into it…

She groaned as uncertainty wrapped around her.

She didn't regret the kiss. Or opening up to Keith about her potential firing. His reaction had made her feel better. Being around him made her feel good. She was enjoying every moment with him.

Hopefully the impulsive kiss hadn't wrecked things. She closed her eyes and tried to sleep, fighting an urge to go back up on deck and potentially ruin things even more with even more kissing.

THAT ONE KISS had set Keith's life completely off course.

Not to mention the contest. His mind and heart in conflict after Monica had retired to the cabin, he'd made a few miscalculations, and they'd drifted farther west than he'd intended once the storm passed over and they'd set sail again. A few hours later, the next flag was supposed to be within sight, but Keith couldn't see the buoy in any direction.

He picked up the map and frowned as he studied it.

"You didn't wake me," Monica said, appearing on deck. She yawned, and his gaze fell to her mouth, where his lips had been the evening before. Where it was a struggle not to let his lips wander again.

He had to focus. He forced his gaze away from her sleepy expression as she took over the helm.

"We're a little...off course," he said.

She looked slightly embarrassed as she nodded. "Right. Sorry. That kiss was impulsive and..."

He shook his head quickly. "No, not the kiss. I meant we're lost."

A relieved-sounding laugh escaped her, breaking the tension and anxiety that had been weighing on his chest all night as he'd pondered his actions.

He grinned. "That's not a good thing." But in truth, it wasn't entirely a bad thing either. Suddenly, winning the contest wasn't the most important part of the weekend. He'd kissed a beautiful woman, and he didn't feel the guilt and remorse he thought he should be feeling. He was conflicted, but not for the reasons he'd expected to be. He was almost ten years older than Monica, and she was a local celebrity. She had married a hot news anchor who drove a flashy car and lived in an impressive condo. He was a retired captain with a modest lifestyle, set in his ways, unsure if uprooting his peaceful, quiet life was something he'd ever entertain.

The future he'd envisioned for himself—growing old with his wife, hopefully enjoying grandkids someday—had been altered when she'd passed away. He'd redesigned the future he'd seen for himself.

Could he reimagine it again?

He was getting too far ahead of himself. Monica might not even be thinking of the kiss as anything more than a spontaneous, unexpected act.

"Afraid I was a little distracted," he said.

She moved closer, and his pulse raced as she reached up to run her hands through his hair. "Should I apologize?"

"No," he said, voice thick. The temptation to kiss her again was overwhelming...but they were drifting farther and farther off course, and he needed to figure out where they were headed both physically and metaphorically before he could kiss her again. "But you should go sit over there while I figure out how to get us back on track," he said, gently removing her hands from his hair. He kissed both before releasing them.

She laughed. "I'll go make us some coffee," she said.

Keith's gaze lingered on her as she headed back inside the cabin, then he released a deep breath.

How did he get them back on course when this detour might have been the best thing to happen to him in a long time?

HOURS LATER, THEY were clearly lost and drifting even farther off course. As much as Keith didn't seem to want to admit it.

Monica scanned the ocean, looking for the contest markers that were supposed to be along the route, but she didn't see them.

Worse, she could no longer see the shore. Any shore.

"Maybe it's time to consult the GPS or something," she said. It was against contest rules, but the sun was starting to set, and she worried that if they continued on the wrong course, they'd really be in trouble by nightfall. She could barely see the lighthouse beacon rotating in the distance.

Keith avoided her eyes as he cleared his throat. "There is no GPS system installed...yet."

Her eyes widened. "What? How is that possible?" All boats had those systems.

He shrugged sheepishly. "The old one needed replacing... But we didn't require it for the contest so it was on my list of things to do."

Okay. Don't panic.

She reached into her pocket for her cell phone. "I'll just use my phone." She glanced down at it and frowned. Two percent battery. She'd charged it the night before while she'd slept. "My battery is dead," she said.

Keith glanced at his. "Mine too. It's being out here on the water. The cell phones are constantly searching for an internet connection, and it drains the battery quick." He sighed. "And even if they weren't almost dead, an online connection would be painfully slow. Impossible to use reliably."

Oh my God... They were adrift on the North Pacific with only their own knowledge to help them.

"Don't worry," Keith said reassuringly. "The unexpected storm just threw us too far off the original route. I'm sure the other teams are experiencing similar problems." He reached out and touched her shoulder, and the heat radiating onto her bare arm at the contact had her momentarily forgetting their predicament.

Her kiss had caused Keith to lose focus. She *wanted* to feel guilty about that.

"I can figure this out," he said.

His confidence was definitely sexy, but an hour later, they were still headed away from the lighthouse beacon, and darkness had enveloped the sailboat. A strong wind blew from the south, pushing the vessel even farther north, and the stars weren't visible beneath a thick cloud cover. Navigating without stars was impossible, even for the experienced coast guard captain.

Keith ran a hand over the stubble on his chin, then placed his hands on his hips as he stared off into the distance. He sighed. "I think we need to call the coast guard."

The irony of the situation was not lost on her.

HIS DAUGHTER WOULD never let him live this down.

As the lights of the Port Serenity coast guard rescue vessel approached an hour later, after his radio-distress signal, Keith sighed. Even if she hadn't been on shift, Skylar would have insisted on taking this call.

Her grin when the forty-five-foot, red-and-yellow cutter pulled up alongside them, emergency lights unnecessarily flashing, said it would be a long time before this story wasn't a favorite topic of conversation at family get-togethers.

Thank God, he was officially retired. He'd never be able to face his old crew without so much tormenting and teasing.

"Captain Beaumont. Navigation issues?" Skylar said over the radio. The hint of glee in her tone made him swallow his pride. So, he was the one needing rescuing today. He wasn't exempt from having problems at sea.

If only it had been a bad calculation or judgment error that had sent them off course. But it had been Monica and that life-altering kiss. He couldn't exactly tell his daughter that... Right now, he could barely meet her gaze, for more than one reason. "Requesting coast guard assistance back to the marina," he said.

"Wait? Why the marina?" Monica asked, next to him. "Just ask them to point us in the right direction, and let's continue on."

He loved her spirit, but he shook his head. "Receiving assistance immediately disqualifies us." He hated that he'd let her down during her first time competing. He hadn't exactly demonstrated sailing expertise.

"But that shouldn't stop us from at least finishing the contest," she said with such sexy determination—such a show of character—Keith found himself speechless. He stared into her beautiful expression, illuminated in the glow of the moonlight, and he suspected she could easily set him off course in more than one aspect of his life.

And he might not care.

From the corner of his eye, he caught Skylar's interested stare from inside the cutter cabin. His daughter was watching their interaction with keen interest. Could she sense the attraction between them?

He cleared his throat. "You sure?" he asked Monica.

"Absolutely."

Guess they were finishing the race. Was it too much to hope that prolonging their time together was part of her reason for wanting to continue?

"Requesting coast guard assistance to simply put us back on course," he said over the radio.

"You can't win now," Skylar said, her surprise evident in her tone.

Keith felt like he'd already won, being out here with Monica. "We still want to finish," he said, his gaze locked on Monica's.

"Okay. Set your course eastward, and follow us," Skylar said.

Eastward. The complete opposite direction. Good thing

they'd put in the call, or they could have been hundreds of miles from Port Serenity by morning.

Though Keith couldn't say that would have bothered him one little bit.

CHAPTER FIVE

THE NEXT DAY, hours after the other contestants had arrived, Keith and Monica sailed through the opening of the inlet and crossed the finish line. A large crowd—about a hundred locals—was still gathered along the marina, and they erupted into applause and cheers.

He and Monica had finished the race, despite going off course, and their dedication to finishing was being celebrated as if they'd placed.

All because of her. Keith glanced at Monica, standing behind the wheel. He'd been ready to call it the night before, but her insistence had encouraged him to stay the course, finish what they'd started.

She maneuvered the sailboat into the dock, and they waved to the crowd as people started to disperse. A familiar-looking man blew a kiss their way, and Keith was certain it hadn't been meant for him.

Monica blushed slightly as she motioned the man toward the sailboat. "That's Brent, from the station. He's reporting live in my place," she said.

Brent Clauson. Her ex and current coworker.

Keith nodded. "Oh, right…"

"He's probably going to interview us," Monica said.

Wonderful. Keith had been hoping he and Monica would have some time alone before they parted ways. Before she went back to her life as a TV celebrity or wherever her career took her next if the network did let her go. And he'd be setting sail for his two-month voyage the following week as planned.

The idea that one kiss should give either of them pause—to the extent that they changed their individual plans—was absurd.

He lowered the gangplank, and Brent hurried up to the boat, grabbing Monica for a quick hug before turning his attention to Keith. "Captain Beaumont! Huge honor to meet you."

Keith shook the news anchor's hand. On TV, the man looked a little younger, taller and more muscular than he did in real life. Keith could definitely beat him in an arm wrestle. Still, Brent had charisma and celebrity status. And Monica used to love him.

Still loved him?

They hadn't really covered that in their discussions. They'd gotten close in the last few days, but they were still essentially strangers…

"You two had quite an adventure," Brent said, glancing back and forth between them as his camera operator joined them on deck.

Monica blushed again, and Keith nodded awkwardly.

"Well, we interviewed the other contestants as they arrived. First place went to Ainsley and Bishop, second went to Carlisle and Sharpe, and third went to Addison and Myles," Brent informed them.

Keith nodded and offered a solitary clap for the winners. All worthy competitors for sure, and if they'd all successfully navigated the unexpected storm the day before, they deserved the wins.

"We'll get your story, and then we should get back to the station for the noon broadcast," he said to Monica.

She nodded and smiled. "Of course."

Obviously the two were still close and respected one another as coworkers. They seemed friendly and comfortable with each other.

Keith struggled through the interview, his cheeks flushing with the camera pointed at his face as he recounted the comical, ironic call to the coast guard.

Luckily, the interview was short, and within moments, Brent signed off, and the camera stopped rolling. "That was great," he told him. "Viewers will love this story the most. You two stole the broadcast from the winners." He turned to Monica. "Ready to go?"

She hesitated. "I'll meet you at the van," she said.

Brent shot her an intrigued look and glanced back and forth between them, then Monica jerked her head to say *Get lost*.

When Brent and the camera guy had disappeared down the dock, she turned to him. "Sorry about the way things turned out. I know you were hoping to keep your winning streak."

How did he tell her that, out of all his years competing, this contest had been his favorite? That despite not coming close to winning, he'd enjoyed this year more than any other? It had been special. One he'd never forget. "I feel like I did win," he said gently. "I won...a friend."

She nodded, with a slight look of disappointment on her face. "To new friends." She checked her watch. "I should get going."

He didn't want her to go. He wanted to ask when and if he could see her again. But tongue-tied and conflicted, he simply nodded. "I better get going too. Thanks again for filling in for Bob."

"You're welcome. Anytime."

After she disembarked the sailboat, she turned to wave, and Keith fought every urge to run after her and say all the things he wanted to say but didn't know how.

THIS WOULD BE her last broadcast.

Decision made, Monica was going to tell Calvin before the noon segment of the news that she was resigning.

He'd likely be relieved that he wouldn't have to be the one who broke the news that they wanted to replace her.

She wanted to leave the station on her own terms. Her own time. It would be torture going to work every day knowing any time could be her last.

She suspected they had a list of new candidates at the ready, anyway.

She took a deep breath and squared her shoulders as she knocked on his open office door and entered. "Hey, Calvin. Can I talk to you?"

He waved her in. "Absolutely."

Static glanced up at her with a weary expression as she approached Calvin's desk. She bent to pet the lovable dog to give herself a moment to gather her thoughts. When she stood, she said, "I think it's time for me to leave the station."

Calvin frowned. "Where are you going?"

She had no idea. This hadn't exactly been something she'd planned so she hadn't given it much thought. "I'm not sure…but we both know that my time here at Station Five is limited." A lump formed in her throat.

Do. Not. Cry.

Calvin nodded slowly. "You got an offer from another network, didn't you? I bet it's Weather Beat in Anchorage, isn't it? I knew we'd never be able to compete with them." He shook his head, looking truly defeated, and now it was Monica's turn to frown in confusion.

"No, there's no other offer."

Calvin looked relieved. "So then, why?"

"Because I'm getting older, and the station was planning to replace me," she said. Obviously, they hadn't been ready to tell her yet, and it was slightly embarrassing to admit that she'd overheard the conversation.

"Why on earth do you think that?" Calvin asked.

"Because I heard Maxwell say something the other day..." Had she misread the situation?

Calvin laughed as he shook his head and sat back in his chair. "We were talking about *S-t-a-t-i-c*," he whispered, spelling the name so the dog couldn't understand.

"The dog?"

Relief ran through her. She wasn't being replaced.

"Think on it, okay? We definitely want you here," Calvin said.

Monica nodded as she left the office to do the broadcast that now wouldn't be her last one.

"You and Captain Beaumont seemed to really hit it off," Brent said casually when she met him on set.

She applied a thin layer of lipstick before answering. She hadn't been home to change or shower. Her hair was salty and windblown, and her outfit was slightly wrinkled, but she didn't care. "He's a really nice man," she said simply. How did she tell her ex that she'd kissed the captain? How did she tell him that for the first time since their divorce, she'd felt a true, real connection to another man?

Nice? That's it?"

She sighed. "Okay, so he's attractive." And kind and gentle, but his kiss had held a passion that revealed another layer. He'd been vulnerable and open and yet so in control when he'd been leaving her breathless.

"Are you going to see him again?"

"I'm sure I'll see him around town." Until he left on his two-month sailing journey. One that sounded incredible. By the time he got back, any connection between them would have dissolved like a fragile early mist on the ocean.

"I meant really see him. Like a date," Brent said with no trace of jealousy or judgment. Just the tone of someone who knew her far too well.

"He didn't ask."

"I hadn't realized it was the 1950s," he said with a smirk as the makeup assistant applied pressed powder to his face.

She laughed. "Look, he's a widower. It's a different situation than ours." The divorce had hurt, and moving on had been tough, but they both had. They were better as friends, and they still had one another. Things were different for Keith.

"I get it, but I also saw the way he looked at you—like the sun rose on your command," Brent said. Then he added gently, "The way I do. That's real, Mon."

She released a deep sigh as the crew gave them their two-minute countdown to air. It was real. She'd felt it.

But had Keith?

"I THINK THIS PHOTO needs to be framed," Skylar said, sitting across from him at the Serpent Queen Pub as she scrolled through her cell phone.

"Mmm-hmm," Keith said. He scanned the local hot spot, which was bustling with a Sunday-night crowd. Loud music played over the speakers, and the Sealena statue stood proud in the center of the pub. He didn't come here often. It still felt a little weird, despite the family feud being over, but Skylar had invited him out for a drink, and he needed to tell her his plan to set sail the following week.

"Dad? You okay?"

Keith shook his head. "Yeah, great. Why?"

"Because I just threatened to frame the photo of you stranded in the North Pacific and you agreed to it," she said with a grin, setting her cell phone aside and leaning across the table. "What's going on with you?" Skylar asked, her gaze piercing. "You haven't been yourself all evening."

"Nothing. I'm fine."

The eight-o'clock newscast started, and his stomach lurched at the sight of Monica, looking as pretty as ever in a light blue suit and white blouse. He'd only spent two days with the woman. He shouldn't be feeling this odd sensation of missing her. They'd had a connection on the boat, but what did it mean?

He was so out of sorts, but he had no idea what to do about it.

Skylar followed his gaze, and her eyes widened. "Oh my God! You like her!"

Keith shook his head so quickly his neck cramped. "She's a lovely woman. Great sailor." Incredible kisser. Wonderful companion. Interesting conversationalist.

Skylar leaned closer, her eyes shining with interest. "You've always had a crush on her. Did something happen between you two?"

"No..."

"Dad..."

He sighed. "Fine. We kissed. She kissed me. I had nothing to do with it," he said, feeling the need to clarify. What would his daughter think of him kissing another woman?

Skylar laughed. "You had nothing to do with it?"

"I might have kissed her back, but it didn't mean anything." If it had, wouldn't she have reached out by now? Sometimes a kiss was just a kiss. An impulsive act in the moment. They'd shared a connection. Didn't mean it would lead anywhere…

"*Didn't mean anything?* Dad, this is the first woman you've been attracted to since Mom died. You should totally go for it." Skylar's encouragement wasn't a surprise. She'd been wanting him to open himself up to the possibility of a new love for a while now.

"I don't think she would be into me." It was easier to believe that than to have hope or to admit the real reason for his hesitation.

"She kissed you, right? Now's your chance."

Keith stared at the liquid in his beer mug. "It's too soon."

"It's been seven years. It's okay to move on, Dad." Skylar reached across the booth and touched his hand. "Mom wouldn't want you to not live your life. And she wouldn't want you to take that sailing trip alone."

He frowned as he glanced up at her. "How did you know?"

Skylar shot him a look. "Oh, come on. As if you'd buy a cruising sailboat, fix it up and then not take that two-month excursion you always talked about."

He laughed gently. He should have known she'd figure it out. "I was planning to set sail next week…"

"Invite her to go."

He shook his head. "We just met…"

"You're not getting any younger."

"Gee, thanks." He squeezed his daughter's hand on the table and took a deep, contemplative breath. "You'd be okay with that?"

"It would make me feel better to know you had someone to help you if you steer off course again," she said with a wink.

"Couldn't resist, huh?" he said with a laugh.

But his daughter had definitely given him something to think about.

A week later...

THE RUMOR AROUND TOWN was that Keith was setting sail the next day.

She'd heard it two days ago from a fisherman she'd interviewed about the largest catch of the season, who'd heard it from a member of the coast guard, who'd heard it from Skylar.

So it must be true.

Walking along the marina, Monica's heartbeat echoed in her chest as she saw *Wind Dancer* docked. It had taken two days to get the nerve to come see him. He hadn't reached out to her since they'd parted ways after the contest, and she wasn't sure what to say exactly.

Bon voyage? Happy sailing? Take me with you?

That last one had played on her mind more than was safe the last forty-eight hours, and she feared it might be what she would actually blurt out.

Brent had noticed a connection and said that he thought Keith was interested in her, but what did it mean? He was a widower, still unsure how to move on after a broken heart, and she was...

She was ready. Ready for the possibility of a new relationship. Ready to love again.

She casually glanced toward the boat as she passed, but she didn't see him on deck, and he wasn't visible through the cabin windows.

But *Wind Dancer* looked in fine shape. He'd applied

another coat of paint, and the fiberglass hull sparkled in the summer sun.

What an amazing journey he was about to embark on. Two months at sea. Alone with just the sound of the wind and waves. A beautiful way to reconnect with nature and truly feel the force of the ocean.

What she wouldn't give for an experience like that.

"Hi."

Keith's voice behind her made her breath catch in her chest as she turned to face him. She knew she had to say goodbye and wish him a safe trip, but standing here now in front of him, she wasn't sure how to say the words.

She didn't want him to go. But obviously, she'd never tell him that. That would be selfish and ultimately embarrassing when he chose his journey over her.

"The boat looks amazing," she said, turning to look at it. Looking at him was too hard when she wasn't sure where they stood.

"Thank you. I finished the last of the renovations yesterday, and you'll be happy to know the new GPS system is fully functional," he said with a gentle laugh.

A sound she'd been craving for days. A sound she hadn't realized she was going to miss until that moment.

"That's a relief. Though, I'm sure without any distractions, you'd do just fine without it."

He stared at her pensively as he nodded. The reminder of the kiss lingered in the air between them, and he cleared his throat. "I'm sorry I kinda panicked…before. After the contest, I wanted to reach out…"

Hope rose in her chest. "You did?"

"Yeah…"

"Good," she said, relieved to know he'd been thinking of

her too. The last week, he'd been constantly on her mind. All she'd thought about was how easy it had been to be with him. He was kind and gentle, but confident and sexy. He was the kind of man she'd like a future with. Maybe even *the* man.

"Good?" he asked.

"I mean, I would have liked that. I wanted to reach out too, but I wasn't sure…"

He nodded, and a long, awkward silence fell between them, full of unspoken feelings.

"What did you want to say?" she asked, prompting him.

"I wanted to ask if you had plans for the next two months," he said, the words coming out quickly. As though he needed to say them before he could let reason hold them back.

Her eyebrows rose, but she smiled, a thick warmness enveloping her. "That's an awfully long first date."

He laughed as he nodded. "It was a long shot."

"I'll go." It was an easy decision, really. Keith's journey sounded like the most wonderful adventure—a trip of a lifetime—and the opportunity to spend time with him was too good to pass up. Life was short, and second chances at love didn't come by every day.

His eyes widened. "You will?"

She stepped toward him, excitement creeping into her chest at the unknown possibilities that awaited them. "On one condition," she said, wrapping her arms around his neck.

"Which is?" he asked, his tone low and gravelly as he wrapped his arms around her.

"You get us lost as much as possible," she said, standing on tiptoes and placing a soft kiss on his lips. One he returned with all the affection in his heart.

There was no rush, no agenda. Just two months at sea, getting to know one another and discovering if maybe they could make a future together in this unpredictable adventure called life.

* * * * *